Mark of the Cat

/

Year of the Rat

by

Andre Norton

Meisha Merlin Publishing, Inc
Atlanta, GA

MARK OF THE CAT/YEAR OF THE RAT

An MM Publishing Book
Published by Meisha Merlin Publishing, Inc.
PO Box 7
Decatur, GA   30031

Editing & interior layout by Stephen Pagel
Copyediting & proofreading by Teddi Stransky
Cover art by Hoaug
Cover design by Kevin Murphy

ISBN: Hard Cover 1-892065-52-5
        Soft Cover 1-892065-53-3

http//www.MeishaMerlin.com

First MM Publishing edition: January 2002

Printed in the United States of America
0 9 8 7 6 5 4 3 2 1

Table of Contents

In Memory of
KAREN KUYKENDALL
1928—1998

Artist, Dollmaker, Costumer, Jeweler
and
Creator of the Outer Regions

Introduction to the Outer Regions

The "Outer Regions" were created by the artist Karen Kuykendall, whose book of paintings, *The Cat People,* and her justly famous Tarot cards immortalized these fantastic lands and peoples. There exists among Ms. Kuykendall's records a complete "Travelers' Report" upon which this book is based.

Each of the five queendoms—The Diamond, Vapala; The Sapphire, Kahulawe; The Ruby, Thnossis; The Topaz, Azhengir; The Emerald, Twahihic—varies greatly. Each is ruled by a Queen, but all pay full obedience to the Emperor. It is a carefully preserved custom that these rulers come into power not by inheritance, but through election, although in some queendoms candidates come from only one House. The Emperor is chosen from selected candidates, through a series of severe tests.

The territory of these queendoms is mostly arid desert, and the harshness of the environment has shaped both people and cultures. What appears a frightening and barren world to stray travelers from the hardly known inner regions is accepted as home, and a loved one, by the five nations, the inhabitants so attuned to the "essence" of the land that they are unhappy and adrift apart from their roots.

The principal food of four of the queendoms comes mainly from algae beds, for the whole region contains a vast shallow thermal of briny waters in which live many kinds of these plants. Only in Vapala, which is a mesa territory, is other vegetation to be found—true plants—though some of these are grown in the glass-bubble-protected oasis cities of Twahihic. Both people and animals, however, depend mainly on the algae for food and water.

Kahulawe is a land of slickrock isles which are pitted with caves and crevices, and crowned by weirdly carved sand spurs sheltering the algae pans. Between these (most of which are owned by the settlements of Houses and clans) lie stretches of barren sand. The weather is very clear and sunny, so much so that most traveling is done by night. There are periods of death-dealing storms which may last for days. The people raise herds of oxen-like yaksen, and the oryxen used as mounts. They produce fine leatherwork and jewelry and are a most prosperous and quiet folk. Their independent women are noted traders and often the leaders of the caravans.

Volcanic Thnossis is in direct contrast to this quiet neighbor. Quake prone, with rocky potholes and crevices which breathe out steam and gases, it trades in sulphur, pumice, iron, glass, and weaving. There are many noted smiths in Thnossis. This is the most unstable of queendoms, and its people are fiery of temper, moody, and fatalistic.

Most desolate of all is Azhengir, for it consists of wide salt flats and baked alkali lands. Its weather is very hot and clammy near the large salt pans, and as the other countries, it suffers from the sweep of violent sandstorms. Salt gathering is the main industry, though there is some manufacturing of limestone and gypsum products and glassware. The people accept their hard life fatalistically and find their main source of escape in music, singing, and playing on a wide variety of instruments.

Twahihic is known as the sand queendom. The terrain is undulating with great sand dunes. The glass-dome-protected settlements cover the oases. There is almost no rain. Smothering sandstorms and tornadic winds are always threatening. The inhabitants provide recreation for tourists from the other nations. Dune skiing and flying are very popular. Twahihic is also the center for fine glass and ceramics.

Vapala has the distinction of being the formal seat of the Empire. Situated on a huge mesa tableland, it has orchards, grasslands, and farms. There are two seasons, wet and dry. Farming, some herding, diamond mining, and the mechanics of solar energy provide work for the inhabitants. A profitable and stable country with the most advanced technology, its people are arrogant and inclined to consider those of the other four queendoms to be "barbarians."

Animal life has an important part to play in all five queendoms. The heavy-coated yaksen are both beasts of burden and sources of wool and meat. Oryxen, much lighter, larger, antelope-like creatures, equipped with murderous horns, are kept for riding. It is usual to clip the horns, though some expert horsemen and women are proud of mastering the more wild, horned mount. One with clipped horns is known as a pa-oryxen.

Within almost all homes are kottis, small cats, independent of character. These choose the humans they wish to associate with and are highly esteemed. To deliberately kill a kotti is considered worse than murder and the offender is subjected to the death law.

The royal leopards have long been the symbol of imperial power. In fact, the Blue Leopard of Vapala is first guard to the Emperor and has a part in selecting those taking the tests for that position.

On the other hand, the larger Sand Cat is dreaded, as they dispute territories with human settlers. They are highly intelligent and have customs of their own. This species is distrusted and yet held in awe by the humans.

However, both Sand Cat and man have a common enemy in the packs of huge rats which prey upon all living things, befoul the algae pans, harry the herds, and are a source of death wherever they strike. Their hunger is never eased and they turn upon their own kind if no other prey is near. They breed continually and the litters are very large.

As to the customs of the queendoms: There are no formal marriages. Women only accept mates when they come into heat and not all of them ever do. Children are greatly desired but the birthrate is low. In Kahulawe, Vapala, and Thnossis a mating partnership is for life. In Twahihic and Azhengir polygamy is practiced and in those queendoms women who fail to come into heat are treated as servants and laborers. Children, being relatively few, are cherished and families are close-knit for the most part. However, unfit children and adults are put to death, since the community at large cannot support the unproductive. In Kahulawe and Vapala, where the normal deaths are fewer, the population of both people and animals is carefully monitored by a Minister of Balance and surplus of either humans or animals can be condemned. It is the quality of life rather than the quantity which is desired.

Belief is in the Cosmic Order and the Essence of the lands. Human sacrifice has been known in times of great drought. Often a ruler or person of importance volunteers as victim. Organized religion does not exist.

Only Azhengir practices slavery. In other countries servants have a firm social standing and dignity of person.

The solo—a rite of passage—is practiced in Kahulawe, Azhengir, and Twahihic. To be successful in this severe test, a young person must prove his or her ability to be accepted as a full adult.

In Kahulawe, Vapala, and Thnossis the Queens are elected by a council of representatives. The Queen has absolute power for life. In Azhengir and Twahihic the monarchy is hereditary; a Queen who does not bear children can be replaced.

Warfare used to be known between the isles of Kahulawe and in struggles between Houses of Vapala and mining towns of Thnossis. However, there has now been a long period of peace. Warriors still follow the traditional training, but their only duties are the protection of caravans against the periodic raids of outlaws and the search for travelers lost in the harsh country. However, there is constant intrigue between the Great Houses of Vapala, with assassination and quiet murder often ridding some lordship of an enemy.

This then is the land and people as they are in the here and now, but there are hints that all is not well and the future may be clouded as we come to the end of the reign of the Emperor Haban-ji. The waves of history are known for their rise and fall.

Mark of the Cat

1

The night sky of Kahulawe arched over me. I had seated myself some distance away so that I could no longer see the lamps and torches about my father's house. But I could not close my ears to the songs and the drumbeat which inspired the lingering dancers.

There was no small furry body curled beside me, no gentle nudge of head against my arm, no low, crooning purr to assure me that whatever I might be to my family I did not lack at least one to whom I came first. There would never be that again.

The raw heat of anger gripped me as it never had before in my life. That I was a disappointment to my father, an object of disgrace to be bullied by my brother, a servant for my sisters—I had accepted, fought to accept. Many, many times I had come to this perch on the roof of my own hut with hurt, even some despair, inside me. Then that which is the very essence of my birth place had rearmed me, encased me, as a mother might welcome a hurt child to her arms.

I was Klaverel-va-Hynkkel, son to Klaverel-va-Meguiel, the last full commander of the Queen's forces before the proud regiments of the past shrank to the guards who now patrol the land against those who would prey along the caravan routes, or seek those gone astray from those same routes. I was his son and in his eyes I was a nothing. That I had learned to bear—or thought that I had. When I was younger I dreamed of accomplishing some act which would make my father turn eyes of approbation on me. But what deed could it be when I was not a bearer of weapons, one of those youths now strutting down around the house I refused to look at?

My brother Klaverel-va-Kalikku—now he—My nails scratched against the rock blocks fitted together beneath me as I drew two deep breaths, fighting once more the rising rage which burned me as greatly as would the sun at full height—My brother was all in my father's reckoning that a son should be. It was he who skillfully rode the most vicious and hardly tamed oryxen, he who had hours earlier sent arrow and short spear to the heart of the test target, he who roared out the old war songs and danced the Advance of the Five Heroes.

I had accepted that to my father, this is what a man is. And what am I? A servant, a caretaker of stock, a trader who goes to town when necessary, one responsible for things which no warrior considers needful—not unless all would suddenly cease to be done.

Once more I strove to put aside the unhappiness of others' judgment of me and think of what I had which was my own. Whereas any oryxen would shy and lower horns to my brother, I could lay hand to its skin and fear no lash-out of horn or hoof. All our yaksen came to my whistle and made grateful noises deep in their throats when I groomed them, for none of my father's herd wandered matted of hair or needful of salve for hoof.

I was able to know with a single glance when those algae beds which supplied the major part of the food for ourselves and our herds needed to be double trimmed, and usually I was the one who harvested the major portion of the crop. Though at times my sisters would come with carry trays, to select for drying those bits which had special properties.

It was I who went to the market to trade yaksen hair to the weavers and select those needs which we could not supply for ourselves. The market—I shivered and leaned forward, resting my head on the arms I had folded across my knees.

No longer could I put off facing—and conquering in myself—what I must conquer. Let me then begin at the beginning, which lies with my sisters.

Melora-Kura—Her mind and her hands were truly filled with the essence of our land. I brought back for her such turquoise, agates, and other stones of color-life as she could use. She would sit and stare at such a piece for sometimes near a day and then her hands appeared to move of themselves, for many times she still looked only at the stone, to draw upon a sheet of cured skin that which she was moved to make. Jewelry from designs of Kura was greatly esteemed, so greatly indeed that outer traders from beyond our own marketplace would bring her commissions. She had never come into heat and I do not think that she regretted this, for she gave life with her mind and her hands and not her body. Not for her the wide-known feasting of a choosing such as occupied my younger sister Siggura-Meu this day and night.

Was Siggura satisfied now that she was engaged in something which Kura did not experience? That she had envied Kura I knew well. Too many times had I transported lopsided and strangely shaped pots of her manufacturing—such as she affirmed loudly were indeed works of art of a new kind—to market, where they were ignored or treated as a matter for laughter. No longer need she try to be as Kura: no, she would make her choice of those showing their prowess (if she had not already done so) and ride off to start a household of her own.

The market—No matter how my mind skittered away from the path of memory I would force upon it, I grimly returned to recall that. There I had always found a manner of acceptance. There was Ravinga, the far-traveling doll- and image-maker from Vapala.

And there was Mieu—My hand reached out to nothingness and there was a filling in my eyes, a tightness in my throat, which were as painful as would be my father's 'epron whip laid across my shoulders.

The kottis are our friends, our companions, our luck. They are much smaller than the wild Sand Cats which all men with reason fear, but they have that proud look about them, that independence of spirit which is shared by even the Emperor's great Blue Leopard, the very sign of imperial power.

Mieu had chosen me in the market of Meloa. She had but lately left whatever birthing place her dam had chosen, but there was already showing in her all the pride and intelligence of her kind. She came to me like a queen, her gleaming white, longish body fur jewel-patched by the black of onyx, the orange of fine agate. She was a treasure beyond all price and she made me hers.

From that moment we were as blood kin such as the bards sing of—comrades between whom there are no barriers. She took her place proudly beside what I had to offer in trade, even as she shared my sleeping mat and my food at home. It had been she—

I raised my head. For the first time I was realizing something I had forgotten, and I held to the scene in my mind. Yes, it was certain that Mieu had called me with her particular small urgent summons to Ravinga, running before me to where the dollmaker had her stand.

Ravinga was not in attendance at her sales place. That was occupied by a girl whom I had seen with her twice. She was very slender and her hair was the white flow of all Vapalans, though her skin was darker than Ravinga's as if she had spent more time in our hotter land.

Ravinga to one side was running her hands over the head of her great pack yaksen. The beast was lowing and shaking its head. Ravinga saw me at once and signaled with upheld hand, stepping aside, for it was no strange thing that I tend a sickening beast.

It would seem that something plagued this one and I thought perhaps a salsucker had managed to embed itself in that thick covering of long hair. Such were sometimes to be found around the algae beds where the yaksen browse, and they tortured an animal which could not rid itself from them, jaws gnawing into the skin.

I took my curry comb from my pouch and hunted, parting and lifting the hair. However, what I found was no dark green slug of a parasite—rather what looked like a tiny bag deliberately knotted into several strands. I changed my comb for a knife and sawed the thing loose. Once separated from the hairs it opened in my hand and I found myself looking down at a tooth.

The desert rats are the curse of our people and slain wherever they are found. I had killed many from my childhood on to keep clean the algae beds which they befouled and poisoned. Thus I was well aware what I saw now was one of the fore fangs of such a creature. It had been scored in several places and those markings filled with red paint, but the lines so formed held no pattern I had ever seen.

I heard a hiss from the girl. But Ravinga struck my hand, knocking the bit of leather and its uncanny contents to the ground. Then she seized upon two rocks—flat pieces of yellowish stone which appeared so quickly in her hands that I do not know whence they came. These she clapped sharply on either side of that fang and ground them around as one would grind for paint powder. There had arisen a furl of what seemed smoke and a puff of noxious odor. When she pulled the rocks apart there was only a dead-white dust which she set her foot upon, to tread it into the sand.

Having done so she stood looking straight at me. It seemed that there was a question in her eyes. I had questions also—in plenty. Yet it appeared I could not voice them. Now her hand went to her belt and she brought out something which gleamed.

"No!" The girl put out a hand. She was frowning and she certainly regarded me with no liking.

"Yes!" Ravinga denied her. She took two steps forward and I now saw that she held a round pendant swinging from a chain. At her gesture I bowed my head, then the chain was in place about my throat, and I looked down to see resting on my breast the finely wrought mask head of a Sand Cat, fashioned from that ancient red gold which we seldom see in these times. I was well aware through Kura of good workmanship and had heretofore believed that no one could surpass my sister. Yet there was something in this which I had never seen before. The inset yellow gems forming the eyes almost appeared to have life.

"To you," Ravinga said. Then she repeated some words I could not understand. Once more breaking into the common tongue she added:

"This is for you alone and it shall be a key to that which is meant. Do not let it go from you."

When I protested that such a piece was worth a fortune she shook her head.

"It goes where it will. Now it is yours—I think—" She frowned a little. "No, the fate of another is not for my telling—take it, Hynkkel, and learn."

I had other luck that day, obtaining a very fine piece of turquoise which I knew would delight Kura, and I returned home, the cat head still on my breast, Mieu croon-purring on the top of my loaded yaksen.

However, I quickly found that I was wrong in believing that Ravinga's unexpected gift was a mark of good fortune. That I speedily discovered shortly after I reached the rock island which was home for my House. One travels best by night and certainly never under the full punishment of the sun, and so it was dawn when I passed the last of the towering carven sentry cats and saw my brother and Kura both heading towards me as I plodded wearily along.

Kura I expected, for my sister was always impatient to learn how well her wares had sold and what raw materials I had bought to build up her store. However, that Kalikku would pay any attention was certainly new.

As usual he was fighting his mount as he came. To Kalikku any animal must be harshly mastered, and most of his, so ridden, were so vicious that none other of the family chose to go near them. He felt always deprived because the days of war when one family or clan turned against another in open battle had passed, listening eagerly and with close attention to my father's stories of past engagements. Hunting and forays for caravan raiders were all he might look to, and who would become, he thought, a hero from such petty trials of strength?

I halted, waiting for them to join me, which they did speedily, Kalikku reining in with a swift cruelty which made his oryxen rear, sending sand showering. Mieu sat up and growled, turning a very unfriendly eye upon my brother.

"Foot padder"—that was one of the least cutting of the names my brother could call me, and did—"make haste. Your labors are—" He did not finish; instead he leaned forward and stared, not eye to eye, but rather at the pendant I still wore.

The oryxen snorted and danced sideways as his rider urged the animal closer to me. "Where got you that?" my brother demanded. "How much of our father's store money did you lay out for it? Kura," he said to my sister, "perhaps it was your market profit this one has plundered."

Now he favored me with that ever-present challenge I had seen most of my life, silently urging me to retort either by fist or voice. And, as ever, I refused to give him the pleasure he had once taken, when we were very young, of beating me at will.

"It was a gift." Beneath my journey cloak my hands clenched and then by the force of my will loosened again.

"A gift!" My brother laughed scornfully. "From whom could such as you receive that! Though I wager you certainly would not have the spirit to take it by any force."

Kura moved closer also. Seeing the interest in her eyes I slipped the pendant from my head and handed it to her. She turned it round and round, running her fingers over it. "No," she said musingly, "this is not from the hands of Tupa" (she mentioned one of the greatest artists of our people). "It is too old and also it is—" She hesitated and then added, "Truly finer work than I have ever seen. Whence did it come, brother?"

"From Ravinga, the dollmaker of Vapala, whom I have met several times in the market."

My sister held it as if she were caressing the fashioning of stones and metal.

"Whence did she get it, then?"

I shrugged. "That I do not know and—"

However, I had no time to finish what I would say, for Kalikku made a snatch for it, one which Kura was fast enough to avoid. "It is a treasure for a warrior, not for one who labors by his will," he proclaimed loudly, "Rightly such is mine!"

"No." For the first time I refused to be bullied. During all the night hours of my travel, that had rested not far from my heart. A belief had grown stronger in me with every step that it was indeed now a part of me. I did not really know what it portended nor why I should feel it now so, but I did.

"No?" My brother showed his teeth in a grin like that of a Sand Cat seeing its prey at easy distance from it. "What is this dollmaker then to you that she gives you a treasure and you would hold it—your mat mate?"

"Stop it!" Kura seldom raised her voice. Ofttimes she was so intent upon her thoughts and plans for her work that she hardly seemed to be with us.

She dropped chain and pendant into my hand again. "If Hynkkel says this is a gift, then that is so. And one does not take gifts except for good reason, nor does one then surrender such to another. Hynkkel, I would like to look upon it again and perhaps make a drawing of it for my files, if you are willing."

"I am always at your service," I said.

Among us we have no slaves—that is for the barbarians of Azhengir. Our servants are free to come and go as they well please—but usually as a caste they have their own well-earned positions and a different kind of pride. That I should be as a servant in my father's house was because I was a failure as a son, a son he thought was not worthy of his notice. I was early a failure at those very things a warrior must know or do.

Bodily my strength was never that of my brother and I disliked all that went to make up his life. Though I had buried deep within me the pain—I always knew that my father denied me—I was content in other ways. I worked with our herds, I was careful as a tender of our algae beds, and I was always willing to go to the market. However, to my father's mind I was no proper one to inherit his name. It is true that I have always been something of a dreamer. I longed to make beauty with my hands as did Kura—but the one awkward figure of a cat guardian I chipped from stone was far from any masterpiece, though I stubbornly set it up beside my door, even as my father and brother had their "battle" standards beside theirs.

So, there being no middle way, I was a servant and that I tried to take pride in—making sure I served well. Thus I used a servant's response to my sister.

"You are needed." She drew a little away from me now as if, though she had taken my part, that was only in fairness and now we were back again in the same relationship we had been in for most of my life. "Siggura has come into heat. We must have the feast of choosing. There is much to be done. Already messages to other clans have been sent by the drummers."

Kalikku laughed. "Do you not envy her, Kura—the feasting, the coming of many wooers?" His tone was meant to cut as might the lash of his riding whip.

She laughed in turn but hers was honest laughter. "No, I do not." She lifted her hands and held them out, letting fall the reins of her well-trained mount. "It is what these can do which gives my life meaning. There is no envy in me for Siggura."

Thus I had come back to pressure of hurry. Not all of our women are designed to wed. Some never come into heat. I do not know whether many of them regret that or not. But I did know that Siggura was one who would make the most of this chance to be the center of feasting and attention, which might last for a week or more, until she was ready to announce her mate choice.

So it was that I got scanty sleep that day but hurried to oversee the checking of supplies, the dispatching of the others of our serving people to this or that task. The cat pendant I did not wear—I had no wish to stir up further comment. Rather I placed it in the small coffer where I kept the few things I truly prized.

To my surprise Mieu, instead of treading at my heels in her usual fashion, established guard there beside the box. So she remained for most of the time we took to arrange the housing of guests.

Siggura made her choice of the ornaments Kura spread before her, a collar of gold with ruby-eyed kotti heads, bracelets of fine enamel, and a girdle of shaded agate beads—the very best of her sister's stock, for she was always greedy. To match these she had new robes fashioned.

I saw very little of her, though I offered formal congratulations; words which she received with the smug expression of one who had achieved what was due her.

Our guests arrived, in both families and separate companies of youths ready to display their skills and their persons. There were dome wigs worn by men who had never seen any battle, even with the raveners of the trade trails, and much time spent showing off trained oryxen, singing and dancing. So our portion of the land was awakened from its quiet by the pulsing roll of drums, the lilt of flutes, the finer notes of hand harps.

I was heartily tired of it all on the night before Siggura was to announce her choice, when festivities were at their height. Also I had had several occasions to know shame, for there had been remarks made within my hearing about the disappointment I was. There was no brightly colored clothing for me, no jewels. Even my hair knot was held only by a small silver ring. But I had sense enough not to wear the pendant, for my showing of such a treasure would be questioned.

Wearily I came to my own small house. There was a glow light on and I expected to hear Mieu's welcome even though the singing was so loud. She always greeted me so.

Instead I heard a muffled curse and then a cry so full of pain that I threw myself within the door. My brother stood there. He was nursing his right hand with his other and I could see the blood dripping from what could only be bites and scratches of some depth.

He turned and saw me, and his face was the mask of a rat as he raised his hand to suck the blood from his wounds. My casket lay on the floor and—

There was a pitiful whine. I went to my knees and would have caught up that bundle of bloodied fur, yet was afraid to touch it lest I add to the pain which racked it. The small head raised a fraction and eyes which were filming with death looked at me. Under that head lay the pendant.

I already had my hand on the hilt of my knife when I swung around. Kalikku was backing out the door. Before I could move he hissed at me:

"Killer of kottis!"

"You—" My throat nearly burst with what I wanted to shout.

"You—there is but you and me—and who would Father believe?" He reached out his unwounded hand and caught up a flagon from the shelf near the door to hurl at me. I was not quick enough and it struck my head.

There was blackness and I do not know how long that lasted. Then I moved and was aware of the smell of the potent wine which my father had refused to have served at the feasting lest the drinking of it lead to quarrels.

I was dizzy and the world swung around me. Then I somehow got as far as my knees, holding to the stool for support. Still clinging to the stool, I edged about. My companion of little more than a happy year was only a fur bundle —unmoving.

Tears seemed to wash away the dizziness. I handled the body.

A blow, and then perhaps a kick—I felt my own lips flatten and draw back against my teeth. My tunic was wet with the wine and I jerked it off, for the fumes seemed to make my head spin the more.

I was able to think straightly again as I bunched together the sodden cloth and hurled it from me. As if it were as plain as an oft-told ballad, I knew what had happened.

To kill a kotti was death. Yet, for all his known harshness towards animals, my brother's word would be accepted. The story was very plain—I was drunk—I stank of that very fiery wine which was supposed to arouse men to the point of insanity. I was drunk and I had killed! Was Kalikku already on his way to tell his side of the story?

Or maybe he would tell it only if he were openly accused. That I would go into later and face it when I had to. Now there was something else.

I gathered Mieu to me. That pendant seemed to catch in her matted fur. I worked it loose and would have hurled it from me for the misfortune it had caused. Yet once it was in my grasp I could not force my fingers to loose it. Instead I wreathed the chain once more about my neck.

Mieu I rolled carefully into a scarf of green which was striped with copper glitter, a fanciful thing I had bought for its color on the very first day she had come to me. Then I carried her out under the stars, speaking in a whisper the while to her essence, even though that might have fled from her. There I laid her even as she had always curled her own body in sleep, and above her I built a cairn such as we erect for those furred ones who honor us with their friendship.

Then I climbed to this point on my hut and I tasted hate and found it hot and burning, and I tried to think what life would hold for me here now, with this thing ever in my mind. Below me the guests departed and the loneliness I craved in which to order my thoughts seemed not too far away. I watched the stars and tried to be one with that which is greater than any of us.

2

The morning came with the rising fierceness of a wind. Afar I caught the warning boom of that nearest signal drum, which was always to be heeded when a storm was imminent, to raise the sand with such a flesh-scouring force that death was the answer if one were caught away from any shelter.

Below my father's spread of house the tall cat, riven as a sentinel from the rock which formed our home territory, throbbed in answer. I was shaken out of thought, out of my self-pity, if that was what had gripped me, and hurried about my duties of seeing the stock sheltered. Even my father joined in this, and Kura, who has a particular bonding with animals and could soothe and bring to obedience a contrary oryxen or fear-savaged yaksen, was there with the others of the household all aroused by the need for haste.

Working so, I forgot all except what was right to hand and drew a breath of relief when, at the time of the second heavy drumbeat, we had all secure.

I had not approached Kalikku, nor he me, during that time. Since my father had not summoned me to face his full wrath, I could believe that my brother had not indeed told the tale he threatened. Not that that betrayal might not yet come.

The storms are capricious. Often the warnings by which we live come to naught as the whirlwind-borne sand suddenly shifts in its track. Yet never can we be sure that it will not strike. Thus we sit in what shelters we have, waiting. We strive to be one with the essence of all about us, to be a very part of the slickrock islands which support our homes and settlements and of the treachery of the sand in between. For each has a place in the whole, rock and man, wind and sand—are we not all a part of our world? Storms may last, at their worst, for days, and we in tight-held houses drink the particles which ably find their way in to film our water, grit it between our teeth as we chew on dried meat or an algae cake. It brings tears to the eyes, a gritty coating to the body, gathers in the hair, weighs upon one. Still we learn early endurance until the violent essence of the land is stilled.

This day our wait was not long, for there came the sharper note which was the signal from the distant drummer that we were not this time the chosen victims. I had spent that time of waiting sitting with the pendant in my hands trying to guess why Ravinga had gifted me with something which had brought such sorrow with it.

She had seemed to be grateful when I had discovered that foul amulet in the hair of her trusted trail beast. But her words had been cryptic, at least to me. Was I indeed not only awkward and clumsy with weapons, disliking all which seemed proper for my father's son, but somehow thick of thought, slow of mind into the bargain?

What did give me peace and contentment? To think upon what lay about me with curiosity, to have a warm rush of excitement when I heard some song of mine echoed back as I followed a stray from our herd, to examine the varied colors of the algae, marking the subtle difference in shade against shade, to look upon the handiwork of Kura and strive to find for her those desert stones, as well as those that traveling merchants brought, which would fit in some pattern of her dreaming. She had said more than once I almost seemed to borrow her own eyes when I went trading, so well was I able to fasten upon that which served her best. This was the inner part of me—as was the friendship of beasts, the companionship of Mieu—

I had thought around in a circle and was back once more to face that which had burned its way into my mind as a flame might burn determinedly its path. Almost I could see Mieu on her back, her four paws upheld, her eyes teasing me for a romp—or feel her soft, gentle touch of tongue tip on the back of my hand.

However, this time I was not to be left alone to chew once more on my bitterness. There was an impatient rap on the door of my small house and one of the herdsmen told me that my father wished to see me at once.

I was cold in an instant as if our sun had been struck from the sky. This then was the ending Kalikku had planned. Still I did not hesitate, but went to stand before my father's tall battle standard which already had been wedged back into place.

There I shed my belt knife, laying it in the trough provided for weapons. My brother's knife was there, the sullen red jewels on its hilt looking to me like the drops of blood he had shed. Also there was Kura's, bearing the fanciful design of small turquoise pattern which she loved most. My brother, yes, I had expected him, but that Kura had been summoned—Only, of course, as a member of the house she would be there to hear the sentence pronounced upon such a criminal as I would be named.

I whistled the small call and was answered by my father's deeper note and then I entered. He was seated on the chair fashioned of Sand Cat bones which testified to his hunter's skill, and it was cushioned, as the floor was carpeted, with the skins of those same mighty killers.

Kalikku was on his right hand, my sister on his left, but I had more attention for my father's face, for by its expression I might know whether I had been already judged and condemned. There was no heavy frown there, just the usual distaste I had met with for years.

"Hynkkel, there were words said among our guests which were not good to my hearing. Most were spoken behind the hand, but others more openly. You have reckoned some twenty full seasons—five since you man-banded your hair. Yet you have not soloed—"

"Let us name him ever untried boy and be done with it!" my brother said. "There is no spirit in him, as we all know." He gazed at me as if he dared his judgment to be denied.

However, it was not for him to say I was this or that—my father remained the Head of this House. And it was to him I spoke:

"Lord, none have spoken to me before of this thing, nor is it my place to do so."

Nor could I help but think of how this might go with us, should that between father and son have been easy. My brother had soloed four years ago, Kura three. And each time it had been an occasion of feasting and joy, even as it had been for Siggura this day past. They had been escorted out into the unknown blindfolded, riding for a night beside my father and most of our kin and a greater part of the household. When there appeared one of the slickrock isles unknown to any and unsettled, my father had raised his hand and struck the honored blow, rendering unconscious the one who must prove his survival skills to return home in triumph. There Kalikku had been left with weapons and some scanty provisions, and Kura likewise at a later time.

Triumphant had been their returns, proving that they had indeed been supported by their Essences, accepted as man and woman, adult and fit to choose their own way henceforth. So it was with all our youth. If they did not solo they remained always thought of as children, simple and of little worth, with no words of theirs ever listened to.

However, it was always those who were the House Heads who selected the time of such a solo, and my father had never so spoken of it to me, this being another thing which I thought he did that he might express his lack of feeling. Now—

"You will solo, Hynkkel. Though," he paused, surveying me from head to foot, "I expect nothing from you. Always have you stubbornly shown that you have no warrior mettle in you. Even your weapon—is it a spear, a sword? Paugh—it is a herder's sling—and a staff. When any other man's tool is put into your hands you are as awkward as your sister always was with those lopsided pots of hers—I trust she will not continue to inflict her 'art' upon her chosen, Koolkan-va-Kastern, in the future.

"Yes, you shall solo but I shall not expose this House to any more gossip or tittle-tell. There shall be no feasting where all can look upon you and see what is so woefully lacking. You may solo—but it shall be at my wish—and in my way!"

I swallowed and bowed my head. Even now there was no softening in him. He only wanted me out of his sight in a manner which would seem correct and leave him feeling he had done his duty, distasteful as it was. There were three of them, and me—but in my father's house I was alone.

So warned, I returned to my quarters and made my preparations: the sand-shedding cloak, the boots, the wide-brimmed hat against the sun. When I picked up that, a bit of fluff fell out, a pinch of Mieu's shedding, for when she was smaller she liked to sleep within that hat. There was my water container, and a packet of algae cakes, the rope coil and a few other things which, by custom, I might take. The last thing I did before I lay down to rest for the day was to gather those hairs of Mieu's shedding and weave them into the chain of the pendant before I set it once more about my throat. This was a symbol of the pain I would always carry.

I thought that I would not sleep but the weariness of my body subdued my thoughts and I went into darkness. Perhaps I dreamed; if I did, I did not remember. But at my awakening I found my cloak-cover twisted, my mouth dry, as if I had indeed fought some inner demon.

Forgetting for an instant, I looked about for Mieu, who always shared my sleeping mat. Then I remembered and rose to dress in the coarse journey clothing kept for travel. One of the herdsmen came even as I was latching fast my overtunic, bringing a bowl of thick soup, a small measure of the juice crushed from algae.

Thus again I was made aware of how my family considered me, that a servant and not kin brought this. Yet I was so accustomed to this usage that I ate and drank and, taking up my sack of permitted supplies, I went down to my father's house.

There were the three of them and in none of their faces did I see any concern. My father turned his usual mask upon me; my sister could have been one of the carvings she so patiently made and fitted into settings for her most elaborate jewels; only my brother showed in his eyes feeling and it was not such to warm my heart.

My father snapped his fingers and I went to him so that he looped over my head the blinding hood. Perhaps it was Kalikku who pushed me up so roughly into the saddle of the waiting pa-oryxen, which I had seen to be the most worthless and expendable of my father's herd. Someone jerked the reins and the beast under me gave forth a cry, nearly a moan, as if it were being urged to do something beyond its slender strength.

There was no sound of any company gathering about us, no singing, no beating of drums to wish me fortune. I might be an outlawed one on his way for a ceremonial casting forth from his House, so meanly did they think of me then.

That same anger which had first arisen in me when I had witnessed Mieu's death became a steady fire. There is in all my race this need to be one with the homeland, with kin, yet my need was not acknowledged in the sight of all by this shabby exit on my solo. I held to my anger, for if I did not keep that as a shield, I had no strength to battle that great feeling of loss which was like a stone resting on my heart.

Kalikku talked, but never to me, or of anything concerning me. Instead he set himself, as I had known him to do many times, to interest my father, draw to himself the full attention in which he basked. He spoke of a prospective Sand Cat hunt which the youths had planned, of an expedition to the city to see and perhaps buy some of the weapons new come from Thnossis which were rumored to be of better metal than men had seen before.

At length my father was wooed into answering him. But I did not hear the voice of Kura, though the drift of her own spicy scent reached me now and then in spite of the blinding hood.

We paused for no nourishment nor rest, but plodded on. I was more used to tramping on my two feet when I journeyed to market and I felt stiff in the saddle. Nor, without seeing the stars overhead, could I begin to guess in what direction we were now headed.

There could not be too many unoccupied rock islands, for my people ever search for more land where we may build. This is an anxiety that occupies the mind of the Head of each House, for the Master of Measures and Balance stands always ready in the imagination of even the most steady-hearted of our people.

When it would seem that we occupied too much living space, when we began to outgrow the resources of the land— then there could be an accounting. And that was a ritual I think even such as my father feared to face. Flocks could be decimated upon the command, even people given to the sword's edge, that their fellows might have living room. There had not been an accounting of that kind for many years, yet the thought and threat of it always overhung us.

I had much time to think as I rode so. Though I had taken merchant roads many times, had fought off the attacks of the rats which preyed upon every algae bed and the other life that had to gather there, yet I was not one to count myself a seasoned traveler. I had listened to the accounts of those who had undergone this same challenge and now I found I remembered best the disasters rather than the triumphs.

Our small party came to a halt at last. There was a quick jerk to remove my hood after I had been dragged roughly from the saddle. I had barely time enough to see that there was a dimming of the stars overhead before the blow caught me and I was enclosed once more in the dark.

I was in a furnace—one of those they tell of which are parts of the mountains of Thnossis where they use the inner heat of the earth itself to aid in the shaping of metal to their will. With all my might I strove to free myself from the bonds laid upon me to hold me to such torment, and opened my eyes.

My head and shoulders lay within a shallow hollow of rock but the rest of my body was positioned in the full heat of the sun. I speedily drew farther back into my small shelter. My head ached and before my eyes both rock and sand were in sickening motion. Slowly I was able to raise hand to my head. Back of my right ear there was a place where touch brought instant pain. And that pain cleared my mind so I knew where I was and why.

My pack lay in the direct rays of the sun. I lurched forward to grasp and pull that to me and as I did so something glittered and fell into view. My fingers closed upon an armlet of burnished copper such as my sister often chose to work with. On the wide band there was set a pattern of turquoise twined to glistening yellow stones such as are those set in the eyeholes of the guardian cat statues.

I held the gift, turning it round and about in my fingers. Its color and fine workmanship would raise pride of possession in any beholder. Yet to me it brought a chill. Resolutely I slipped it up above my elbow, thrusting back the sleeve to view it against my skin. It was such an ornament as would be worthy of several well-trained oryxen if offered in the city. A thing made to please and honor, yet with that chilling message of its own—for I was sure I read it aright—this was my sister's farewell to me.

Did she believe that I was going to my death? Perhaps that was also true. Yet I lived now and that new stubbornness within me said that I would continue to live in spite of all the omens against me.

So I made fast the ties of the bag which held my supplies, shouldered that, and looked about me. By the width of sun outside my crevice night was not far away. And night would bring stars. None who ever ventured on the merchants' trails lacked knowledge of those as guides. I would see what lay above me and then I would move—and keep moving—

3

Ours is a land of great color and beauty. The slickrock islands are rugged, baring jagged fangs to the sky as if some Sand Cats lay upon their backs thrusting up their well-clawed paws. Many are the forms of these rocks also, besides such spires. There are even domes which might mark homes, yet no man's hand carved them so. Others take on the shape of strange beasts from the ancient tales. The winds sound with voices of their own, sometimes with the mocking notes of speech or song one cannot understand.

Under the full sun the rocks blaze forth hues of the colors of Kura's gems. At nightfall their splendor is not fully quenched, for then there lies a silver glimmer over the drifts of sand, glittering at the slightest shifting of grain against grain. This world is a part of my kind even as are the smaller bits upon which we build our homes.

I scrambled to a higher point on the island where I had been left. There was still a streaking of grayish purple and muted gold in the sky, but already some of the stars shone palely. As I looked around to view all that I could before dark took over, I saw that this place of temporary exile was larger than I thought it might be. That such a stretch of available homesites had not been colonized was a puzzle.

Throwing back my head I drew several deep breaths. There are three scents one may pick up on slickrock formations, two of which may mean death, while the third is just the opposite, being rather a promise of existence.

Two species protest the rulership of my own kind. Firstly there is the rat. Though these run in packs they have no real kinship with each other, even for the dams which bear them. Much larger than the kottis, they are personified avid hunger given legs and the freedom to hunt down what will fill their ever-empty bellies.

They can live on algae but do so stupidly, wasting and befouling the bedding pools until they poison the whole of the crop so it may take years before it will recover from their visitation. Being able to burrow deeply and rapidly under the ground, they can shelter so from the sun and emerge only when the worst of the day's blaze is gone, issuing forth to kill and eat, kill and eat. If they cannot find aught they turn upon each other—even the young upon their dam or the dam against her own offspring. There is nothing but evil in them and their stench is enough to bring vomit into the throat of those who must face them.

Our yaksen with their thick coats of long hair have some protection against any small party of such raiders but a large pack can surge over them in a space of breaths, even as the full wind can bury in sand anything alive. The oryxen, on the other hand, though vicious fighters themselves when their horns are not clipped, can be easily slain.

Rats have two enemies—my own species and Sand Cats. We have our long-practiced strategies, our spears, swords, sling-pellets, hunting knives, knife-staffs—yet there have been unfortunates pulled down and left only well-gnawed bones.

The Sand Cats, which we also fear (it being a test of manhood to go hunting such and to bring home a trophy of teeth or hide as a matter of praise from family and kin), have not only a wily and clever form of battle, but jaws and talons which they put to excellent use. Like the yaksen they possess a thick fur coat which is an aid against all but the most well placed and forceful bite. It is probably their presence here and there which keeps down the possible fateful ravages of the hordes of the rats, for the latter are moved entirely by their hunger and will keep fighting rather than retreat because of the constant gnawing of their bellies.

The cats, also, have their scent—a muskiness which is not unpleasant, and a sharper odor with which they carefully mark the boundaries of their hunting territories. They do not gather much together, there being perhaps only one mated pair to a single rock isle, and they have but one cub at a time, that one striking out for itself when it reaches a certain stage of growth. There is fighting between the males for both territory and mates, and the loser often becomes a roaming rogue, always a danger.

Tonight I smelled neither rat stench nor cat trace, but rather the third scent—that I wished for. That was the one which might mean my own survival. The algae pools and pans mean just that to those of my race. For it is on those waterlogged plants that our principal food depends. We have the product of our herds also, but those beasts themselves feed only upon the algae. The only thing else which grows on our brackish soil is the fus-melon, which must be harvested just at the right time or is too hard to be edible.

If this islet on which I stood had an algae pool, I might also encounter some wild yaksen which could furnish sun-dried meat for future traveling.

Traveling which way or where? I looked up to the stars which were growing steadily brighter. Each of us who travels the trade trails is familiar with those points of light which mark the passages we use. However, we are not a wide-roving people, being too heart-bound to our land and our homes to venture far afield. I knew the position in the sky of those which would spell out my own road from home rock to the market at Meloa and return. I could not mark those from where I stood now, nor did I expect to.

It certainly would make the solo of no purpose if he or she who was to make it were placed so as to find their path of return an easy one. But there were other guides and if fortune favored me I might well find one of those.

Among our people one who has been given certain benefits by fortune or who has escaped some dire peril, or wishes to honor an ancestor, might order carved, some place along any known trail where there stood rocks more than life high, the likeness of a kotti—to be supplied with gem eyes to glint in the sun, or a collar of stones which served the same purpose. Many of the main trails were very well marked along their lengths with such sentries, but even lesser known ways had one at least at some important point.

Could I sight one of these—I sighed. There was no firm belief of future fortune left in me.

My eyes adjusted enough so that I could see something of what lay ahead. It would be best I decided to move along, as best I could, the edges of this island until I was able to see how large it was and whether it had—

At that very moment there came a sighing of air which is sometimes born of the evening, and what it brought to me then was the very welcome scent of algae! Nor was there any taint to suggest that this was a poisoned pool which had been deserted. The footing was rough and I went slowly, never knowing when a crevice could confront me suddenly. Also the surface might turn treacherous and a wrenched ankle or broken bone would soon put an end to not only this venture, but me.

I was able to follow the scent, alert to any faint stink of rat or the acrid odor of a cat marking. So far it was only the wholesome breath of growing things which reached me.

At length I came out on the edge of a drop and, in spite of the roll of shadow beneath, I knew that I had indeed found the pool, and one of some size—which added to my puzzlement that this was not already colonized or rat-haunted.

I found a cave of some promise and shifted my pack from my shoulders to store there before I essayed the climb down into the pocket of the pool. Though I was no master of sword or spear, there were two weapons with which constant practice during my duty with the herds had made me expert. Even my brother had never challenged me to a duel with a sling—he professed to find this not befitting a warrior's warrior but rather the weapon of a servant. The sling I had with me, as well as that herder's stout staff, which a twist of the wrist equipped with knife edges protruding halfway down its length. My knife I loosened in its sheath before I swung over, hunting foot- and handholds. I made it only partway down so prudently, for then one of my footholds broke loose and I slid, to come up with a painful slam against rock.

The algae had a night glimmer of its own, some varieties of it giving forth more of the pallid light than others, so I could see that I was not far from the beginning of the bed. However, as if my jarring fall was a signal, there was a boiling up out of the ground not too far away of a slavering pack, red eyes agleam, the fangs in their gaping mouths a faint green. They squealed with ear-punishing shrillness and the stench of their bodies and breath near made me vomit.

I was not foolish enough to have made that descent unprepared. The staff slung on my back seemed to flit of itself into my hands—the knife edges extended as far as possible.

With my back close to the wall down which I had come, I made an outward sweep with my staff. Two of the rats were caught near in mid-air and sent sprawling. In a flash the laggers among the pack were on their fallen fellows, but I was busied with those who came at me. There was not enough room for me to use my sling; I had to make do with staff but that use I knew well.

I swept away two others and snarled myself as my staff was seized in the jaws of one that was larger by half than its fellows and whose red eyes promised full vengeance. Quickly I released my grasp on the staff, now knife in one hand. Use of that I also knew well. This was not the first time I had faced the fury of a rat pack, but never had I been alone. Before, when I had defended the home herd, I had given the signal and knew help would be there speedily—while the yaksen, well aware of their longtime enemies, had lowered horns and trampled with sharp hooves. There was a sudden sharp pain like the bite of a sword at my thigh. I stabbed down with my knife. Luck had provided me with a place to make my stand where I was sheltered in a crack between two projections of rock wall. The rats could only approach me two at a time and those I could meet. However, there was only one of me, and my enemies numbered more than I could count as they whirled about, moving with the speed which was part of their nature. One came from behind the two which were engaging me, leaping across the backs of its fellows for my head and throat. I flung up my hand and the impetus of its leap brought it smashing into the knife. The force of the meeting sent me back, my hand numbing, but not before I had felt the smashing of bone.

The attacker fell with a squealing shriek at my feet, striking about it dazedly, and so bringing down the attack of those two that I had been holding off.

There was a flurry of battle which kept the others of the pack away from me. My shoulders grated against the rock and I breathed heavily. Such a respite could last but a moment and then they would be at me again—For all the strength I had learned in my own way as herdsman and trader-traveler I knew that I could not hope to last out against another determined attack.

I was afraid, yes, but I also knew anger that I would lose my life to fill the bellies of these monsters. As many as I could take with me, or feed to their own, that I would. My staff lay there but the fight of the three rats before me raged over that and I had no chance of retrieving it.

There was a shifting of the pack. In this light they were only black shadows with those fire coals for eyes. I stiffened, waiting for the last rush to bring me down.

They were backing away! I could not believe that—though the rats were thought to have little or no intelligence, these might almost be withdrawing to take council how best to attack me without so much loss to their pack.

However, more and more heads were lifted, not toward me but to the sky overhead. Then there rang out a single shrill cry, to be picked up and added to by a second and third. Those three rats entangled before me still gouged. One lay beneath, trampled upon, but its fellows were at each other's throats for the privilege of consuming it. They alone did not display the strange behavior of the pack.

Once more the cry arose. I thought I read into it not an urge to battle but a warning. I found myself also head high, listening, trying to scent more than the stench of the pack. There was a whirl of breeze and I knew what had altered the behavior of my enemies. We who are a part of the land, and live close to it, are readied to catch its changes.

Storm—I had heard no warning drum, none of the far-carrying vibrations picked up by the road sentinel cats to be relayed. Instead there was that strange prickling of the air itself which sent a tingling of the skin down one's body.

The pack, squealing in chorus now, were gone. Even one of those in the struggle before me tore loose and went limping after. They were seeking the shelter which all life must have if it were to survive the coming blast—as I must have.

I leaped over the two bodies so near my feet and sought the side of the algae pool. Such storms had been known to last for days and I must have some provisions to supplement the few rations I carried. With a sweep of hand I gathered algae, storing it in my jerkin against my body for want of better carrier. Only three such garnerings dared I allow myself.

The cliff down which I had so unceremoniously descended had to be faced and climbing was always far more difficult than descent. Yet I schooled myself against such haste as would deposit me once more at the bottom of that drop unable to find shelter before the menace born of wind and sand struck.

Panting with the effort, I did regain that small cave where I had left my gear. Dumping the soggy mass of algae I had managed to bring up with me onto the rock therein, I set about making my cloak into the partial shelter which a traveler could depend upon. The cave was cramped but I was lucky to have it at all.

Now I formed a protection with the cloak, wedging my staff to hold it as secure as I might hope to make it. Then I huddled down, a handful of algae in my hand to suck upon, waiting for the storm to strike.

Strike it did. There was no escaping its fury. My preparations were as nothing against such constant blows. Sand as fine as grit reached me. My skin was scoured raw by that. I was deafened. And I was blind, binding my scarf over my eyes so that I would not lose them to the ever-present torture of the sand. When I was driven by a hunger which seemed as demanding as that of the rats, I strove to choke down bits of the algae, only to feel within each bite the grit which shifted through my poor protection to coat everything within.

One loses count of time when one becomes a prisoner of a storm. I must have slept because I remember one wild dream wherein I confronted a Sand Cat and felt the slashing of its claws, the rasp of its rough tongue. It was playing with me as a kotti plays with one of the vine beetles. There was no welcome escape, no death—only darkness. Into that I sank thankfully, no longer able to summon up the strength to fight. Still in that darkness the roar of the storm deafened me and there was no peace to be found.

Was this to be the end of my attempt to prove myself before my kin? No, something in me would not accept that! There was a part of me which endured through darkness and pain—which held stubbornly to life.

4

There came an end in time and with the deafening howl of the wind out of my ears I awoke out of the darkness which was not true sleep, only to lapse again into the slumber my tense and aching body craved. All I realized in those moments before I fell asleep was that I had survived by some chance such fury as could wipe out a caravan with ease.

It must have been a dream—certainly I did not in truth act out what was so vividly real to me. There was a room lighted by lamps which gave off an amber glow like unto the eyes of giant cats, so that I seemed to stand before some judge who held as much right over me as one of those dreaded masters of the desert.

There was movement and into that area of light came two I knew, Ravinga, the maker of dolls, and her apprentice. Ravinga held in her hands, with the care one carries something precious, a doll whose like I had never seen before. Such was the art of its making that it might indeed have been a man in miniature. Then I saw that indeed it had the likeness of a man and that man was me.

She came two steps forward and held the doll out and her eyes went searchingly from it to me and back again as if she would so make sure her likeness was correct in every detail. Then she nodded and spoke.

But the storm might have indeed rendered me deaf, for though her lips moved I heard no words, nor did she address me, but rather her companion. The girl moved forward also and it was plain to me that she came reluctantly and that whatever was happening was against her will. Still she came. She put out her hands, palms flat and up, side by side, and Ravinga laid the doll which was me across them. The girl bent her head, and her tongue showed forth its tip from between her lips. With that she touched the face of the doll three times while Ravinga's lips moved again as if she sang or spoke. Like a snap of the fingers they, the lamplight, all of it was gone. I opened my eyes.

Clawing away the scarf I had bound above my face, I saw that I lay in darkness and when I tried to move there was a heavy pressure against me which brought a start of fear. The driven sand must stand high against my frail protection of cloak and it was as if I were sealed into this crevice.

When I struggled to free the staff which had pegged that down from within, I could feel a sliding and some of that pressure lessened, setting me to quicker action, to be free of what might have been a grave.

I worked out into the night. There were no ominous clouds of whirling sand. The stars hung as well-tended lamps. Trembling and moving stiffly I got to my feet to look around. I smeared my hands across my face striving to free it from the caking sand dust and there followed pain from my blasted skin.

The algae pool! Not only should I find there the food and moisture my body needed, but there should also be some of the growth meant for healing.

It was then that I felt that other, that I was not alone here. Yet when I steadied myself and looked about I could see nothing but rock where runnels of sand filling every depression were sifting across the edge of the ledge beneath which lay the pool, as might a trickle of water drain away. I had never seen such in my life, for free-running water would be a marvel almost past believing—though I had heard that such did exist in Vapala.

I did have one gift which I cherished but which had never impressed my father, that of being able to sense something in trouble. That impression was with me now, sending me wavering along, not down to the pool which my own body demanded, but rather on the edge of the depression which held it.

There was pain in that sending, strong enough to make me wince in spite of my own raw skin. Pain, and a suggestion of fear.

I lurched on, leaning on my staff, striving to avoid those dust-filled cavities which might bring the careless down with a broken limb. Then I halted, for the scent came clearly. The musk of a Sand Cat, overlaid with that of blood and the beginnings of infection—a wounded animal? But how had such been able to survive the storm? And a Sand Cat—

The tales of their ferocity and cunning were a part of our lore. We honored any man who slew one. By all we knew there could be no peace with such.

Still the pain lay heavy in my mind. If the creature were badly wounded and suffering—would it not be better to put it out of this misery of life? I have had to cut the throat of a yaksen that had served me well when I found it rat-torn and in agony. Pain—no living creature should be left to face such a slow descent into death.

I passed now the end of that cavity in which lay the pool. The scent of the Sand Cat was heavy; still I could not sight any trace of the animal. There was a sudden low growling. I faced around, to see a dark opening in an arching rise of the rock.

With my staff grasped in both hands before me, ready to forestall any leap as best I could, I crept forward. Unbidden by any thought, I found my voice as if some instinct I had known nothing of before now spoke through me.

"I come in peace, Strong One—Peace—" Then I fell to humming softly as I did when I tended some hurt of one of the herd—having early learned that such seemed to soothe any fear of me.

There was movement in the darkness. The night glimmer of the sand pools about gave aid to my night sight. Indeed within that hollow was a furred body, and the smell of pus-filled wounds was foul. Pain—but with it now menace—defiance—

I strove to balance my own thoughts, to subdue any of the fear that this one's kind arose in me, as I went to my knees before the mouth of the cave.

"Great One, I come to help—" As I leaned forward the cat pendant fell outward from the folds of my thickly sand-powdered travel shirt. It startled me, for it gleamed and with a greater life than did the shimmer of the sand. My hand went to it, but there was no heat as a lamp might give forth—only the light increased.

That rising snarl from within the dark cup stopped. Pain I could still sense, but there was something else now which I could not define. I only knew that if I crawled forward I would no longer need my staff, nor the knife at my belt. So I laid aside my shaft and went ahead.

Great golden discs of eyes met mine.

"Great One—" I said slowly. Then I caught that other smell—the stink of rat—and my hand rattled away a well-gnawed bone. The light of my pendant had increased and I could see that this was a male, with mangled paw, now swollen and giving forth the stench of corruption. It might be too late to offer anything but a clean death, but I could try and that, I knew deep within me, I must do.

Those same water plants with which I had thought of relieving my own scored skin—could they draw the infection out? At least I could offer the animal water and something which might lighten a little of its present torment.

"Great One—I go for that which will comfort—" I spoke as I might to an injured kotti. If my fear had matched his, so was it now decreasing.

The descent to the algae pool was difficult. My sore hands were as if burnt by the time I reached the pool side. For the first time I remembered the rats which had been driven away by the coming of the storm. I listened, drew deep breaths to pick up their smell. There was no sign nor scent of them. So I got to the pool, plunging my own hands and arms deep into the mass of growth there. There was no strong light to show me the graduations of color necessary to tell one type of plant from another. I merely gathered all that I could within reach and, with that bundle, won once more to the surface of the rock and so to the cave.

The wounded beast must have scented what I carried. He growled once but then was still. Carefully I squeezed some handfuls to the stone where he might lick it off, and then turned my attention to his wound.

To my relief, from what I could see by the light of the pendant which had obligingly flared up again, there was only one wound. Moving quietly, again humming, striving to project to him that I meant no harm, only good, I crushed another mess into a paste, and, with all the care I could to spare the pain of a wrong touch, I began to spread it across the wound.

The paw twitched, I saw those wickedly sharp claws show. He raised his head from where he was licking up the last of the algae and once more stared at me round-eyed, unblinkingly. I refused to be so easily cowed, finishing my task as deftly as I could. Then I settled myself not too far away, sitting cross-legged and eating avidly what was left of the store of algae. Part of it was bitter but I was sure that it was no different from the crops grown in our own home pool, and the moisture it carried to my body was as soothing in its way as the touch of it was to my skin. The rats had had no chance to befoul and poison this bounty.

The Sand Cat finished the rest of the algae. With his good paw he pushed at one of the gnawed bones and I knew that he craved more than the stuff from the pool, but I carried no dried meat with me. To deliberately seek out and kill rats was a test I was not yet ready to face, though I was very sure that it must come sometime.

I had withdrawn to just outside the cave space this strange new companion was using for shelter. My body ached with fatigue. The pounding of the storm and my exertions since then had brought me close to exhaustion. Already the lights of dawn showed along the horizon I faced, from the place where I had dropped down onto the rock. Those supplies, my cloak, all the rest I owned and had left behind when I had sought out the source of that unvoiced call for succor were some distance from me.

Still I could not just leave this creature who had given me an unusual portion of trust. Judging by my past knowledge of animal tending, his wound would take some time for

the healing, if heal it was going to. To leave him here unable
to find food, a prey to the rats whose scenting ability when it
came to any living thing (and all life was their prey) would
speedily bring them seeking him when they issued again from
their safe burrows—No—

"Great One," my hand had gone unconsciously to the pendant, "I must go but I shall return. This I swear by—" my
fingers closed about the mask, "by this which is a thing of
power." And when I said that, I knew that I spoke the truth.
Where this had come from, for I was sure it was not of the
craftsmanship of Ravinga, I did not know. Kura had said it
was of such workmanship as she had never seen, and my sister was always one avid to collect any new pattern or design
which she did sight; also that it was old.

Somehow I pulled myself to my feet. At the pace my body
would allow me it would take me some time to reach that
crevice which had saved my life and I must do so before the
sun was up enough to be a menace. I leaned heavily on my
staff as I went. There was a querulous sound from behind me
and I looked over my shoulder. Those eyes were fastened upon
me. They did not hold the glow they had showed in the dark,
yet they compelled. Once more I offered assurance:

"Great One, I shall return."

It was almost as if my words were a message he could
understand. His large head dropped, rested upon his good paw,
he blinked, and his eyes closed.

So I made a toilsome way back to my own place of refuge,
taking good care as I went to sniff for any taint of rat. The
rocks around me were taking on day color now, yellow, red-
brown, here and there some point like a small cliff layered
with a hue nearly red between two dull yellows.

There is a beauty in our land which travelers may call harsh.
But there is born in us a feeling that we are a part of it. Even
as our skin is bronzed like unto some of those shades of red
and rich brown, we choose to wear colors which are brilliant,
so we may even feel that we have indeed been hewn from the
very stone which forms our dwelling places. It is our custom

to open our hearts and minds when we are alone to the land, the sky, all which may be about us.

At this moment as I so painfully trudged back to my camp I paused now and then to look about me, breathing deeply of the air which was now free from any trace of sand powder. However, each time I surveyed the sand which lay beyond this perch there was no sign that any of my blood had been here before me. There certainly were none of the rock-hewn cat markers to be sighted.

The heat of the day was already up when I reached the crevice. My stiff, sore body protested as I made as swift a business as possible of folding my small store of possessions into the pack and lashing it so with the rope.

I went to the edge of the rise and looked down at that portion of the pool which lay below and then I changed my plans and decided that to follow along the shore of that, close to what moisture the pool exuded, would be a better plan than to keep to these sun-baked heights.

Though the descent was a cruel test of my body, I made it and came almost immediately upon the body of one of the rats which I had killed during the attack. Perhaps it was the fear of the storm which had kept it out of the stomachs of its fellows. Save for some torn flesh it was almost intact. Remembering the gesture of the cat, reaching for the tooth-stripped bone, I stayed long enough to butcher the dead thing, taking legs and haunches from it.

These I lashed together with the end of my rope and added to the weight of the pack. At the edge of the pond I stopped once again and ate of the algae I recognized as the most nourishing. Later I could harvest such and dry it into cakes so that when I would move on again I would have fresh supplies. When I would move on again—

I hesitated over the thought. Prudence would suggest that I do so as soon as possible. Still something, perhaps the stubbornness which had been born in me so that I could not be the son my father wanted, told me now I had a task before me whether I wished it or not.

Men said that there was no greater enemy to us than the Sand Cats. They prey upon our flocks, and, it was widely believed, upon such of my own people as they could take. Teeth, claws, and hides of them were proud possessions of the hunters among us. There was an insurmountable enmity between my species and theirs. Yet now I could not leave this one to certain death.

I stirred algae with one hand and tried to sort out my thoughts, to understand. The pendant in this light had lost all its glimmer of the night before. To any eyes it would seem merely a finely made piece of jewelry, a little strange perhaps. I began to remember that odd dream or vision which had been mine during the storm—of Ravinga and the doll which had been made in my likeness. My dripping hand went up, not to my mouth, but to touch my face, as I remembered the action of the girl, the unwilling action.

Had that only been a dream? Or something else? Dreams could seldom be recalled as vividly as I did this. Suddenly I knew that if I came through this time of solo and was free to go my way, I would seek out the dollmaker. I wanted to know more, not only of the mask I wore but the meaning which lay behind it. That there was such a meaning I was sure.

Having eaten my fill and noting that the sun was now near a period when I *must* seek cover, I started on around the edge of the pool, my staff ready. Heat of direct sun might well not keep the rats from my trail; they were always too avid for flesh.

Walking here was more even and I was able to make good time until I came to that portion of the wall which I recognized as my path when I had sought out food for the cat. I made the journey up and then hoisted the packet of my belongings by the end of the rope.

There was a muted growl. The cat raised his head. His lip drew back a little to expose those fangs which are so fearsome a weapon for his kind. Then his head dropped again upon his paw as if in weakness.

I freed the rat meat and brought it to him. He lifted his head a little and his tongue licked at the offering. For a moment I was afraid that he was indeed so near death that he could not eat, but it seemed that that licking aroused him, for he planted his good paw on a portion of the meat and started tearing at it, seeming to gulp it down without chewing. While he so disposed of the food, I searched through my scant belongings and brought out a small leather bag which held some yaksen fat into which had been worked certain strains of algae I knew were healing. This I kneaded until it was very soft and once more I approached the cat, humming again as I did so.

"Great One—" he had finished most of the meat and had been licking at a leg bone, "give me leave to tend your wound."

His stare was a measuring one and then he actually moved, as if he did well understand my words, pushing forward a little his wounded leg. As carefully as I had applied the algae poultice, so now I pulled it free in flakes. I was sure that the limb was less swollen than it had been last night, yet I could not altogether depend upon that.

Now I could see clearly that the wound was a nasty tear, almost as if a portion of the flesh had been detached from the bone, and I thought it was a rat bite. That it might well be infected was the problem. I could only hope that the small knowledge I had gained concerning the hurts of animals would be of help.

Once more, as gently as possible, I covered that expanse of angry-looking flesh with the salve. When I had done he dropped his head to sniff at my handiwork and I feared because of the scent of the grease he might set to licking it off again. But he did not.

Meanwhile I set about making a resting place of my own. I envied my companion his cave, for I had to make do for a shelter with my cloak stretched between two upstanding fangs of rocks. However, there was a third, higher pinnacle which did give me a dark shadow for cover, at least for now.

One of my final preparations was the finding and choosing of stones suitable for my sling. Those I piled in three places where I might have to take refuge if the rats did come sniffing along the trail.

There was little more I could do and I curled within my own cramped shelter, hoping the cat would give warning if we were attacked. The full heat of the day was now upon us and perhaps that would be our greatest defense.

5

I had good reason to be glad that I had chosen ammunition for my sling and had that within reaching distance as a growl from the cat—one which heightened to a roar of defiance and rage— brought me sharply out of uneasy slumber. The stink of rats was strong. In spite of the fact that the sun was still high enough to light fire heat on the rocks, the creatures were on the hunt.

That they ventured out into the full day to do this was surprising. It must have been that they had picked up not only my scent but that of the cat, so altered by his wound as to make them think that he would be easy prey.

I brought down two and sent a third howling and stumbling back, one foreleg dangling. As was usual their pack mates closed in upon the injured as well as upon the dead. But there was something else which surprised me above the natural heat of battle.

The pack milled about the foot of a taller spur of rock and on the top of that there was a black spot which in spite of the sun's glare I at length made out to be another rat. But this one was different from the others. The shape of its head, as I made it out against the red of the rock, was too large and almost misshapen.

Even as I was able to see that much, the creature raised its head and howled, a sound different also from the squealing of its fellows. It was on its feet and I could see that the thing was at least twice the size of the pack members below, formidable as those were.

As if it had voiced some order the pack surged forward towards us. Still that brief pause had given me a chance to use my sling to good advantage. Two more of those attackers went down, one snapping at its own side where my rock had thudded home, as if to bite at the thing which had hurt it. This time those who fell were not set upon by the rest. So that small advantage was lost.

I had already moved so that my back was to the cave wherein the roaring cat was fighting to get to its feet. I had jerked with me the cloak I had set up to use as a sunshield and this I swirled out with one hand, to engulf the first of the rats coming within reach.

A moment later I had thrown my knife, taking a desperate chance upon something which was just a suspicion. It struck deep, not into one of those upon whom I was now using my staff in the sweep which was the best answer to their charge, but into the neck of that thing on the rock point above.

Its peculiar cry was cut off, as I was busy with the rest. One of them would have taken me from the side, but the cat, as handicapped as it was, smacked that down with a single blow of its good paw.

The whirlwind of their attack was finished as quickly as it had begun. Dark forms, their skin patched with the green muck from the pools, drew back. They once more waited at the foot of that spur where the larger creature had taken its stand. Only, the body of their leader (and when had any rat pack known a leader?) was flopping until it rolled from its perch to fall among them.

Then the remainder of the attackers acted in the true style of their kind, throwing themselves upon the larger form, tearing and fighting among their kin for a chance to devour the swiftly dead. However, then I saw a strange thing indeed. Those who were nearest to and even had their jaws in the flesh of the dead suddenly flinched back from the body, fighting each other to get away. Moments later they all turned and slithered off, quickly concealed among the spurs and tumbles of rock.

There were left the bodies of the two killed nearest to the cave, a third dragging itself away uttering cries of pain, apparently its spine broken, and the partly tattered bundle of skin and bones of the one that had watched from above.

For moments I crouched where I was, unable to believe that the rats had given up so easily. I surveyed every blotch of shadow, sure that at least some of them lurked there ready to jump again if I relaxed my vigilance.

However, such a maneuver was foreign to them. Though they might indeed have swept men and animals from many of the islands by sheer might of numbers, they had never been known to show any such signs of intelligence, only the blind rage and hunger which brought them out in rush attacks. I looked to the cat. His senses were more acute than mine. I longed to be able to communicate with him, to discover what he thought of this strange withdrawal.

He still growled, but his battle cry was stilled. Then he reached out his uninjured paw and drew towards him the body of the rat he had slain and began to eat avidly. That he would do so in the face of the enemy was something I did not believe. So to the sound of crunching bones I made my way across the sun-heated stone to look down upon that one which I had knifed.

To the eye its torn body seemed no different from the others I had seen all my life, save that it was so much larger— almost equaling the size of the Sand Cat. It was the head which showed the greatest difference, as I saw when I used the end of my staff to roll what was left of the body over so that it lay more straightly stretched upon the bloody rock.

The skull was domed to a high level, and, though that had been crushed in its fall, there was something else, a glint which flashed from the shreds of torn skin. I had no desire to touch it, yet I needed to get my knife which, I saw, to my satisfaction, was buried in the neck where it joined the shoulder.

It was not the knife which had glittered. I knelt and now used the tip of that knife as a probe, lifting forth a thing which was certainly not native to any rat.

It was well smeared with blood. I tipped it onto the rock. What I saw was an oval of what could only be worked metal and in the center of that a stone or perhaps another bit of metal which was a dead black in color.

From where I had lifted it there came the knowledge that it had been embedded in the fore of that oddly shaped skull. Surely the creature had not so encumbered itself. I fumbled in my belt pouch and sacrificed a piece of dried algae to clean it, handling the thing very gingerly.

There was that about it which made me wary of touching it, even when it was clear of blood and spattered brain stuff. Nor did I want it to be with me even to the extent of being bundled into my pouch. Instead I hooked it up with my knife point and returned to the cave, turning it out on a stretch of rock under the sun which was now well towards the other horizon and so less of a menace.

The cat stopped his meal to look from me to the stone I had laid in sight. Once more he growled.

"We have here a mystery, Great One," I said. Though he might not understand me, still it seemed good to express my thoughts and perhaps fears aloud. "That one which fell to my knife had this embedded in its skull. Yet this is of the making of another and not any badge of true rat."

I thought of my father's Leader banner which stood proudly beside his house. It is true that my species were given to such badges and sign posts of position and honor. Yet it was also true that for generations there had been no story of any leader rat that would impress its will on the remainder of the pack. Each was an enemy to the others and always had been. That they traveled together might be their way of life but it meant no cooperation among them.

"Great One, why should a rat one wear such? Do they now change their way of life? If so this is an ill thing for all of us who dwell in this land. It—"

I stopped almost in mid-word. For I had been watching that thing I had taken from the dead. The center stone which had been shiny black, its setting which had glinted like red gold, had lost color as if the heat had leached it. And under that touch, light as it was, the piece crumbled as might a bit of sand which had been temporarily shaped but could never hold for long. Powder it became, with a twist of thin metal also crumbling into nothing.

Metal I knew, stones I was well aware of. At times I had watched Kura at her work fashioning that jewelry which was a source of pride to all our House. Nothing I had learned of her, and she was always ready to talk of her art to a serious listener, had suggested that there was such material as I had just watched fall into nothingness.

"Great One," I said now very slowly—though the sun still could reach us, I felt within me a chill—"this is of evil—" Of that I was very sure. But what kind of evil and whence it came, who knew? Were I to travel to the Emperor's court with such a tale, who would believe me when I could bring no tangible evidence?

The cat growled again. Its eyes were also on that pinch of dust. I suddenly got to my feet and swept out my staff, sending the remains of that dark object away from us. Then, to keep my mind away from speculation which was of no value, I set about butchering those rats which had been untouched by their fellows. I had no liking for rat meat but a man needs to feed his body, and strips of flesh, sun-dried, would be welcome to take with me when I moved on.

That night I climbed to the higher pinnacle of rock which had been part of my shelter and tried to trace the star paths overhead.

There was nothing I could identify, but I settled myself, staff across my knees, striving to put from my mind all the tumult of the day, and open the inner part of me to the essence of the land about, as is the custom of my people. Thus there came a measure of peace though one part of me never relaxed sentry duty.

We had driven off the rats which had come by day but they had been acting out of nature doing that. It would be more likely that they would make another try, under the usual cover of darkness which they favored.

Though I had good reason to expect so, there were no more attacks in the dark. I came down from my high perch and spread out the skins of the slaughtered rats. I had neither the time nor the materials to do any curing; still I scraped them as best I could and spread them out on a level rock where the sun's heat in the morning could produce a manner of very crude drying. These I would need to patch my boots.

No footgear had a long life for anyone on foot in this land. It was the custom for any traveler to carry several pair of boots in his luggage as well as tough hide for repairs. To the best of my ability I worked with what I had, and every time I glanced up I could see the glowing eyes of the cat watching me closely.

So as I worked I talked, though there came no answer. But I put into words what lay in my mind, addressing the cat as I would some very old and wise one of my own species.

"In my father's house, Great One, I am the least of those under the protection of the kin. Perhaps it is that I have carried with me some curse from my birth hour, for my father takes no pleasure in my company, and my brother—"

The heat of that anger I had buried deep within me was stirring a little though I would not give it room to grow.

"—is my unfriend, though the reason for that I do not know either. Save that I have no wish ever to be a slayer—"

Then the incongruity of that struck me as I rasped the knife over the skin. Who was I to speak so who had fought and brought to death that very creature whose hide I now claimed for my own?

I settled back on my heels. The glimmer of the sand, the light shining from the cat mask which swung free outside my overshirt, fought the dark, though nothing could reach within the many shadows, for I had no lamp.

"Great One, how does a man learn in truth what he is? I say I shrink from taking life, I have laid hand and voice upon beasts and soothed them into peace. Yet since I have come to this place I have killed and killed. Though no man can stand with empty hands against the rats and it may well be that in the end, should one's own life be at threat, one takes up the nearest weapon—"

I turned to look straight at those unblinking eyes. For all I knew, the cat might be an instant enemy, more deadly than any rat, to be slain lest I be slain. Still within me there was no wish, no fear, to act as would my father, my brother, any of warrior stock.

All this time the feeling had grown in me that this wounded warrior of another sort was far greater than any beast. He presented more and more of a riddle and one I was drawn to solving.

At last, putting aside my work on the hides, I went downslope to the pool to collect more algae and returned to dress again that wounded forelimb. There was no growl now, in fact the animal stretched out his leg, though I was sure that that gesture caused him pain, in order that I might work the better on it. When I put a portion of the algae down where he might lick it I heard a rumble which I realized in surprise was a purr.

So encouraged, I put out my hand and laid it for a moment on his head, feeling the soft thickness of the fur there, even thicker than that Mieu had worn, and longer. However, I did not take any further liberties. I leaned back to eat my own portion of the growth I had harvested—as well as smearing some on my still tender skin—though that also was healing.

The night went swiftly. I was ever on the alert for any move from our enemies. In my pouch there was a twist of cloth which held certain stones which I had found when I had been hunting for ammunition for the sling. There were two lumps of turquoise, which made me think of Kura—though they were of inferior color, and my sister would doubtless scorn using them in any of her work. There were some agates also, and those I had set aside for the color—for they were boldly striped in several hues even as were the rocks about. I had seen such in which those lines, were the stone to be skillfully enough cut, seemed to make pictures of sand and rock.

All these offered in a market might bring me food. In a market—did I then plan to return to Meloa where I was known? Rumor flies from rock isle to rock isle, from market to market. Those who were servants to my father had tongues in their heads. I did not in the least doubt that many times our affairs had been a matter of curiosity-led discussion. That

I had gone on this solo in such a shabby manner would be a matter of comment which would well reach afar—before I had the chance of even discovering any marked trail. And if I went to Meloa, then it was certain I would be expected to return to my father's house.

My father's house, where there was no longer any place for me!

So close are kin to kin among us that such a thing was hardly known. In fact when I even thought of it now there was a sickness in my throat as if I must spew forth the food I had eaten. What place was there for me?

I was fingering the stones I had harvested, passing them from hand to hand. What could I do? That I had a good hand with herd beasts, that I had trained oryxen so that even my father had accepted mounts I had gentled without question, that I knew was perhaps my only gift.

In Meloa I had once seen an animal trainer. She had been out of Vapala, sent to bring back some high-bred oryxen for one near the Emperor. Her I had looked upon with respect and longing—longing that I might hold such a position.

It was the custom for a younger son to be apprenticed to some trade—or such was true in families which were not of the ancient warrior blood. Could I by myself arrange such an apprenticeship to some beast handler? That could well mean leaving all that I knew—even this land—for such a chance would be quicker found in Vapala than in Kahulawe. Again that sickness was sour in my throat. To leave—turn my back on all which had been a part of me—I—surely I could find some other way of survival—

Survival! If I were to survive the immediate future, and there might be little chance of that, it was better to fix my thoughts on what was immediately around me and not strive to read the future as certain women were supposed to have the gift of doing.

Dawn came at last and there was light enough that I could look upon the wound of the cat and see it well. The swelling was down. In two places the ragged tear was knitting, I noted, as I replastered the hurt for the second time.

I had emerged from the cave and was standing, striving to set in place once again my cloak and staff shade against the coming heat when I heard it—and from behind me—the menacing growl with which the cat had announced the coming of the rats—and yet this was not from the animal I tended!

6

I schooled myself against any hasty action, knowing well that such might bring attack at once. Why had I accepted so easily that the beast I tended was the only one of his kind on the isle? It was well known that the Sand Cats lived in small family groups.

Very slowly I moved and at the same time I hummed that soothing sound I had made when I had first found the hurt one.

Crouched on one of the higher lifts of rock was indeed another Sand Cat. Now I heard growling, was sure I saw a tenseness of shoulder and leg which suggested that the newcomer was well ready to spring and bring me down. My staff I had just wedged into a crevice to support my improvised tent. I had only my knife—my opponent was too close for me to use my sling.

This was a female. Rounder of body, amber back in striking contrast to the white spots, the clump of white fur growing longer between her ears and along her spine, about her broad muzzle and underparts, she was majestic. Her club of tail was held spear straight, and her great eyes centered on me. She was but slightly smaller than her mate.

For what seemed to me far too long a time we faced each other eye to eye. Then my senses were acute enough to see that tenseness begin to leave her. If she would attack, it would not be at that moment.

Still humming and continuing to face her, I sidled around until I could reach for some of those strips of rat meat I had laid out for the sun's drying. With several of these in hand I edged back towards her.

"Great One," I kept my voice as low and as even as possible, "to your lord I mean no harm, nor any to you. Accept this guesting gift."

Suppressing all my unease I ventured to the very foot of the short height on which she was still in crouch and there laid down the meat, edging once more well away. She had growled warningly when I approached her but she had not sprung.

Now, having eyed me intently, she did leap lightly from her perch to sniff my offering. She took a long time at that as if she were still suspicious of my good will and distrusted the gesture. Then, apparently having satisfied herself that I had indeed presented her with no more than it seemed, some meat, she took up two of the pieces and in a bound was at the side of her mate.

As he bent his head to sniff at the meat and then bolt it, she in turn dropped her nose to only inches from his hurt and then put out a tongue to lick at the poultice I had smeared upon the wound. From that examination she raised to tongue her mate's head, grooming his fur between his ears. I could hear again the rumble of his purr.

The feeling grew in me that they had some form of communication. Yet when I took a step towards them she was instantly on her feet, her lips drawn back to show fangs, warning me off.

She was well away from the path I must follow down to the algae bed and there was a need to gather more of the crop there, shape it into cakes to be sun-dried like the meat. I felt it safer to have a supply of food to hand than to continue to risk more and more separate descents. We had certainly not accounted for all the rats, and their knowledge that we were here would bring them again. Of that I had no doubt at all.

The female cat watched me go towards the cliff. She did not stir from the side of her mate. Still I felt as one might when trying to slip by a horned oryxen, as if I dared my way past an unsprung trap.

Two trips down and up I made, transporting masses of algae. The second time I came to my improvised camp I saw that the female was stretched out beside her mate, but still she watched me with what I believed was a lively suspicion.

I set about fashioning cakes of the algae, separating that which I had brought for the tending of the other cat's wound. Selecting a fairly flat section of rock I spread out my supply, though I kept some for this day's food.

As I leaned forward to pat the last of these cakes into shape, my cat pendant swung free into the sun. There was a brilliant spot of light dancing across the rock near the mouth of the cave, the sun reflected from that metal.

The heads of both cats turned, were watching that dance of beam. From the female came a sound which was not a growl, rather something close to a mew. Her eyes were now on me as she sat up, or rather fixed on what I wore that gave that ray of light birth.

Now she arose. I made myself remain where I was as if any fear of her was forgotten. Those great paws, either of which could tear the very features from my skull, as had been done with some unwary hunters, were lifted and replaced deliberately.

However, she was not heading in my direction but rather for the rock where lay the already leather-stiff meat. One strip she picked up by its very end, then she did turn in my direction. Coming to within a distance which would allow a blow of her powerful forepaw to flatten me, she sat again, and with a slight movement of her head tossed her meat so that it fell half across the toe of my nearest boot.

So—Almost I could not believe. From all that I heard about the Sand Cats, I knew that they were wily opponents and that they could match men often by some act of intelligence which caused the older people to whisper of demons and the like. For generations beyond generations my kind and this beautiful beast before me had been enemies to the death. Now of her own wish she had made the same peace offering to me that I had earlier made to her.

I picked up the strip of meat and set tooth to the toughness, striving to worry off a mouthful which had the consistency now of a dried melon vine, almost beyond my dealing with it.

Grimly I chewed and swallowed and hoped that the brittle fiber of it would not abrade my throat as it went down.

"My thanks, Great One, so we share upon share—" Of course she could not understand me but I hoped that the tone of my voice would make clear that there was peace between us. On impulse then I slipped the chain of the cat mask over my head and held it out, letting the pendant touch down upon the rock not too far from her.

Instantly her attention was all for the mask, now a blaze of fire in the full sun. She inclined her head and her tongue came out. Delicately she touched the pendant with its tip.

Memory came to me of that dream—of how the girl who shadowed Ravinga had made something of the same gesture towards the doll her mistress held. There was no resemblance between that slender girl and this massive cat form—save they were both female—but somehow my thought linked one to the other.

The Sand Cat drew away, back to the side of her mate. Him she nuzzled and then, without warning, she leaped outward from the mouth of the cave, was past me like a stream of bronze fur. To the top of the same height from which she had first viewed us she went, but not to linger—instead she disappeared almost instantly from view.

I went to pick up the pendant and restore it to its place. The heat of the day was advancing quickly; it was time to take to such shelter as I had. And that I did. The Sand Cat had withdrawn farther into the cave and I thought he was asleep, an example it might be well for me to follow.

I did not dream and I awakened quickly to sound—the growl of my companion. There was no need for explanation— rat stink was heavy on the air and it was evening. Yet the enemy did not come boiling out at us as I expected. I could indeed pick out forms slinking from place to place and they were ingathering. To dismantle my shelter in order to free my staff for battle took but an instant or two.

After, I made my way quickly to the edge of the cave. For both our sakes it was better that we stand together against the surge when it came. The fact that they had not already struck at us began to add to my uneasiness. All my knowledge of the creatures was being questioned and the tactics I had been taught to use perhaps would not now be of much service.

Was there out there somewhere another of those giants wearing that evil thing the other had borne? Rats answering commands—it was unnatural and so doubly threatening.

I could hear low squeals now, picked up by some chance of the rocks about us and echoed back. There was no telling how big a pack we might be facing. The other cat—we could have well use her strength and fighting ability if she had only stayed with us.

Out of my shirt I pulled the cat mask and instantly the light it had shown of itself before was there. From slightly behind me my companion gave a howl, surely a challenge. And that the rats answered. They slipped and slid around and over rocks to come at us, a vicious dark flood of death.

Again we fought and this time the cat had drawn well towards, even a little before, me, swiping out with his good paw and smashing the brutes away, sending their bodies back to crack bones against the rock, while I swung my staff, fighting with what was to me a new assurance and strength. I began to note that the rats would not face me squarely, that whenever I moved and the light from the mask touched any one of them, it would squeal and leap away to darkness.

It was to my utter astonishment that the attack suddenly withdrew, for this was completely out of rat nature. I remained alert listening intently to the noises out of the night. The hissing of the drifting sands was a monotone but across that came a series of squeals and to my mind they seemed to make a pattern. There was the skittering sound of rat claws on rock and I braced myself for another wave.

It was gloomy within the chamber. Ravinga had ordered the curtains drawn at dusk. Not only did those, thin as they were, keep out all the lights of the Vapalan city but much of the air, so one could no longer smell the flowering qutta trees in the garden. Instead there arose curls of aromatic smoke from the brazier placed on a tripod in the exact center of that secure chamber.

I sat straight-backed on the stool my mistress had indicated, holding in my hands the box she had pressed upon me. This was not the first time I had assisted at such a ceremony nor would it be the last if I were to achieve my purpose and gain the knowledge I desired, for such wish was as an ever-eating pain within me.

Ravinga herself crawled across the floor, pulling with her the square of painted oryxen hide. That design had occupied her for many nights, sometimes with long pauses between one touch of a paint-thick brush and the next. It was as if she must drag the pattern from very far depths of memory.

On that hide now rested small figures. These were not the dolls which we sold in the markets to gain our bread but were far more elaborate ones. The small face on each had been molded over and over until the features suited my mistress. Some I knew well—

There was the Diamond Queen of Vapala with all her crown and formal robing. And the Topaz Queen of Azhengir, that most barren and forbidding of lands. Here was also the Grand Chancellor of the Outer Regions with the Sapphire Queen of Kahulawe.

All were fashioned of Ravinga's secret clay mixture which gave the appearance of living flesh to heads and hands. And they were all garbed in fine bits of fabrics, miniature jewels so perfect that one wondered indeed at the maker's great skill.

By each Queen stood her Minister of Balance, his features rock hard as if he fronted some period of a weeding of flocks and perhaps even of people.

There was also Shank-ji, who was not one of such an exalted company by any right of office. Son to the Emperor he might be, but our lord took no formal wife and any get of his held naught but a position of minor nobility. I looked upon Shank-ji and I remembered—my thoughts straying from the pattern I had been set to hold. Old hatreds run deep and cannot always be kept under control, at least not by one who has not followed the rituals into the Higher Plane.

Ravinga glanced at me with anger. She, being who and what she was, could read emotions, if not minds. Resolutely I made my eyes move on from the doll which was Shank-ji; the next was the Emperor—not as he had appeared at the last great court, a curiously shrunken figure with a hand which shook when he held the leopard staff of authority, as if that shaft was too heavy for him. No, this was a representation of the Emperor as we had not for years seen him. And beside him his Chancellor.

The four remaining figures were not human but animal. There in all his majesty of office, first bodyguard of the Emperor, was the Blue Leopard, and with him two of his own following. But the last certainly had no place in any company save that of death itself, for it was a faithful representation of a rat.

That did have meaning of a sort, for it was a symbol not only of death but also of evil, which could not be touched nor in any way governed by even those who held to the old knowledge and were such as Ravinga.

She reached the other side of the brazier and there three shadows awaited her, Wa, Wiu, Wyna, the black kottis that had been a part of her household ever since I had taken refuge here. They sat erect now, their eyes upon Ravinga while she began to place the figures upright on the floor as if they might indeed march off about their business.

Emperor flanked by the two Queens and they in turn by the Chancellor and their Ministers of Balance, before the Emperor the Blue Leopard and the guard that one commanded.

But the rat remained lying upon the hide, under its carefully fashioned body a symbol drawn in a red of fresh-spilt blood. Ravinga did not reach for it, rather she snapped her fingers. I answered at once to her signal.

From the box I brought her she took out two more figures, each rolled in a fine silken cloth. The cloth covering one was the gold of clear citrines and there was a wandering thread wreathing through it of the rust red of certain rocks, such as I had seen in our travels to Kahulawe. This she drew away to display that doll which she had showed me before when she had begun this ritual days ago.

A youth—yes, I even knew his name—Hynkkel—and I had heard of him, too, and not only from my mistress. What she appeared to approve, others found a reason to disparage. Second son of a gallant warrior, he refused to follow the trade of arms. In his own family he became a servant, and not even one of prideful background since he had not gained that position (as most of the low-born may) through his own efforts.

He was a herder of beasts, a runner of errands, one who bought and sold in the market, one who those of his own rank would pretend not to see.

Yet Ravinga had dressed his representation in the fine robes of a great lord and had by some magic of her own given him the look of one who would rightfully wear such.

Now she placed him directly facing the Emperor. There was also a staff of honor in that small hand of his but the insignia topping that was a Sand Cat. Seeing what she did I wanted to decry it all. This youth was no leader of men, no bearer of the old blood of Vapala—no, he was a barbarian and held by his own people to be of little worth. Ravinga—what strange fault of thinking had made her shape him thus?

She was already taking out the other figure. This was one wrapped in a dirty white, the shade of the sand of the Plain of Desolation. Here and there was a pattern in black of small skulls, both those of men and beast. She did not unwrap this one and I knew the reason for that.

What lay within that coil of cloth was no body, no carefully fashioned replica of a living person. For Ravinga knew not as yet the person of the one whose existence she could only sense. That stranger kept about him a barrier which no dream search could penetrate. We had even tried together, I uniting my smaller strength to hers, to find the presence of the enemy, spy out who or what that was.

Now Ravinga set the shrouded doll up and placed it beside the rat on the pool of scarlet. Sitting back on her heels
she began to sing. I squatted opposite her and my tongue also
shaped words, the meaning of which neither of us knew—old
and old and old was that chant. Only those who had the true
gift could even mouth them, so twisted awry they were from
our normal speech.

The doll things answered—that is, all did save the rat and
that which stood by it. The Queens raised their arms and held
forth their scepters, the Emperor took one step forward but
only that, for Shank-ji strode about until he faced his father,
his head up arrogantly. Now the Chancellor moved in from
one side and the Ministers from the other, all of them turned
so they faced Hynkkel and the Emperor's son.

Ravinga's voice soared and quickened until I found it hard
to match her word for word. I saw her hands knot in the folds
of her robe as she leaned forward, as if she would bring about
some other movement in the small people she watched so intently. But those now were frozen in place.

What did move was the rat. From lying on its side it
scrambled up, baring fangs and moving at Hynkkel. Shank-ji
stepped back to make room for its coming. The doll Hynkkel
swung his cat-topped staff and the rat withdrew step by step.
Then that muffled thing which had shared the creature's stand
shifted awkwardly and the rat came to it and lay down at its
feet (if feet were hidden there). Hidden one and rat were still
and as I watched, that illusion of life left all the dolls.

There came an instant dawning of weariness to Ravinga's
face. Her hands were now clasped loosely in her lap.

"So be it," she said and there was deep unhappiness in her
voice. "One can only do the best that one can. It rests now
upon the land and those who dwell here. We must have strength
against what comes. But the strength must declare itself and
that I cannot force."

She raised her eyes from the dolls. They trembled as if all
strength had been removed from their small bodies, then they
tumbled to lie face up or away as they had fallen.

"You have seen, Allitta?"

"I have seen, Caller of Shadows." I made the proper answer.

"And in your time you shall see more." As so often before, she ended some ritual with the same words.

Did I want to see more? Did I want to drink of all the knowledge this woman could offer me? Yes—for I had a purpose of my own. In spite of all of Ravinga's warnings I would seek that purpose in the end and that I knew past all doubting.

That which was in the brazier had nearly burned away but Ravinga made no attempt to gather up the dolls. I knew that her energy was now at a very low ebb, yet I could not help her, for with these dolls only her hands could deal. I went to the nearest window to draw aside those muffling curtains, to let in fresh air to banish the last scent of the burning spice wood.

At that moment there came a chime from overhead. Someone in the shop? But at this hour? The curtain twisted in my hand and I saw that there was sun without—what had begun in the proper darkness which would nourish the power had finished with the coming of day.

Ravinga paid no attention to that summons but I went swiftly. Our servant, Mancol, would have opened the shop for the day and usually all simple sales could be left to his management. He got around very spryly for one of his manifest age and he treasured the dolls with a fervor, taking delight in showing off the most clever and beautiful of them.

However, when I entered the shop room I found that there was a customer, or a prospective one, who would indeed not deign to deal with any underling, though she would with me, as I would not disturb Ravinga for this one.

The First Maiden of the Household of the Lady Yevena stood there, her sandaled foot tapping an impatient tattoo which echoed the lighter sound of her long fingernails as they ticked against the counter which ran across one side of the shop. Above were the cases of dolls, new-conceived ones directly in a middle one. Mancol had come from behind the counter, was dragging a cushioned chair intended for our most profitable visitors towards the Maiden, though she had so far not taken any note of that suggested comfort.

In the doorway lounged two shield men, an escort for which there was certainly no need here except for purpose of display.

I bowed my head in courtesy as I would to any except Ravinga—for her I would have made the bended-knee salute if she had ever allowed me to. That curtailed gesture I knew would irritate our caller. She was frowning and there was a flush of red under her clear skin. She gave a little toss of her head which sent a-tinkling the nodding, stemmed jewels of her headband.

"Where is Ravinga?" she demanded harshly.

"This morning she is indisposed," I returned. "Does the lady desire some new treasure for her collection?"

I took Mancol's place behind the counter and pointed to the glass-fronted shelves in the prime place. "There is, as you see, a new Topaz Queen, she who ruled in the days of the Emperor Tampor and was accredited the most beautiful woman wearing a crown in that time. And here is a fanciful one of Ravinga's own dream design—" I indicated a very life-like (in miniature) Sand Cat, but this one wore a necklet of rubies and opal agates and had emeralds for eyes. Also, it was sitting up and between its forepaws it held a Kifongg harp. I snapped open the case to take forth this temptation and touched a small button at the cat's back. Straightway it began to play and there was a thin yet pleasing music to be heard.

The Maiden's attention was taken for a moment. When I set the small wonder down she put a finger to its head and I knew she could feel the outer covering of fur which made it seem all the more lifelike.

Then she snatched her hand back and once more there was anger in her face. "Behold this," she was sneering now. From a wrapping band in her hands she shook out with no care a doll, but one which had lost its head, though the head rolled out with it.

Though it was not as perfect a resemblance to Shank-ji as the one I had just seen Ravinga put away, it did look close to that arrogant young warrior, fully clad in all his trapping, from fuzzed-out silver wig to small, perfectly fashioned sword.

"Broken. Three days only has my lady had this in her hands and when she would bring it forth to show his lordship she found it broken! An ill omen and if he sees or hears that it has happened so—" She drew a deep breath—"My lady is not one to be made to look foolish or worse!"

She glanced across her shoulder at the two guards who had accompanied her here. "Those of the Six Families have their ways of attending to such problems."

Her suggestion might be one of pique. Only one who could recall certain events in the past would understand just what a person of the Lady Yevena's type might be moved to do. The old families were jealous of their distinction and city-backed power. They sometimes held themselves even above the Emperor, chosen as he was by chance, in family and breeding.

"Maiden, I shall take this straightway to my mistress and let her see what is—"

"Let this maker of dolls come to *me!*" That was almost a snarl. Again there was the sign of that touchy need for difference which was ever a part of one of close intimacy with the Six Families.

"I am here." Ravinga did not address this messenger with any honorifics. She was outwardly her usual self and I hoped that inwardly she had recovered from the ritual.

I moved away to let her see fully what lay there. Because I knew Ravinga so well, had been ever alert to the small changes in her features, even the little tension of her hands when she was deeply aroused about anything, I now could read that she was moved.

She touched the head and then picked it up and surveyed carefully where it had broken away of the neck. In turn she examined the body closely.

"The Lady Yevena was warned that these must be carefully handled," she said. "These are not dolls for the pleasure of children such as those," she waved to the right-hand case, "but things, one each of their kind, and to be kept carefully.

This cannot be repaired—for a treasure once damaged loses its value to all. The Lady Yevena is collector enough not to wish any repaired piece in her display. We can offer to make another—"

"She wishes to have the saying of that! She has ordered that you attend her at the fourth hour."

Turning her back on us, she walked out with as near a stamp as her flat sandals would allow.

Ravinga nodded to Mancol and he hurried to draw the door shut. She was already bending closely over the doll, running her finger back and forth across the broken neck, then she gathered it up quickly and went off to her workroom.

When I would have followed to give what aid I could, comfort even, for her dolls were indeed treasures to Ravinga, she made a quick gesture for me to remain where I was.

It was true that no two portrait dolls were ever made alike. Some of them were fashioned as copies of deceased members of the House. There were even several past Emperors on display in the palace. Some were made for love gifts—had the Lady Yevena intended this to be such a one?

Mostly they were made to order, unless they were historical like the famous Queens on the shelf above, or as some fantastical object such as the Sand Cat who played its harp.

I put this back in the case and snapped the lock. But I was thinking more of Ravinga and knew some uneasiness over the whole affair. Little troubles could lead to disaster, just as it had for me when I was so small I could not have seen the top of this counter. Ravinga saved me then. But could there be anyone to step in and speak for us if the House lady wanted to cause trouble? A merchant said to sell imperfect goods got short shift in any market.

7

A raging furred body sprang over the rocks. Beside me the female cat took up position. The rush attack I waited for did not come. Nor did the cat make any effort to go seeking it. Instead she backed against her mate, though she did not relax at once. I could no longer hear the scrabble of nails after her war cry died away. Then there arose a second squall. But not from either of the cats which were with me.

Sounds of battle and that too died away. The female snarled and turned her head to wipe her tongue across her mate's ears as if in assurance. He was growling deep in his throat, still facing outward, trying to rise to his feet although the female, flanking him, threw out a huge paw and, as she might to some disobedient kitten, rested that on his shoulders, pushing him down once again. From her now issued a series of small sounds much like the "talking" of the kottis, as if she was reassuring him.

Then she faced outward. It would seem that I was wrong in hoping our ordeal was past, for both cats were alert. I reached for my sling and the supply of the rocks I had garnered as ammunition. At least I might be able to take out one or two before they reached close enough for staff work.

However, what crossed the rocks towards us now was no wave of rats, but rather another Sand Cat. Open jaws showed that one of this male's great fangs was broken off. His fur was clay-colored and ragged. There was a bloody tear on his flank where one of the rats must have bitten him.

The male beside me roared a challenge and again struggled to get to his feet. I realized that what we confronted now was a "rogue" who had been driven from his own holding and wished to fight both for this rock isle and the female. Against my companion he might well triumph, for he was at least steady on all four feet and the rock ruler was still weak from his wound.

Once more the cat beside me challenged. Now he was answered with a deep-throated roar of pure rage. I whirled my sling and sent the stone flying, aiming as best I could.

My missile thudded home not as I had planned, for the great rogue had flattened in preparation for a leap. Instead the stone struck on the beast's shoulder and he snarled, turning his head to bite at his own flesh where the blow had fallen.

Then a newcomer went into action. The female stalked stiff-legged towards the rogue, a beginning hiss rising into a screamed threat. He hissed in turn. She leaped, bowling him over so his body struck against a spur of rock and he yowled in pain and fury. The surprise must have been great, for among their kind the females and the males do not fight each other. It appeared that she was intent on taking on the battle in place of her wounded mate.

The rogue squalled and appeared to be trying to withdraw from battle. Claws had raked him viciously and now he shook himself free and ran, the female hounding after him. Her mate was still growling deeply and had completely arisen as if wanting to follow—while that plaster I had put on him shifted.

"Great One. Warrior of Might." I went down on one knee beside him, "Not yet are you healed enough to do battle. Let me tend your wound again."

That I speedily did as he lay down and stretched out the injured leg as if he understood perfectly what must be done.

The rest of the night I stayed on guard, having dragged the rat bodies within reach to one side. The air was foul with the stench of blood and the natural stink of the creatures. However, I felt that I could not take them out of sight lest some of their kind still lingered below the rocks waiting for our watchfulness to falter.

I had expected the female to return and began to worry. Could it be that the rogue, once he had gotten over his astonishment at her attack, had turned on her with the full ferocity of which he was capable? Yet there was nothing I could do, except hope that we would see her again and soon.

It was near dawn and I again made my way down to the pool and harvested for the day's food, restored my rough camp. The soothing aid of the dressings I had applied to my own sand-scored skin had done its purpose. I kept on exercising, so that the new skin forming there would stretch fully. I fed my companion and brought two of the corpses from the night's battle that he might also restore himself with the flesh his kind craved. There were the skins to be taken and worked upon.

Certainly I had never expected to settle on this isle but I could not walk away until I was sure that the cat was able to care for himself. At least he had the female—but now there was a rogue ready to do battle, and that was another thing.

I slept away much of the day. Again before I awoke at the sun's descent I dreamed. It is said that in the very ancient days, before our five countries drew together under the Emperor, there were those born with certain powers and talents. Yet these had been hunted down, and their whole family lines wiped out after the last great battle so that no one might again arise to use such gifts—or curses—in the name of some leader.

The last and greatest of these had been driven into the Plain of Desolation and that was so many generations ago that only the keepers of the records could count them. Nor were any ever welcomed to even study those ancient accounts, they being under seal.

So, though there were vague stories of such things, powers and dreams, even those tales were not the subject for any bard, nor teacher, to mention.

Yet this night I dreamed.

There was a darkened room where a single lamp gave light to what lay on a table. There was a pair of hands which came out of the shadows beyond the tight focus of that lamp, handling, with delicate fingers, what the light showed very clearly. It was a manikin or a doll, and it lay in two pieces, the head snapped off at the shoulders.

It was the head which interested those hands the most. With a knife hardly thicker than a large needle, the puffy silver wig was worked loose to display the coiled hair beneath. That also yielded to the probing of the knife point, and the top of the skull, if one might deem that so, came off.

Now the knife was set aside for a pair of fine pincers such as my sister used for her most important work of setting the smallest stone. Those were inserted into the cavity of the head, to emerge holding a tiny ball which flashed like a diamond in the light. One of the hands disappeared and returned in a moment with a small metal box into which this bead was dropped and the lid clamped down with a force which seemed to say that this was a very precious thing, perhaps one to be kept secret.

Swiftly the doll head was restored to what it had been, and the hands withdrew, leaving the broken warrior lying where he was, still headless.

So strange was that dream that it remained vivid in my mind and I was surprised when I opened my eyes to find that I lay in my rude tent. What had it meant? I had nothing to do with dolls—no, those were Ravinga's. But never had I seen among the stock she had brought into the market any such fine product as this, smashed though it was. That was no lifeless doll face which had been turned up when the hands were busy with the head—rather I might have been looking at the small figure of one who was alive, or had been so. I remembered that other dream which had been of Ravinga and her apprentice, and another doll.

I put my head in my hands and tried to think clearly. Certainly I was caught in that which I did not understand. The very fact that I had been able to establish a fleeting relationship with a Sand Cat and his mate was something I had never heard of and many strange things are always eagerly told and listened to in the marketplaces. Sand Cats were deadly enemies—yet I no longer saw them as so. Last night I had even known something of pity for the rogue—like me he had been driven from his proper place and sought his old life again.

Would I come to seek my own return after this venture? That thought I pushed sharply away as I crawled from my shelter to welcome the cool of the night and see to my charge.

I was greeted with a throaty sound from the Sand Cat, who was clearly awake, instantly aware of me. However, though I had expected to find her there, his mate was still missing. And I felt uneasy. Though a male might not attack a female, yet when she had carried war to the rogue, it might well be that he had turned on her and she lay somewhere on the uneven surface of the isle in pain and torment just as her mate had earlier done.

"Great One," I had gone to my companion to examine the dressing on his wound, "is there trouble in this place which has taken your lady?" I tried to open my mind, to sense if there was any uneasiness in the male, even as I had done when I served as herdsman and had striven to seek out some disaster among the beasts for whom I was responsible.

There was nothing of tension about him. When I uncovered his now closed but still tender wound, he set to licking it after the manner of his kind when they tended their own hurts. I left him to his own treatment and once more went to the pool.

A shadow moved, took on a slinking form. No rat but the rogue, one ear half gone, a visible tear along his shoulder, was slipping down to the pool on the opposite side. I saw a lift of lips, heard a rumbling growl. Then he looked to me no more but pulled himself forward to the moist edge of the algae bed and mouthed torn masses of the stuff as if his belly was completely empty.

Looking upon him so, I knew that there was no danger to be feared from him. Clearly he had forced himself here for what succor the pool offered but he would not try to dispute it with us again, keeping to his own side.

I watched him feed and then he withdrew, but no farther than a slight distance. He moved with such labor that I thought he was badly hurt. When I had climbed above again with my own gleanings I took up two of the rat bodies and passing

along the edge of the rise near to where the animal now sheltered, I tossed them over. They did not fall too far from his
chosen shelter. His blood-smeared head came up and he looked
at me. But his eyes were empty of any expression I could
read.

Once more I skinned rats and tore meat apart for the drying. The scraps I tossed down a narrow crevice in the rock for
which I could see no bottom. The skins I had scraped earlier
were hard-dried now and I began clumsily to stitch them across
and around my boots.

As I worked so in the twilight I spoke aloud, for I felt very
much the need of hearing speech in this vastness, even if it
were my own.

"Great One, there is much in the world which is beyond
understanding. Why has it come to me that I must be a part of
something which—" I stopped the punching of holes in hide
with my knife point and looked out at what lay about me.

There was a change. I slewed around, my hand going for
the staff which I had laid close to hand. Another form came
out of the dusk and I greeted the female.

"Lady, your lord does well." She crouched beside her mate
and first sniffed the wound I had left uncovered after sponging
it off with the algae, then began to lick it.

She raised her head for an instant to gaze at me and then
went back to her licking. The male was purring, the rumble of
his sound attune, it seemed to me, with the peace of the night,
perhaps perilous and short-lasting as that might be.

However, we perhaps had proven ourselves to be too much
of a danger even to the rats. For it was not us they attacked
this night: rather I heard their squeals from across the pond
and the roars of the rogue doing battle.

The female was instantly on her feet and her mate struggled
to stand beside her. I ran, staff and slingshot in hand, to that
place from which I had tossed the meat earlier. There was still
a portion of twilight and more vision of what was happening
below than I had thought. I used the sling and saw two of the
things fall. Then I turned to the throwing of stones.

Halfway I feared that they might turn on us at this attack, yet I could not leave that other to he savaged, enemy though he might be. A clean death by hunter's spear or knife was one thing; to see a helpless beast eaten alive, as the rats handle their prey, was more than I could allow. Now I was hurling rocks with my hands and saw a third one of the attackers fall. There was movement beside me and the female went into battle, taking the descent in one great leap and landing full into the middle of that pack where she used her claws and teeth in a whirlwind of well-delivered death.

The squealing of her prey rose to a high point and through that sounded that same strange howl I had heard in the battle wherein the great rat had died.

On the ground the rogue was rolling, his jaws fastened on the scruff of a rat's neck and surely the creature he was striving to pull down was near match to him in size.

I lifted a rock with my two hands and, running forward to the very edge which hung nearly above that struggle, I hurled my crude weapon out and down. By some chance of fate it actually struck the rat which had just torn free from the rogue, not fair, but well enough to make the noisome creature stagger. In that instant the rogue reared up and closed his massive jaws on the neck of his enemy and gave a sharp swing of his head. I could not hear above the clamor of the pack the sound of the snapping neck but I saw the thing go limp.

Again the pack, upon the death of this one, withdrew, scrabbling away, some of them actually plowing through the algae pan. There was a silence as if the night with the complete fall of darkness had swallowed up all their company.

The rogue was panting heavily, the sounds he made close to whimpering of pain. He strove to crawl out of the algae into which he had rolled, and made such an effort that he did draw himself free of the growth, only to collapse.

Nor did he pay any attention now to the female, who was licking down her fur. As far as I could see in this dim light she had suffered no deep hurt, a guess which was proven when she came clambering back up the slope to join us.

I listened for any return of the rats. The suffering of the rogue troubled me. That he would be minded to tear a hand from anyone who strove to touch him I well knew. But I could not leave him there untended. Also I must know more about the last of those things he had killed—whether it was like unto the other we had found.

Thus I descended to the pool and, with care and wariness, rounded the end of it to the side of the animal. There was a faint snarl: he lifted his head a fraction and showed his one fang now dyed with blood.

"Great One." I held out both hands and in the swinging light of the pendant he could certainly see that they were empty of any weapon.

His eyes picked up the gleam of the cat mask and followed that to and fro for an instant as it swung.

"Great One, mighty have you been in battle. Now you are hurt, suffer it that your wounds be tended."

His untorn ear flattened to his skull and his body writhed in a futile attempt to get to his feet. Then he fell flat once again and I could see that there was a great gash across his back and he could not move his hind legs.

There came a sigh from him and his head dropped forward to rest upon one paw as if, worn by the roaming of a day, he would sleep. His eyes closed and I felt at that moment that his essence was at last freed, and, for all his lonely wandering and his many wounds, he was now one with the land and all that is about us even as we all wish when the final end comes.

In his time he had been a warrior and—I stood to look about me. At the last he had been searching for a home. It was not in me to leave his body to be devoured by those filthy monsters upon their return—and that return I did not doubt.

In the wall of the cliff to the north was one of those gash openings, not quite a cave, for at the top it was open to the sky. This could be a place of burial for one who deserved honor.

I found it hard to move the body. Worn by privation as he was, he was still a load more fit for a yaksen, and I had to take the task by degrees. However, at length I had the body well within the opening. Then it was a matter of gathering stones to wall it in and that I did also, though my shoulders ached and I was gulping great gasps of air by the time I had done with it all, unable at first to summon even enough energy to reclimb the wall.

When I looked up I could see the glint of four eyes watching me and I knew that the other cats had witnessed all I had done, though that they might understand why, I doubted. If I should die by rat fangs or starvation here, there would be none to raise any monument to me. As I sat there in the night I thought of that and what I could do to make sure my body did not lie as scattered bones.

Once more I searched the stars overhead for some sign I could recognize. There was little use in my staying on here. The Sand Cat was healing well, and, with his mate, could hold his own against the rats, once more ruler in his own place.

What place remained for me?

I got wearily to my feet, believing now that I had the power to reclimb the cliff. The night was surely far spent and tomorrow, tomorrow I must make my preparations for moving on. I had been caught in such a venture here as few men would believe—one that I could not voice lest I be declared a braggart and a liar.

Taking a step forward I nearly stumbled over a contorted body—that of the giant rat. I made myself do grisly work upon it—to find once more the same evidence that this was no common desert menace.

Having exposed to the destroying air that ball of stuff I had picked out of the skull of the rat, I was remembering in detail two hands which had plucked forth from the head of a doll a similar implant, save that had been a brilliant diamond rainbow-endowed piece and this was dully evil, so I was careful not to touch it with my flesh.

What further mystery might hide here I did not know and at the moment I was too tired to care.

8

There was the thud of a heavy body landing chose by. I lifted my head and saw that the female cat was watching me with curiously narrowed eyes. There was something about that gaze which I found measuring, making me uneasy—wary—As if the truce between us had worn thin.

Before I could move or defend myself she was on me and her great jaws closed about my left wrist bringing such a thrust of pain as made me cry out. My throat next, I thought dazedly—but why—now?

Blood spurted out of my torn flesh. The cat drew away from me and I crawled to the algae pool. I must staunch that bleeding if I could. Through the haze of torment I hunched my shoulders, waiting now for the full weight of the beast to flatten me, claws to find my throat and shake the life out of me as if I were the giant rat.

I rose to my knees and pitched forward, my mangled hand plunging into the smarting water thick with the plants. I thought I had known pain many times before in my life but this blow dealt me out of no reason seemed to sap my strength almost in moments. I met the cushion of algae with the forepart of my body and then there was nothing.

How long I lay so I did not know but there came back to me a kind of hazy consciousness which sent me crawling once more. How I made the way back to the cliff foot I will never know, but once there I knew that I could not manage any more. Still the cat had not put an end to me. However, to even turn my head now to look and see what she might threaten was beyond my strength.

There was the heat of the red-streaked stone about me and that heat sank into my body, became a part of a fire which seemed to seek to destroy me. The nothingness which had held me earlier was gone and I had not even that escape.

My head had fallen sidewise so that a stone bruised my cheek and that small torment seemed to make all the rest worse. When I opened my eyes I saw no pool, no green and orange of algae—only the long stretch of red which could be some plain as great as that of Desolation.

Then across that something moved, coming in bounds. The cat! I tried to move my arm in some feeble defense which would be nothing against her attack.

Yet what came to me was another. Mieu leaped towards me and from her mouth swung the mask pendant. I felt her paws heavy on my wounded arm, and again cried out as she dropped the mask on my breast. Her tongue came forth and I could feel the rough rasp of it against my cheek: she might be washing a kit in reassurance.

I talked with her and she answered me, but what we two said to one another I could never afterward remember. However there came a quiet into me for a space and it made the pain recede to a bearable distance.

There was more movement on that plain of red sand. Fine as dust the grains spurted up to clog the air behind a rider. There my brother pulled up his oryxen and sat at ease in the saddle though the beast bucked and fought his control as always, until he aimed a heavy blow behind one of its tender ears.

He struck his mount almost absently. His full attention was for me, and I saw his lips curve in a smile which became sneering amusement.

"Weakling!" He leaned forward a trifle, as if to view me the better and gloat over what was left of me. "No man—child always—accept what you are and leave true life to your betters." And his laughter was as loud a roar as that of the cats offering battle.

I could not rise to any challenge now. He was right—I was a weakling and even my body refused to obey me.

Once more he laughed and then urged his oryxen closer, now coming to me spear in hand until I thought that he would do what was unknown even among the most brutish of barbarians, put kin to death.

However, it seemed that what he strove to do was hook the point of that spear into the chain of the mask, to make that finally and undisputedly his own. Mieu was on her feet. Hissing, her small body swollen to nearly twice size, she struck at the metal point with a paw, only to have him make a sudden sweep with the spear, send her tumbling away with a cry of pain and defiance. Then I struggled to rise, and still laughing, my brother rode away. Yet the mask of the cat was not yet his.

Though that metal still rested on me, yet I also saw it rise through the air until it crowned a staff as might the Honors of a House. Still, no House would bear such a device.

It was past the hour of nooning. Even here in Vapala, where nature dealt the easiest with humankind, these few hours were a time when merchants put down their shop curtains and fortified themselves in the shadows those barriers gave to the full heat of the day.

Mancol nodded and dozed on his cushion behind the counter, now and again waking himself with a snort of snore to look bewilderedly around for a moment before sinking back into the languor none of us could avoid.

We had an inner court where green things grew—such as were found nowhere else in the five lands. That was Ravinga's storehouse wherein were rooted many plants which were not ever to be seen, except perhaps in the gardens of the Emperor where gifts from the eastern lands, more than half legend to most of us, grew, though not easily.

Small winged things swung from one bright patch of flower to another, and there were others which crawled upon the ground, or hopped. These, too, were only known in the mesa land. Under the sun spicy odors were drawn from the growth. Seated now on her padded mat, my mistress looked out over her small domain. Yet there was no satisfaction in her expression. She could instead have been reckoning up omissions and mistakes for which a strict accounting might be well demanded later.

Before her was a small lap table hardly larger than a tray for mid-day food. On this were several rolled scrolls and one which had been spread open, its curled edges holding so because planted on either side were two of her delicate tools. By her knee a carbon box, yellowed by great age, showed beneath the flung-back lid rolls of sewing thread, as rainbows in their many shades.

I had my own task and I kept to it, though when I had come to Ravinga I had not been too handy with a needle, for in those days I had ridden and hunted, and knew freedom beyond what was given most of my caste. Yet I had set myself to the learning of what would be a part of my craft from now on—and I had mastered with dogged effort most of the intricate stitches which Ravinga taught—briskly and sometimes impatiently—for she had to school her belief that all could be as accomplished as was she, if they would only try.

What I dwelt upon this day, being very careful to match colors and set the slant of each stitch just right, was a patch which might have served for the shoulder bag of some highly placed servant in one of the Six Houses. Yet it had no connection with any that I had ever seen or heard tell of, for it was the head of a Sand Cat so perfectly designed as to seem that the mask of an actual cat had been stripped from its skull and reduced to miniature size.

While such heraldic beasts, for the purpose of badges, are usually shown expressing defiance, each after its own way, this was calm, as if the cat were all-knowing and observing that which lay about it, not yet ready to take part in affairs.

The eyes were gemstones, very well cut—those we call citrines for their clear yellow. These were not faceted as such usually were, but smooth, and when I studied them closely I was almost sure I could see, deep within them, a hair-thin line of black set as a pupil.

I had finished most of my work upon the head of the animal and was now dealing with a frame of sunstones and bits of filigree, so fine and pure the gold that one might inadvertently bend them during the task of making them fast. These made a frame for the mask and, as elaborate as it was, still it did not subtract from the forcefulness of the less ornate head.

When I set aside one threaded needle and reached for a second I saw that my mistress's eyes were closed. Her breathing had slowed until there were unnatural pauses between each lungful. The signs were unmistakable. Though Ravinga had made no preparations for an outseeking, she was indeed caught in the forestages of one such.

Slower and slower came her breaths. Her hands had fallen to the surface of the small work table and there were clasped lightly together. Ravinga now walked shadow ways which I had taken once or twice, knowing full well the terrible fatigue of body and mind one must expend thus.

She drew a last sighing breath and then it was as if she had done with all outer life. I moved uneasily. To anyone who watched another in this state and knew exactly what dangers it entailed, this was always an uneasy business. I, too, allowed my work to slide out of a tight grasp.

It was my part to play guardian. Ravinga usually retired into her bedchamber, behind a safe locked door when she went far questing—that she had not today was a matter for concern. I reached slowly into my belt pouch, made sure that no gesture or sound I might make inadvertently would break the spell she was weaving tighter and tighter. My fingers touched a slick smoothness which was the result of time's long use and I brought out a herdsman's flute.

Back and forth I followed the road of soft notes, watching Ravinga. We had played these roles before and I knew what had to be done: still there could always be a first time of failure. To those who gather power, that brings awe and fear and if it does not—then that dabbler in forbidden things is a lackwitted fool.

Ravinga's skin was darker than that of the usual Vapalan, which I thought came from her many travels across the five nations. She was no fine lady to go veiled against the sun. Now I saw a flush creeping up under that brown skin. Her lips parted a fraction and her breath came pantingly as if she struggled for air. I watched her very closely. No, it was not yet time for me to take my part in any awakening. Did I so too soon, I would rightfully earn her wrath.

There was a shadow of change in her features also. Her face looked a fraction leaner, wearing small signs of some past struggle. I saw the darkness of a thickening shadow on her upper lip beginning to bracket her mouth and then I was almost startled into some bitter mistake. Before my very eyes, as one would assume a traveler's cloak, my mistress was drawing on another identity—and this masculine!

Hynkkel! Why? My grip nearly broke the flute in two. I had seen such shadow masks worn by Ravinga before when she locked herself into deep seeing—but what was so important about this cast-off son of an old army officer, a family which had lost its importance long ago and had with this very son (if rumor spoke true) come to an ignominious ending?

There was more than the heat of the day walling in the two of us. The fire was of the body, as if my mistress was consumed by some flame of disease. For the first time her hands arose from that limp clasp on the table and moved as if she were pulling towards her something of vast importance. So would a healer—

I had the flute to my lips, though I still did not send forth its summons to the wandering spirit. This Hynkkel suffered some ill and my mistress was striving to turn it from him!

Ravinga coughed, her upper body arching a fraction as if that came as a painful stretching. Her hand groped outward as if she sought something she could not see. I caught up a goblet standing to one side, my quick motion disturbing its contents so that the liquid within swirled around and gave off a strong scent of herbs. This I pressed into my mistress's hold and she, still unseeingly, raised it to her lips and drank. One long draught near emptied the goblet as she swallowed.

I knew that what she did was not for herself alone and that the medicine which that container held was meant to pass farther in the way of inner healing from her to Hynkkel.

There was no trace of blood on that thin green robe which was all she wore. Oftentimes a famed and blessed healer could project upon her own body any hurt or wound which marked the one seeking help. No blood—except—she had dropped her left hand once more to her knee and turned the wrist outward to show dark, puffed lines, a wound which might well have gone bad.

I did not need to be prompted now. This had I done twice before when I had learned how to sever the power of Ravinga. I took the goblet from her. There still remained a mouthful or so of the drug at the very bottom of its bowl.

My own work slipped unheeded aside, I snatched up a small bit of soft cloth and sopped up that remaining liquor in the cup and then, holding Ravinga's hand with force against her own knee, as for a moment or so she tried to jerk away from me, I wiped the sodden rag back and forth across the lines of a wound another truly wore.

Twice Ravinga hissed and attempted to free herself with a jerk but I held on and she could not be free of me. The mark there had been a welt, raised above the skin it disfigured. I was able to feel that upthrust of the very red flesh.

In my own throat rose the hum which was part of this treatment. My flute I could not use as long as I held the cloth to her arm.

I vacillated between two opposed beliefs. One that I wrought for good, the other that I sustained what was better left alone. Now the welts were subsiding, even as they paled in color, that dangerous darkness fading.

Out of nowhere came words I could not translate as I mouthed them. The strange wound on Ravinga's wrist was being banished. Nor did I believe that it would again threaten my mistress.

Her skin bore only a scar. I put aside the cloth which I had used. The slender length of the pipe slipped easily through my fingers. I raised the flute to my lips and began to play.

Nor did I stretch or seek for any notes, rather such came to me, following fast one upon the other as if I unconsciously held to some pattern of music I had once known so well that I need not think on what I played.

As I played, so that pressure of which I had been so aware eased. Ravinga's head fell forward on her breast as if she had worn herself out at a task which had been nearly beyond her.

The flute was quiet. I dropped it from my lips and sat with it between my fingers. Now there was no mark on Ravinga's right wrist, but the wide bracelet she always wore as a cuff on the left had slipped and beneath it lay a scar—an old one not unlike the one I had seen. Her eyes were closed and she breathed evenly as might one in refreshing slumber.

I looked down at the cat head which I had been fashioning. The citrine eyes—almost I would swear those were alive! For me there was no explanation of what we two had done. save that Ravinga had carried to its end some ritual of great strength.

Heat and pain—save that the latter was now less, a lash which fell only lightly across my body to bring back the memory of what I was. I stared straight up. Over me was the night sky. There was the rasp of a great rough tongue across my cheek and I saw that on my right crouched the female Sand Cat. Only her eyes were clearly visible in the night's dark, but those held me as I strove to lift a hand.

"Great One." My voice was a harsh whisper.

"Friend—" My head ached as if I had spent time striving to make sense out of sounds alien to me. I gave a cry of wonder, for I was sure that this was no dream, that I had indeed sorted intelligible sounds from the noise issuing from that furred throat.

Only this was a time I could not rise to take in wonders. I was still prisoner to all which had overtaken me when the cat's teeth had closed upon my wrist.

But I seemed also to hear a pattern of music I had known so long that it had been a part of me.

They rose, they fell, those notes, and it was almost as if I saw water falling in droplets as might a trickle poured from a jug into a basin.

There followed silence at last, and I slept.

9

I lay on my back, the folds of my cloak wrinkled about me. The pain had been leached from my wrist. I felt light, content to be where I was. Another dream? No, I was sure that was not so. Certainly I had heard, and understood, moments earlier the exchange between the Sand Cats when the female had gone off and left her mate to play sentry.

Klaverel-va-Hynkkel—I was him. My eyelids were heavy. It was hard to clear the haze which seemed to wall me in. There was a wind against my desert-dried skin. I blinked at puffs of sand carried by that breeze in arcs against the darker rock. It was a place of desolate loneliness, I thought—for a space—

"Myrourr—" I twisted my speech as best I could to form that name.

A lazy, questioning sound answered. The great head lifted from its position on forepaws, and golden eyes surveyed me critically. This was as one might feel on the weapon practice ground of my home isle—just as that huge body of gold-grey fur could have matched the broad shoulders and well-trained body of my father's marshal at arms.

I could talk, be understood, be answered. Sometimes it was as if I shared camp with one of my own blood. Death crawled below—there had certainly been no wiping out of all the rats. Still I pushed the thought of these from me for now.

"—Metkin of Rapper's Way—" I caught those words clearly. The cat had been doing some inner shifting of my memories.

"That one was a hero of many battles. On the days of remembering he is called and from him came stories that his clan stood proud of reckoning." The deep-throated rumble of speech was akin to a purr. "Before him Myart of blood of the Five who fought for the many." The great cat drew his paw towards him leaving parallel scratches on the rock surface. "Behind that one Maslazar—and others—many others. Myroe—Meester—" He yawned as if reciting these scraps of history brought a need for slumber.

"And did these heroes company with my kind?" I had to feel my way word by word, unsure as to whether my alien voice could shape these names which held a slurring difficult for me.

Myrourr's head moved in the negative, his sleepy eyes half closed.

"Our clan far from roads of others, Myfford went to death where blow winds of great harshness. He spoke with one living apart, asking for knowledge. Only able to re-member a small part of that told him. But as was the begin-ning, so the end."

Now his slitted eyes closed. Mine followed, for what he had given me in fragments whirled in and out and made no strict sense. Nor had I any desire to probe the deeper.

My sleep was a drifting in strange places where there was always one beside me, striving to pressure me to do some-thing, though I slipped aside and evaded easily the control which would have kept me at labor.

I was aroused at last by another sound, the grate of claws on rock. So I levered myself up on one elbow to see the better. Not too far away was the female cat. And she was not alone. Copying her solemn stance, watching me with the round eyes of inquiring childhood, was a half-grown Sand Cat. Its mouth hung a little open and it was panting.

Though he was colored like his elders, his spots were more indistinct, his fur was less thick, and his feet oversized as is the case of many cublings. But he gave full promise of equal-ing his sire in time.

Maraya, the female, used one paw to urge him forward.

"Murri—" Her voice was hardly more than a purr. "This one is of our get, smoothskin. As is among your kind we also have a time when the young go forth to learn. Murri will be as a little brother, lifting claw and fang for you."

She paused and again I strove with the word sounds of the furred ones.

"Great lady, do you entrust your cub to me, who am one with those who hunt you?"

The Great Cats might not laugh but there is humor in them and that colored her answer to me.

"Entrust him to you, youngling? No, rather we trust you to him."

"But—"

"It is thus, youngling," Myrourr spoke. "In this place strange things have happened. I lay open to your knife. Yet you took no life, rather worked to save me. We fought side by side, foul things of the inner dark."

"And the old one," Maraya cut in. "You felt for him and did not leave him to the foul ones to worry."

"Nor are you any longer what you were," Myrourr continued. "For in you now is blood of our blood. To our kind you are sealed."

I glanced at my wrist. There was a scar there but the wound had closed cleanly. I had heard traveler's tales that some people afar signed adopted kinship so. But that any had sworn a pact with others than their own species, that had not been told.

Myrourr and Maraya exchanged a long look. If they communicated so, I could not follow. The male arose, stretched, his huge body nearly as large as that of a bull yaksen. Then he leaped, as lightly as a grain of sand upward borne by the wind, to the top of a rock spur. There he stood, facing outward over the sand beyond the isle, so still he might have been carved from this stone. His head went back and he gave voice to such a roar as might well challenge a storm in fury, once, thrice, and yet again, each time turning a little to face in another direction.

What he sought I soon learned. Across the distant sands, sometimes so much the color of the land that they could not be detected save that they moved, came Sand Cats in scores beyond my counting.

There were those as great in size as Myrourr, there were females coming in pride, bringing with them young. All approached the slickrock isle and made their way up it to where Myrourr and Maraya waited with the dignity of rulers among their kind. The visitors touched noses lightly with the two who waited them and then scattered out, forming small family groups, waiting—

With the coming of dusk they gave tongue. My people have a love of song—the bard is ranked high among us—but this wild music was to no pattern that I knew. Yet the longer it continued the more it sounded right to me, so that I raised my own voice, timidly at first, to join in their ululating wails. There were some who led the singing, perhaps selected the songs. Maraya was one of these and twice all other voices died away allowing hers to echo to the sky, as proud as any challenge.

Singing was only the beginning. Now they danced. First one and then another leaped upward. By some trick of breathing they were able to draw air into them. Their fur fluffed out until they looked like great soft balls as they leaped and floated for distances I would not have thought possible had I not seen it. They rolled, they twisted, as might cublings at play in the air, as they arose above the crags of the isle.

Their exertions had another result, for the fur of the airborne ones gave off sparks of light. I watched and I longed, too, to so float in the wind. I could leap, yes, and twist somewhat, but there was no escaping the pull of the earth on my body and I could only stand, panting from my vain efforts, to watch the whirl of the dance. Now those aloft singled out one another and spun together, dipping above or below their partners. Once more they sang. I saw cublings try to climb the sky but with hardly better success than I had had. Twice Murri came to me, short club tail switching, striving to pull me into the midst of the youngsters' wild circling on the ground.

I did what I could, for my childhood was not so far behind me that I could not remember certain tricks I had learned from entertainers in the marketplace, somersaults and leaps. My clumsy, probably foolish, efforts appeared to excite Murri and led him to more attempts at soaring, rising to the point where he could circle my ground-bound body.

Soon I was the center of a circle of cublings and they watched me with unblinking eyes as if I were some marvel. However, I was soon panting heavily and the strength drained from me so at last I seated myself just to watch.

I was not the only one tiring from that wild revel as more and more of the larger cats touched surface and settled as might kottis before a fire, though their bush tails were too short to curl about the forefeet as did those of our home companions.

Myrourr and Maraya threaded a way through their resting kin and came to me, to stand one on either side. From Myrourr there came an order that I show this company the mask pendant.

Straightway when I pulled it into the air it took flame, as if it drew from those about the sparks of fur light. It blazed forth brave as any torch, save there was no heat in it. I held it up so it could be clearly seen.

For a moment there was complete silence, no scrape of claw on rock, no pant of breath. Then from all that company arose a hum which could be reckoned a great purring—and the sound shook me. They moved in upon me, marshaled as if they were warriors in review before a Queen. Each halted but a moment directly before me, head a little forward as if to sniff at what I bore and then at me. Even though I had shared, in my very small way, their dance and song, I found this a little daunting. To be surrounded by the cublings had been one thing, but to be encircled now by those I had been trained from childhood to consider prime enemies of my kind, awakened uncertainty within me. And still they came.

It might have been that they wished to store in memory a scent to recall again in times to come. They were accepting me as one of their own, something no one of my species had ever known—at least as far back as our bard songs went.

For three suns that company remained. The pool algae was shared by all, and there was a determined night hunting for rats. For the first time I witnessed that the Sand Cats would seek those out even in their burrows beneath the surface of the ground. There was a concentrated digging and runways were laid open, nests of the vermin uncovered, those within being speedily taken care of.

On the third night the first of the gathering began to drift away, followed by more and more. They made no formal farewells to their host and hostess, nor did any of them seek me out.

During the meeting the cublings had engaged in mock battles of their own with much snarling, hissing, and even flying tufts of hair. Murri rendered good account of himself in two such encounters and his trot took on something of a proud roll when he came to me afterward that I might smooth his fur and hail him as warrior.

Once the company left and the silence settled once more on the isle, I helped the family sweep the debris of the meeting into deep cracks and fissures. Again I took up scraps of rat hide, softening it from the stiffness of sun drying by pulling it back and forth across the edge of the rock.

I could delay no longer. The future I had refused to meet must now be faced squarely. Where I would head when I left the safety of this isle I had no idea. We were not too far, I believed, from that stretch of death-dealing land—the Plain of Desolation. But I still lacked any guide.

As I worked packing sun-dried pats of algae, more strips of rat meat, whatever I believed I could carry that might mean my life later on, Myrourr came to me.

"There is a road." His speech was easier for me to understand the longer I listened. "Masca Broken Tooth said it lies so—" He lifted his head and pointed outward from the isle.

"Where does it lead?"

"Who knows?" He made it very clear that the trails of my kind were of little account to a Sand Cat. "But some pass along it. Twice has Masca had good hunting from their beasts. Murri—!"

He summoned his young son, who squatted before him. I received a jumble of thought impressions and knew that the cub was being instructed by his sire. Since the Sand Cats were lovers of the desert lands, certainly they must possess powers of direction which were more than even the knowledge of our far-ranging patrols.

When Myrourr had done, Maraya followed with more warnings and instructions, ending that her cub was now to be the comrade and protector of another, and one who was not properly taught.

How long it might be before we found another such refuge as the one which had served me so well here, I had no idea. The more supplies I could carry with me, the better our chances.

I made up two packs, one containing my own few belongings and all I could cram into it of the dried food. The second pack was not a heavy one, for neither the algae cakes nor the meat strips were of weight. I enfolded this in a crude covering of skins lashed together and showed it to Murri.

He backed away, looking at me and uttering sounds of refusal.

"To travel," I told him with what authority I could summon, "one must feed. Thus we bear food in case we stray days from new supplies. I can not carry two packs. On the trails comrades share burdens."

Murri's measuring gaze went from me to the two adult cats as if he expected them to back his proud refusal to carry a burden like a yaksen. But neither of them moved nor made a sound. Then he looked back to me and I nodded.

Showing by every muscle movement of his lithe body his distaste for what I asked, he advanced a stride and stood while I made fast the pack, settling and securing it as best I could to accommodate his movements. I took up my staff and then it was my turn to face the older cats. Farewells come hard. My people are clannish and find it difficult to cut any ties. This rested upon me now even though I fronted Sand Cats and not kin of my own kind.

I bowed my head, as I would to the Head of some House and spoke the words of going forth—as I had not been encouraged to say them by any of my blood on the night I left my own home.

"To Myrourr and Maraya, this visitor within their land gives thanks for hearthright and homeright. May the Great Essence of all enclose and keep you, and may the end of the trail be that which you most wish."

Myrourr answered me:

"Smoothskin, I have taken the gift of life from your hands—as none of my kind have done. Between us there is no claw nor fang, no knife, no spear. Those are for ones who have no understanding. Go in peace to follow the trail set for you— there is more than chance in what you do."

Then, with Murri trotting confidently in the lead as if he followed a visible marking of foot and hoof prints, we left the isle of Myrourr and Maraya. I looked back once over my shoulder, but so akin were the marking of their fur to the color of the rocks that I could not see if they still watched us, or if they were already about business of their own.

Murri appeared to be entirely certain of the way, and I could only accept his confidence in hope that he knew what he was doing. The coming of day found us passing out of the sand waves onto a bone white land where there was only a spread of sharp pebbles under foot. Our pace slowed as each step brought with it pain, for those pebbles could be felt even through the boots I had cobbled over with dried skin. Murri began to limp well before the coming of morning.

There was no sign of another isle where we might be able to find shelter or food. From our two packs, my cloak and staff I devised a limited cover from the glare of the rising sun and set about treating Murri's bruised and torn paws, smearing them with algae salve. Over them I then tied foot coverings fashioned from rat skin, making sure these were tightly lashed into place. Murri aided me as best he could by the stretching of paws.

We ate very little of our supplies and then huddled together within the shelter knowing we had the fire blast of the day to get through.

10

"Allitta!"

I set the square of black-painted hide carefully on the table so that the beads laid upon it in intricate pattern would not be shaken from the lines upon which they were to be firmly attached. There was the scent of incense in the room and I turned down the lamp under the basin where the tree gum from the far east simmered. I was purposefully deliberate in all my movements, having learned long ago that haste was the enemy of many of the tasks left for my hands.

Now I passed from the workroom into the shop. Mancol was gone, having his list of errands for the morning. So the outer curtains were still pegged into place, leaving the interior in shadows.

Though I knew very well all which was about me, I felt as always that uneasiness which plagued me in any half light in Ravinga's house. I had seen all, or most all, of those tiny bead eyes, set in place to give a lifelike appearance to the ranks of dolls. Still the skillful fingers of my mistress appeared to have awakened all images into life so that they stared at me, weighed me. Almost I could believe that I was the object of gossip among those eyes' owners when I was not present.

There were times when I was sure that Ravinga's skill was far too great—that now and then a doll passed out of her hands which was so akin to a living person that it might have been an illusion projected from flesh and bone.

During the past four seasons a new, macabre demand had arisen among the Vapalans to keep Ravinga busied—a fashion for portraits of the newly dead. Even to being clad in scraps from the favorite robes of the deceased, these foot-high figures had been fashioned as permanent records of friends and kin lost to their Houses. The making of these had not been introduced by Ravinga. In fact I was certain that she made such against her will. Yet she had not refused to accept a commission no matter from whom—grieving lifemate, sister, brother.

I remember quite well the first of her making—it had been of Wefolan-ji, one of the elders of a House now prominently represented at court by Giarribari, the Grand Chancellor, and the customer, Ravinga was informed, was from the far eastern inner lands which are legend to us.

Since then Ravinga had wrought a full dozen more, and I heard that such were now on display in the halls their models had once known in life.

Very recently it had not been only the dead that friends chose to honor so—but upon the coming of anyone into fame, those of the House would order such a figure to be clad in full court dress.

Two such lay even now in boxes behind Ravinga on the shelf, well wrapped and sealed against any jar. Now her hands were busy shuffling through a packet of dried and beaten tav leaves on which were drawings in color, plainly the specifications of another such representative of the living, or the dead.

She did not look up as I drew closer, only fanned the last of the leaf pictures out upon the counter where a low-trimmed lamp banished the shadows immediately around.

"Haban-ji." Her voice was very close to a whisper.

I shivered. There was that in her tone, in the tense stance of her body, which was a warning.

"Who brought this order?" I kept my voice low to match her own hiss. "And why?"

"Who—the confidential clerk of Giarribari. Why—?"

The Grand Chancellor was not one to draw upon Ravinga's skill in a need to flatter her lord. All knew her for what she was, a shrewd, somewhat calculating autocrat, true servant not of Haban-ji—rather sealed in loyalty to the office she now filled. To Giarribari the laws, rights, very life of the Empire were infinitely greater than any one man.

"She does not wish to flatter," I spoke my first thought aloud. "There is no need for her to do so. She knows her own worth and weighs well the worth of him whom she serves—"

"Haban-ji has been more than thirty storm seasons on the throne. There have been no speeches against him."

Ravinga nodded. "Nor has there been much speech for him. There has been no true testing of him."

"But truly there was! Otherwise how would he carry the leopard staff?" I protested.

"True—he won the crown testing. However, matters change through the years. He who was a bold young hunter becomes, when lapped in power, another. There has been much coming and going lately between Vapala and the far eastern inner lands. Their merchants make journeys hither lately in large numbers. And each of those pays two tolls—"

Now she was repeating a rumor of the marketplace. Though the Six Houses were long established and among them controlled most of the trade, still they might well be complacent now, not too quick to follow up some whisper that one or another of their kind had sudden access to luxuries unknown in the outer lands.

However—the Emperor! One who had passed through the great trials to reach the throne—what need had he of foreign merchant favor or greater riches than his office gave him?

"There was a difference in the past," Ravinga continued. "Then an Emperor did not gain the throne and forget he might have to struggle to hold it. For there was once a set period of seasons and then he knew the challenge might come. We of Vapala now speak of such action as barbarian and not for us to follow. Yet it was once the law that the Emperor was to be the nourisher of his people—he was to give all himself to the land, strengthening the Essence in a free surrender. Now he is not the sacrifice but rather makes token offerings and such are accepted."

A token offering! I looked to the patterns she still shuffled back and forth as one might treat papers which carried ill news, wishing to throw them away and yet unable to do so.

I need not ask the question in my mind—she had caught it.

"A token? Perhaps. If so—" she shook her head slowly, "that is sensible reasoning. Yet I wonder. There is Shank-ji."

Our rulers, the five Queens, the Emperor, do not take lifemates. Though that does not mean that they live celibate lives. However, any children born of such matings had no standing above any others of noble Houses, nor were such ever recognized at any of the courts, unless they won to high place by their own efforts. For the past three seasons we had heard much of Shank-ji, the Emperor's son in all but formal name.

He was said to have openly vowed, before the great ones of the court, that when the time came that his father died he would enter the contest for Emperor and that he fully meant to take the High Crown.

"This is," Ravinga's hand curled into a fist and she brought it down upon the lined leaves, "an honor doll for which there is no honor to celebrate. Therefore it can become—"

"A death doll!" I clapped my hand over my mouth even as I said that. "But there is no talk of the Emperor ailing—more than the general ills of age."

"Just so," Ravinga agreed. "Yet this is also the season of fevers. Haban-ji is interested in curiosities from the east. There have been reports from the sentries at the far border that there is grave sickness beyond. One caravan was discovered with all the traders dead about their beasts. They did not die of any sword or knife thrust—their killer was a thing unseen. Let Haban-ji be given some toy from such an infected camp—or seem to be given such—and there can well be good reasoning for a death doll."

"And the Grand Chancellor?"

"Who are such as we to know the intrigues of the court? They have little to do, those noble ones, and thus they may play some odd games such as we commoners would not try. Yes, there are changes coming. Have you not also foreseen it so?"

"And if I have? I tell you, mistress, I will have no part in such! Have I not been life twisted already, and by none of my own doing, because there are those who clutch with greedy fingers? There is no longer any House of Vurope."

I was angry. She was pushing me into paths of memory I had no wish to travel—paths I had worn so deep over the past seasons that they were only too open to entrap my course of thought.

Ravinga had put together in one packet those leaves and now she placed them in a flat envelope. But that did not join the rest of the patterns in a side drawer, instead she pushed it into a seam pocket of her robe.

"You will make it then?"

"What excuse can I rightfully raise to refuse such a commission?" she countered. "I delay by this much. I have asked for the proper jewels with which to fashion a crown of state. Outwardly, Allitta, this must be accepted as any other order. However, there is also this—"

She half turned to pick up from the shelf immediately behind her a box of some dull black substance. There was a strange look to the surface of that container, as if it could swallow light, a devouring shadow, so that any color or gleam of metal, even warm lamp glow, was dimmed in its presence.

Ravinga had jerked from a crumpled mass of dust-laden cloths such as Mancol used each morning to rid the counter of debris, a square which was streaked with black back and forth. Some artist might have used it to wipe a brush upon it.

She used that to handle the box, spreading out the dirty cloth beneath it. We often received oddly protected materials in the shop, and this was not the first time my mistress was so very careful about how she handled some such container.

Ravinga now pressed at either end of the tightly sealed lid. There came a whiff of vile odor, like the stink of a waste pit under the sun. When she raised her thumbs again the lid adhered to them, was so carried up.

The inside of the coffer was splattered with red which had thickened in some places into gummy bubbles. Amid this rested, not such a doll as I had more than half expected to see, but rather the representation of a beast.

We of Vapala might not he threatened by the desert rats but I had seen their carcasses enough to know what this was. Still keeping her flesh covered, Ravinga levered up the creature and dumped it on the counter between us.

It had been made of some material I did not recognize—seemingly of a bit of real skin stuffed, but it was manifestly too heavy for that, for it landed with a heavy thump. Save for its size it was complete in every detail, even to the bloodlike spots which glistened as if it had been recently slaughtered.

The head of the creature moved! There were sparks of yellow-red fire filling the eye cavities and which I sensed were aware of me, of Ravinga. What I thought of was the skitter of clawed feet on stone, many such.

I watched my mistress pinch together where the cloth lay beneath the monstrous thing. There she held a grip which made her knuckles stand out.

"So—so it is—" I said and then I moved. From my girdle I jerked a short rod carven from fire-born rock such as gushes out of the mountain crevices in Thnossis. And I flailed out with that, the end of it catching the creature on the side of the head even as it lifted lip to me in threat.

At the same moment I armed that blow, Ravinga also jerked her hands. The touch of my rod rocked the figure, and it fell back into the cloth. Then my second blow followed the first. The beast's body jerked—simulating life which I was sure it did not have before it crumpled into small crumbs.

I stood, rod ready for a third blow, staring down at the broken mass.

"I was right! I was right!" I said and my breath seemed to hiss between my teeth. "It was no dream—but the truth!"

Anger as hot as the stuff of my wand had once been surged in me. Behind me arose all the times I had heard a story, only to be told—soothingly by some, angrily by others—that I had fastened on some dream and claimed it for reality.

I had learned through pain of both mind and body that the truth of one is very often lost by the will of many.

Now, once more, I saw the mat bed—and the woman who lay upon it, the struggle of childbirth and pain twisting her. Imposed upon that scene the half-seen face grinning, grinning with a second mouth which opened wide inches below the one nature had granted him. I saw once more the vicious gleam of those eyes, which only I had seen alive then. I heard my own voice, a much younger voice, cry out protests and pleas as he held me in a grip which near tore my skin with its savagery, and I felt the flash of red-hot fire about my shoulders again and again!

So beaten had I been that there was hardly a shred of life left to me when I was thrust into a place of darkness and knew, through the pain, that this was only the beginning of suffering to come.

However, I did not meet that death. I never knew whom I had to thank for that. A spark of stubbornness, of the growth of that need for vengeance, had set me crawling through a place of shadows. I sensed that there was that also crawling through the dark which was even worse than he who had attacked me.

I looked to Ravinga again and her eyes met mine. "What and who?"

It was true that my hot-tempered father had had the two rights over me—life which he had given me and death which was his for the asking. He had many enemies—which one of them had devised such a scheme, one to attack me past any hope of either belief or forgiveness? Yet it was not the battle of kin which I had ever fought, but more my own. Nothing dampened my wrath, but I had learned to bury it deep for a space.

"Who—why?" My mouth was so dry those two words came as croaks.

"Who—why—?" she echoed me. "Someone tries now a variation of a game played so well before. There is an order for a ceremonial figure of Haban-ji—then comes this filth secretly. Mancol found it on an upper shelf of the store room this morning. Tongues wag freely—an Emperor ages—perhaps dies. In my hands there is an honor image—with something far worse to be found if the guard comes to search. Was it not something of the sort before, girl?"

I was not too overwrought by memories of the past to see the dark and threatening logic of what she said. A web woven.

"Someone fears—" I said slowly. "But why me? Power is yours, but who has anything to fear from me?"

Ravinga swept the stained cloth together and thrust it into the box which had held the rat. She pulled towards her the brazier meant to scent the air with burning powers. Into the coals which still existed in the heart of that she slammed the cloth and the now empty box.

There was an explosion of raw light, a noise which hurt through my ears far into my head. The upward blaze of the flames obscured the box at once.

"There may be two who play—one may be a searcher into lost knowledge who strives to turn bits and pieces into weapons—the other—the other may also be a seeker—of other things. For this time what can we do but watch—listen—sense—We must be the guardians of our own lives and freedom."

11

For as long as I can remember I had heard tales of the Plain of Desolation, a heat-blasted land closed to all life forms save bands of rats. These seemed to have become adjusted to its lack of any water except algae beds so minerally poisoned as to kill the wanderer with the first mouthful.

Even the most desperate of raiders would not venture therein and there were accounts of outlaw bands turning at bay on the edge of the Plain to face a death they knew, rather than a worse one than any sword or spear offered. Traders made lengthy trips to north or south to avoid that death trap.

Where Murri and I now traveled was the very edge of that ominous waste. It was not speedy travel, as the sharp pebble footing slowed us. The stores we had started with I stretched as far as possible. Murri might outlast me, for the great predators were better used to going longer without food. Yet there would come an end to strength for both of us unless we could find some sustenance in time.

Murri's pack was exhausted first, though he was clever enough to take no pleasure in that loss, knowing how much we needed every algae cake, every scrap of rat flesh which each day we divided into smaller and smaller rations.

I was losing my confidence in him as a guide. After all, though the cats did roam outward from the isles each pair claimed, yet I could see no sign of any heights ahead, or any break in the baking enormity of the Plain. Our journeying was by night. Always Murri seemed certain of the way. The parched white stretch of land about us had the starkness of bone, and, while there was no night-awakened glimmer of sand, yet we were not altogether without a ghostly light which sprang here from the pebbly ground.

We were five days out from the isle when there showed a promising break on the skyline ahead. Within an hour after we started on the fifth night, we came to traces of some who had dared this path before us. Bones of both beasts and men had been dragged apart and splintered by teeth. Three wagons still stood roped to the shattered remains of yaksen carcasses. Some traders' party had come to an end here. I moved among the dead unable to tell one set of remains from another, so hardly had all been used.

Without very much hope I dragged open packs from the wagons. These had been near torn to tatters. I could guess food supplies had been in some. But two were intact and when I unrolled them there were inner pockets full of rough gemstones, unpolished and showing little color. Still I had been schooled well enough by Kura to recognize the worth of what I had found. There was a bundle of notes of sales and that I took. Were I ever to escape this deathway, what I had discovered might be returned to the heirs of those who lay here.

There were in addition two knives and a sword—trade goods of high value—and those I gathered up eagerly. What small training I had in sword play had given me far less skill than that of my father or brother, but a good blade in the hand was in a way heartening and I was more than pleased with my find.

Murri had been prowling around the scene of the disaster and now he came to me.

"Cat—smoothskin—other—"

"Other?"

I let him lead me to a place where there were five of the skeletons huddled together. The glint of jewelry showed among splintered bone. However, that was not all—two skulls lay with their empty eye pits pointing up to the sky. And the very center of each was blackened and turned to crumbling ashes as if they had been in a fire.

I squatted down on my heels to view them but I did not put forth my hand, even my staff, to touch them. The bones were clean, the death about us one I could understand.

Sand Cats could well strike so, even though there were no traces of any of their dead—

"Here one!" Murri had taken two long strides and there lay another skeleton, plainly one of his own species. The massive skull of that was charred from behind as if the animal had been brought down as it fled the scene of the other deaths.

Who killed with fire? We could tame that into lamps and torches to carry with us, lanterns even, to set up for night guards along the trade roads—though those signals are carefully imprisoned in cavities in the heads of the carven cats, the light to shine through their eyeholes.

I could imagine some desperate traveler of my own blood using a torch as a last weapon. A cat could have been so felled. Yet here, too, were the fallen of my species showing the same traces of grisly wounds.

"Other cats?" I asked of Murri.

"We honor dead," he returned shortly.

"Why then—?" I nodded to the skeleton he had found.

My night sight was good enough to see the rising of hair along his spine. He growled.

"This is of evil." He turned aside and picked up in his mouth a long tatter of one of the supply bags. With a flick of his head he sent that flying so that it fluttered down across the bared bones. One tip of the torn hide fell across that blackened hole.

Flame is red, yellow, many shades of those colors, as anyone who has watched the dance of fire tongues can tell you.

The hide drew something else—it was grey, as if this country had even bleached the life from fire itself. But that strange flame leaped into being as the hide curled, giving forth the stench of its burning. When the last of it was ashed there was only the blackened hole and no sign of anything which might still lie in wait there. I had seen that happen. Such was totally beyond any traveler's tale I had ever listened to with the greed of one who wished to know yet hesitated to venture forth to learn for himself.

Now I went back to those other two skulls which bore the brand of the strange burning. This time I impaled a tatter on the end of my staff and gingerly shook it free so that the stained ribbon might fall upon the human skull.

There came fire again—only this burned with a sickening greenish hue—and was as quick to finish off what I had fed into it. Two kinds of fire? Or only one which answered in different ways because the prey differed?

What had happened—

I started back, tripped over the bones of a yaksen, and fell on my back, as helpless for a moment as one of those brilliantly colored beetles the traders from Vapala offer from time to time.

Again—

Sound, a moan of sound—then pattern of notes—as if someone lost in this desolation was singing his own death melody.

Murri snapped around but with care for his footing. He was facing outward, away from the ill-omened battlefield.

Again—now there was a continuous background hum from which came notes, or even sounds like a much repeated refrain aroused. And since the first shock was over I realized what it was—that there was one playing a Kifongg harp and with it singing a dirge which was only rightful for this country.

"Life!" Murri's whole body stiffened into a point.

Had someone escaped massacre? The law of the trail was plain: it was my duty to hunt for that survivor.

Or—I glanced once more at the blackened skulls—was this a trap?

Murri picked up that thought. Perhaps it had already occurred to him.

"No trap—life, cave, food—" He was impatient.

I had stored my finds into my pack. Now more than ever were I to reach some authority I must report our discovery. Leaning on my staff a little as the ever-crunching and moving gravel cut at my boots, I moved on into the night after Murri.

As suddenly as it had sounded out of the night, so that dirge ended. We had passed out of the treacherous footing that lay on the edge of the Plain and once more faced the rise and fall of the glimmering sand dunes. Here the wide, furred feet of Murri made better time than mine and I had dropped a length or so behind when I sighted a spark of light ahead. It seemed so high in the sky that first I thought it was a star, yet it seemed too bright for one of those dim beacons which had so far not served me at all.

We came upon our first-seen spur of rock. And a moment or so later, I was sure that this was not altogether the work of nature. Rather it was a part statue of a way cat, the head and shoulders of which had been snapped off to lie as a partly shattered mass to one side.

Not far beyond that a second way marker reared, and this one was not only intact but within its head a small fire had been kindled, for there were yellow beams to mark the eyes. It was a work of cunning art and it wore also a necklet of dullish jewels, certainly so eroded by the sandstorms, as well as rings at the tips of its well-shaped ears. Yet there was that in its outline which suggested the Sand Cat rather than the harmless kottis with which we were always so glad to share our shelters.

The statue was faced partly away from me so that I saw only the one eye clearly. As we passed it the land began to slope downward and we had to fight our way through shifting sands, which in places were like to swallow Murri to his belly fur and me to my knees. It was the sloping of this way which had hidden, by the aid of the night, the fact that we had entered a great basin. Nor was the cat with the burning eyes the only one who was set there on guard. There were three others, and a second of these also showed the burning night eyes.

We won through the slopes of the dunes and came out upon a more level space. Here there had been erected a whole clan of cats, some showing signs of wear, and others standing as straight and tall as if they had just been set in place. Not too far away was a line of darkness blotting out some of the sand glitter—surely the outermost shore of one of the isles!

Murri held high his head, his ears pointed a little forward, his nostrils expanded. My senses were so much the less than his but I knew that scent too well to be deceived—there were yaksen ahead! Though that did not mean that we had come upon some outpost of a holding here—for the thick-coated beasts of burden roamed free in many places.

We came to where rock sprouted upward from the sand. Murri uttered a small sound. Water! Somewhere not too far beyond us now was an algae bed and there lay what we needed the most.

Still we were not utterly disarmed by our need. Murri yet took the lead with a spring which carried him up into a shelf extension of the rock and I followed with greater effort.

I heard the snorting of a herd bull that must have picked up our scent. Murri was inching along an ascending ledge, his claws unleashed to make sure of every small advantage to come from hooking them into the seams and crevices.

"Saaaaaaaaaa!" It was almost the snarl of a cat and there bounded downslope, only inches away from my defenseless head, a rock, full double-fist large. I flattened myself until my cheek ground into the stone.

The musky smell of the yaksen was strong. I could almost hear the click of their hooves.

"Saaaaaa!" Again the rising cry of a guardian herdsman. How many times I myself had uttered such when on duty?

"We mean no harm." I had to moisten my lips twice with my tongue before I could shape those words. "Traveler's rights, herdsman. These we claim!"

Traveler's rights for a Sand Cat? To any there would be folly in such a suggestion.

"Saaaaaaaa!" Undoubtedly the voice was farther away. The watchman was true enough to his service to urge what beasts he could out of range.

My hand flailed upward, caught at the stone, and I had a firm enough grip to hold, to pull myself up on a flat surface. I got to one knee and then made it to my feet which were shaking a little as I forced myself away from the stone to look around.

Five yaksen, two of which were hardly more than calves, had moved away. I could see no more of them than blots which stirred uneasily.

"Traveler's greeting." I tried again. And to prove the rightness of my claim for such consideration I added:

"I am Hynkkel of the House of Klaverel. I am faring forth on my solo."

"You bear weapons." The voice was thin, wavery, almost as if it had been but little used lately.

"Only such—" I was beginning when I remembered the arms we had taken from the massacre camp, "only such as a man may need hereabouts."

"You company with that which brings death—" There was accusation in the voice which had now taken on something of a whine.

"I company with a friend." I returned firmly. "This one is blood brother to me. Murri." I called to the Sand Cat. "This is a friend—"

"A Sand Cat has no friends among smoothskins," he spat.

"Then what am I?" I countered. That this stranger so well hidden in the shadows could make anything of our exchange I did not know. But having reconstructed a course of life after such a near acceptance of death, I was not going to surrender.

"By the blood which unites us," I spoke only to Murri now, "swear that we come in truce, as is the way of the land."

There was only silence and my frustration grew strong. If Murri was ready to separate me from my own kind after this first smile of fortune—

"Murri, I wait!"

"And die?" there came the cat's answer.

"Death! There has been too much of death!" My voice rose ever louder.

Once more there skimmed by my head a weight of hand-thrown stone.

"I come in trust," growled Murri. "But this one surely could not understand cat talk."

There was silence, broken only by the click of yaksen hooves. The small herd was moving.

"Stay then." The words were now lost in a heavy coughing and I heard a scrambling sound as if he who had spoken was now gone. All the taut readiness went out of my body and I fell rather than seated myself on the rock surface, depending upon the few small sounds my ears could pick up to assure me that, for the moment, there was to be no other attack.

12

The first streaks of pre-dawn were washing out the stars. Twice I had called upon Murri but the cat had not answered. That he was on the hunt I could be sure and a yaksen was no easy prey, especially if more than one were to be found. Their thick fur gave them some protection, and the heavy horns with which they met any assault, head down, were danger, for they fought in head fashion, the males and barren females surrounding the calves and any nursing mothers. Murri, as large as he seemed when one compared him to a kotti, was not nearly the size, nor had the brutal strength, of his sire and dam.

There had been no sound since that scrambling which had marked the retreat of whoever had challenged us, he and the beasts whose scent had so surely drawn Murri. Somewhere and not too far away was an algae pool, that I could smell, inferior as my senses were compared to Murri's. My body's need for what that offered grew so strong I could no longer withstand it.

It was my turn to thread a way among tall spikes of rock. As the light grew stronger I could see that many of these had been worked upon by chisel and hammer. More than half of them were fashioned into cat guardians, their faces turned towards the death plain from which I had come.

The first were roughly made, with very little skill to give them life, but, as I worked myself inward, that skill improved, as if the artist learned by his mistakes. Yet there was a sameness in position and raise of head which argued that the one carver had wrought them all.

Finally I was confronted by a line of such, fast-wedged into an opening before two towering walls. The guardian cats were not so well based here and it was apparent that some had been fashioned elsewhere and brought to this place, packed into a wall one against the other.

I shed my pack, attaching one end of my rope to it, and set myself to a climb. The rough rock was scorching my skin, still not yet completely recovered from the torments of the journey. However, I doggedly fought my way to the head of the largest cat and looked down.

There was an algae pond right enough, but an ill-tended one. Here had been no careful pruning to discourage growth which forced out that more edible kind which was meat and drink for my species, while in other places the nourishing kinds had been too close-cropped, as if a herd had not been properly moved.

There were yaksen here and, in the morning light growing ever stronger, it was plain that they had been neglected for some time although they were not the smaller species which roamed free. Their heavy coats were matted and, with some animals, dragged on the ground, adding crushed algae and even small stones to a burden from which they could not clear themselves. Now and then one of the beasts would utter a small cry of complaint and strive to reach some weighty mat, biting fruitlessly at the foul caking of hair.

Of men there were no signs, save on the opposite of the pool there was a hut of sorts—certainly no house such as any man of respect would claim, its walls a crazy patchwork of stones of all sizes, each fitting at rude angles into any space where it might be forced. On its crown was a reasonably smooth place and there was a patch of green-blue color, showing vividly against the red-yellow of the veined rocks.

Such a woven rug could have come only from Vapala, where, it was said, there were growing things not rooted in pools, which put forth tall stems to delight the eyes with new colors.

From Murri there was no signal which concerned me, but the yaksen were bunched together. Now and then a young bull would toss head and give voice to a bellow which was more an expression of uneasiness than any challenge.

By the door of that patch-upon-patch hut there was movement as a man came into the open, an algae-gathering basket
in hand. His body was thin and old and I could see the most of
it for he wore a kilt of fringed bits of rags, as if that garment
was the last of a hard-used wardrobe.

His hair was an upstanding ragged mop, strands of which
fell to his sharp-boned shoulders, giving him the look of those
sand devils of childish tales. In one hand he held a staff much
shorter than the one which served me, lacking metal tipping
and edges. That he needed it for support was apparent as he
tottered down to the pool.

"Ancient One—" His accent, in spite of the grating notes
of his voice, had been that of the son of some House, no
common trader. I did not know what title to give him. "Ancient One, I am no enemy of yours."

His head was cocked a little to one side as if so he could
hear me the better.

"Not Vapalan then. Kahulawen to be sure. Traders? Have
you wandered from those who now follow you? This is a forgotten place, you will find no succor here. There was—" He
paused, frowning. His eyebrows were very bushy and beneath
this overhang I could sight that one eye carried a fog-film.
"There was a Sand Cat—"

"There is—my almost brother. It was his people who
gave me aid when I needed it. They have accepted me as
friend."

"Sooooo—" He drew the word out until it was near a hiss—
such as Murri might give. "And I suppose now you will say
that you are Emperor-to-be? If it is difficult to be a man, how
much more difficult it must be to be a ruler. It has been a long
time. The ancient ones—Karsawka—and by all rumors
Zacan—should now also be waking. But there is nothing for
you here, even though you carry the mask. Leave me in peace.
I have nothing for the aiding of heroes, no matter how powerful they once were."

"You have what any can offer, Ancient One. I am no hero
but I need food and drink—"

"If you are truly son of the Essence, that Karsawka who will be once more, as testify the very ancient songs—" he frowned again and his expression was of one trying to remember, "then what man can deny you? Many songs have grown from your deed." Then he did what I never could imagine such an elder doing. He flung back his head and sang. There was no rusty coarseness in that singing—no break or difficulty. To close my eyes was to listen to some bard fit to eat at the Emperor's table.

"From the sand draw the light.
From the rocks learn the strength.
In the storm wind walk without shelter.
There is that in the land which enters in.
And such holds two lives within it.
That which is gone, that which is to come.
Walk swiftly in the chosen way,
For the time of shadows is upon the kin,
Only he who shares life can live it."

I recognized the song, not in itself but for what it was—a puzzle. The Vapalans, who consider themselves the only truly civilized members of the five nations, have a taste for such, binding into words some hidden meanings to which only few have a clue. Some of the cliques and Houses among them have refined this to the extent that only a handful out of their whole land may understand—no one from outside their mesa country can hope to know the meaning.

As his last word was echoed faintly back from some distance the bard leaned forward on his staff, that feat of song seemingly having weakened him. He was regarding me intently as if I were enough a countryman of his to see to the heart of his "tangle."

"Truly," I said and I meant it from the heart, "that is bard gift. Never have I heard its like—"

"Never is perhaps right." There was a scoffing note in a voice once more hoarse, perhaps even more so from the strain which had just been forced upon it. "There are bards and bards, stranger. Of them all the great ones are of Vapala." He continued to stare at me under his bushy eyebrows as if striving to detect any protest I might raise.

"Lord Bard, so will I agree. Also I would swear to you that I mean you and yours no harm. I have no power to claim guest right. However, this isle lies within the borders of my own land and so is bound by the laws of my people—"

"Guest right." He mouthed the words as if he chewed upon them. "Yet you travel with one of the killers of the desert. Does he claim guest right also?"

"Murri—" I raised my own voice, giving it the particular twist which was the closest my human lips and throat could come to the speech of the Great Cats.

He came, seeming to rise out of the rocks themselves so close in color was his coat to their surfaces. Padding to me, he turned, as my hand rested on his head, to also face the bard. Then to my surprise he opened his jaws and there poured forth a medley of such sounds which I had heard uttered many times during the festival of the cat people.

"Cloud—evil—not of night—" I fitted together the growls and snarls. The bard leaned still farther forward, an incredulous expression on his wrinkled face.

"No blade can slay and still protect,
Two battle as one—as it was—
So shall it come again.
Zacan rouses, stretched forth claw to rend.
Where then is the LAW?"

The bard had been tapping out a rhythm on the length of his staff as he listened. Before the echoes of Murri's voice died he spoke:

"Old am I, cubling, and once I was known to many because I hunted forth the most ancient of songs and introduced them again. It was idle sport—and many held puzzles we could not solve. But it became a badge of proficiency among us to know, to try to understand. What—who was Zacan in truth? Lost." He shook his head and the long locks of his hair brushed back and forth across his shoulders. "But then they would tell us, these delvers into old stories, that nothing is lost—it may be hidden for a space and then brought once more, perhaps by chance, into the light—even through folly. It is enough that bard speak with bard, whether one wears a furred skin or goes bare-armed."

He took a step backward. "Into the land of the House of Kynrr enter freely, you who come from the desert." He pushed with the much worn butt of his spear, winding with it a floating mass of algae. This he then offered us, the host gift which would make us free for at least ten days on this holding.

However, in this bargaining he lost very little, for after accepting I made myself busy. Once more I worked at an algae bed, transplanting and encouraging new growth. I tended his yaksen also, grooming them, cutting out odorous mats of hair to free and cleanse them. The clipped hair I soaked and then combed it straight.

Kynrr's hut was the better for a cleanout, too, and that was what it got, perhaps the first in years. While its owner withdrew to a seat on a spire of rock and kept staring so intently in the direction from which I had come that I was led several times to turn and search that same direction—only to see nothing but rock and sand. He never gave me any explanation of what he so sought.

Murri went off by himself hunting. Through some delicacy he did not bring any game with him on return. He did inform me that this isle had its share of menaces, mainly at another algae pool which was attracting rats.

During my cleaning of the hut I found a Kifongg harp which in its day had certainly been a master's instrument. Kynrr watched me examine it with reverence and then signed me to bring it to him. He then began abruptly a series of lessons.

As all children, I had in my time been taught to use the Kifongg but I had never displayed any proficiency which led my father into having those lessons extended. Now I discovered that I had fallen into the company of a master musician and one who wanted not only a captive audience but a student.

The stiffness wore out of my fingers and I kept at the exercises set me. Mainly because Kynrr's eyes were ever upon me, I attained a measure of skill I never dreamed could be mine.

Perhaps because Kynrr had been so long alone, to have company now was like someone opening the gate of a corral to allow an impatient herd beast down to the pool. While what my mentor talked of between bouts of music was the glories of Vapala of the Diamond Court, never did he tell me what had exiled him from all the luxury he had known and I knew better than to ask. However, it was plain that his position there had been a high one and he had been on familiar terms with the inner core of lords who dealt with great affairs.

He seemed to take pleasure after time in describing in detail court ceremonies, interrupting his accounts of such with scraps of gossip. It seemed more and more to me as I listened that the High Court was indeed a place of masks—that no one therein was, or wanted to be, himself, but behind their faces their thoughts moved in strange directions.

There were six premier Houses which had kept their position and identity through countless generations of time. There were other, newer ones, upon whom the six looked with emotions ranging from faint contempt to sneering intrigue designed to bring them down.

It was my belief that Kynrr had been caught in some such clearing of lesser Houses and had to flee Vapala for that reason.

On the surface the major occupation of the court appeared to be participation in endless and dull-sounding ceremonies which Kynrr related in detail. The dress, the action, even the sex of those in such interaction had a great deal to do with success. To humor him I became a sort of puppet acting out for him some bit of this purposeless play. Yet he took it with all seriousness and was so upset at my numerous errors of speech or action that I attempted to do his will to the best of my ability.

Murri found this dull. He would watch a bit from some perch among the rock and then disappear silently—rat hunting for the most part.

So days passed. I thought often of starting off again, but it was growing plainer all the time that the Kynrr's sight was failing more and more, that it was increasingly difficult for him to care for himself, let alone the dozen yaksen who were growing sleek and tractable under my ministrations.

It was one night when we sat together on a ridge, looking at the stars—rather I looking, and Kynrr striving to point out guides he could not see any longer, that he spoke with some of the sharpness he used when trying to drive a bit of court etiquette into my thick head.

"Hynkkel, you are not made for a hermitage. Where will you go?"

I answered with the truth. "I have something of a gift with animals, Kynrr. It might be well to go to Vapala, as you have been urging on me, and there see if I can apprentice myself to a trainer of beasts."

"Trainer of beasts!" He cackled, then clapped his hands together as might a child delighted with some jest. "Yes, a trainer of beasts, and a rare one you shall be." He changed subject abruptly.

"The Emperor ails. Before your coming, there was a trading caravan off its course because of a storm. They had news— much news. With the Emperor dead—then there will be a choosing—"

It was my turn to laugh. "Ancient One, if you are suggesting that I set myself up for the trials, then indeed you have a poor opinion of my common sense. I was the least of my House, so poor a son to my father that he will show little sorrow at my non-return. I am no fighter, no doer of deeds which will make my name one for bards to remember. No, I am not of the stuff of which heroes are made. And that suits me very well."

I went off to check the herd, be sure that the rats were not a-prowl. But as I went I smiled as I thought of my brother's face if he looked upon the candidates for the Empire trial and saw me among them.

13

Still I could not bring myself to desert the old man. Though I tried, even bluntly at times, to discover whether any of his House might be concerned with him, he evaded any answer, sometimes even getting up and walking away or shutting his eyes as if he had fallen into one of the sudden dozes which strike the elderly.

On all other subjects he was talkative enough and the longer we were together the more he talked. At times his voice took on the tones of one lecturing students and he would spring questions without warning, keeping me alert to all which he said.

Murri, for the most part, kept out of sight, though when the old man slept heavily he would come to me. The Sand Cat was growing impatient. Having been released by the custom of his kind from the isle of his birth, he was eager to be about his search for territory of his own to claim.

Though he might not be in sight, he sometimes lay in the shadows and I believed that he understood much of what Kynrr said. But it was the singing of the bard and his playing on the Kifongg which appeared to enchant the cat the most.

I certainly could never qualify for the place of bard before the high seat of any House, but my playing was better than most I had heard, and that is not a boast. All of us of the Outer Regions have a liking for music—from the roll of the lookout drums which signify the coming of the storm to those small songs one sings to soothe a fretful child, we are surrounded with music from our birth. I had known to the last word some half hundred songs, both the genealogical chants which were the duty of each House child to be able to recall, to fragments of very old verse children used for counting-out games among themselves.

However, now I found that what I knew was nothing when compared to Kynrr's store and many of those I was able to keep in mind, though the riddle songs had no meaning and perhaps had not held any for centuries out of time.

I experimented with the Kifongg when Kynrr passed it to me, striving to fit chord to chord until I could mimic in part the singing of the cats as I had heard them at their great meeting. Kynrr might close his eyes during such efforts on my part but his hand kept time, settling with little trouble on the underlying beat of what I battled to bring into being.

"Soooooooo," he said one morning, "that is what lies behind the Lament of Lasre. Here." He reached for the instrument and began to pluck the strings, tentatively at first, then with more assurance, so that even I could hear the thread of purposeful melody.

"What is the Lament of Lasre?" I asked when he was done and sat with his hands lightly grasping the harp, staring past me at that coloring of the rocks which faded subtly one into another.

"It is a tale." He sat up abruptly and started to wrap the instrument in its silken covering. Kynrr might go in rags himself but his beloved Kifongg fared much better.

"A tale," he repeated to himself as if he had a need for reassurance. "There are many tales from the old days, boy. Most of them nonsense. It is said that there once was knowledge open to certain of our people which is now long forgot. That there was a time of darkness which was worse and thicker than any night across our land. And then one Lasre went forth into the very heart of the darkness and there he sang, and the Essence of all the land and everything which dwelt upon it, within it, was gathered to him so that he broke the cover of the dark. And at that time all which lived were kin—even as you, boy, claim kinship with that great beast of yours.

"And what will you do with him when you go on? For such as he are hunted and slain wherever they may be found."

From time to time that same thought had troubled me. If I picked up the caravan trail and made it into Vapala, certainly

Murri could not accompany me openly. He would be the target of every frontier guard who sighted him.

If there was to be an answer to this it was not made plain that day when Kynrr's yaksen returned from scrambling over the rocks. They divided their grazing between the pool where Kynrr had built his hut and that which lay at the side of a breakneck ridge of rocks. This time answer did come when there was a calf missing and his dam lingered behind, giving long, mourning cries, pausing to look backward.

I was up on my feet, reaching for my bag of pebbles and sling, my staff already to hand. Though it was still early morning the heat was already arising from the rocks. I whistled to Murri and he appeared around a rock spur ready for action. Though it was difficult to track on the bare rock, there was only a narrow way the herd followed. I had not gone far along that before I found evidence of a rock slide, breaking off of the narrow ledge.

There was no sound from below. I crawled, belly down, as close to the edge of the depth as I dared. Having anchored my rope to one of the rock spurs, with the other end of that fastened about my middle, I swung cautiously over.

As I slid down the last portion of the rope, there came a wild squealing. The earth at the bottom of the crevice around the half-buried body of the calf was heaving. There broke through baby rats already jumping to fasten teeth in the long hair of the yaksen and pull it away from the flesh they longed for. I realized that what I had ventured into was a trap—some one of the females had established her nest underground nearby and her offspring, ravenous from the moment of birth, were seeking anything which they could devour.

From above I heard Murri howl a challenge and swiftly answered with my warning. There was no room in this narrow space, half choked as it was by the fall from above, for the Sand Cat to maneuver. We could only get in each other's way disastrously if he tried.

I backed against the nearer wall of the crevice and was using my staff. Luckily the lack of room was also a difficulty for the rats, and these were very young, though among them squirmed the body of the dam trying to head for me.

A well-placed swing of my staff bowled her over and instantly two of her own offspring were at her throat. It was then that I felt the tug of the rope against my body. But I dared not turn to face the cliff wall and so uncover my back to what was left of the ravening pack.

There came a shout and a rock sailed down from above, striking between me and the ratlings. A second rock more perilously aimed, for it nearly struck me, landed and I realized that what help from above which could be offered was on the way.

I made a last sweep with the staff, thrust that through my belt, and whirled about to face the wall. It was rough. There were plenty of finger- and toeholds, but how many of those were strong enough to take my weight? A fall might land me helpless in the midst of that pack of monsters below.

Another rock thundered by me. I forced myself to test my handholds and not be reckless in my choice. Then the rope about me grew taut and I knew that I was being drawn up.

There was a blow against one of my boots, the sharp shooting pain of a tooth slash which had cut through the layers of hide as if they were the softest of skin. That was a spur which sent me reaching for a large knob of rock, giving me energy I would not have thought I would have had.

I was reaching to hook one hand over the edge of the cliff when I felt the pull of the life-saving rope loosen, but I managed to make it on my own to sprawl forward.

Kynrr lay crumpled against a rock and beside him Murri was spitting out the rope. It was plain that they had united in getting me out of that trap. I crawled to Kynrr.

The old man was breathing in gusty gasps and I could see the fast rise and fall of his bare chest. Murri had moved out to meet me and was pulling at my cut boot, bringing the slashed hide away from the blood-spurting flesh beneath.

I managed to staunch that flow of blood and Murri lay licking at the wound while I saw to Kynrr. At first I believed that each of those difficult breaths was going to be the last for the old man. For a space we huddled together. Murri went back to patrol along the edge of the cliff. The loud squealing from below was silenced. It could be that the ratlings had turned on each other as they were well known to do and that we had no more to fear from them.

To get Kynrr back to his hut was a task which took far too long under the sunlight. Thin as the old man looked he was not a light weight, but somehow I managed to get his body over Murri's back. The cub was smaller than his sire but I was able to take a good portion of the weight and the bleeding on my leg had stopped. Perhaps there was indeed some virtue in the licking the beast gave to a wound.

But we were both winded when we reached our goal. Luckily the algae bed was not too far away and it did not require any climbing for me to reach it. When I had recovered my strength somewhat I crept down and plastered my hurt, bringing back a supply for Kynrr in turn.

Towards nightfall the old man roused from the restless sleep which had held him throughout the day. I managed to get him to eat some of the algae, feeding him with my own hands as if he were a child. Twice, though he did not open his eyes, he carried on broken conversations with those who were with him from memory.

The longest of those dealt with Vapala, and he spoke as if his words were caresses offered to some enshrined lover. These broken pictures he so drew for me were indeed of a land far removed from the rock isles and ever-encroaching sands of my own country. He spoke of countryside covered with grow-ing green which was not always rooted in pools, of scented woods and rich stretches of grass where yaksen and oryxen grazed in peace, where there was no hunger, no fear of storms or failures of the pools which supplied our only chance of life.

He began to sing and his voice was full. The melody he shaped brought with it a peace I had never known before.

Perhaps it was his own voice in song which brought him awake, for now his eyes opened and he focused his full sight on me.

"Of your heart kindness, desert born, let me see the coming of the stars once again." His desire to do that was very great as he levered himself up with more energy than I thought was left in his wasted body. So I hastened to help him to his favorite place on the roof of his hut and, because he always had it with him when he went so, I also brought his Kifongg to him.

He smoothed its arched sides back and forth with his hands. Then, with care, he tuned it, until he had tightened the last string and it lay across one bone-thin knee.

From his chosen place he could look out for limitless distance, if his clouded sight allowed. Now he began to point out the stars.

"There is Gurpan's Necklace—and it points to the Tree of Avor. Beyond lies the Gourd of Hinder—Mark them well." Some of the authority of the teacher returned to his voice.

"Follow the Sword, desert born—under it lies your fortune—" He hesitated and then actually cackled with a laugh which left him coughing. "Your fortune, yes. There lies Vapala. You have yet a space of the Waste to cross and that will be a testing—but not such a testing as you shall know later."

His eyes fell from the stars to me. It seemed that in the dusk they had a hint of glow, if only a hint, to be found in a Sand Cat.

"I do not seek Vapala." For at his words there awoke in me an uneasiness which threatened, but why or how I did not understand.

"Some men do not seek fate, that comes seeking them. Try as you will, desert son, you will discover that Vapala awaits you, twist and turn though you strive to do."

Once more he began to sing. Though the words could be understood one by one, their meaning was hidden when he fitted them together:

"Yellow bright, gold of the sun in glory,
Black as foul as the breath of death the rats serve their prey.

Mask of cat, jaw of rat—so shall it be.
One and two—a hosting of small powers, joined.
The path is set, the gate is passed—"

His voice grew weaker, was gone. Then he spoke:

"We can carry nothing with us when we return to the greatest Essence of all, save what we have made of the gifts, doubts, fears, weaknesses, and strengths with which we came. What we take lies here—and here—" He touched his forehead and then his breast.

Then he took up the Kifongg with both hands. It might have been a child of his blood, cherished and much beloved, the way he held it. This he offered to me.

"Take it, desert son, return it whence it came. And say to her who waits, that the meddling is well begun and there is no turning back now."

I accepted the harp and then set it aside and took Kynrr into my arms, for he was coughing and from between his lips there dribbled a bead and then a flow of blood. As I eased him back his eyes once more sought the stars.

"There is a thought—Malquin said it once—that the stars mark other worlds. If that is true then on them men must live and die, be remembered, then forgot. Who was Kaland?" His voice grew stronger on that demand.

"I have not heard that name."

"I have not heard that name," he mimicked me. "Forgetting comes easily with the passing of seasons. Thus one who stood against the Great Dark has vanished from memory, as so *she* will, perhaps much faster. I lay this on you, desert son, by the Zancan and the Orb, by the Diamond and the Sword—"

I could not stop those words and I shivered for I did know what lay upon me now—a geas! And by the old tales the geas of a dying man was a burden no one would willingly receive.

"Get you to Vapala." His voice was fading again. "Tell— tell my lady that I have fulfilled my oath—let her see that she does likewise." His head settled back against my shoulder and there came from his lips a single clean, high note of a song which would never now be sung.

I was alone with the dead, and upon me lay the burden I could not forestall. Go to Vapala I must.

14

There was no escaping the sound throughout the city. The singing of the smaller mobiles was so much a part of our lives that we forgot they existed. But the beat and clash of the Emperor's seemed to rock the very walls about us. There was no sleep for us this night and Ravinga was putting the time when that usually held us into labor.

Around the chamber the curtain fell into place and I doubted that the smallest glimmer of lamplight could be sighted without. Yet there were six lamps, three set along each end of the table, and in the brilliance those gave us, not the smallest detail could be hid from notice.

Ravinga's fingers twisted and turned, handled needle, small soldering iron, tools so tiny that they were difficult to hold to their work. Beneath her hands the man doll took on shape and substance. As her last client had ordered she was busied with a mortuary doll—one of the Emperor himself.

To me she had given another task. I had never been set to work with those special chants to be spoken, those gestures to be used as I picked up one of the delicate tools or another. What I fashioned was not a man but a Sand Cat. The kottis of the household sat to one side watching with deep attention.

I had my guide unrolled on the table before me, each corner of that painted square held down by a carven weight. Those too were things of power. One was a replica of the Blue Leopard such as served always he who was Emperor, one was a yaksen herd cow, proud in the strength which made her guide and leader for her kind, then came a kotti carved of some very dense black stone, glassy smooth to the touch and unusually heavy for its size, the fourth a man doll, whose features were too well set to be aught but a portrait. And a likeness of one I knew—a trader about whom they whispered behind their hands—that he was so lacking in manhood that his own family gave him no proper position—Hynkkel of Kahulawe.

I was twice as slow as Ravinga, for this was the first time she had set me such a task to be done by myself. It was hot in the shrouded chamber and I slipped out of my overblouse and ran the heel of my hand across my forehead as I concentrated on the miniature Sand Cat.

Ravinga fastened the last infinitesimal gem into the crown of the doll she worked upon. Then she turned it slowly and critically about.

Three times had I seen the Emperor close enough to mark well his features. Doll this might be, yet there was so much life caught up by Ravinga's skill that I would not have been surprised to see him slip down between her fingers and stand alive, his own master.

She stood him with care upon a block of black stone and then whirled that around with an impatient gesture so now he faced me.

"It is well?" and she meant that question to be truthfully answered. In all the years I had seen her as another pair of hands I had never before been asked my opinion of her work.

"By all I know, mistress," I replied quickly, "this is in truth an image of Haban-ji."

Now her one hand gestured but the other kept still a jealous guard between her and her masterwork.

I glanced down at what I myself had wrought. It, too, had a lifelike air to it. Almost I could feel this image looking at me measuringly as if it were indeed true one of the great menaces of our land.

"Call!" commanded my mistress.

I wet lips, desert dry, with my tongue tip, lowering my head so that my eyes were on a level with that of one image.

"Hynkkel," I named the name of the doll which stood to my right hand anchoring the cloth. "Desert warrior—"

The yellow eyes did not change. There was no sound of an answer—had I expected such? Using one of the small tools I still held as a pointer, I spoke again, quietly but not allowing myself to be denied.

"Enter!"

It was the desert cat, stretching as might one of the kottis— its front legs spread outward, its hind quarters stiff, again as a kotti before padding out on a nighttime prowl. It moved from the center of the cloth and there was something lightsome about its fur which matched a bit of the ancient markings on the skin it had rested upon as I worked.

Ravinga was not through with either it or me. Once more she turned the figure of the Emperor Haban-ji, now to face the beast I had wrought.

She had whipped up from behind her a length of fine silk embroidered with silver leopards and swung that swatch about the Emperor doll, hiding it from view. I had no more the feeling that the doll was what he seemed—that which had been life in him had departed.

The same was not so of the cat. Its head turned as it looked to the image of Hynkkel. One could believe that there passed between them some spark of communication. Ravinga reached forth across the table and caught up that miniature of the Kahulawen.

She put him down beside the cat and eyed the pair narrowly as if she was searching for one small error in craftsmanship.

Then again she gave her order in a single word:

"Speak!"

"Hynkkel," I obeyed. I was still and tense, disliking this thing that was not of my willing. She had taken me, I saw clearly over the years, to establish her will, overriding mine. This carried the bite of old anger. Yet she never appeared to sense that I was not one of her tools, to be discarded at will and reused again at a whim.

I saw the thin shadow of a smile about her lips. Whatever game she played Ravinga surely believed that she had it under her full control.

Long back during the years I had spent with Ravinga I had learned that there was a time one did not ask questions. What she did in the privacy of the back of her shop was secret and often I never knew what it was. I studied her now with some of the same old unvoiced demand as she was turning on the doll Hynkkel and the Sand Cat I had wrought. The heat of the room was more oppressive. I did not believe that she felt it.

Then putting man image and beast one together in the middle of the table, she brought forward the wrapped replica of the Emperor.

Opening up the small box of minute gems, from which she could reproduce in miniature the heavy jewelry of state, she thrust the end of her most delicate tool into the massed bits of color and then lifted it out, a thread of chain dangling from it. Pendant from that was a tiny mate to that cat mask which she had given to the feckless young man at the trading square almost a quarter of a season back.

She dropped the circlet of that thread-thin chain over the manikin's head and sat him, so adorned, to face the Emperor, whom she had unwrapped. Game—this was some game. Bits and pieces I had witnessed, words overheard here and there, they drew together in my mind.

The old puzzle was at the root of it. Who—what was Ravinga? She made no parade of any arts beyond what anyone might see: her use as a maker of dolls. Yet there was much more—very much more.

I had come to her not with any real hope drawing me to her household. For nightmare days and demon-ridden nights I had been hunted. And I knew just how much I was worth to any astute enough to break my disguise and spy me out.

When I was very small I had made a great discovery for myself. If I believed myself unseen, undetected, then it appeared that was the truth. First my nursemaid, and then old Vastar, my tutor in things suitable for a maiden of any House, could pass within touching distance and yet see me not.

Because I was a child in a household of adults, and ancient adults—the lady ruler being my grandmother twice over—I went much my own way.

Six Houses ruled Vapala and, through the Emperor and their support of him, they ruled our whole known world. Not outwardly, but in devious ways of their own. I was sure that the very deviousness of their dealings with each other gave them a cold yet intense pleasure.

Below the six, there were the twelve. More ambitious these, and more active outwardly, for they yearned to see their House standard set as near to the square before the palace of the rulers as possible. They had promise of gaining such heights. It had been done so far three times in our slow-moving history.

The twenty and five came next. And they were the doers, those who fought more openly for place. Among them it was not unusual for the Head of a House to challenge an equal, knowing that survivors in such a constant hidden war were the winners. These hunted for unusual powers and sought out knowledge long since forgotten.

There had been one such House lady under the banner of my line, and she had set herself up against the ruler of her own House, dooming it to extinction. I was nameless and clanless. No one in the whole of Vapala had so before brought to naught as old and mighty a House.

Ravinga bore a twisted scar across her shoulder which she ever concealed with a scarf. That brand I owed her recompense for.

From the first she gave me an established position in Vapala. Having declared before the council that I was her chosen apprentice, I was removed from the wreckage of the House and even out of the ranks of the nobility, which did not bother me in the least.

My education was strict and I was put to learning things which a year or so earlier I would have argued did not exist. I discovered that, just as within the Houses there are intrigues, so did veiled action continue elsewhere, not only in Vapala but in all the queendoms. It was very much a matter of not accepting the surface but relying on one's knowledge of what lay below.

Now it would appear that my education was to be furthered. Ravinga planted her elbows together on the table and cupped her chin in the palms of her hands, her attention now on the two images, man and cat.

"Last season," she began abruptly, "there came one from Azhengir, a trader of salt, the one I told you afterward to keep well in mind."

I remembered clearly the woman she meant, hard as a lump of her own dusky wares, her skin dried and chapped, her eyes buried in protecting wrinkles raised against the shifting, smarting dust of her country. She had walked into Ravinga's shop with the sure tread of an expected visitor, though I had never seen her before.

Once inside she had done an unusual thing, dropping the heavy butt of her traveler's staff against the door so that it denied entrance to any following her.

She had shrugged off her pack, giving a wheezing cough as she set it down.

Then as if she had seen Ravinga only an hour before, she said:

"I've come—the waiting is done with." She had made a gesture before her breast as if tracing some symbol there. A twitch of the rope which fastened her backpack together followed and the hide cover, rimmed with crystals of salt, opened stiffly.

My hand had gone for my knife and then a moment later I knew that no active defense was needed. The thing crouched stiffly within her pack was truly dead.

Much of the body was gone, showing a lattice of bones, but the head, frozen in a snarl, was still intact. I have many times seen the bodies of sand rats, had even fought against them and had drops of their dark, sour blood eat into my flesh. But this dead creature was many times larger than the only ones of its kind I had ever seen.

Also the skull was misshapen with a high dome of forehead as if to give room to a man's bulk of brain.

"I see." Ravinga made no attempt to draw closer to the displayed creature. "This came from whence?"

"Our caravan was attacked just at the border of the Plain. And there were four such as this which kept its fellows at battle to the end. Since the Fire Dawn there have been no changes in men or beast—though they tell us that before that time there were such unchancy things. The winds blow, the storms strike, caravans are lost, our kind dies for one reason or another. Why else were we given wardenship of the Waste in the far times but that we watch for such?"

Ravinga shook her head. She spread her hands wide as if she would measure something invisible to us. "What do I know, Bissa?"

The woman showed her crooked teeth. "Ask rather what you do not, Voice. But the time grows short, I think. I have heard that the Emperor fails."

Ravinga nodded.

"How long since we have had a Watchment for the ruling? Perhaps we should ask that?"

"There is no way of influencing the choice."

"They tell us that the Emperor must be the Essence of our countries if we would stand tall, unbroken. And the people have some rights—"

Ravinga's eyes had narrowed then and she had spoken coldly. "They need demand no answers from me. I am only a watcher—"

"See that you be more when the time comes," the other had answered and began to rewrap her package.

Ravinga had spoken once more. "For the time there is no one we can appeal to. Watcher, that I am, yes. And perhaps can be more when the time comes." But the woman had picked up her burden and gone quickly without glancing at the dollmaker again. Nor, to my knowledge, had she ever returned. And surely Ravinga had never mentioned her again.

"What would she have you do?" I asked, daring as I never had before.

Ravinga shrugged. "Perhaps she herself could not have said. One cannot fight mist and shadows with steel of knife or spear. However, the seasons have turned, Haban-ji is dead, and now we must look to another. He comes, oh, yes, he comes! There shall be changes in plenty." She picked up a strip of crimson silk and tore it in two with jerks, wrapping half about the man and the other half about the Sand Cat. I needed no spoken word of hers to dismiss me.

15

Murri and I made what preparations we could for continuing our journey. Though all my instincts were to cling to the land to which I was bound by birth, as is the molding of my kind, yet it became more and more apparent that perhaps Kynrr had been right. I would best cut free from a past which no longer held anything for me and begin such breaking of bonds by going to Vapala, which, like or agree with the belief or not, we of the outerlands accepted as the paramount center of our being.

At least I knew by Kynrr's drilling how to reach the nearest caravan trail and we would not be striking out too blindly. Though how long a journey we faced I could not reckon.

Kynrr's hut formed his burial place and I worked as carefully as I might to seal it past any entrance of rats or storms. I took nothing from it save two water bottles and the Kifongg which the bard had given me and which I would cherish, not only for the fineness of workmanship but also because it kept alive when I held it all the close companionship I had shared with its owner. Kynrr's stories were now sealed into my memory and, while my voice could not even echo the glory which had once been his, I had a number of ballads which he had taught me. Though coming out of nowhere, and with no patron to speak for me, I could not hope to be accepted as more than the humblest of tavern bards in Vapala.

I gave careful tending to the six yaksen that formed Kynrr's small herd. Made sure they were carefully groomed, their hooves inspected for any cracking and then well smeared with rat fat. The algae pool was a small one but its harvest would be entirely theirs after our going. Murri was making sure of that, systematically clearing out all the rats, and showing me new skills in such hunting. Their stringy meat went onto drying lines and their hides were used to cobble together foot covering.

I had selected Bialle, the oldest of the cow yaksen, for our beast of burden. She was calfless, perhaps past the time of bearing, but her senses were still acute and she was well trained as a sentinel for the herd.

Also she must remember best the ways of the trail. Once so trained any beast that had been of the caravans would fall naturally again into the journey patterns. With her broad back for burdens we could hope to carry far more in the way of supplies.

I had lost measurement of time—my illness among the Sand Cats might have lasted a number of days' duration. However, the season of storms could not be too much longer delayed.

Along the marked trader trails there were shelters set up for the protection of travelers. Once pointed along one of those roads, what safety this land knew could be counted upon. Still I could find one reason or another each day to keep me there, away from the actual carrying out of the choice I had made.

I had baled up a good amount of dried algae cakes and gone over again all my equipment. That evening when I visited the yaksen for a final check, I stroked each animal, speaking to it, though its language I did not know. Mainly I did this for the comfort it gave to me to hear my own voice. Murri had been casting out from the isle on prowling of his own kind.

His impatience was growing and I knew that I would not be able to delay much longer. Thus we set forth from our refuge, Murri scouting ahead, I matching my speed more to the plodding of Bialle.

I watched the stars, steering the course Kynrr had sketched out for me earlier. His Kifongg rode in its own soft casing on top of Bialle's load. We crossed a short strip of sand in no time and found ourselves once more treading sharp pebbles. Bialle also wore boots to protect her hooves but I discovered that her greater weight made those wear out the quicker. At the end of the first night's travel when we set up camp, extending my very badly worn cloak with the quilted patchwork of rat hide, I checked all our footwear and discovered that I must indeed reshoe the yaksen.

This open land under the full light of the sun was a torment which grew every day. I had thought that we could be not far from the caravan route Kynrr had spoken of—yet, though I checked the stars, and Murri scouted a wide fan of countryside ahead, we came across no suggestion of a trail. Murri and I might have made better time together. I began to wonder uneasily if I had made a mistake in bringing Bialle, even though the amount of supplies she could carry was an advantage. Her hooves cut through the hide coverings now in half a period of travel and our own supplies for the gear we needed to keep from going lame were fast being used.

Sometimes I wondered if I were deceiving myself, if Murri also suffered from some evil in this land, which forced us to go in circles and that we had not in truth traveled any distance, though the isle of Kynrr's exile was out of sight.

To push on was more and more of an effort. The flesh melted from us and sometimes the smallest of acts came as an almost unsurmountable burden.

It was on our sixth day after leaving Kynrr's isle, or so my stumbling thoughts counted, that misfortune struck, as hard as if we had lain between its paws from the start of our journey and now it tired of the game and would put an end to it.

Bialle no longer walked at her steady pace; rather she staggered from side to side, her heavy head but two palms' height from the rough ground. Now and then she uttered complaints which were like a man's sigh increased a hundredfold. She needed frequent rests and I would stand panting beside her. Murri I had not seen since the start of this night.

A yowling cry of fear aroused me. That it was Murri in difficulties I had no doubt. But where? By what could he be menaced to bring such a cry from him? For if he were prepared to give battle his voice would not have held that wild appeal.

Bialle bellowed, swung her heavy head, and moved forward at a stagger but I was in front of her, though the treacherous footing slowed me. Then we were on the edge of a slight hollow. Almost this had the general shape and size of one of the algae pools. Out in the depression Murri was struggling, more than half of his body gripped by one of the worst of the land's traps, a hidden sucking patch which gulped greedily anything unfortunate to come within its borders.

From where Murri flailed, trying to find some firm land, there came puffs of foul stench as if indeed it were the mouth of a living creature and not the ground itself which struggled to engulf him.

I shrugged off my small pack and loosened the coils of rope.

"Murri," I used the cat sounds as well as my human voice could utter them, "do not struggle—you break the crust all the more. Be ready, take up the rope when it reaches you."

I fastened the end hurriedly to Bialle and pointed her away from that hidden trap. Then, lying belly down, searching the ground for any mark which might guide me, I wriggled forward, my staff holding a loop made from the other end of the rope. My hands shook from the effort of keeping that above the grip of the sucker pot, and yet close enough to the surface to make sure Murri could reach it.

He had stopped his wild threshing about. However, his fear was as plain as the stench which set us to coughing. My eyes watered and stung from the fumes and I had to keep blinking out the tears which made my vision waver.

"Bialle—Var!" I shouted the herd cry which the yaksen were trained to obey. She gave a second bellow but she was moving, if only at a clumsy, tottering pace.

Now it would depend upon me. I had once seen this type of rescue when on the trail. There was so little time. The Sand Cat was submerged now nearly to his chin. I angled the staff and it shook back and forth in my hand though I summoned all my strength to hold it straight.

Murri made a sudden desperate twist of his head and a second later the rope snapped taut along the staff. I pulled that back and the rope, shaking free, was still tight and stiff.

Dropping the staff, I edged around so that the part of the rope in my hands was now across my shoulder. It was a struggle to get to my feet without losing grip on that but I made it, though the power of the sucking pulled me backward as if to join me in Murri's danger.

"Var! Var!" It was more of a breathless cry than a shout of encouragement. But the rope tightened yet more as the yaksen gave her strength so we pulled together.

Though Murri was little more than half grown he was certainly heavier than I. His compact body, even thinned as it was by privation, was still too much for me to draw free by my own. I could only hope that Bialle's ability to pull, developed as her breed had been used for generations to drag carts along the trails, would provide the extra power we must have.

I slipped to my knees once, skinning my legs on the sharp pebbles, but, by fortune, the shock did not make me lose that hold on the rope. There was no longer in me breath enough to call to the yaksen.

Back! I was being drawn back! I dared not waste time nor effort to look over my shoulder to see how near I now was to surface of which I could be sure.

"Var!" No shout this time but a dry-mouthed whisper. However, as if Bialle could hear that, she gave a sudden lurch ahead and I threw myself into aiding the pull.

For the space of several hard-drawn breaths we kept on. Then the rope was not so taut ahead. It was as if Bialle could no longer maintain the extra effort which had won us so far.

The fumes from the sucking pot were stronger and a racking cough reached my ears from behind. Although—if Murri held the rope in his fangs as I believed, that might endanger all our efforts. Yet the rope was still drawing against my shoulder, chafing through the clothing I wore to erode the skin below.

"Bialle—" I called that beseechingly. I knew that I was very close to the limit of my last surge of strength. The hard traveling of the past days had taken its toll of all of us.

Once more the rope ahead stiffened, there was a forceful pull, and I added to it as I stumbled on. There was a sudden sharp give from behind.

"Murri!" My cry was more a scream. The loosing of that bond had brought me once more to my knees. I must force myself to look back, to accept the fact that our best had not been enough, and all that strength, beauty and lightness of spirit which had been my companion was swallowed up in foulness.

Somehow I made myself make that turn to look.

There was a black blot against the faint glimmer on the ground. Part of it moved feebly from side to side, then eyes opened and were lamps to guide me.

"Murri!" I flung myself toward him, my rope-burned hands catching fur matted with the evil-smelling substance of the trap.

"Brother kin—" The words were only a rumble in his throat. He was still fighting to rise and I added my strength to his, getting him somehow to his feet. Then we wavered and weaved back well away from that place of death to collapse together.

Just as Murri's cry for help had urged me on before, now did a low beast moan pull me upright again. There was infinite pain in that—could this whole countryside have been hollowed by such traps and the yaksen now caught in turn? To free her would be impossible.

I crawled to the top of that rise which formed a rim around the sucking pit and saw a large bulk staggering ahead. Praise Essence, she was not caught in one of those fearsome pits.

No, she was not a prisoner. Still this treacherous land had dealt her a death blow. She was struggling to get to her feet as I reached her, but that was impossible, for it was plain that she had broken a foreleg, that some one of those punishing rolling stones had brought her down.

She turned her head to look at me. Yaksen eyes by night did not hold the gleam of those of the cats but I felt her pain and knew her despair. That we could hope to heal her here was beyond possibility.

"Bialle." I knelt beside her, my hand smoothing the heavy mane fur about her ears, scratching and smoothing as I did when grooming, actions which always relaxed the great creatures. "Bialle, Great One, Strong One. For such as you there is pride. Great One, open wide your heart, let in the essence of the land, of the spirit, be one with the land and with all living things. Pain shall go and that which is truly Bialle shall be free, even as is all life when the time comes—"

As I spoke I loosed my knife. Might the spirit of all this land be with me so that I did not falter but would strike true. Though I could not see their glow I knew that her eyes were turned upon me and that she knew what I would do and welcomed it as the kindness of one who had never wished her anything but good.

In the past I had done this as herdsman and always was it like a second blow struck deep into me.

"Bialle," I held my voice steady as I would when leading her to a full pool and fresh growth within it, "go free!"

I struck the blow with all the strength I could summon, hoping that it would need only one to loose this valiant friend. By fortune's favor it was enough.

But still I crouched beside her, drawing my fingers through her sand-matted coat. Freedom from all the ills of life, yes, I must look at it so. Her patience and her last life gift would ever set her sharp in my memory.

There was a rattling of pebbles. I looked around. Murri was belly down pulling himself along, by one paw outstretched and then the other, to join me. When he reached the body he lifted his head and gave forth a squalling cry.

16

I try to shut out of memory that last gift which Bialle had for us. It followed the rigid custom of travelers and yet it was such that no one can lightly take, nor is it spoken of among us who have wandered far. We are assured that we are all linked, not only to the life about us, but to the very land on which we live. Therefore if one life or body may serve another, then that is the proper following of what may be demanded of us. Thus I put my knife to a second purpose, one so against my wish that I fought down revulsion even as I doggedly worked. Though I sensed it was not so to Murri.

Bialle had been one with us, yet he accepted, as was true of all his kind, that that which was the inner part of her had departed and what was left behind was no longer to be considered a trail comrade. That he would think my squeamishness to be a flaw I knew.

At least we need not fear that the scent of death and meat would draw rats down upon us. This land was too bitter and barren, not even the Sand Cats would range this far.

I sorted out our gear and made packs as large as we could carry, Murri, despite his loathing, having to again bear one.

So when the time came that we must stagger on, we bore with us that last food and moisture we could hope to find—unless I could discover the trail Kynrr pointed me to. I had not discarded his Kifongg though it was perhaps foolish of me to cling to such as part of my burden. Now I strove to keep off the demons of despair by humming and thinking of all the old bard had spread before me as a source of knowledge. If—when—I reached Vapala I would need his information to serve me until I did find some labor.

Still, how could I who had been but a servant, a herdsman, a family trader for a people considered by the mesa dwellers to be primitive barbarians, hope to find some outlet for my future? The traders' guilds would be closed to me as a single tradesman with no link to any House. If all the stories of Vapala were true, the inhabitants were more strictly allied to House clans than even my people, and there would be little welcome for outsiders.

I tasted dust and with it an ever-growing despair. Still there was not that in me which would allow me to sit in this dreary wilderness and wait for death to come. As long as I could move, I realized that I would place one stumbling foot before the other and shuffle along.

The stars I steered by were there but certainly I could not be sure, having periods of dizziness from time to time, that I was still on my course. The constant rustle of the shifting sands—

Rustle of the sands! But there was no sand! I came to a halt and looked about me, aroused from that haze of fatigue and self-pity which had near overcome me.

The harsh pebble footing was gone. We were back in the cushioning of true sand. I looked about me, fully alert now.

Thus I saw the light a little to the east. From there carried also the distant scream of an ill-tempered oryxen, an answer to that as sharp and warning. I turned a little and was able to plod faster, even though my bruised feet sank sometimes ankle deep in that very welcome sand. I could only be heading for a camp—

Traders? For that I could hope. That there were others who hung about the edges of the Waste was also true. However, if I had indeed found the trail, those would be wary about approaching a track which was constantly patrolled by the scouts of Kahulawe.

Murri dropped back, flanking me now instead of forging ahead, and I realized that, while I might be traveling towards safety and help, it was not so for a Sand Cat. Too long had our species been at enmity with one another. He growled and I knew that that same thought was shared by him.

First light and then sound! There were voices singing. I could not separate the words as yet but the tune I knew well. It was a traditional one much liked by the traders, and each party seemed to have their own version, for they added verses concerning their own ventures and any strange thing which they had noted or endured during that trip.

Then that sound was suddenly overlaid, drowned out—the beat of drums—storm? I threw myself forward, digging in with my staff to pull myself along at a faster gait, hoping to reach the trail safety offered by the camp ahead before wilderness struck at us. Then I realized the distant beat of that warn drum was different. What message could be of such importance that the drums only used for the greatest warning would be set to beating out this different pattern?

The singing in the camp had ended. Yet still the drum, distant, kept on. Now that rhythm was picked up by the order drum of the traders, transmitting the news, that it might be carried on through the night as was always done.

"Ssseeeeeeee!" the traditional hail of the traders came as the drum ended. Some sentry had sighted me.

Though my own travels had heretofore been limited to the short trails, I knew well the answer I must give. My throat and mouth were so dry that I found it hard to raise above a choked answer.

"Kkkaalawwa—" The recognition of my own people. I knew, however, that I would be under close observation until I reached the open light of the fire and that there would be those casting to be sure that I answered with a truthful sign.

Again that drum in the distance had taken up a steady beat. Not a storm warning, not even the former message, but a second I could not translate, warning against some uprising of outlaws?

The outermost limit of the fire touched me, by the way of torches upheld by two women, swords out and ready, but with their brands in the other hand. They were of my own people and one I knew.

"Kinsha-va-Guara!" I hailed her crack-voiced.

"Who out of the night bespeaks my name?" I saw that her grasp on sword hilt had tightened. She was peering at me and I realized what a strange and perhaps even frightening apparition I must be, in my rent clothes, my back bowed under my pack, the marks of my ordeals upon me. And there was also Murri—

"Klaverel-va-Hynkkel—and Murri—" I spoke the cat's name even as he was of us. "I have come from my solo—"

"Bringing death on four feet with you? That is a thing which has no meaning—" She relaxed none of her forbidding stance and her companion moved a little to her right so that if there was an attack she would be ready to give battle from another angle.

"I bring a comrade with whom I have faced death and to whom I owe my life. We are brothers by blood oath" (indeed the ceremony which Maraya had used was enough like a swordsbrother's life essence sharing to be termed that). "There is no death threat from us, trail mistress."

She stood staring at the two of us for a moment and then gestured us ahead with the torch, still holding her weapon in plain sight. I moved forward and Murri also, keeping close beside me. I was sure that the Sand Cat was not in any way afraid of any attack, being fully confident of his own strength. However, wariness was well bred into his kind.

"Off this!" he mouthed at me, giving a hard shake to his body to dislodge the pack he was wearing. That he hated the necessity of such service I well knew and appearing before strangers so beladen was highly hurtful to his pride. There was no reason why I should so humiliate him thus. I leaned down and cut the thongs so he was able to allow it to slip to the sands.

That second strange beating of the warn drum had died away, but its message was being echoed by the drum of the caravan. So we could exchange no more talk with that in our ears as we entered the heart of the camp.

There was an ingathering of the traders. As was often common among my people these were women. They have always been good at the task and early made it theirs. The color of their fringed tents was touched to brightness by fire globes, proving this party rich enough to transport such travel luxuries. While their own clothing might be the drab stuff worn by travelers, their profusion of gemmed belts, headbands, bracelets, necklets made them appear as wealthy as the Vapalans.

She who had questioned me motioned again to the center tent and there I saw the drummer, her hands flying as she struck with the flat of her palms. Behind her was an older woman, one who, by her wealth of jewelry, which she wore with pride and taste, must be the leader of this caravan, though it would be made up from several small groups, each commanded by the most experienced among them.

She I knew also. This was Elwene Karafa, truly a mistress of far trails who regularly made a full journey through the queendoms, gathering produce of each along the way and then heading for the great market of Vapala by the year's end.

I allowed my pack to slip from my bruised shoulders and thrust my staff deep into the sand, resting both hands on it. Murri swung his heavy head from side to side and, apparently deciding there was nothing to fear for the moment, flopped down beside me.

"Klaverel-va-Hynkkel," I announced myself. "Murri of the furred ones."

The drum sound had stopped and there was silence so that I could be easily heard and I added:

"To Elwene Karafa be all good fortune. May the trade be rich, the trail easy, and no storm of land or trouble strike her path."

I met her regard squarely. She looked from me to Murri, her eyes widening a little as she met his golden ones, and then her gaze shifted once more to me.

"What do you on the trails, not-warrior?"

Not-warrior. Instead of making me feel shame this time, I found myself able to hold my temper steady. It was the truth, was it not? I came from a warrior house but the sword was not mine for the taking. I knew well that the tittle-tattle of the feastings had dealt thoroughly with me who was counted a disgrace to his House.

"I have come from my solo, Lady."

She continued to study me and then she turned her head abruptly and spoke to the older of the two women who had brought me in.

"This one came out of the Waste?"

"That is so."

Now I suffered her regard again. "I think there is a tale in this. Trail welcome to you, Hynkkel, and also to this companion of yours. Yes, truly a tale lies behind this. A night of wonders to be sure. First we hear the death notes of the Emperor's passing, and long has he reigned. Then comes the summons for the testing. Yes, a night of wonders. Guest rights be yours, and later we must hear this tale."

Once they had accepted me, it was as if I had always traveled with this train. Food in quantities and of the best possible obtainable when marching was set before me, and a goodly supply of well-dried meat, not the rat flesh which had been his fare for so long, was given Murri. At first the traders were wary of approaching the Sand Cat and I fed him from the huge bowl they had placed before him before themselves withdrawing to some distance. When they could see that he communicated directly with me they drew closer, watching us both as if we were entertainers on our way to some feasting.

It was the caravan leader who showed no sign that this was more than any meeting which might happen along the trail, seating herself as my hostess within such reach as she could pass to me at the ending of the meal a bowl of the dried fruits which were such a rarity that the very offering of such established me in good standing in her sight.

I searched for some comment with which to begin a conversation, since, to plunge into the tale of my own adventures so baldly, without a second invitation, was beyond the bound of good manners.

"The Emperor dies—" I thought of Kynrr and what he had told me of the court at Vapala, of the bedazzling throngs who gathered there, always mindful of the least wish of the man, who, by his own endeavor, achieved the rulership. No one came to the Leopard Throne without undergoing such trials as would make even a warrior as seasoned as my father consider well. The struggle of one in solo was as nothing compared to that one who aspired to rule must face.

The late Emperor had been young when he had stood in the center of the Great Mobile and so triumphantly claimed his reward. He had reigned before I was born, and all I knew of his deeds were what had been repeated and repeated as news spreading out from Vapala.

He had been of the House of Vars, not one of the Great Houses of Vapala, but of the second rank. By custom he went without an official mate but stories had related his temporary arrangement with women from the Great Houses and even, when he was in the powers of mid-life, with the Ruby Queen. He had offspring, only the birthing charts knew how many, but Kynrr several times repeated in stories of the glittering past that most of his get had been daughters, only one son living to full manhood. That was Shank-ji. And Kynrr's tale of him was that, past all custom, he had several times openly said that he would try in the testing.

"The Emperor is dead," Elwene agreed. Taking up a pinch of sand between two fingers, she tossed it over her shoulder. "He was old, but in his time he did well enough."

Certainly faint praise for the ruler of the outer lands. Yet Kynrr, with all his detailed memories of the court, had never retailed any outstanding feat, save that Haban-ji had been able to keep down the eternal struggles for hidden power which had convulsed Vapala several times in the past. The Great Houses no longer reached for advancement by the way of sword and spear and the gathering of armed warriors. However, their many intrigues continued.

Though the trial for the Leopard Throne was open to all from every one of the queendoms, for several generations now the winner had been out of Vapala and it had become accepted by those of that nation they had first right to it.

I had listened to the talk of my brother's comrades, even to some of the discussions in my father's great room when he had guests of his generation. This matter of Vapala's supremacy was moving, through the years, from a small grievance to a major one. There would be champions from every nation and should Shank-ji triumph there might well be trouble among the restless, power-hunting young men.

We had so long been at such peace as to not need warriors, save for the patrolling of the trade routes, that men of martial tastes found little way of discharging their energy.

"It will be an interesting testing—" Elwene smoothed the stuff of her richly patterned cloak across her knee. "Some deem that the leopard has too often stood guard for a man of Vapala. I hear that this son of Haban-ji thinks to change the course of custom. We shall see. Now, brother of the trails, tell us your tale, which can be no common one—"

So I launched into my own story and perhaps some of the coaching of Kynrr came to the fore, for I found myself moving at times from the common speech into the rhythm of a bard—having indeed enough to deal with for the fashioning of any bard's song, even if it dealt only with the actions of one who was deemed a failure.

The dawn had well arrived when I finished the last of that story. They had all gathered to hear it. Only at times sentries to be relieved coming in and their comrades going out on station. But the newcomers settled down, eating as they listened.

Elwene nodded when I was finished at last. "Surely a venture unlike any other we have heard tell of. Perhaps, man of Kahulawe, you should be the one to stand for our land in the testing. It would seem that fortune has favored you many times over."

I shook my head. "Fortune favors no one for long. I have no desire to reach for any crown." At that moment I could not conceive of anything I wanted less. Though, a small inner amusement stirred, I was indeed at present a man without any work which was mine.

"At least if you plan to go to Vapala," Elwene said, "you are welcome to ride with us."

That offer I could accept and did so eagerly.

17

There were near a hundred dolls laid out on the table before my mistress—each a replica of Emperor Haban-ji in his coronation robes—all ordered to be delivered as soon as possible, The Great Houses of Vapala would pay honor to their late ruler in the formal and proper manner—by placing one such in display in their gathering rooms. At the accession of each new Emperor such were prepared to await the call. These had waited for more years than I, myself, had to count. Haban-ji had reigned for a long time—

Ravinga inspected each minutely for any deterioration brought about by years of storage. I noted that she withdrew four, taking them into the workroom, though she had pointed out to me no reason for repairs as she usually did, to increase my knowledge in such matters.

Now she brought them back and fitted them in their proper place in line. Within a chime's time the stewards of each House would be calling to pick them up and transport them with due reverence to their proper niches in different halls.

As Ravinga laid them down she was frowning and once they were out of her hands, she stood, fingers pinching her lower lip, which signaled, for her, deep thought. Then she glanced at me side-eyed, and crooked a finger so I joined her on the other side of the table.

"Girl, are these in proper order? Need they any changes?"

I was a little agape at that question, for we had inspected them together last night when we had taken them out of storage and then to me they had seemed intact. I had not even caught the minute flaws which had led her to the morning's work. Obediently, I drew up a stool and seated myself. Taking up each doll in turn, I gave it the most searching inspection I could make. Then I paused and picked up a second doll, to hold it comparingly beside the one I had just taken, studying first one and then the other.

Haban-ji had not been portrayed in these as the man of many years that he had been when he died, rather as one in his full prime as he had been when he first ascended the Leopard Throne. He had been a noted hunter and patrol officer of native Vapala stock, the son of one of the middle-status Houses. Thus he was presented in the two dolls I now held. Yet there grew plainer and plainer to me that there was a subtle difference between the two.

The stance and the magnificent robes, the crown worn by both with a certain prideful arrogance—those were alike as far as I could determine to the last tiny jewel, the last stitch.

It was the facial expression, I decided. The one I had first taken had the impassive features of a doll, an image meant to depict a real personage and doing that faithfully. But the second doll's eyes—there was a spark deep in them! Also I could believe that they were observing me as intently as I was studying them!

The first doll I laid down but the other I kept to hand for comparison as I examined the others. At last I had lying to one hand those dolls which Ravinga had taken into her workroom and each had the same peculiarity: living eyes!

Pushing back a little from the table to look up at my mistress, I had questions but I did not know how to frame them. That what I had discovered had some important meaning I was very sure. Yet I schooled myself to wait, for I had learned long since that Ravinga parted with knowledge at her own time and by her own choice of methods.

When she did not speak I was driven by curiosity (had she not asked me to make this discovery?) to say:

"The eyes, mistress. They might be all-seeing—"

"Just so, just so. And for good reason!"

However, she did not seem inclined to add to that assertion. Instead she turned and reached down two other figures from a shelf behind. Both of these she held out, not as if I were to accept them, but rather for me to only look. And those I knew.

There was the Sand Cat and the youth from Kahulawe. The same two she had evoked during that ceremony days ago. They, too, appeared to have living eyes.

"Come, there is yet much to be done."

I got up and followed her into the workroom. There she settled in her high cushioned chair where she spent so many absorbed hours. Settling the two figures before her, she opened a small box which had been standing to one side. Many tools were stored in similar cases in the workshop and I knew well the use of all of them, had held most in my hands. However, these she brought out now were needle delicate, and were of some substance unlike those we used commonly. They were a milky white until she took them up, then from the place where her fingers touched there spread a threadlike streak of blood red, suffusing the whole of the handling rods until they glimmered as if lit from within.

Picking up the Sand Cat, she settled the figure in a small padded vise which would hold it immobile. With her blood-fused needle tool she probed into the head just above the nape of the neck. The tool was turning white again as if the color drained in some fashion into the head of the cat.

As she did so she uttered words I, too, had learned, though I had not been instructed in their meaning. Each craft has its own mysteries and there are certain patterns of action which each creator uses to seal her work. I had always thought it a matter of wishing good fortune on one's labors and that formality I was well attuned to believe.

When the tool Ravinga held was completely white again she freed the Sand Cat and set it to one side. Then she arose and motioned me to take her place, much to my surprise. As she leaned across my shoulder to set the likeness of Hynkkel into the vise she spoke:

"Matters will move fast. There is dire trouble ahead, Allitta. I am not an old woman grumbling at senile faces. Nor are you completely what you believe yourself to be. There is that in the Essence forming, the wholeness of our being which at times seeks out those who will best serve its purposes. You would have come into my household in any case, for I saw in you the skills needed. But there are other skills which can be sensed but must be more subtly studied and honed, as one polishes a weapon or a tool. Those you have also.

"Now comes close the time when those who hunt will sound the drums and those unprepared will be the hunted. We must prepare for such battles as our people have near forgotten. The musty intrigue between House and House, as vile and bitter as it often has been, is as nothing compared to that coming upon us.

"Here." She held out to me the same tool she had used on the Sand Cat doll. "Do you also to this one as you saw me do. Use the care you would with the setting of a small jewel—you have such dexterity in your hands and you have been well trained. Do as you saw me do!"

I knew that this was no time for questions. There was arising within me an excitement which was usually the result of my carrying out some very delicate piece of work, as if I and I only could do this properly.

Leaning forward I studied the doll. The hair was looped up in the usual knot of one who does not wear a ceremonial wig, and that neck, which I could easily have snapped with my fingers, fully exposed. I glanced at the tool: as it had been in Ravinga's hold, so now it was red again. My fingers tingled. It was as if something of my own was feeding into that tube, that a kind of strength I had not known I possessed was being drawn upon.

I pressed the tip into the proper point on the back of that very small head. It slipped in easily for a fraction and I felt that strange drawing growing the stronger. Then I knew that whatever task I had to perform was done—the needle rod was clear and there was now a lifeless feel, as if it were only a tool and not linked in any way with me. So I took it forth.

Ravinga set free the doll and placed it together with the cat. I slid out of the seat and she retook her place there. She placed a fingertip on the head of each figure and closed her eyes for a long moment and then nodded.

"So far it moves as it should. We must prepare for visitors and for what those shall bring." Drawing a deep breath she leaned back in her chair. Her hands were now clasped under her chin and she looked straight ahead.

"It begins, at last it begins!" There was a note in her voice which I associated with a demand for deliberate action. It was as if she could fashion time itself to her pattern even as she did her dolls.

Well fed and with the warmth of acceptance of those who, if they were not kin, were yet of my own land, I settled in to sleep. There was yet the long trek into Vapala before us, though the excitement which gripped the caravan at the thought of the coming assembly at the capital had begun to flower in me also. Vapala had been for so many years a storied place that the chance to see this proudest and wealthiest of the queendoms was something to look forward to.

Yet it was not Vapala, or even the trail ahead of us, which twisted my dreaming that night. Once more I stood in a strange room, one different from any I had ever seen. The walls rose into a darkness so far overhead that I could not distinguish any ceiling in that gloom. They also stood far from the surface on which I stood. Around me were great boxes and coffers, some taller than I and many nearly as large as my small dwelling at home.

I was not alone. Murri stood by me, as still as if he listened for some faint sound which would release him eager for a hunt. What I saw above me were great twin orbs of a silver brightness, and these were set in a vast expanse—

A face! So great a face that for me the features could not easily be fitted together. It was as if some craftsman had turned the whole of an islet into a single giant head—not that of a boundary cat but of a human. The eyes moved, blinked.

That I was the object of their survey was very obvious. I strove to move. There was that in that regard which I found vaguely threatening. Yet I was as frozen in place as if I, too, were a fashioned thing and not of flesh, blood, and bone.

Then I strove to speak to Murri. But that power had been taken from me also. I was a mind, an awareness, locked into an image.

"You will come—" I had expected any voice from that vast overhang of face would roar like thunder—but this was no true voice. It was an order which flashed into my mind. "You will come—" There was a repeat of the same words and then an addition. "Ravinga waits—"

The face vanished, the walls, the very surface on which I stood was now gone; rather it was as if my own eyes had been detached from my imprisoned body and looked down from the sky on what could only be the sprawl of city buildings— but such a city as if my well-known Meloa had been enlarged a hundred or more times over.

It spread farther and farther, the details became ever cleared as I dropped nearer to it. Now I could see that, unlike Meloa, it had a wall about it and there was a wide gate. Warriors moved there. Their battle wigs were the clear white of mar-stones—their skins also paler. Those who came into the city (they were but shadows shown me in no detail) must stop by these warriors as if to assure the keepers of the gate that they had a rightful business there.

Starting from the gate, that which was the part of me was sent upon a strange journey swinging over a street, pausing above a building which had about it a very large space, in which sheltered many oryxen, and I thought that it might be an inn. My sight of that lasted for only a second and then was pushed on, down a short side way, keeping to more of such passages, away from the main thoroughfares where there was a constant passing of the shadow people, until I came so unto a dead-end court and halted (or my sight did) before a building which showed marks of age—in fact at one time it might have had another story, for the top was ragged-looking.

The court was a narrow one, its room shared only by two other buildings, one of which was definitely a ruin, its roof long gone and only part of the outer shell still standing.

Here was no stir of the shadow people. Only it was made clear to me that I should remember well this place and seek it out.

Once more I was drawn back along the same way I had come and I found that I could easily remember every turn or change of small side way and alley which had brought me here.

I had returned to the inn when there was a loud sound, one which shook the whole of the scene I looked upon, as if that was a curtain stirred by a breeze which rent it.

There was no longer any city. Only darkness—

"Rise!" That I had certainly truly heard. I opened my eyes.

One of those I remembered from the night before—one of the caravan guards—stood beside me. The sun was near down and the whole of the encampment had come alive.

Yaksen were being harnessed between the shafts of wagons or stood patiently waiting for their packs to be adjusted.

"We move out," she who had awakened me from that very strange dream said impatiently. "There is food at the kettle fire but that will soon be gone."

Remembering my bondage in that dream, I half feared that I could not move now, or was this true reality? I rolled that extra sleep cover I had been loaned and stuffed it into my package, making very sure that the Kifongg, Kynrr's gift, was well shielded from any chance breakage.

I was not the last to fill my bowl at the fire—the others being sentries of the last watch. Murri had kept close beside me and accepted from my hands a second bowl. I had feared that being among the yaksen and the two or three oryxen which were the mounts of the caravan leaders, he might cause trouble with the animals who would very quickly pick up the scent of an old enemy.

However, it would seem that there was some sort of a truce among them. He did not venture too near, and, though they turned heads and moved nervously as he passed, they did not stampede. For which I was devoutly thankful. If I had had to choose between Murri and this company as to which might be my only salvation, I feared I could not have faced that choice with any fortitude.

As it was we took up our position at the tail of the caravan. The sun was gone and the twilight welcomed travelers to the road. Somewhere along the strung-out line of riders, beasts of burden, carts, a voice started a song and the rhythm of that singing carried us at a steady pace as one after another picked up the refrain.

We halted at intervals to rest the beasts. Dried fruit chunks were passed from the forage cart. These were a treat which only the best of the caravans could afford, for fruit was a great delicacy. My own people never tasted it except at ceremonial feastings, and I found the gummy sweetness could be chewed for a long time, well satisfying any thirst or need for other food. Even Murri, meat-eating predator that he was, appeared to relish it.

There was much talk of the future, speculation as to the choice of Emperor. There would be one trial for each queendom, and only when those of that section of the land accepted the candidate as a success in his endeavor, could he pass on to try the next.

The dead Emperor had had such a long reign. In fact so long that those of my father's generation had been children or quite young when he had taken the trials in triumph. He had displayed successful power of character from the first. It had been he who had put down the custom of duel wars between the Houses, and had not been greatly beloved among his own Vapalan country people for that slighting of what was their cherished belief in "honor."

However, though they might not still fight openly, there were still personal grudges and struggles in the dark between House and House, yet all would close ranks against outsiders. The oft-stated opinion of those I now traveled with was that it was time for the rulership to pass from Vapala, that a winner from one of the other nations would bring welcomed changes at court to be the benefit of the others. The Vapalans, with their noted arrogance regarding all other peoples, needed a taste of a few new changes.

Since this was a Kahulawen caravan, there was talk that it might be one of our nation who might achieve this. But no one name seemed to come to more than one or two at a time.

"It will be Vapalan once again," Lara Musa, one of the guard who shared paces with me, stated, "if Shank-ji has his way. They say he is a man of power. We may see changes which will not be good if he wins. It has never been our way that the reign should descend from father to son. So would one House, one land, easily gain power over all. Such a change of custom might be welcome in Vapala but I think that we of the outer lands would not greet it. It has always been that the tests, which are of the essence of each land, make sure that he who commands the Leopard Throne be above all House allegiances, free from such ties, that he may treat all equally."

"How long before these trials?" I asked. There would be many coming in from each of the queendoms to celebrate something which only happened once in a lifetime. I was sure that my own kin might well choose to be among those.

"The Emperor must be sealed," she answered, "and the Grand Chancellor and the Voices of the Essence make a deal of that. They must wait until the Queens are gathered before they may proceed. But even before the sealing there may be marshaling of those who will be committed to the testing." She nodded to the carts ahead.

"We have a good cargo and there will be a profit when we market it in a city full of visitors. Prices will go up." She nodded with satisfaction.

"Also," she added a moment later, "we shall be early in and our mistress can have a chance to arrange for a very favorable market site."

With this indrawing from all the queendoms, I thought, surely I would be able to find some employment, which, if only temporary, would keep me for a while. I shrugged my pack to relieve shoulder strain. There was the Kifongg. I was no trained bard, but then I would not be seeking employment at any lordly House. I might find myself singing in some inn or even in the marketplace and garner in enough to keep me and Murri while I waited for an opportunity to do better.

18

We made good time, keeping a steady pace between the necessary halts, and on the second day there loomed up, from what I thought earlier might be a bank of clouds, the bulk of the great tableland, well above the sands, which was the Diamond Queendom. I had often heard it described but that telling gave no good impression of the vast cliffs which supported Vapala.

Our slickrock islands varied in degree of shape and size, but this was something far removed from what now would seem a handful of rocks tossed idly to lie hither and thither on the Kahulawen sand waves.

As we drew closer (we now marched by day) that cliffside was daunting indeed. We began to hear those crystal-noted chimes of the mobiles which kept ever in song on the surface of the mesa well above.

Also, for the first time in my life, I saw patches of vivid green. For Vapala was not dependent upon algae beds. There grew plants, even the fabled trees. It was a land rich in many things that we of the outer lands did not know.

There was a guard outpost below, flanking the beginning of that road which climbed slantwise up the cliff wall. Looking at that pathway, the mere fact of its being was overwhelming. How long had it taken the determined people from above to carve that way out of rock? Surely whole lifetimes had gone into its construction.

Yet the fact that it was the only entrance into Vapala made the Diamond Queendom a well-guarded fortress instead of just a country. Warriors would find defense of that roadway an easy thing. Only a few bowmen, stationed well above, could sweep the path of any invaders and keep it clear.

Before we came to the border station the caravan mistress appeared on her mount from the fore of our outstrung line of travelers and spoke to me:

"That one," she pointed with her whip to Murri, "will not be welcome here. You had best free him—"

"Free him?" I interrupted her. "Murri is as free as I—he is a companion, not a serving beast. Do you speak of freeing kottis? There are a number of those with the train, are there not? Do you haul them along so by collar and lead rope?"

She considered Murri, who eyed her straightly back.

"To those of Vapala he is the prey they prize. Those of the Houses count hunting his kind as a sport, while others who have beasts look upon Sand Cats as a menace to their herds. There will be arrows in him as soon as he is sighted from the post."

She was right. Yet also I knew that there was that which linked the two of us, Murri and I, which would not be denied. I spoke to him now in the language of the Furred Folk and he nodded his head.

"True," he growled. "Yet not true. There is no sleekskin who can command one of the Free Folk. Tell her what she wishes to hear and—you will see what can be done."

"This is a well-guarded place ahead—safe only for such as I," I answered him. "It can well be that you would be attacked on sight."

He blinked his eyes. "On sight—maybe. If there is sight. Let me handle this, brother-by-the-tooth."

There was nothing I could do for the moment but answer:

"It shall be as you point out, but be of great care."

Then to Elwene I added, "We shall take your warning."

She nodded and rode on to her place at the head of our line, ready to answer the challenge of the guards. Murri watched her well away and then approached the last of the carts, one which carried our food supplies and was now riding light since those supplies were near exhausted. Two of the kottis rode in the back, peering out of the opening of the covers with the usual curiosity of their kind.

They centered their gaze on Murri and then drew apart, leaving a space between them. The Sand Cat, so many times their size, leaped up into the cart and disappeared, while the kottis drew together again. Their eyes swept coolly over me and it was as if Murri had never been.

Surely the guard would investigate the caravan wagons, all of them. I had traveled so long with Murri that I was hardly aware any longer of the slightly musky odor of his fur. Would the presence of the kottis be enough to conceal their larger kinsman? Luckily Murri was still far from his full growth, or there certainly would not have been any way of concealing him.

I chose to tramp beside that slow-moving vehicle. I had no idea what I might do if his presence was discovered. I only hoped that I could somehow distract any guard long enough for the fast-moving Sand Cat to get back into the dune waves.

The caravan came to a halt. Some of those ahead took the opportunity to sit as if they expected a wait of some time. Apparently there were formalities to be observed. From the heights above, the chimes of the wind-blown mobile makers of music sent their clear notes down. These mobiles were the pride of the Diamond people, but the greatest one of all—that was a symbol of the very land. It was only unhooked and freed to ring upon some great time of emergency—Though it was pent again now, it had chimed upon the death of Haban-ji.

Music it made, yes, but also it was death—a deadly and slashing death. Any who had committed certain crimes past all redemption were forced into the circle of the unevenly hung chimes, which were set with diamonds along their separate plaques so that they slashed cruelly as the chains which held the whole Great Mobile were kept whirling by guards well trained to the job.

Also—it was the last test for him who would set himself up to be Emperor. He must pass through the freed chimes successfully and without hurt to reach the crown set at their core. I wondered at the skill and courage of those who had

tried it in the past—they must have possessed the agility of a
master swordsman or of a great dancer in order to tread that
path. One moment of faltering, one mistake in judging the
swing of one plaque or another, and they would die painfully,
as if they had been set up for targets for the practice of inept
swordsmen.

There was a drum note from the head of our line—we
were to be on the move again. What was the penalty, I wondered dourly, for one who tried to smuggle a Sand Cat into
Vapala? Would he face the dance of the chimes? Yet I followed the cart at the steady pace set by those ahead.

To proceed was a test, almost as great as that endeavor
wherein I had brought Murri out of the sand trap, as the tail
end of the caravan passed between the rows of guards to start
up that precipitous way to the land above.

I looked from right to left, taking the measure of these
warriors. They were brightly accoutered, their armlets, breast-
plates, belts bejeweled with more elaboration than even that
worn by the Head of a House among my people.

Their hair was hidden under the massive wigs, those sil-
ver-white wigs which were surely sprinkled with diamond dust,
so did they glitter in the sunlight. Each was armed with a spear
but also carried a bow unstrung at his back, and their prowess
with both weapons was very well known across all the
queendoms.

They stood in two squads, one on either side of the entrance of the upper road, and their officer, holding a tally in
one hand, was a little to my right. It was apparent he was counting and checking both carts and people as we went. As I drew
near he looked straight at me, snapping his fingers, the gesture
one used to summon a none too reliable servant. I bit my lip.
Was it coming now? My staff and my knives were my only
weapons and surely those were nothing against the metal a
trained warrior could bring into service.

"You—what name?" He spoke with a strange clip to his
words and certainly not as he would address an equal.

"Klaverel-va-Hynkkel, Sword Lord."

"She of the caravan has said you were solo lost."

"That is true."

"Your plans here, outlander?"

"To see Vapala of which we have heard so much in the outlands," I returned. His voice and attitude were such as I had faced before—from the companions of my brother and the elders who visited with my father. How could he have faced some of the ventures which lay behind me now, for all his diamond dust, his war art, his place as keeper of the door to Vapala? For the first time I felt not the usual half-apologetic reaction I had done in the past. I did not wear a sword, but I had survived and in that much I was his equal. I rubbed the healed tooth mark wound on my wrist. No, I was even more!

This one might hunt Sand Cats, but I had seen their councils, shared in part their starlight dancing, was blood kin to them now. There was none in Vapala who could match that!

It was growing near twilight before the whole of the caravan finally reached the top of the mesa. That was a chancy path, one which was usually only taken by day. Late-comers camped by the guard post would have to await the next dawn. To my relief the guards had made no inspection of the last wagon. The kottis continued to sit together, lazy-eyed, covering the space they had made for Murri's entrance. I began to wonder what communication might exist between them and their much greater distant cousins.

The feral leopards, who had not joined the guard of the Emperor or those of the various Queens, were rumored to be enemies of Murri's people, though of any actual case of one attacking the other I had never heard. There had always been a bond between the leopards and my people, though perhaps not as close and familiar as that the kottis granted a household or a single person.

I thought I knew what to expect when I reached the top of that climb, for the greenery natural there had been many times described. The ferocity of the few storms which hit all our lands from time to time (little to our aid, for any fallen rain was very quickly sucked up by the sand) might strike here but the water did not escape. Those of the Diamond people had studied such problems from time immemorial and had their way of funneling such downpours, not into sucking sand but into reservoirs in the foundation rock. From those they drew to irrigate symmetrical patches where they induced growth, even trees tall enough to reach above a man's head like some tall rock spur. These were a marvel in themselves. As we passed along the upper road on our way to the city, I could see rows of these well tended and heavy with fruit. Between their columns were shrubs—some which gave off the tang of those spices which brought such high prices in the outlands.

There were other wider spaces, fenced, in which were fine herds of yaksen, even once such an inkeeping where oryxen of plainly high breeding had gathered to watch our passing, several exchanging challenges with those being part of the caravan.

Though my own House was considered prosperous and we had a good herd of yaksen and several finely bred oryxen (in fact my father, though he was inclined to make little show, lived as well as a noble might), no one of such standing had such a show of land wealth as I saw here.

However, looking around at all this spread of growing things, I found them strange, and I longed for the rock isles and algae pools of my own land. We are a part of our homes and I think there will always be a feeling of loss and ache within when we cannot longer actively communicate with our own special places.

Now I was overwhelmed and began to think ever more strongly that I had taken a wrong path. For all the disappointment and heart loss I would have had to face had I returned home, yet I was of Kahulawe. The Diamond Queendom could bedazzle with its richness and it did. At the same time the stranger here must be more of a stranger even than elsewhere. Those of Vapala might think the outer lands too harsh—for barbarians only. However, for untold time they had lived so until they could not conceive of any other way of life.

We were still a day's journey from the city, since it was situated more in the interior of the country. That night we tail-circled in a place prepared for caravans—and there camped. Elwene summoned all her staff (there was no need for sentries here) and began to lay out their program for setting up an impressive booth in the market—discussing prices and duties of those who would take care of the actual sales, and those who would continue to care for the beasts and the possessions of the caravan.

"Raffan is holding room at the Three Leopards," she said. "Vara brought us assurance of that. He is tight-fisted and it is needful to stand up against his overpricing, but he knows better than to try to take any high-nosed stand with me. What we put in his treasure pouch at the end of the marketing will be reasonable. As you know his beds are clean, he has a weekly immersion room, and the food, if it is plain, is well cooked."

Immersion room! Those two words struck me. Such was an often-told wonder of the Diamond Queendom. Many of the Great Houses in their palaces had private immersion rooms. For the most part we of the outer lands are a cleanly people, though we have not the washing use of our tongues, kotti fashion, to keep us so. But we do lave ourselves daily when possible with sponge mats of non-edible algae and even scrub before that with sand. To actually put the whole body into a large basin full of very soggy algae—that was a luxury I did long to try, having been so long without even a renewal of clothing.

Yet the thought of going to the inn was something I must consider. I could not let Murri show himself and an inn was a very public place. Also, though I carried some good lumps of turquoise which I had garnered along the way (also those gems which I had discovered in the destroyed caravan—though those were not mine to use), I could not exchange them for lodging without knowing their true worth here. Being the imperial capital, there would surely be workers in gems, though my own land was most noted for that. I must see about selling what I carried, and I knew enough of the value they had from my

sister to ensure, I believe, that I would not be cheated in a
bargain with a maker of gem-set wares. Also I was not a member of the caravan, and rightly I could not claim a share of the
arrangements they had already made.

I had reached that point in my musing about the immediate future when there flashed into my head the map of streets
and alleys which had come out of that vision dream. If I
deemed it a vision and not just a dream, then I had my answer
to the problem of where to seek guidance as to lodging and
information in the city.

Knowing that, I faced my entrance to the city far more
confidently. Luckily it was beginning to be dusky. The main
thoroughfare down which we passed was lighted with globes
which might have contained the brilliance of diamonds, so
did each illumine its section of the way. The buildings were
white, for the most part not higher than two stories, a precaution they followed from the far past against the worst of storms.
The closer in we drew, the more we could see of larger and
more ornate buildings. Statues of black leopards held some of
the globes and there were traces of color, some mosaics of
small gemstones, on the walls of the larger houses.

This splendor was indeed far from the homes of the isles
and surely meant, in part, to overawe those who came as visitors. I had drawn near to the cart in which Murri still rode
hidden. For him to emerge into this well-lighted place was to
betray him quickly, for there was traffic which thickened as
we came closer to the center point.

That morning I had given my thanks to the mistress and
offered her her choice of the rough stones I carried as my
payment. I had also given her note of the gems from the
massacre, asking that she might perhaps discover their new
owner. However, she had seemed doubtful that might ever
be done. My stones she had refused in such a way as I could
not feel as one given charity, saying that to aid any coming
out of solo was the duty of all wayfarers, as of course it was.
Thus I had now to make no farewells to those I had traveled
with, only to reach the inn towards which we must be bound

and then somehow get Murri to follow me into that maze so imprinted in my brain, using all his hunting skill as a skulker to do so.

When I started to convey this information to Murri, the kottis politely drawing to one side so I could approach as closely as possible the end of the wagon, I was interrupted with a swift answer.

"Know way, shall be ready."

Did Murri have visions also? If I accepted that which had been so offered us—what might be the pay asked in return? I was wary of the future—sometimes there came the feeling that I was being moved, not by my free will, but the power of some essence that I could not understand.

There were lights in the inn courtyard where the caravan drew up to sort out and empty carts, unpack the beasts, and see that they were escorted to the place set aside for them—the extra stable. I was watching the wagon, lingering in the shadow of the gate and keeping as inconspicuous as possible. Murri slipped over the tailgate, the kottis again standing aside, and was gone. I had already shouldered my pack to follow. The street outside was well lighted and there were both walkers and riders but somehow Murri had slid from one bit of shadow to the next while I crossed to the mouth of the narrower way which was the first part of the alley maze.

Once I was sure he had not been sighted we again crossed a wider way. At last I heard a cry and I took firmer hold of my staff and hurried along to act as rearguard if necessary.

It was then that I saw Murri take to an overhead path, making it in two bounds from a single-story roof to a higher one.

We had not been followed after all. And this section of the town had fewer lights, and those of subdued radiance. There were signs of shabbiness about buildings here. No fine mosaic work was picked out on walls and the carving about doorways and windows was often broken. The narrow path into the last court was entirely in the shadows as night had closed in. There was a faint light only in one place, over the doorway of the house my vision had shown me.

Murri appeared suddenly and was waiting by that door even as I reached it. I raised my hand to knock. There was one of the musical mobiles hanging there and it swung and chimed to my gesture. As if I had been impatiently waited, the door was opened at once and Ravinga's girl apprentice looked at me.

"So you have come—" If it was intended as a welcome it was a cool one. But she opened wide the door for Murri and me to enter. The Sand Cat showed no signs of hanging back but went in as confidently as if he were entering some lair of his own people.

19

The foreroom of the house was plainly a shop. Though there was a single light by the door, it did not reach very far towards the shelved walls. The girl held a lantern globe in her hand and the glimmer of that picked up from what stood or was seated on the shelves bright sparks of eyes, as if all those figures there were watching us as we passed by.

I felt wary, as if I were now in a place where there were secrets. The dolls I had seen Ravinga sell at the market in my own land had been very good but always there had been one or two among them so perfect in face and form as to suggest that it had been modeled with great skill from a living person. Those had sold only for a very high price, usually to some collector of curios, for my people had a liking for trinkets as they could afford, and like my sister's fine jewelry, the makers of such were esteemed and their craft stalls in the market were sought out by House lords and mistresses.

I paused now to get a straighter look at some pieces of which I caught a glimpse and would have liked to see the better. There was surely a Sand Cat on one shelf, sitting upright, both forepaws resting on a drum as if it would play for one of those air-floating dances of its kind.

However, my guide was already holding aside the curtain of the door which led beyond and Murri was heading in that direction. The curtain was of light hide and now we did move into a larger room which was plainly made for living and not for a shop, though there was another doorway displaying a light beyond, and that curtain was looped away to show a work table well loaded with what must be the raw materials of Ravinga's craft.

The dollmaker herself appeared there a moment later and
held out both hands palm up as she would greet a favored
guest. To my astonishment Murri raised a forepaw, his wicked
claws well sheathed, to lay against hers, his so large that it
nearly spanned both her hands. Deep in his throat he made
that sound which those of his own kind used in greeting.

Ravinga bowed her head in courtesy.

Then she made the same gesture to me and I hurried to
touch palms. Though I knew that she must have been tending
towards the later years of life, she remained the same as I had
always seen her—from many seasons ago when I had first spied
her work in the market and had stopped to admire a fully armed
warrior figure which had all the pride of my father when he
made his annual visit to court.

She had greeted me then not as a child who must be warned
of meddling with fine things but had spoken with me almost
as if I were a fellow craftsman, taking time to answer my questions concerning the warrior and his gear, which was slightly
strange to me as being that of the Azhengir, those whose
women also once rode to war.

Since that day I had always been glad to see her, though
the last two seasons our meetings had been a little awkward,
as, for the first time, she had brought her apprentice with her,
and Allitta had made it very clear that she had not the friendship for strangers which her mistress showed. The girl had always made some excuse to busy herself with the merchandise,
even to keep her back to me as she fussed about rearranging
displays or sitting in the corner busy on small repairs of the
figures people brought in to have their treasures returned to
full value again.

Now she had already left this room, vanishing through the
other door. I thought her churlish, though I had never sought
out the company of aught but my sisters. It would have done
me no good to attend any festival of first heat where choosing
would be done. It was most plain that I had nothing to offer
any mate-minded maiden. Now in my rags of soiled travel I
must present an even less attractive appearance.

"Accept guest right, Hynkkel," Ravinga greeted me with words more warm than any I had ever heard from even kin.

"You are gracious to one such as me, mistress—I—"

"You were summoned and this is your place for now." She had the same authority in her speech that my father used—an authority which, for the moment, daunted me from asking questions.

She asked nothing concerning my travels but led me on through that other door where Allitta had gone, and into a section which had a kitchen to one side—good smells coming from that making me feel at once the hollowness of my stomach. Murri was seated right within, watching the girl who moved between stove and table. His whiskers quivered as his mouth opened a trifle to let his long tongue sweep across his lips, plainly in anticipation.

Without pausing there my hostess showed me into one of the other small rooms, plainly private sleeping quarters. This was the type of lodging one would give an honored guest. The wall carvings were of Sand Cats in dance and those caught my eyes immediately, for only one who had witnessed the real ceremony could have wrought that. However, there were other luxuries waiting. A very large basin—perhaps not the baths of a House palace but well enough for anyone to wish for—stood to one side, and from my first sniff I knew that the sponge algae within it had been mixed of those kinds which were made to soothe as well as cleanse the most weary and long-journeyed of travelers.

In addition, laid across a cloth pole was a rust-yellow kilt, and a long coat of a blue-green, embroidered at throat and hem with a pattern of small crystal beads. Heel and toe together, a pair of soft oryxen-hide boots waited. I stared at this display as my backpack thudded to the floor.

A night's lodging, food, yes, those were often guest-offered, but this city finery—why? Again that feeling that I was being moved by something I did not understand made me uncomfortable. Yet I could not reject what was so offered without giving offense, that was certain. Though such a welcome to one returning from solo was right—yet it should be in gifts from kin, and not from one who had no blood tie.

I pulled off my rags of trail dress, bundling them together. For the most part they were past wearing. I must see to replenishing my wardrobe as soon as I could.

Then I stood on the wash mat and sponged myself down with the algae. It was warm and my abraded, scarred, and dried skin soaked up the moisture. I could feel my body relax. I no longer even wondered as to why I was received with such a welcome, I simply sank into a kind of yielding bemusement.

The clothing fitted me. Which was another surprise—unless Ravinga was so versed in the making of clothing for her figures she could reckon in her mind my size—even though she had not seen me for a season. The boots were a little large, but no matter for that, at least they did not abrade the skin as did those many-times-mended ones I just discarded.

When I was done I stood and viewed myself in a mirror. It did not show the whole of me, but I thought for a moment that by some device I was looking at one of Ravinga's dolls raised to man height. My face was thin and darker, my hair had grown longer so that even when I pressed the keeping ring about it the ends switched my shoulders behind. My sister's parting gift was bright on my arm, and on impulse I added the cat pendant which I had kept concealed for most of the time during my trail walking. That glinted now against my chest between the open edges of the coat and certainly was such an ornament, even by the famed wealth of Vapala, as could not be easily equaled.

Feeling very much as if somehow I had come into that room one person and was going out another, I went in search of my hostess.

Murri was already occupied with the contents of a large basin when I entered the eating place. Facing him in a solemn row were three black kottis, their attention full upon him, cleaned plates before each of them.

Ravinga waved me to a well-padded seating mat beside her own and there were polished knee tables before us. A third was set at a right angle to Ravinga's and there Allitta seated herself in turn, having placed the last of a series of covered dishes before us.

To one who had been living off the very rough fare of the country for so long this was in truth such as would be provided at only a Great House ceremonial feast. I tasted food which was common here, grown in the fields of Vapala, but unknown, since it could not be transported by any lengthy trailing, in my own land. There was also fresh fruit to end the meal, as well as a drink made from subtly flavored stuff which brought a warmth not only into my middle but into my mind. This night was taking on the quality of a dream.

My hostess did not make conversation, and following good manners I addressed myself also to the emptying of my bowls, twice over—which perhaps was true greediness. Allitta arose twice to bring on further supplies.

Murri had polished his basin clean and used a ready paw to clean whiskered face. Trailed still by the kottis, he had crossed the room and now was stretched full length behind me, though his bulk was not well fitted into the limited space. I could hear his purr, kept to a faint rumble.

When the meal was at last done I ventured to break the silence.

"Lady, your House may rest in pride. Such bounty to a stranger is beyond reckoning. Now—" I hesitated trying to find the proper words, not the blunt ones which were already on my tongue.

She pushed the knee table a little from her and sat with her hands clasped lightly in her lap. Allitta made a quick matter of clearing away the remains of the feast, leaving only three cups of fine design and a flagon of the soothing drink there.

"Now," Ravinga said when the girl had at last returned to her own place, two of the kottis immediately pushing each other to establish favored positions in her lap, "now you have questions, as who would not." She paused again, not looking at me but at the opposite wall as if she saw there something of intent meaning.

"We are a people who have forgotten much, and some of that I believe was induced—as a punishment, a warning, an escape—who knows which? The most ancient of the bard songs hold hints. Hints that predate the wars before the uniting of the outer queendoms. Most of our lands are harsh ones and the lives we have made for ourselves here have demanded that we become what we are now.

"The unification has done away with war between nation and nation and that paves the way for something more. If we have fallen from some former estate, perhaps we are now very slowly climbing back, as ones who would find a way up a slickrock island new to them. But at present we are more like travelers trapped in some sand pit, and hiding our eyes against what is before us—or must be before us in the future.

"We have grown complacent. Oh, some of our customs we have held to—the solo to toughen our young for example." Now she did glance at me. "Is it not true, Hynkkel, that you are different now?"

"I believe so—" My hand sought the cat pendant and I saw the scars on my wrist. Different, yes, a whole new dimension of life had been opened to me. I had danced with those who were the fabled enemies of my kind, I had listened to Kynrr's tales, I had come away from my roots and at the moment I realized that I had indeed broken out of the shell which had once held me.

"My House," she seemed to change the subject sharply, "is a strange one. I have only two of blood kin left—and one is not truly of my nature." Suddenly she stretched forth her own wrist and pushed up a wide bracelet circling that. I saw on her slightly puckered skin scars similar to those Maraya's teeth had left on me.

"For many seasons there has been trouble, trouble which was so faint that even the Great Essence could only dimly convey—and then only to some born sensitive to such nuances. Now this trouble is rising faster. The Plain of Desolation has a lord power."

I think I was staring at her gape-jawed, trying to make sense of such a wild statement. For there could be no life in the Great Desolation—no House for any lord power to use.

Behind me I heard a sudden growl, felt Murri stir.

"Listen—" his throat speech carried. "This is the speech of wisdom."

Even the kottis, those on Allitta's lap and the one which had settled down beside her, opened wide their eyes to regard Ravinga's with that unblinking stare of their kind.

"There are the great rats—" Suddenly I thought of those we had slain and how they were different from their fellows. And I had heard tales of how such large ones have come out of the Desolation—though how they could abide there—

"Yes, the rats—a testing—to see how alert and ready we may be." She reached within to a pocket of her robe and brought out in the hollow of her hand a round ball of a dead-black substance, a black so intense that it appeared to draw light to it for the quenching and the room became darker as she set it down on the table before her.

I leaned forward to take a better look but her hand curved over it instantly, shielding it from my sight. "Not so! I do not know the full power of this. You have one shield—" she pointed to my pendant, "but you have had no training. We do not risk you now—"

"Risk me?"

"From the day that you were able to find the cursing on my beast I knew that you had that within you which might answer." Again she changed the subject. "The kottis, the beasts, they sensed it in you, for in many ways their measurements are more accurate than ours.

"Allitta," she nodded to her apprentice, "is also one who has inner sight. She has learned a little in her way, you have in yours. We shall need those who can stand up to dangers far different from any that our peoples have known for generations."

"I am no warrior!" I protested. Had not all the trouble in my life sprung from the seed that I was not by nature such?

"There are many kinds of struggle, and a sword, lance, or other weapon in one's hand may not be the answer to such. We need others than warriors, though it may well follow, and probably will, that we shall see lances readied against what comes.

"We need more now those who can walk other ways, who are ready to be attuned to the most subtle warnings of the Great Essence. Firstly we are in need of a new Emperor. Vapala has supplied the last two Emperors. There is a candidate very ready here now who would change the source of custom—for it has always been forbidden that the rule should rest in the hands of any one House.

"Though we now dwell in peace as to nation, there are dark workings between House and House." Her hand went out and touched that of Allitta which now lay on the table. There was a harsh stiffening of her apprentice's whole body, an odd sharpening of feature which could be evil memory possessing her for an instant or two. "Yes, there are many darknesses under the surface of our apparent safety. Thus we need no scheming of House against House to add to future danger. Our Emperor must this time have no tie with Vapala."

She spoke as if she were issuing an order and now she turned her head and looked straight at me as might a commander look at his troop.

"No!" the denial burst from me. "I am no Emperor, nor can I be! Nor will I try—"

The girl leaned forward and her sharpness of feature was matched by her voice as she said:

"One does what is demanded of one—or one is—nothing!" She smacked her hand, palm down, on her own small table so the cup there nearly toppled to its side. Her eyes were as cold as those my father had often turned on me and there was certainly a measure of disgust in the curl of her lips.

"I am no Emperor," I repeated firmly. The thought that these two women could see me a candidate made me suddenly suspicious of all the vague warnings Ravinga had been mouthing. That I should offer myself for such a trial—there would rightfully be mocking laughter and I would be ranked one bereft of wit.

But Ravinga now did not seem disturbed. Her hand that was over that black ball raised and under her touch the ball rolled towards me.

"Let us see," she said.

As when her mistress had given me the cat mask long ago, Allitta made a disputing gesture with her own right hand but said nothing.

The ball rolled across Ravinga's table, passed on to mine. I could not understand how it had crossed the short space between the two tops. Then it was before me. Though Ravinga did not order me—she did not this time refuse my study of the object.

It had nothing of a crystal about it. There was no gleam or glitter. The sphere repelled the eye as might a ball of some noxious dried algae. I had no desire to touch it. But it was changing before my eyes. The ball outline writhed, it became different shapes. For an instant only I was looking down at the head of a cat—not a kotti, nor of Murri's lineage, but the sleek one of a leopard—the same leopard which, when blue, was the symbol of rulership.

Leopard it was, but it went on changing and then I saw a rat—the representation of one of those strange and direful larger beasts.

Leopard for ruler, that symbolism flashed into my mind— and rat—rat for the end of all good.

20

For one used to the relative silences of the outer lands Vapala was a place of clamor—though I could not say that my ears were assaulted by raucous sounds. Those musical mobiles which were a part of the inner city were always a-chime from dawn, when they were released to any wind which might be blowing, to dusk. The streets teemed with life, and during the next few days when more and more travelers and trading caravans came crowding in, one had to push one's way through throngs such as an outer dweller certainly never saw gathered together even for a major feasting.

I had hoped for more enlightenment from Ravinga, yet at the same time I did not want to become involved in any argument over the preposterous idea that I would put myself forward for the Leopard Throne. She had somewhat ensorceled me by all the hints she had made on the first night I was under her roof. But in the morning she did not take up the subject again, nor was I minded to do so either.

It was a busy time within the shop. Emperor dolls were in demand—even when they were only clay images of the cheapest sort bought for a couple of fruits, or a small bundle of firewood by those too poor to have anything in a purse. To display one of these over one's doorway, even the doorway of a dilapidated hut, was considered necessary by custom. I saw that Ravinga and Allitta even gave these away to those who looked longingly but had not anything to trade. The Emperor might have been absorbed in the Greater Essence, but it remained that something of his strength might still abide with those who so honored him.

For the time being there was little trade in her other products and I was able to survey them at my leisure. Men, women, and children from all the queendoms, of every rank from the Queens and their courtiers and guards, to the lowest of servants or slaves, were represented in the collection.

Whole companies of desert scouts were assembled with their mounts, their equipment complete to even the deadly boot knives which were now worn mostly for show and no longer settled death duels. There was one entire trader's caravan which marched along a top shelf. The salt gatherers of Azhengir with their crystal-lined branches were there, the guides of the dune sail riders with their light craft from Twahihic. Nor were the miners of Thnossis nor my own people lacking. And in the fore were the lords and ladies, the people of Vapala itself, from the lowest street cleaner to the Queen and her court.

If Ravinga had fashioned examples of all the two-footed inhabitants of the queendoms, she had done as well for the four-footed. There were kottis engaged in all manner of play and hunt, there were oryxen, their fierce horns not trimmed, patient yaksen, with and without carts, and, in a corner to themselves, Sand Cats.

In this land where such were considered menaces and the best of prey I was surprised at the detail and lifelike appearance of Ravinga's collection. Here were free Sand Cats engaged in their own lives as I had seen Myrourr and those who had gathered for the "sing." These had surely never been fashioned by one who had only seen them from a distance, or stood above dead bodies after a hunt.

I thought often of the scars on my hostess's wrist, hidden always by her bracelet. She had not mentioned those, only was sure I had seen them. When had Ravinga entered that other world and why? I had made the point of watching Allitta and she certainly bore no such markings.

From childhood I had been schooled to patience but sometimes now I wanted to confront Ravinga and demand answers, clear-cut answers. Since the night that she had shown me that black ball and taken it again out of my hand while I still goggled over what I had seen and what might be the meaning of it, she had spent very little time with on me, being occupied with the shop—and her work table.

I made myself useful on the second day—the first I had gone to the market to inspect the dealers in stones and jewel work. Twice I had seen pieces which undoubtedly were from my sister's fashioning being resold and at prices which I think would have truly astounded Kura. I began to plan how her work might be brought directly to Vapala so that not only might her fine creations be appreciated by collectors but that she would have the pick of stones and other raw material, the like of which never appeared in our own trading fairs.

Ravinga not only sold from her shop, she had also a leased market slip and it was there that during this time her servant Mancol took the less of her wares. I helped him transport and set up the stall before I wandered about on my own.

The turquoise I had brought out of the outlands I was able to sell for some silver shavings which seemed a goodly bargain to me, though I am sure, had I known better the ways of this market, I could have made an even better trade. But there was too much to see and listen to, so much which was distracting.

Processions wound up and down the streets. There were constant cries from harsh-voiced running servants to clear the way for those of one Great House or another. Youths in their finest were arriving—perhaps not to make the trials—but to mingle and gamble, race their mounts outside the city, drink the wines known nowhere else, generally show their arrogant persons that at times were boorish beyond belief.

Once I saw Shank-ji with a crowd of followers. He was fair-skinned as any Vapalan—but he did not wear the bush wig of a warrior, though he was armed well enough with superbly forged weapons, gem-hilted. His own white hair was knotted back in as simple a fashion as my own, though the clasp which held it so blazed with diamonds.

His face was narrow, clean of any hair on cheek or chin, though most of his companions sported narrow threads of mustache or jawline of beard. There was something oddly masklike about his countenance—no expression showed.

Heavy lids appeared to hide, by chance or design, most of his eyes. There was certainly that about him which drew the attention—perhaps a certain tension throughout as if he held himself in tight rein against flaming action for which he longed.

He was young, though there again one could not say he was like the other youths. Rather there was about him some of the authority which my father has always worn as a daunting cloak. Still, Emperor's son though he might be, he had by custom held no open power in Vapala and ranked lower even than any House lord.

People made way for his party. I observed that some in the crowd looked at him oddly in question as he rode by. Once I saw a woman's fingers move quickly in a sign which in my land was used to ward off ill fortune. On the other hand there were a portion of those who called out his name, though he did not look at who so hailed him or make an answering gesture.

During my prowling of the market Murri had withdrawn to the ruined house in the small court where Ravinga's shop stood. When I questioned his safety Allitta said, with that stiff impatience she always used for me, that the ruin also belonged to the dollmaker and there would be no one to visit it untimely.

My desert-born comrade was bored. Had it not been that at night he could come back to Ravinga's own roof and that the kottis appeared to trot back and forth regularly to his place of refuge, I think he might even have climbed to the housetops again and gone exploring on his own. I took to describing to him in the evening what I had seen. How much human affairs meant to Murri when they did not actively affect his own life I could not tell, but he listened, and once in a while asked a question which surprised me.

He seemed particularly interested in my sight of Shank-ji, though he growled several times and at last stated flatly:

"That one kills—kills not to eat—but to—" He seemed to be searching for some way of expressing a thought important to him in the limited vocabulary we could share. "He kills—to wear teeth—to take skin—for the seeing of others."

A killer for red sport. Certainly that could be true of more than half those I had watched riding so proudly through the streets. Yet Shank-ji, if he shared that with most, had more. Kynrr had been hostile and forbidding at our first meeting, yet there had been that in him which I could understand. Even my brother I could read after a fashion. However, this would-be Emperor—no, he rode alone.

"Not one—" Murri broke in upon that thought, "two—"

"Two what?" I asked.

The Sand Cat blinked. Again it seemed he struggled to make clear some thought. Then he answered:

"Here stands that one." He placed a paw flat on the floor close to my knee. Then he moved his other foot to position several finger lengths behind the first. "Here—other—"

"Other man?"

Again Murri blinked. "Other—" I thought I could sense puzzlement as if he could not truly give a clear answer.

Someone behind Shank-ji? That suggested that the Vapalan's bid for the throne of his father might indeed have covert support.

I had heard enough sidewise comments from time to time since I had reached the city which suggested that there was an unrest under the surface, that all was not as it had once been in the Diamond city, bound by custom into a narrow trail.

That I could get any more out of my desert-born companion was impossible now. I only hoped that what he might know or learn in the future he would share with me.

Night's shadows lay on the city. The shop was closed, and, though the music of the mobiles was still in chime, this pocket of a court which held us was relatively quiet. For the first time since I had entered Vapala I brought out Kynrr's treasured Kifongg and tuned it, glad to see that the hard trek had not affected it in any way.

The bowl was worn indeed, polished very smooth by long handling, so polished that only the faintest of designs remained—an intricate twisting of lines of which I had never been able to make anything. They could have once been a running script such as those of Vapala used for their "high" writing of music and sound.

I moved my fingers back and forth in an exercise to limber them, then dared to strike the chords of one of those songs Kynrr had taught me. Allitta had gone elsewhere in this sprawl of building which I had never fully explored, keeping strictly to the section Ravinga had made free for me. The dollmaker herself came to settle on a pile of mats, sighing as she relaxed, rubbing her back with one hand as if hours spent above her work table had left her aching.

One of Kynrr's songs came easier as I reached the proper strings. I kept my voice low. Murri loosed a rumble of purr and the three kottis gathered in about Ravinga, watching me as they rubbed lovingly about the dollmaker. They were as one in their black coloring and always they went together as if invisibly linked. They had paid me the courtesy of notice now and then, but it was plain that in this house only Ravinga and the girl rated their whole attention and devotion.

I sang the song which Kynrr had himself fashioned in exile, one which spoke of the stars he loved to watch, the softness of the nights, the harshness which came with the day, and above all the loneliness that ate into one apart.

Why that one of all the songs of his own making he had given to me came now I did not know. It was as if this was proper and rightful for this day and twilight time.

"Where learned you that?" The last notes dropped from the strings even as Allitta was upon me. There was not the scornful withdrawal which always seemed to possess her when she looked at me. She was inwardly aflame, almost I could see her hand tense as if to aim a blow.

"From its maker. He who called himself Kynrr—"

"A dead man does not sing!" she hissed as might one of the kottis.

"True. Yet when he taught me this he was not dead. Though the Great Essence took him later."

She raised that fisted hand and bit at the knuckles. Across those she looked at me as if she would reach into my mind and pull forth the stuff of memory.

"But that is not—There was no known Kynrr's song in this tune!"

"I knew such." Swiftly I spoke of the hermit and of his place of exile. Of how he had spoken of Vapala and of how he had died, having given his strength to my rescue.

She listened. Then I saw that her eyes in the lamplight glistened.

"Kynrr," she repeated the name when I had done. "It was indeed Master Kynrr whose blood that one bore. I believed him dead in the night's slaughter. That he won free—" She shook her head slowly. "The last of the sworn ones, and so that was his ending."

She might be speaking to herself as she dropped down upon the cushions opposite me. Some strength could have, for the moment, gone out of her. There was desolation in both her eyes and her voice. Now she reached forward and touched the Kifongg I had put down, touched it as if she might so put finger on a great treasure.

"True enough—this was of Kynrr—and Kiticar treasured it. Had any saved it, it would have been him. Many times I have heard him play—he was one of the great ones, even as was Kynrr long ago, though ever said he was not the master as that one was."

She grasped the Kifongg fully now and drew it into her lap. Her fingers found the strings. What came forth was not the lament which had been born by my playing, but rather small gem notes which spoke of growing things, of the dancing of feasters, of the quickening of hearts. Never had I heard such from the man who had called himself Kynrr, yet somehow I knew that this song was also of his fashioning in another and happier time.

I leaned back a little against the bulk of Murri, who, as usual, had settled behind me to listen in delight. There was something which came to lighten the heart, assure the hearer that beyond all cares lay happiness and beauty.

It was not to last. Sharply came other notes, crystal clear
but with nothing gentle in them. They rang through the walls.
Allitta's fingers ceased to move, she was again stern of face,
shaken out of that which had possessed her. Ravinga straightened in her place.

"Haban-ji goes to his sealing," she said. "A time ends, new
begins."

I wondered what mysteries now were in progress in the
Vapalan House of the Past. How long would this new resident there be remembered? Oh, yes, any child could recite
the roll of Emperors going back for generations. The sing-
song of that roll came even now to the fore of my mind. But
how many of them had set any lasting mark upon that roll,
save for their names?

"Tomorrow," Ravinga had to raise her voice to compete
with the chimes of departing, "they will choose."

I moved, shifted. Must I now again face her belief that I
was one who would make that choice? If she expected some
answer from me she did not get it. After a moment she arose
to go into her own quarters. Allitta slid the Kifongg from her
knee to the floor and abruptly departed also without a word,
leaving me to seek my own bed. However, this night I did not
go alone, for Murri paced beside me as he had in that trial by
travel through which we both had come.

The chimes sounded once more in the morning, all of them
in a clamor which was ear-splitting to one who came from the
relative silence of the desert. Still I was drawn with Ravinga,
and Allitta, and seemingly all those of the households of Vapala
who could crowd into the square before the Hall of the Past.

There was a bright splash of color on the high flight of
stairs leading up to the wide portal of that hall. The Queens
were aglitter with gems; their foremost courtiers made a
back tapestry. Before them were the Herald and the Head
of the foremost House of Vapala. Between those a sleepy
beast wore a netting of diamonds about its ears—the Blue
Leopard, always companion guard to the Emperor, in himself the symbol of power.

For a last time the chimes of the Great Mobile, shining rainbow patterns in the sky above us, sounded and then were silent as the Herald came forward. He had the reaching voice of his office and it carried over the throng massed below.

"The Great Haban-ji is now of the Final Essence. There must be one to follow him. These are the tasks, O men of courage and skill. Listen well and then take oath you shall reach for the triumph of the crown." He pointed to the Great Crown set in the heart of the mobile.

"From ancient times it has been that he who would rule must prove himself to each of the queendoms, that he may well understand the life of those whom he shall rule.

"First: in Thnossis he must venture close enough to the ever-flowing lava river to bring back one of the ruby cats of Qurr from that temple which the river now threatens to engulf.

"In Azhengir he must join in the harvest of salt crystals, proving to those who labor there his fitness to be considered their equal in skill.

"In Twahihic he must harvest from the haunted garden.

"In Kahulawe he must discover and challenge the Leopard Keeper of lasting knowledge that he may touch the talisman and so be given the high power of judgment both good and evil, himself being judged thereby.

"On his return here, he must claim the crown from its place aloft.

"He who can return a victor in all—Emperor shall he be!"

More likely, I thought, he will have passed to the Essence. What mortal man could survive that? Each of the trials was long known to be well nigh impossible. Yet I also knew that there would be no shirking, that it must and would be done even as the Herald had outlined. Among those massed here below was a man who would stand there at last with the crown in his hands, no matter how many lives would be gone to gain that.

21

Massed before the steps on which the dignitaries stood were those who offered themselves for trial. I knew that many of them had started from their homes before the actual death of Haban-ji, when the first rumors of his decline had been spread. Now they were gathered, each in a group of the land of their birth—clad in their best finery, armed, and already on show to their fellows.

To me, well back in the throng, they were one mass of warrior wigs, to be sighted now and then when there was some ripple of movement in the crowd. I heard around me some names mentioned, but none of those except that of Shank-ji were known to me.

The leopard stirred and of a sudden the hum of the gathered people ceased. Though the chimes of the lesser mobiles continued, those of the great would not be heard now until the final test.

Down the steps flowed that sleek animal. The sunlight made an azure glow of his fur, his eyes were fierce gems of a milky grey. He came to the candidates. The crowd about me pressed backward until I was near the opening of one of those streets which fed into this plaza. I could no longer see what was happening, but I knew well the leopard was a-hunt.

There was a rising sound. Those who had come from Thnossis opened their tight group and from that a single one of their number stepped to the second stair to face his Queen, who greeted him as her champion, gave into his eager hands the emblem of this search. From that moment forward he would be free of all other demands upon him, set only to the task ahead.

So was he joined by the select ones from Azhengir and
Twahihic. Then Shank-ji, who could not be taken for any ordinary contestant. Again there was a murmur arising. There had
been no candidate as yet to walk forward from those representing my own land—yet I had earlier marked the number of
volunteers from Kahulawe.

The crowd behind the groups of chosen were in movement and again I was pressed back. I had already lost touch
with Ravinga and Allitta. Those about me were Vapalan towns-
people of the middle classes, exchanging comments in their
own clipped speech. I gathered from what I heard, the information spreading, that the leopard had passed by all the men
of Kahulawe as if they did not exist and was now entering
into the massed throng.

I could see the rippling which must mark the coming of
the beast, those drawing from side to side away from that
embodiment of imperial power. That ripple spread to where
I stood.

Men and women drew away to afford clear passage as the
beast came striding as might the Emperor himself. He halted—
before me!

Moon-silver eyes regarded me, sweeping from head to
boots. Then the gaze centered on that pendant which I had
dared to wear this day. Leopard and Sand Cat were no brothers in blood bond. Leopards had hunted Sand Cats with the
men of Vapala for generations. I saw the lips of this one curl
back to show the fangs which seemed to shine in threat. Still
the beast paused only for a moment before it came directly
to me and then yowled as one which had fastened upon the
prey it sought, though it had not cried out so when it had
made its other selections.

There was a quick surge away from me so that now I stood
alone with only the leopard. It looked once more into my eyes,
and, much as I wanted to slip into the street behind me and be
away from it and what its interest in me meant, I knew that
escape was now past my ability. Between me and those steps
on which stood the four already selected was a clear aisle and

the leopard turned to tread it. Without hope of outwitting fortune I followed behind.

Around me there was a clamor of speech in accents of all the queendoms. I wondered if this had ever happened before—and resented that it had happened to me. I was not any young blood, steeled by desert patrolling, safe in the esteem of House or clan. Those with whom I must vie were certainly as different from me as the burning sun from the cool of the night.

I came to those from Kahulawe and, though some made a path for me, there was another who made a firm barrier of his own body. He had turned to face me as I came and I knew that this, my brother, carried not contempt for me now but something approaching hate. I saw his hands as they hung by his sides open and then clench as if upon the hilt of a weapon. His eyes were narrow, and hard, barriers to veil his innermost being. We could have been enemies from years of struggle instead of two who shared the same blood.

The leopard had passed him to return to its statue pose on the steps. However, Kalikku did not move to let me by. It was plain he was daring me to join those others selected by fate—or the whim of a beast.

"This one is a servant!" His voice arose and those about him gave ear, their silence spreading. "This one is no more than a herder of beasts, a carrier of burdens. He is not fit—"

Now he swung around and spoke directly to our Queen, who had descended a step or two drawn by the strangeness of this selection.

"Great Lady, this one is a shame to those of Kahulawe. It is wrong he should be chosen to disgrace our nation. Surely such a selection cannot stand!"

The Herald was now beside Queen Alompra Eakanna. It was he who answered:

"Be silent! It is not for any of us to say this one or that should try for the crown." His hand went out to almost touch the head of the leopard. "From the beginning it was given to this one and his kind to bring forward those who are on trial. Do you dare to question the one who is the servant of the

Great Essence? If even a slave of Azhengir is so designated as a candidate then he must be given his full chance."

My brother might have been rendered unable for any more protest, but his eyes told me of the fury that gripped him. One of his companions caught his shoulder and jerked him back, leaving me at last a free path. I longed to cry out myself at that moment, that much of what Kalikku said of me was the truth. I was one ignorant of warrior ways, one who had been a servant even in his father's house. Yet I knew that that would avail me nothing. My fate had been settled when the leopard had looked me eye to eye.

Thus it was under escort of Queen Alompra's own guard that I returned to Ravinga's home to take up my pack again. Of Murri there was no sign and I hoped that he was well hidden. That the dollmaker would somehow get him out of Vapala I was sure.

She had ready for me the pack I had brought out of the desert, but its outer wrappings had been renewed with a fine new blanket and she had also prepared for me the clothes of a traveler, the heavy boots, the short coat, the thick leggings— all of outstanding quality. When I had changed and left the finery she had given me earlier, I picked up the Kifongg. This fine instrument should be left here in safety. Allitta stood in the shop and I held it out to her. "Maiden of the House, this is best in your hands now."

"If you wish." She was cool, but then she added, "The Essence be with you, seeker of thrones."

The Queen's guard had a led oryxen for my riding, that resented my pack until I calmed it with that skill I had learned among my father's herds.

I had no time to really speak with Ravinga. But I sensed that she wished me well. As I swung into the saddle I saw her fingers move in a small, nearly hidden gesture which was one to summon the good will of the Great Essence. But what was more strange was that Allitta, now in the shadows behind her, made the sign in addition to her spoken good wishes.

It was the custom that each contestant begin his trials in the country of his birth, and to the border of Kahulawe we moved at a goodly pace. The first night out, as we camped, I found myself very much alone. None of the warriors of this company spoke to me in a friendly fashion, rather only with the aloof speech of the court. I was left to myself largely, though I realized that every move I made was noted and perhaps commented on.

My brother had served his allotted time in the guard. Did his opinion of me hold with these men? That could well be. They had offered me my choice of weapons and though no one sneered openly I took only those with which I was familiar—a wayfarer's staff (though one much better than any I had before seen, as this one had longer blades of fine metal set in the length) and a knife. I was not offered a sling. Doubtless that was considered so far beneath the proper equipment that they did not even possess them, but my own was fastened in my belt loop.

It took us three days of fast riding, changing mounts along the way at the camp points on the traders' trail. Then we were across the border and once more the essence of my own place enveloped me with more comfort than any cloak or blanket no matter how well woven.

Once in Kahulawe I realized that we had a follower, Murri, though I could never catch sight of him, nor could any who rode with me do so. The relief of learning that lightened my mind. There was an ordeal before me which was none of my making but one I could not escape. Twice I dreamed that I sat once more at that table in Ravinga's house and looked down upon the stone of dull black which was first the head of a leopard and then that of a rat.

Rats were a matter of conversation about the campfire at night. There had been a steady flow of information open to the guard concerning packs of the creatures, larger and apparently more intelligent than any we had ever known. They were said to have near completely overwhelmed one of the crystal-enclosed cities of Twahihic, coming up through earth tunnels and slaying more than ten times ten hands of people—such a disaster which none of us had heard of before.

Morning brought the arrival of the Chancellor of Kahulawe and she came to me directly. There was no sign of favor in her manner.

"You go thus—" She turned a fraction and pointed westward. "The rest of this journey is yours alone, Klaverel-va-Hynkkel." Her lips folded tightly together.

It was plain that in her eyes I was no fit representative for my country. Her scorn did not strike me as strong as such had done in the past, for I might not be a warrior, but I had—my one hand clasped and caressed the scars on my other wrist—danced with the Sand Cats, and out there waiting for me now was one whom none of these would face without drawn steel.

I bowed my head with courtesy as I answered:

"Great One, I accept this path."

Once more her lips twisted as if she tasted a sour and bitter mouthful. "May the Essence possess you in this—" The tone of her conventional words left much to be desired.

I laid out my pack to discard all which might make an extra weight, slowing me down. Somewhere ahead was an island of legend. What I was to confront there I was not sure. I could only hope that in this test, which was of my own land, I would not fail.

At twilight I set out and they watched me out of camp. There were no cheering words and about me their disbelief was like a smothering cloak. Only that was a spur to action and not a deterrent.

I had pushed well away from the torchlight of the camp when there was a darker spot against the night gleam of the sands and Murri came to me. He rubbed his head against my thigh and I went on one knee to stroke the thick fur of his head and neck, scratch behind his ears. Our meeting was heartening. Under just such rising stars as these had I seen his kin in their dancing and, even as that memory crossed my mind, the Sand Cat whirled about like a kotti playing tail-I-must-catch, giving voice to a singing purr of excitement.

Hardly knowing what I did, my own steps became not those of one patiently slogging through the sand, but rather I, too, advanced in the formal steps and then short leaps I had used at the feast meeting of his clan.

For some moments it was so with us and then that which I must do broke through the small snatch of freedom. Murri ceased his own bounds to come to me.

"What waits—?" he asked.

I shook my head. "Truly I do not know, save that I must search out the heart of Kahulawe and there face that which guards it—and they say the path lies ahead."

We traveled on in the direction the Chancellor had set for me. There arose out of the sand two of the stone guardian cats, set on a line, with a space between them.

Unlike the other such guide posts of the land, these each held up a paw as if in warning, and the gem glow of their eyes was the orange red of those gripped by the heat of anger, ready to attack all who might dare the road between them. Still they did not stir as I walked between.

Against and rising from the gleaming sands was an isle: dark, very dark in the night. Murri slipped ahead of me, to stand waiting at the foot of what seemed to be a cliff. When I reached him I near gagged at a stench which seemed to be exuded from the very rock.

That stench I knew well. Somewhere, not too far away, was a befouled algae pool. Befouled—by the rats?

My staff I must sling across my shoulders if I would climb. My knife? I loosened it a little in the sheath. Then Murri rumbled:

"Evil ones have been here—"

His natural senses were all much keener than mine. At this moment he must be my guide.

"They are still?"

"Who can tell?" His answer held little satisfaction for me.

Already the cat was clawing his way up the cliff. I dropped my small pack, lashed a rope end to it and the other end to my belt. Then with my staff securely bound to my back I began the climb. It was not to be easily done—the handholds and toeholds (for I had also left my boots within my pack) were not easily found. Had I not been faced by similar demands during my days as herdsman I might have found it even more exhausting than a night's march.

However, at length, I won to the top and found that so I was on the rim of a hollow, almost as perfect in contour as the inside of a ceremonial cup. From that rose an overpowering stink. Under the sun, I thought, that it might well overcome any who dared draw near its source.

So rough were the edges of that cup that, after drawing up my pack, I needed to use both hands and feet in a kind of crawl to make my way around towards that part of the island beyond, which appeared to be again higher.

I had gone only a short distance when Murri, still proceeding me, stopped short to look down into the pool of noisome stench. My staff was in my hands and I squirmed around until a spur of rock was at my back so I was best ready to face attack.

"What you seek is there—" Murri jerked his head forward and then coughed as if the stench had eaten at his lungs. I looked down into the hollow.

The walls appeared even more precipitous than had those of the outer cliff. To venture down into that stench—I had heard of herdsmen and hunters who had been overcome by the reek of spoiled algae. If I was to try that descent and should become light-headed—

Murri was still looking down. One half of the cup lay in full dark, the wall holding it in shadow. The other side was revealed somewhat by the glimmer of the rocks under the starred sky. On that side there was carving again.

A giant cat, fashioned as if it were emerging from the wall, sat upright there. Between the forelegs showed a dark opening into what must be inner ways.

Murri's head swung towards me and his eyes were lamp globes in the dark.

"I not go here. Be place for smoothskin only."

I stared down into the bowl-like valley below. The over-powering stench of the rotting algae was sickening. Could I dare such a descent?

My pack lay at my feet and I stooped to open that and rummage within. There was a mass of soggy algae in a container—the medicinal scent of which reached me even through the overpowering odor about. With my knife I worried a strip of cloth from the edge of my cloak and rolled that mass within to tie it over my nose and mouth. It limited my full breathing to be sure, but still it kept me from the threat of the reek of this place.

Fastening my staff firmly to my back, and looping a rope end around a spur, I pushed over the rim, leaving Murri behind.

The descent was not as difficult as the climb up the outer cliff had been. My boots thudded to the ground in the shadow thrown by the rise behind me, but the cat-guarded entrance I could see very well.

I must pick a careful way to that doorway. The poisoned algae spattered by my boots might well touch skin to raise dangerous blisters. However, it was not algae alone which made a stinkhole of this place. The carcasses of rats were scattered about. None of them bore long fang tears so it would seem that they had not been brought down by their fellows as was the custom when part of a pack turned upon the weaker members for food.

As I approached that dark doorway in the wall, so over-shadowed by the pillar-like forelegs of the cat, I found more and more of the dead beasts and they looked as if they had tried to make some advance in that direction and been mowed down.

There were among these at least three of those larger rats, and one had reached a point nearly between the cat's feet.

I circled by the body and, with staff in hand and ready, lest the darkness ahead could hold some of the pack more lucky, I entered that portal of darkness.

22

I was in utter darkness, so thick that I swung my staff before me, sounding walls and flooring lest I be swallowed up by some crevice. The dark gave me such a feeling of being smothered that I pulled down the mask I had assumed against the stench. Luckily here I found that the odor was much less and continued to disappear the farther I advanced.

As I went I listened for any sound which might be that of a rat that had managed to reach that point, but my own breathing, the muffled thud of my boots against rock, and the swish of my staff were all which reached my ears.

I have no idea of how long that shaftway into the rocky heart of the isle was, though I tried to count strides. To me, in the present case, it seemed to reach forever.

Then, as suddenly as I had come into this thick and stifling dark, so did light break upon and about me.

Here was a circular room but its rock walls were utterly unlike anything I had seen before. They were veined with glittering riverlets of gold, silver, copper. And those riverlets were on the move, twisting and turning, sometimes slowly, sometimes racing, always giving off a light as vivid as a score of lamps.

In the exact center of the chamber was a pedestal, as wide as Ravinga's work table, and on that rested a great ball—clear as glass.

Within it floated, or raced in their turn, motes of vivid color. Those, as light as air, were ever in motion, to form colonies for an instant and then break apart again into separate strings and whirls. Once seen, it held one's eyes, kept one's full attention.

Until something behind it moved. There arose to overshadow that globe and its dancing motes a leopard—not the blue of that imperial symbol—but rather as black of fur as that passage which had brought me here. And it was larger than any leopard I had ever seen, even larger than a Sand Cat.

One giant paw, claws extended in warning, arose to flatten on the top of the globe. The ears tightened against the skull and the lips a-snarl showed fangs which glistened of their own accord as if coated with diamond dust.

"Thief!"

Even as I could understand the Sand Cats, so did that throat rumble make sense for me.

"Not so," I struggled as always to produce the proper sounds with my ill-fashioned human lips and throat.

I laid my staff on the rock floor and did as I would with a stranger of my own species—holding out my hands, palms up and empty, in a sign of peace. My sleeve had been nicked back and the scars of my blooding among the Sand Cats showed.

The leopard eyed me from head to foot and back again.

"Smoothskin—what you—what you do?"

"I seek the rulership—to lead my kin—"

"You are not of the blood—yet you speak—" His ears went up, but his giant paw still embraced the globe.

I reached within my clothing and pulled out that which I had worn secretly while with those who brought me to this shrine—the cat mask pendant. Like the vivid color lines in the walls, that flashed brightly.

The great eyes of the leopard turned upon that.

"I dance with the furred ones," I said slowly. "I wear this, and this." I held forth my wrist still farther that the tooth-carved band might be seen. "I go not armed against the kin." It was difficult to shape throat speech, and how well the guard beast understood I could not tell.

He watched me still, but I thought no longer as he might possible prey. Then he drew back, lifting his paw from the globe. I had been given no instruction as to what I must do in this hidden place to prove my "worthiness" but it seemed that the Essence had its ways of guidance.

I stepped over my staff, moved forward to the pedestal. Reaching out with my hands, though I did not will that gesture myself, I put them palm down against the sides of the globe.

Those spots of color within were set in frantic motion. Patches collected to form the shape of my hands within as if they were inner shadows. The cool surface of the globe began to warm. The more that the colored patches thickened, the more that heat increased.

Now it was as if I had laid my hands against sun-warmed rock at mid-day, then as if skin and bone were thrust into a fire. The skin itself became transparent and I could see the bones through it.

Fire, I was afire and still I could not loose my grasp of the globe. Nor was I aware of anything about me now, nor saw anything but my two transparent hands with the shifting colors in the globe.

This was like the torment which had been forced upon me when Maraya had given me the wound to make me free of her kinship. What would be the consequence of *this?*

I thought that I could summon no more strength within me to counter that pain which ate through my body. Yet somehow I held fast.

It was some time before I realized that that pain was growing less, receding. No longer could I see my bones through the skin. The motes within were breaking up their concentrations, whirling back into a dance—forming lines and blots which looked almost like the words of some very ancient records. I had a feeling that if I could only make a fraction more effort, I could understand what was to be read there.

However, the last of the energy had been leached from me by pain. I dropped to my knees, my hands slid loosely down the globe sides to hang limp. My breath came hard as might that of a man who had made a mighty run or pulled himself up a high cliff.

The play of lights in the globe still held my eyes, though there was a flickering now which might even mean that they knew exhaustion, too. What was the meaning of this test I did not know. Nor could I even be sure of how well I had acquitted myself.

With an effort I broke eye connection with the globe to look for its guardian. There was no leopard there. A little wildly I turned my head from side to side seeking the beast. His black form was nowhere in that chamber. He might have been a dream save that I was very sure he was not.

I settled back and lifted my hands. By the rights of what I had endured they should have been charred and useless stumps. However, those I saw were normal. Then I turned them palm up. In the shallow cup of flesh at mid-point there was a dark spot. My head still was unsteadied by pain and I had a hard time focusing my sight on those spots.

The skin was not truly charred—as the color of those spots indicated. Rather I now bore on both hands a branding—the head of a leopard to resemble the guardian of this place.

Gingerly I touched the brand on my right hand with the fingers of my left. There was no pain; rather the flesh there felt hard as if I had a thick callus won through demanding labor.

Within the globe the motes had formed a single line, coiling from the base to the top. They moved no more, resting frozen in that loose pattern.

I got to my feet. It seemed to me that the lines upon the chamber walls were dimming. The belief grew in me that whatever I had come for in that testing was now a part of me—a part which I would always wear.

When I stooped for my staff I felt as tired as if I had ventured a whole night's journey on foot, and that at a goodly pace.

With my mask once more in place I again entered the thick dark of that corridor to the outer world. In spite of my weariness I felt something else, a small spark of confidence, almost a flare of pride. I had faced the testing of my own land and I was alive and free. One of the trials was behind me.

There were the first heralds of the sunrise in the sky when I came out between the legs of the cat. In this better light the horror of devastation was more fully revealed. I wanted nothing but to be out of the stink, away from the threat of poison.

My weariness, however, was with me still. Even by the aid of the rope it was difficult to gain the heights above the befouled pool. One of the rocks uncoiled proving to be Murri, his fur so much the color of the land about us that he was hidden until he moved. He came to me in a bound and licked the hands I held out to him, the rasp of his tongue moving over those imprinted palms which I was now sure I would wear until I was absorbed by the Last Essence.

"Good—" he told me. "Kin brother—great fighter?"

"Not yet—" I sat down beside my pack. "There will be more—"

"Kin brother do, do as easily as oryxen kill," he assured me.

I was too tired to protest. My exultation had faded. All I wanted was rest and I pulled back into the shadows of a rock spur which was nearly wide enough to be a cave and there fell almost instantly asleep.

I dreamed—but this was a dream which had no problems— nor did I see Ravinga. Rather I roamed the land freely, with no burden of duty laid upon me. Murri bounded at my side and there was a sense that this world was ours together and always would be. The feeling of well-being which that gave me carried over into waking.

The sun rays were already in the west. There was an ache in my middle which I recognized, after an eye blink or two, as hunger. The dried cakes of algae in my pack had little taste, but I chewed them slowly, dividing that Murri might have his share.

I did not want to return to the camp of my escort, yet once more the pattern of duty held me fast.

I found them waiting—Murri had disappeared discreetly before the sentry challenged. When I came into the direct firelight, the Chancellor of Kahulawe stood waiting me. There was no lighting of countenance in greeting, and once more the old soreness of being one not counted as profit to House or clan haunted me.

Not speaking, I rammed my staff point down into the earth and held out my hands so that she and those hard-faced guards behind her could see the signs I now bore.

"So be it." No congratulation in her voice, only a murmur from those gathered there. I wondered, first dully and then with growing anger, if they had been willing for me to fail and that my success was only to be recognized grudgingly.

So be it, my mind answered that thought. Now there was born a determination in me—I would no longer be swept into this by custom, an unwilling participant in this time of trials—rather there *would* come a day when I would reach for the crown and my hands would close upon it! These who still looked upon me as nothing—they would learn!

We were five nights of travel away from the border of the land where my next ordeal waited. But only one day were we in open camp. Instead we were given hospitality by various House-clans, and the last night we approached the isle owned by one of my out-kin—the sister of my father.

She was older than he and even in my childhood I had counted her ancient and kept away from her, for her sharp remarks and piercing looks always weighed and discarded me, or so I thought. But as we came to her guesting house at sunrise, one of her serving maids waited with the message that I was to come to her.

Though I had no robe of presence to wear, being less well clad than her servants, still I was enough in awe of her to answer that summons after I had done no more than clean the sand dust of travel from my face and hands.

The woman I had remembered as majestic as our Queen in her person sat now in a pillowed chair. At her feet was a grey-furred kotti—its color the same as that of my hostess, for not only had her hair dulled to the color of fas-sand but her skin had paled. Still there was the same vibrant life in the eyes she turned upon me.

"So, Hynkkel, you come as a stranger—after all these years. Also you come as one who attempts much."

Those were statements which needed no answers. I had only murmured the conventional greeting before she had spoken. Now she leaned forward a little among her cushions. Out of the dusk behind her quickly moved a maid with a cup she held ready for her mistress. The clawlike fingers of my aunt curled about that and to my deep astonishment she held it forward in a gesture which meant I must accept it.

Never had I been offered the guesting cup which was the greeting between equals. That she should do this now—

Part of me wanted to put my hands behind me and refuse to accept what had never been so offered before. Another and stronger part took the offered goblet.

"To the House, the clan, to she who rules here, may all good fortune come. May the Essence of all be hers—" I said.

As I took the ceremonial sip and returned the cup to her, she accepted it with one hand, but her other shot forward. Those claw fingers braceleted my wrist, turned up my hand so that the marks the globe had set upon me could be clearly seen.

"To he who comes with the favor of the Essence." Still holding my hand in that grip, she drank from the cup which the maid then took from her. Now she peered up at me.

"Judgment may be made too quickly at times," she observed. "You are far more than you have ever been thought to be, brother's son. May you prosper in days to come."

Her eyes fell from my face to the mark on my palm and then she ran her fingers over the scar which I wore as a bracelet.

For a very long moment she stared at that. The kotti at her feet suddenly reared as if some morsel of food was dangled just out of its reach. I saw that her tongue tip ran across her lips.

"You have danced, you have sung." There was a note of awe in her voice. "So it has not been with any for ten generations, and never with one of our House. Truly you have a strange path to follow."

I asked then:

"Have others known the Great Cats?"

She nodded. "There are tales. But who can sift the truth in such ancient matters? Go you, brother's son, to your destiny, and may it be that of the Old Ones long before you."

She sank back again in her nest of cushions and her maid came forward hurriedly, raising a hand as imperious as her mistress's to wave me out.

However, I was left a new thought to chew upon. So one of my own blood knew of the Sand Cats, and said that in the past others had also danced under the stars and watched the great beasts actually take to the air, and heard them raise their voices in song. Yet never in all my life had I ever heard of such a thing until it happened to me. Ravinga's half revelations, which had certainly never gone far enough, returned to my mind. Her belief that I was part of a pattern—What I truly wanted was the freedom I had dreamed of.

I was ready to go on the next night, impatient to do so. For it seemed to me that the farther I traveled into this maze before me, the quicker I might learn of why it was so.

When we came to the border we met with another company. There rode the guards of Thnossis and with them one of the candidates, he whose homeland it was. We had no speech with one another but the very fact that we had met was assurance that he had completed his task and was eager for the next.

Thnossis was a land of raw violence, or so it seemed to me after the quiet of our own sand desert and rock islets. There were rocks here also but they were tortured into grotesque shapes, uplands showing against the sky before us where trails of smoke twisted from the tips of certain heights. This was where there was no peace. The inner fires of our world were still alive and now and then broke forth to send waves of sluggish streams of molten rock wending down their sides. The sky was overcast and the sun was overveiled in haze, while the air one breathed carried with it the stuff of chemicals which led to fierce coughing.

The people of Thnossis had long ago mastered both the use of these sullen undying fires and the metals found in the mountains wherein the earth fires lay. Their work was such as no other race could equal. My own staff with its skillfully planted deadly edges had been cast here. And those ingots of gold, silver, and copper upon which Kura depended for her fine work with gems had been mined and melded within the hills ahead.

Truly it was a harsh land and those who lived there were a rough-and-ready people, far more aggressive than my own kin.

There was far less ceremony practiced among them and I knew that a man was judged here for strength and courage above all else.

We were three days reaching the foothills of the mountains. I found it difficult to slip outside the camp with food for Murri and it seemed to me that the cat was growing gaunt and finding this trail a hard one. We had come to rocks underfoot and these chafed my boots. How much worse were they for Murri's pads? Yet when I suggested that he stay behind he violently refused—as if he, too, were being put to some test he must face.

At length we camped in the upper foothills below one of the mountains which coughed forth smoke. There awaited us the Chancellor of this realm and his private guard. He was harsh of feature and there was little in him to suggest that he in any way wished me well.

The mountain before me was my path forward and near its summit was all which remained of a very ancient shrine to the fire essence. Twice had flows of lava near overwhelmed it and the way to it was now menaced by fire holes and crevices from which came gusts of the stifling fumes.

I was allowed, however, the equipment of their own miner-explorers—the prospectors for new source of ores and gems. So I changed into far more sturdy boots, and into outer clothing, a hood lying over the shoulders ready to be drawn into place as a guard against inhaling the worst of the exudations of the country. One of their master miners instructed me briefly in the proper way to cross the more menacing sections of the trail. And I knew what I was to do—the threatened shrine held a series of cat figures, each carved from a single great ruby—one such I was to pry loose and bring back.

Though I was equipped as well as any who dared the climb could be, the same was not true of Murri and when he joined me after I had put a ridge between me and the camp, I pointed out that this climb was not for him.

"Not so," he rumbled in return. "Kin have come into Thnossis. There are fire lizards—good eating—" His tongue whipped across his whiskers.

Older and more traveled Sand Cats might well have dared to hunt here but Murri had no experience and I was worried, though I was sure there was nothing I could do which would turn him from his chosen course.

So we started up the trail which had been shown to me. The rock was not only sharp-edged but in places brittle. I was near to death once when a great puff of yellow smoke burst upward from a crevice near to. I jerked the hood over my head just in time.

Murri! I peered through the eyeholes in the hood, sure that I must see him overcome. But he was well ahead. He had lengthened stride to bounds, nearly as high and as lengthy as those I had seen in the dance. And he appeared to have an almost uncanny ability to avoid all the dangerous crevices and the fire holes.

Twice I had to make detours around those. The heat gathered inside the clothing I wore; it was almost as if I were traveling now under the full sun of mid-day. At times I had to stand still for a breath or two to fight giddiness. I felt sick also and wondered if the fumes had somehow found their way inside my protections.

I marveled that these of Thnossis accepted such venturing as an everyday way of life. At last I came to a place where the paths appeared to be wiped out by an emergence of wide crevice from which curled the deadly fumes. However, those did not hide the form of Murri as he was airborne in a great leap which carried him forward through that deadly haze. Though my protective clothing was heavy upon me I could see that I must follow the Sand Cat's lead.

Edging back, my attention all for the spot where Murri had taken off, I then ran forward once more and jumped, not daring to think at the moment of what lay below. I sprawled on solid rock, sliding along as if my suit was a slick blob of algae.

Murri turned his head to look at me and I saw what nature had given my companion in the way of defense in this land of ever-churning flames. Those great eyes were narrowed into slits, and there appeared to be skin flaps masking the nostrils in his wide muzzle. It would seem that Murri and his kind *were* equipped to hunt here.

He was already on his way upward again. I chose to follow his path with care. There were no more leaps over runnels and at last I saw, through a haze of throat-rasping cloud, what must be our goal.

It was a squat building, one end of which teetered on the very edge of a drop into a much wider river of slow-moving lava. Sooner or later it must be engulfed by that but there was still part of a doorway showing.

A doorway—rather a hole meant for one of the lizards Murri had mentioned. To enter there a man must go on hands and knees and there was no other sign of door—I thought of being caught within if the whole would sink into the rock flow.

Murri crouched flat and inched forward toward that portal as if he were a-hunt. I went down on all fours reluctantly, knowing I could do no less.

So I squeezed into a room. It was dark, for none of the mountain fire penetrated these walls. I felt the nudge of Murri's shoulder and reached out a hand which struck painfully against the wall.

Then that small point of light which was a fixture of my hood was triggered and I could see a little. Underfoot was a mass of stone and what appeared to be shattered glass but which glittered brighter than I believed glass could.

23

This broken mass was a barrier between me and a shelf along one wall. On this sat three figures of cats. There had been more as the jagged remains showed but some catastrophe (or perhaps malice) had struck. Of the three remaining all were at the far side of the room. They must be over that portion of the structure which hung above the river of lava.

The shards on the floor were a threat to even the stout mining boots which had been supplied to me. Murri had edged back by the door. It was plain that here he dared not risk his pads to such a menace.

In the very limited light I tried to pick a way which offered the least threat. The stuff crunched underfoot and splintered ends scored my boots. I won to the shelf. Now I had to venture to the left along it to lay hands on the first of the figures.

The cat was about the length of my forearm in height and when I tried to lift it I discovered that it was firmly affixed to the rock under it, almost as if it were an extension of that. Since it would not come free from its upright position I attempted to turn it around as one might unscrew it. But it remained adamantly in place.

I carried no tools with me which I could use as a lever. So I crouched lower to search among the debris on the floor for something I could employ so. Now I thought I could understand the shattered fragments. They must be results of other battles in this place.

Murri moved and I glanced quickly to him.

"Wait—" Even through the wrappings of my hood I caught that word.

His head went down; he had extended his claws and was worrying away with his teeth at one of them. I had often seen the kottis do so, shedding the outer covering of a too-long claw to give that new growing more room. So did it happen with Murri. He spat forth a curved length of old claw perhaps as long as my hand.

My fingers in the protecting gloves were too clumsy. I shook off a glove and picked up that claw. This, too, if it were like those discarded by the kottis, would be brittle. I was not sure of what use it would be but I could try.

I edged back to the shelf and examined with desperate care the base of the figure. It met the stone so tightly I could not see even the mark of a crack—though I was sure it was *not* an outgrowth of the shelf itself. I remembered that there had already been one successful candidate here—I had seen him at the border of my own land. Thus what I attempted could be done.

With the point of the claw I drew a line completely around the figure, making sure it met the juncture of rock and gem. There did not show even a scratch to mark my efforts. Then, drawing a deep breath, I dared to force the claw between one of the foot paws and the shelf.

There was movement! I exerted more pressure, this time at the other paw. Finally I had gone completely around the base of the figure. With the care my sister would have shown in the intricate setting of a gem, I grasped the ruby cat with both hands and slowly turned it—there was no result as I tried it to the right, now I reversed and tried it to the left.

It gave grudgingly as I did it, only a fraction at a time. Yet it moved. Still, though it would turn on the base I could not raise it. I was panting now, my breath coming in gasps. This end of the room was hot—The cumbersome suit which was my protection weighed on me, and my shoulders ached with the effort of trying in so delicate a fashion to achieve my ends.

One felt the desire to jerk, perhaps so to destroy utterly the figure. Impatience had to be contained, subdued.

Again I inserted the claw and held it in place while I turned the figure slowly. It was tipping when it met that obstruction. Suddenly opposition gave and I nearly lost my balance, staggering backward, crunching over the debris, but with the red cat in my hands.

When I turned I saw that Murri was gone, and I knew a thrust of fear. Had this venture proven too much for the Sand Cat, even though he had boasted that his people came to hunt here?

Cradling the figure against me I got out of the door, crawling at the best speed I knew until I was able to stand. There was a fountaining of fire not too far away. The noxious haze was thick and I realized that I could not mark the path by which I had come. I had relied too much on Murri's leadership and had not memorized any portion which might now prove a landmark.

To my right, I could see only in small wisps of time as the smoke and haze eddied, the land appeared to slant downward. I had climbed to reach this place, so it was only reasonable that I must now descend.

In spite of the fumes and heat, I dared to unfasten my miner's garment and place inside the cat for the best safe-keeping I could devise. Then I began to edge downward.

It required constant alert inspection of the way ahead to avoid dangerously ridged rock which might trip even the most careful, or the flame- and smoke-emitting potholes. My legs trembled, not only from the strain of the climb and this descent but from my inner fear of taking the wrong step. Also I looked for Murri—

Had the Great Cat been overcome? If so how might I carry him down? Though he was far from being as large as his sire, yet he was a burden I was sure I could not bear.

I dared to halt, to raise the edge of my hood, and I cried aloud:

"Murri?"

There was movement through the haze which was not a fountain of fire. I turned in that direction. My furred companion stood there, his head dropping forward, his huge body trembling visibly. I reached his side and laced my fingers in the stiff ruff of fur at his neck. His head came up a fraction, turned. I saw that his great eyes were fully shut.

"No see—"

There was panic in those two words and that panic fueled true fear in me. Had the fumes blinded Murri? How would we find our way down? That I would part company with him now was impossible.

I pulled at his ruff and he came with me step by staggering step. Meanwhile I tried steadily to tell him what lay before us. It was not until we got to the chasm which he had leaped before that I faced the fact there might be that I could not do for Murri.

"Go—call—many times call—"

Such a hope was impossible. He nudged me with his head.

"Go—call—" Then he coughed heavily.

"You cannot—"

"Go—call!" This time he showed his fangs at me and his words ended in a snarl.

In the end I went, thinking that perhaps this was the only chance for both of us.

I found what seemed to be the best place for a takeoff—the opposite side I could see now and then through the haze which was less heavy here. So I leaped and was flung forward on the rock at the other side, though I had wrapped both arms about the treasure that I bore, lest it be crushed. By some miracle it was not. Then I moved back a fraction from where I had landed and I loosed my hood again and called and kept on calling "Murri!"

He came, though he did not land well, his hind legs slipping over the edge of the crevice. I grabbed frantically for his ruff, twisting both hands in that and jerking him towards me.

That was the last major barrier that it was needful for us to transverse. I could pick a way around the other traps and bring Murri with me. Then we reached the last of the downslopes. Between us and the camp there was still the ridge. Murri—I could not leave him so and yet those encamped beyond would meet him with steel.

The time had come that Murri must be accepted as my companion. Surely my own position as candidate would give weight to my demand that he be tended. That I had been selected by the Blue Leopard for this round of journeying and life risk must have made some impression on my escort, little as those who formed it appeared to esteem me.

Murri offered no objection as I led him on by my grip upon his ruff. In me the fear that he was blind for all time hardened. To such as the Sand Cats this would be far worse than any death. Yet it was our custom—as I had done for Bialle—to release to the Greater Essence those who suffered past hope.

Though I had never been called upon to grant such escape to any of my own kind, I knew that that was also done upon occasion, and in this instance, were I as Murri, I would have welcomed the mercy knife quickly.

Still there was a chance. No one would venture into this land of fire and poisonous vapors without some manner of relief for burns and the like. I held to the hope that those who had brought me hither knew of such.

We ascended the ridge and paused there for a moment. I had thrown back that hood which had curtailed my full sight and now I looked carefully at Murri. His eyes were still closed and there appeared to be a yellow crust forming along the edges of the lids.

"You hurt—brother?" I asked.

"No pain—now." He held his head high as if he could see and I noted that those nostril flaps had folded away and that he was sniffing the air.

"They wait—" he rumbled.

That I could well see. Those I had left in camp were drawing in to the foot of the ridge. Two of them held bows with arrows nocked. And they were eyeing Murri.

I tightened my grip on the Sand Cat's ruff and moved so that any taking aim would find a target in me instead.

"This one is not for the killing!" I raised my voice in a shout to carry above the rumble of the tormented mountain behind me. "This one is under my protection."

Did that statement mean anything? I could not be sure. However, he who led the company of warriors made a gesture and the bowmen lowered their weapons.

We went together down the slope. Lucky here the footing was smooth enough and Murri, though he could not see, confidently set paws in places which kept him steady. Then we were on as level ground as this place offered.

I halted only a sword's distance from those staring at me. Thrusting my hand inside the protective suit, I brought out the ruby cat and, when the Chancellor made no attempt to take it from me, I set it on the ground.

"You have aids for wounds," I said. "Give me such. I have fulfilled your task, therefore you of Thnossis have no more power over me."

The Chancellor gestured, and one of his guard picked up the ruby cat, yet there was bared steel still before us and they looked to Murri as if they expected an instant charge.

I held forth my wrist, pulling back the sleeve to display the ring of the tooth scar. "This one is blood brother, after the rules which all warriors know. I bear the mark of it. Give me that which I can use now for my brother's easement."

There were two points I held fast in mind—first, that the persons of the candidates were to be guarded between their times of testing and what they asked for in the way of aid during their travels must be given them. Second—blood brothership through the exchange of vital fluid was not uncommon among warriors. And, while I could not be counted such in their eyes, certainly no one could deny that Murri was of noted fighting stock.

Now I acted as if this was only the proper thing to be done. Moving forward, my hand still to guide Murri, they did give way before me without question, though the Chancellor and several of the guard looked bleak enough.

However, I brought the Sand Cat into the camp and I was supplied with a bag borne by him who was delegated to be the healer, though he only laid his supplies on the ground and stepped back, giving me no assistance. I could only act for Murri as I had many times in the past for herd beasts and kottis. There was a tightly closed jar which held some paste and that I recognized, by its odor, to be a prime remedy for wounds.

Whether it would react on the Sand Cat's eyes I could not tell, I could only try.

Scooping out a finger end full of the paste, I spread it across each of those yellow-crusted eyelids. Then I caught up one of the squares of soft woven stuff from a neighboring packet and began, with the lightest touch I could hold my fingers to, to work at the edges of that encrustation. The stuff came off in small flakes which must be carefully cleared away lest they work into the eyes themselves and it was not an easy business. But, at last, I had rid Murri's eyelids of the last bit.

The Sand Cat did not open his eyes as yet. I scrabbled among the contents of the medical packet until I had found a package which was squashy to the touch and from which I could pinch out bits of water-soaked algae. With these I washed the lids twice over and then sat back on my heels, a fear still in me. Could Murri see? If my ministrations had done nothing—!

"Brother," I worked with lips and tongue to form my command, "look!"

Those eyes opened. To my sight they were as ever, round yellow gems, with only the thread of darkness in their centermost point to suggest that they were not the stone they resembled.

Twice Murri blinked. He raised one paw as if to wash his face, but did not quite touch his muzzle.

"See—little—"

Since I could not look through those threatened eyes I had no idea of limitation or whether that would be permanent. I squeezed out more of the wet paste and smeared it on another length of cloth, this longer, plainly meant to be a bandage. Murri had already closed his eyes again and I tied that as firmly as I could so that the soothing stuff was in place.

It was then that I took off the suit which had been given me. Glad to see the last of it. I wore only the breeches of my trail garb, while on my chest swung the cat mask pendant.

There was a stir behind me. One of the Chancellor's servants had brought my other clothing, but he laid it down some distance away and I saw that the company who had come with me ringed me around, watching. The archers had set aside their bows, and swords had been sheathed, but I could feel their watchful eyes, sense strongly their unease not only for Murri within their camp, handicapped as he was, but also for me since I had claimed blood kinship with their ancient enemy.

When I had pulled on the rest of my clothing I looked to the Chancellor.

"I have done what I was set to do, Ruler's Voice," I spoke formally. "Is this agreed?"

"It is agreed." His answer was short and he turned away, his leaving breaking that ring of spectators about me. I noticed that two of the sword bearers did not leave, though they kept their distance.

There was food and I divided my share with Murri before I guided him to the small tent which was my private quarters.

That night we slept together. In Thnossis travel was mainly by day, much of the terrain being too treacherous to try to cross except under the brightest of sunlight, punishing as that might be.

Sleep did not come easily. I could not share my doubts with Murri. He had curled up, bandaged head on forepaws, and was already asleep. If in the morning his sight was still gone—

I must be on my way to Azhengir, that perilous waste of desolate salt pans, perhaps to all save those who lived there the cruelest of countries. No Sand Cat could venture there. No beast could, except the ever-present rats. I dared not take Murri, for I was sure I could not trust those with me to help the cat were I to fail. Nor could I leave him blind and helpless here. It would all depend on how well the remedies would work.

My own body was aching from exertion, and sleep came upon me in spite of the thoughts teeming in my mind, the worries which besieged me.

There was light, not the hard striking rays of the sun. Lamplight—soft and glowing, somehow soothing after my ordeal with the fires of the mountain. I stood on a floor of

polished wood nor could I move. Then hands came from overhead, reaching plainly into the beams of the lamp, hands large
enough to grasp my whole body.

They held an object which had the golden fluff of fur as
they set beside me Murri. There was no bandage across his
eyes, they were alive with the glow I had always seen. Yet
when he was placed there he did not move. He might have
been a figure such as the ruby cat I had worried out of its
setting upmountain.

The hands now rested on the flooring a little before me
and I studied them. Each finger bore a ring which was wide
enough around to serve me as a belt. And each of those rings
was of a different design. They had been fashioned to resemble heads, a man with a warrior's wig, a woman with an
ornate crown, an oryxen with wicked horns which gleamed
silver bright, a yaksen, a kotti curled at ease, its supple body
forming much of the band of the ring. Those were on one
hand. On the other there was clearly wrought a setting akin
to the cat mask I wore, beside that a second crowned woman,
then something which was not a head or face but an intri-
cately entwined symbol, next a dagger fashioned so that it
extended up and down the finger beyond the bounds of the
ring band, and, last of all, what could only be the representation of a rolled scroll of high learning, the kind which each
family guarded in their archives.

For a space those hands lay at rest and then they arose a
little and the fingers moved, not joining together but as if each
were fastened to a strand which must be woven back and forth.
Then darkness enfolded me and beyond that light, the sounds
of the camp awakening, drumbeats still troubling the air.

Murri sat at the entrance of our small tent. His bandage
was in place. But he turned his head a little.

"This one would see—"

If you only can, I thought, but did not speak that aloud.
Instead I tugged at the fastening and the strip of cloth fell
away. To me his eyes looked normal once again but that he
could actually see—

Murri held one of those lengthy stares which were of his kind and then a sound like a great sigh came from him.

"This one sees!"

I threw my arms about his shoulders and for a moment buried my face in his ruff. Far greater than any bringing back of ruby cats out of places besieged by fire was this!

"This one goes. Here is no welcome—" Murri arose to his feet and stretched as any of his species arising from sleep.

What he spoke was the truth. But how complete was the cure? Was it only temporary and he would go forth from this camp to be again stricken where there would be no aid? I had no time to voice any protest, he spoke again:

"This one—no go—salt place."

"If you—your eyes—"

"We meet again—after salt place."

He was already out of the tent. People were stirring within the camp but he took two great leaps which brought him to the outer limits. My last sight of him was his flying in the air—or so it would seem to those who do not know his kind—out and away. From his direct line of flight I knew that he could see and I must hold the hope in my mind that that was permanent.

For six days we crossed this world of unstable land and fire-breathing mountains. As usual my guards exchanged few words, and only those of necessity, with me. However, to my surprise on that first morning after the withdrawal of Murri, the Chancellor reined in his oryxen to match the pace of mine and addressed me:

"Blood kin to cats," he began abruptly. "And how did you win such a distinction?"

There was little formality in his speech. The words were more an order, though I felt resentment and I schooled myself not to show it. After all he who advised the Queen of Thnossis perhaps had reason to so weigh me as less.

I told my story in as few words as possible and it came curtly enough. He listened, I saw, with the same care he might give to some report of importance.

At the end I turned my wrist for him again to view that scar which was my key to the councils of those who had been so long the enemy.

He was frowning a little when I had finished. "That might he a bard tale," he commented, "save that you have shown us what you can do. Strange indeed, for between our kind and the Great Cats there has always been war."

"Always?" I was remembering then the half legends Ravinga had spoken of—of a time when man and Sand Cat had been fellow warriors against some great but now forgotten ill.

His frown grew deeper. "You speak of things which are not for all ears." He sent his oryxen forward, leaving me once more to speculate upon what seemed to be an unseen web which had somehow gripped me fast.

Nor did he speak to me again. On the fifth day we came to the border of Azhengir and saw there the guard and Chancellor of that land waiting. But this time there was no lucky candidate in their midst and I could guess at a failure, how disastrous a one I did not yet know.

24

We are all deeply akin to the lands of our birth. The essence ́ of that enters into us so that no other place can mean so much. I had faced the threats of the fire-ridden Thnossis yet that in its way had not seemed as fearsome as did Azhengir, into which I now passed.

There were no insects in the slickrock country, nor had I suffered from the attentions of such in either Vapala or Thnossis. But here the salt pans sent up winds of them against all comers. They bit, they crawled across any exposed skin, they sought out the corners of eyes and mouth until their assaults were maddening.

Also, in some way the very Essence here was repelling. I felt that, following each stage of our journey into Azhengir, there grew stronger the feeling that I was an intruder to be routed, that the desolate world about me would spew me forth.

Yet to the guard who had met me at the border this land was a way of life, barren and hard as that might be.

The salt pans were in themselves traps. Azhengir's one export was salt but that could not easily be dredged from the pans, as its collection was a thing of peril. There were thermal pools within the pans and those grew no algae, or if a few plants made rooting there they were not of any use—either for eating or the soothing of any body hurt.

However, those of Azhengir planted in these scattered pools branched rods which resembled those of the trees of Vapala. Upon those branches there gathered in the course of time clear crystals of salt. These were the harvest which brought the trade to supply those who gathered such crops with the bare necessities of life.

However, to plant those bushes and then reclaim them with their fruit was a perilous undertaking. The harvesters were equipped with long rods of their own to sound out a path ahead, as the scumlike surface hid sucker ponds which could draw into a speedy death any who broke their crust.

Nor could they depend upon landmarks to set a clear trail to any pond no matter how many times they made that journey. For the undercrust traps moved and changed in thickness. Thus each trip to the harvest was a test of skill in judgment, as well as a matter of sheer fortune.

On the fourth day after we had crossed the border we entered one of the small villages which was anchored firmly by the same rock ridge which formed the only road.

It was a squalid place, the buildings hardly more than huts, and, as far as I could see, no attempt had ever been made to ornament any of them. No guardian cat statues stood beside doorways, not even that of the largest hovel in which the chief of this village sheltered. No color relieved the dirty grey of the walls, no banner, save a large pole encrystaled with salt deposit, stood before that place of rulership.

The people turned out to greet us. Though I fought off insect clouds, those of the salt lands did not seem to mind when such crawled over them, raising a hand only now and then to drive away some more persistent attacker. The natives were dark of skin but it was not a ruddy darkness such as I myself show, or that possessed by the miners and metal workers of Thnossis. Rather this appeared to have an overshadowing of grey which was as repelling as their homes and echoed the lank locks of hair which hung about their gaunt faces. No one tied back those straying strands with any band, nor did their women wear the bright metal combs and catches I was used to. In fact there was very little metal in sight.

They watched us without expression and, as I slid out of the saddle, I knew that they were mainly eyeing me. Then he, as gaunt and colorless as all the rest, who stood before the chief hut beckoned, making no move to step forward. It was as if in this place even the courtesy of guesting was unknown.

So I was led into the presence of Dar-For-It, Voice for the village. He was very old, a veritable skeleton figure crouched on a stool within the hut. One of his eyes was filmed as grey-white as his straggle of hair.

Behind him was a gathering of what must be his personal guard, though the only weapons they carried (if weapons those were) were long rods, the tips of which reached well above their unkempt heads. There were both men and women there, the Heads of various Houses, I judged. Yet none were better arrayed than the crowd of commoners without.

In the center of the chamber was a fire which was hardly more than a ruddy handful of coals. Over that, supported on a tripod of legs, was a bowl of discolored metal from which a lazy curl of smoke arose.

"You have come a long way to die." The greeting certainly was not in any way one to encourage. "He who was first here was of our kind and yet he is now gone."

There did not seem to be any answer to that.

The old man stared up at me through his fringe of hair. "It is only right that he who would wear the Great Crown must first share life with those to be governed, say you not also?"

"Yes," I made short answer. All knew the purpose of these tests—that the Emperor-to-be must know the life of others.

The chief nodded. Then he lifted a hand. Those who had stood behind him spread out, some of them circling behind me. I did not like the feeling which came with that encirclement. Again the chief signaled.

One of the others, a woman who looked as old as he and wore the first ornament (if you could call it such) that I had seen—a necklace of what could only be rat teeth threaded together with beads of salt—knelt by that slowly simmering basin and dipped into it a misshapen cup which, brimming with a sickly greenish liquid when she brought it forth, I saw to be an oversized rat skull.

"If you would be one of us—a harvester," the chief said, "then you will prepare even as we do to try the ever-changing trail. Drink, outlander!" The last two words were uttered as a firm order—one against which no argument could be raised.

The stuff gave off a vile odor and I guessed it would have an even worse taste. However, I had no choice. Somehow I choked it down and then had to fight against nausea. To spew it up again—I was sure that was what they expected. I would not please them so much.

The nausea remained and with it came gnawing pain in my middle. Poison? No, I was sure that they would not dare to dispose of any candidate of the trial. The cup I had put down was taken up by the women, refilled twice, and given so to two of the others.

That answered in part my question. It must be a required ritual for those setting out into the pans.

Somehow I got out of the hut, fighting the revulsion which gripped my body. A rod was pressed into my hand and I summoned strength to grasp it.

With at least half the village as an escort we made our way down from the firmness of the ridge to the edge of the pan. The chief did not accompany us, but the seeress was very much to the fore and I saw her eyeing me with a grin of anticipation.

Those two men who had shared the potion with me were already moving out on the crust, their poles swinging before them, testing the way ahead. They were well away from the edge when they stopped and looked back, giving voice to a queer cry. The seeress was at my side now.

"Go, outlander. Our men have shown you the art of pan walking, it is now yours to do it also—there is a salt pool straight ahead, and the crystals there are well ripe for the gathering. We have kept it so for the testing. But to gain it you must watch where you tread."

My stomach still twisted with the drink. However, using the pole for sounding my path, I made a cautious way out on the crust. I could not take either path those other two had followed for they stood firmly in the way. I must prospect for my own trail.

I strove to center all my attention on my footing though the pain twisting in me, the clouds of insects which buzzed about, were hard to set aside. Twice my pole struck through the crust and I must stand on one spot of safety and cast on either side for secure footing.

At length I crept past where both of the others had halted and before me was only open pan. Neither of the experienced harvesters moved to accompany me. A cold bite of realization came: they would make no effort to rescue me if I chose wrong. From now on I had no one to depend upon but myself.

I did not look back. My attention was all for what was underfoot, or rather before foot. My shoulders began to ache at the constant swing of the pole in a short sweep from right to left before me. Once more the tip cut into a treacherous thin crust and this time I nearly overbalanced to follow. That I kept my feet was a sign of fortune I dared not hope might be mine again. I forced myself to a slower pace, tried with insect-attacked eyes to make sure that the next step was solid.

Before me at last opened the salt pool. From its surface projected the ends of those branched rods which were the collectors. I was heartened by so much and gained another step.

Now the swing of my pole proved that the way before me was a trap. I moved to one side at that first testing, thinking to approach from a different angle. Again the pole proved that could not be done. So I struggled on, trying to find a way in. There must be such, or how could the villagers reach their crop? Which now appeared a carefully guarded secret, one which was not to be shared with me. I leaned on the pole and studied the pool.

Those branches were planted around its edge. Apparently there was no way of working them out into the middle of that pond. The nearest? I might be able to touch it with the end of my pole if I exerted my strength and extended it so that my grasp was barely on the end. However, the smoothness of the pole was no use in snagging a branch which I was sure had been firmly planted.

My clothing was that of a wayfarer. And I had no rope such as I had taken with me on my solo. I did wear a belt, though that was heavy with ornamental metal medallions. Now I unlatched that strip of hide and began to pry loose those rounds of copper and gold so that it would not be weighted down. At length, my fingers sore and gashed from the effort, I had a length of oryxen hide which was more supple without its decoration.

What I faced now was the need for skill. Could I put into service some of the ability which I used with a sling?

I attached the belt in a loop to the end of my pole, bending two of the gold medallions which had decorated it about the ends, testing what I had done with vigorous jerks.

Then I cast for the nearest of those branches in the pond. Four times I made that throw, pausing between each to rest my shoulder, trying to control the shaking of my arms.

This could not continue forever. At the same time I must not allow need to push me into a frantic struggle which would not serve any purpose save to use strength I needed so badly.

I stood, panting, looking at that branch. It inclined the least fraction in my direction. Once my improvised noose had struck against it, but not encircled it.

Now I measured distances again and upended the pole, thudding it to my right once again. To my relief it struck a firm surface and I stepped sidewise. It seemed to me that I was indeed closer to that branch. I reversed the pole and made my cast.

The belt struck against the branch, encircled it, slid down as I dropped the pole little by little. Delicately I moved the staff in a circular direction, twisting, or trying to twist, the belt which had nearly sunk from sight in those side branches which were spaced along these salt catchers.

Drawing a deep breath, I dared to exert strength to a pull.

To my joy there was resistance! The belt was securely entangled. Now it remained to be seen whether that hold was enough to withstand a strong enough jerk to loosen the branch.

I pulled, there was no answer, but at least my belt did not lose hold. There was only one thing left. I had no idea how the salt gatherers plucked these out of the ponds, but they could not be set so deep that they did not come loose easily, for there was too much danger of overbalancing and perhaps ending in one of the crust-closed traps.

Putting both hands to the pole I dared all in a single sharp jerk. I slipped backward as the branch yielded suddenly. One foot went off the safe spot on which I stood. I fell to my knees, striving to throw my weight forward. With the crystal-beaded branch swinging over my head, I drove the other end of my support rod as deeply as I could into the secure footing and fought to draw myself towards that one hope of safe support.

For a moment I was afraid that I could never exert strength enough to draw myself to complete safety. Then I huddled at the foot of that planted rod, while over me swung the branch. For the first time I became aware that the day was near done.

Could I make my way back to the ridge land in twilight? I struggled to my feet, still holding on to the anchorage of my rod. Then I untangled the branch and, with my belt for a sling, slipped it onto my back. I edged around to face the direction from which I had come.

Those two salt gatherers who had flanked me when I had entered this morass were gone, but I could make out figures on the ridge. My legs trembled, not only with the reaction to the peril I had just escaped, but also from the strain I had known since I entered this place.

However, the coming night might leave me marooned here and that I could not allow. I would be no more ready to face return then, perhaps even less.

My rod swung out, prospecting for the next foothold, and I forced myself to the task of moving. Twice I again nearly lost my balance when the crust appeared to hold the rod and then it went through. My whole body ached with the effort I expended. The only small relief was that with the growth of twilight those ever-attacking insects were gone.

I kept my attention all for the next step, not for anything ahead, and then at last, when I was sure I could not travel farther, my rod thudded home hard enough to jar my whole body. I could not really believe that I had made it back until one of the salt gatherers confronted me and for the first time I saw a trace of emotion on his face.

He offered me a hand but I drew myself up and did not accept support. Rather I staggered up the rise to the main part of the ridge and there confronted the woman who wore the necklace of teeth and salt. It would appear that here she stood as judge. Swinging off my branch, I dropped it at her feet.

25

I was not the only outsider to shelter in the salt-gathering village that night. There was a merchant who had come through
the land which I was to transverse the next day. His complaints
sounded loudly from the chief's hut. He had been boldly attacked by rats, two of his yaksens had been brought down,
and he had been forced to retreat leaving behind the packs of
goods they carried. One of his men was under treatment, having had one arm mauled to the point that he might never recover from the wound.

However, the merchant had brought with him one of the
attackers, dead of a skillful spear cast, in order to prove his
point that this was no ordinary foe. Like those I had seen dead
after our encounters in the rock isles, this limp carcass which
had been dragged along after the merchant's oryxen was large—
in fact larger even than those others I had examined. It could
have equaled Murri in size, or even been a fraction the greater.

The villagers gathered around to inspect that trophy and it
was very plain that they were shaken out of that impassivity
which had welcomed me and my guard. I heard mutters which
told me that the like of this creature had been sighted before
and that one had slain an experienced salt gatherer, seeming
able to follow the man across the salt pans by some uncanny
knowledge of its own.

"There are enough of these vermin out there," the merchant declaimed as he came forth from the hut, still loud in
his complaints. "But these—they are such as could take a
whole trade party if they pushed attack. And what if they
do?" He turned slowly as if he would catch the eyes of all
those ringing him in. "Can any traveler stand up to such a
pack? Can your village stand against them? I tell you that

there is trouble brewing and you had best be prepared for more of this at your doors." He kicked at the carcass before he strode off.

However, at that moment I was more intent upon crawling into the center of my sleeping mat. My stomach still pained me and I had no desire to take my place by the cookfire of my escort. There was only this much in my mind—I had completed three of the five tests—and I realized that inwardly I had never thought that I could do so.

I was able to eat some breakfast the next morning. There was no explanation for the potion I had been forced to swallow—I could only believe that it had been done deliberately to make my task the more difficult and I felt far from kindly towards the village, very glad to see the last of it.

The guard rode at alert, a scout sent ahead. They were prepared for some such attack as the merchant had suffered. Still we made the six-day journey across this dreary and forbidding land without having to face any enemy. Twice we stayed in villages and I heard the officer who commanded my escort question the inhabitants closely about such attacks. The news he received was not encouraging.

That merchant who had brought proof of the nature of the enemy was not the first trader along the route who had been attacked. But the other had been far from lucky. A pair of villagers traveling along the ridge way had come across the remains of a small caravan where the stripped bones of both traders and their beasts were all which could be found. Even their packs had been gnawed open and the contents dispersed and befouled or missing.

It was the latter point which puzzled both villagers and guards the most. For it was plain that, while the rats had feasted on all food stuffs they had managed to find, why would they drag off trade goods? The accepted answer seemed to be that the scene of that battle must have been later visited by outlaws, who had made the most of their discovery. Though that any outlaw would be willing to linger in this land was more than I could understand. The villages certainly had little worth stealing, while their inhabitants, I was sure, had their own deadly methods of defense. Even I, who had little liking for them as a people, could agree to that.

As we approached the border of Twahihic a scout, sent ahead, reported that an escort was already waiting there and with a successful candidate in their care. We passed into that territory just at nightfall and for once the two parties camped together.

The attitude of the other escort towards their charge was far different from that I had met. And seeing him I believed I could understand the difference. This was Shank-ji. Instead of wearing drab trail garb he was decked out in the finery of a warrior in full dress. He laughed and talked animately with those who had ridden with him.

I wondered how he would survive the treacherous paths of the salt pans, the fiery roads of the mountain, and last of all how he would confront the leopard whose mark I would always bear.

Custom kept us apart. Perhaps it was thought that one might advise the other on the trials ahead, though I believe the rivalry which was strong among candidates would not have led to that. However, we did view each other from a distance. His contempt was plain to read, yet there was a shadow there of something else—perhaps a very angry surprise that such as I had lasted so long.

He might believe himself favored. The trial offered in Vapala was last, only to be made when all the survivors had assembled within the city. I knew that one other at least had been successful in several of the trials, and that another had failed and was probably dead. Which left three of us to be accounted for.

The guard feasted that night and Shank-ji was very much a part of the festivities. Several of those who had accompanied him were wagering he would be triumphant and they found no takers against him. I watched from a distance and finally sought my sleeping mat to lie looking up at the stars.

That I had no well-wisher suddenly seemed to me to be a hard thing. I had ridden from one land to the next with the guard sent by each Queen in turn, yet none of them had shown any friendship, nor given me any wish for fortune, or applause when I had accomplished my task. While Shank-ji, who had faced so far but one of the trials, acted as if he were already victor and also appeared to be accepted as such by his fellows.

I faced this self-pity, tried to open my mind to the Essence that it might wipe clear this feeling, which was weakening. Then I discovered that it was true what I had always heard of Twahihic. As the camp quieted down the haunting silence of the land closed in.

There was no whisper of sand—yet ahead were those mountainous dunes which the inhabitants had put to such good use. For the only purpose of this arid waste before me was to provide a play place for those of the other lands who were drawn here for sand-skimming races and the like. There were cities, each cupped within a bowl of green glass, cultivating within some the fruits which were only known elsewhere in Vapala. Each of the cities had its specialty in what it had to offer the visitor. There were contests of musicians, trained troupes of dancers, those who acted out some of the old legends of each land, as well as inns which specialized in fine foods, held gambling sessions in their top rooms. Here were women and men prepared to offer any entertainment which might be dreamed by those who came. Young people who vied with each other in the dangerous sport of dune skimming had their other desires catered to within the domed settlements.

However, now what I felt was a barrenness of spirit. Were there any here who sought out their private places and opened their minds and hearts to the Essence, waiting to be filled with that blessing which can be obtained only by long and diligent search? I felt nothing—it was as if a door had shut firmly between me and that sure knowledge of being one with the land, with all the life upon it.

We traveled on from that camp. Those of the escort who had been so cordial with Shank-ji kept aloof from me. We exchanged only the formalities necessary for everyday tasks. As I rode, the emptiness I had felt on the first night within the border here continued, wearing on my spirit in spite of all my battles against it.

I longed for Murri—had he indeed survived his ordeal on the mountain of fire? Was he again on the trail of our party? I began striving to somehow touch him, picturing him firmly in mind and then making the struggle to project my call.

On the second night I was answered!

"Brother-one—" It came very faint as if from afar.

"Murri!" There is a strength in names, perhaps that call of his would bring us closer.

"I—here—" his reply seemed to form in my mind. But where was "here"? I could not believe he might survive in this barren land of towering dunes, any more than he could have survived among the salt pans.

"I wait—"

Though I tried to reach him again there was no more. Wait—where—for what? Nor did I sleep well that night.

We pushed on until a four-day journey was behind us. Once we halted in one of the bubble villages. I dined as might the Emperor, slept soft, but still I was walled from all about me. Again I speculated whether this was not done with a purpose, that communication with any who might aid me in my set task was forbidden.

It was the second day after we left that luxurious stop that we were joined by the Chancellor of this queendom. She straightway summoned me, looking me up and down as if I were an oryxen of dubious value being offered her for sale and then she spoke sharply:

"Beyond those dunes," she indicated the towering mountains of sand to the left, "lies your task, man of Kahulawe. There is a village in which no one dwells, for an unseen evil lies within, and near all who attempt entrance disappear. Yet in its gardens grow malons.

"The nature of these fruits is that they must be watched with care for they ripen very suddenly. And they must be plucked when ripe, for otherwise, if left on the vine too long, they are as quickly taken by rot.

"He who would be judged by our land must enter into that shunned place, find two malons, and bring them forth untouched by any rot. Nor can anyone tell what other fate awaits there, but it is dire."

I could believe that she was striving to overawe me. Yet I knew that the peril of death *did* cling to each of the trials and there was undoubtedly some evil connected with the place.

She made no more move to direct me to the site of my testing. Nor did my escort. I strove to pass around the side of the dune in the direction she had pointed, wondering if these so feared what might lie within the shunned dome that they did not wish even to come into sight of it. Yet others—at least Shank-ji and the candidate who was of this queendom—had done this thing, and Shank-ji had plainly been successful.

I twirled my staff and watched the sun glitter on the blades which issued from its sides. Shank-ji might have gone in with better arms, but of what good was a sword to me who had so early proved that I was unhandy with such a weapon?

Slipping and skidding I won my way to the other side of the dune. There, as the Chancellor had promised, arose the green bubble of a dome. It was of lesser size than I expected. Perhaps its original population had been no more than what my people would reckon a single clan or House. The green glass was opaque, though I knew from my visit to the city that that did not prevent the entrance of sunlight, only screened it somewhat so that the heat and light of the outer world were tamed.

"Brother—" Out of the sand which was so close a shade to his own fur Murri arose, shaking himself.

The golden eyes turned to me were indeed unclouded as far as I could determine. Yes, he was as he had always been, save that he seemed to grow the larger each time we were parted. I dropped my staff, throwing out my arms as he approached, burying them in his ruff, while his harsh tongue rasped against my cheek. All the inner emptiness which had gripped me since I had entered this too-silent land vanished. What need had I for any comrade save the one I was welcoming now?

He raised a giant paw as he would to one of his own kind and rolled me over on my back, with a mock growl which I endeavored to echo as well as I could. At that moment I longed for the ability to take to the air in one of the great springs which marked the cat dances to prove how light my heart was.

Murri at last settled back to look at me inquiringly.

"Where go?"

I pointed to the green dome. "There." I explained as best I could in my limited grasp of his own tongue what I must do there.

"Not hard—" he commented.

"It must be," I continued, "or they would not have sent me here to do this thing."

"It gets no less, waiting—" I untangled that much from his complicated series of sounds. And he spoke the truth.

I picked up my staff again. Feeling able to face anything which might lie ahead as Murri paced beside me, I approached the dome.

The big entrance which had allowed access to the city was absent here. There was a portal no wider than would admit two walking side by side or a single beast with rider or driver. Across it was set in place so wide a metal bar as to suggest that what lay in wait within possessed more than human strength.

The bar was hard to shift. It had settled well into its hold-hooks and certainly had not been much moved for a space. Perhaps only by those candidates who had been before me here. I allowed it to thud into the sand which had drifted high about the surface of the door and pulled that forward, discovering that I had to exert some strength to open a space wide enough for Murri and then me to slip by.

The first thing I noted was a tangle of growth which had near buried the few buildings I could see. Loops of vines reached as high as the upper curve of the dome in places. There was a strong smell, not of the algae to which I was accustomed, but rather like that I had met when I crossed the fields of Vapala.

In that other Twahihican village had been a wealth of scents, perfumes, spices, all those which proclaimed enticement for visitors. Here was only one. After a moment or so I found it rank and unpleasant.

There was no sign of any of the malons here. But there were marks, almost effaced by growth as if that which rooted here had been very swift to veil the damage done, a path forward which had been slashed and cut through this net. At least those I followed on this quest had accomplished that much for me.

Murri swiped at a tangle of growth with one paw, his talons cutting branches and leaves. That opened up even more the entrance to the passage which had been recently cleared and I began to use my staff, its blades extended to their foremost, to beat and slice my way.

Murri paused, his head turned to the left, and I saw the swell of his large nostrils as he tested the air. Then he swung out with a paw and slashed at the growth, jerking a wide swath of it out of whatever rootage it had found. I saw what it had hidden—a tumble of bones, among them a skull which leered up at me hollow-eyed. Undoubtedly the remains of one of my own kind.

Though there were no signs of clothing nor any weapon, I had the feeling that death had not come too long ago, clean-stripped as those bones appeared. One of my fellow candidates who had fallen to such evil as was hidden here?

Murri was still sniffing. He might have been seeking a trail. Only what he said was:

"Bad—danger—"

"What kind?" I demanded. That alertness I had learned as a herdsman was what I called upon now, searching for any clue as to the nature of the peril encompassed here, from which direction it might spring without warning.

There was no sign of any malon among these vines matted to encircle us, save for the path we had torn. It would seem that we must venture farther in.

Murri had not answered my question and I gathered that he was also at a loss as to what danger might lie in wait. Yet it would seem he had no intention of turning back; rather he attacked the tangle before him vigorously.

We had passed the first of the buildings, so embowered now that one could see only small patches of wall, but no windows nor doorways. Suddenly Murri gave a cry, not only of startlement but also fear. The paw he had just put forth to claw his way forward had been noosed by a thick greyish rope of sorts and a second one had snaked out across his body as he strove to use his teeth on that first binding.

I moved in with my knife-staff swinging. The blades rebounded at first from the ties which were fast netting Murri but a second slashing at the cut left by the first severed that which was tightening around his body. It uncoiled, fell to earth, and straight-way twitched and writhed, a thick yellowish stuff pouring from the cut to release a foul odor.

This was no creature as I knew, rather a tendril of the growth about us. Across Murri's back, where it had tightened, the fur was wet and slimy and patches of hair were missing.

He spat out that which he held in his mouth, and pawed at his jaws from which the spittle ran yellow. I feared that there had been poison in that thing he had chewed apart, for he behaved as a kotti who had swallowed a fur ball, vomiting a watery substance.

This I saw only with half an eye, as it were, for I was alert for another of the vine nooses. They appeared to spring out of the piece of ground we had cleared and were certainly vines, for the ends, still rooted, were putting out small leaves, of the same sickly yellow, veined in red.

I chopped, swung, chopped again and again. Then the ends which came wriggling up to the surface from the dank soil vanished. We at last had a space in which to breathe. I nursed skin across which one of those flesh-stripping horrors had passed, leaving welling blood behind it. The sting of that contact was worse than all the torment I had suffered from the insects in the salt land.

There was still no sign of any malons. Yet to venture deeper into this mass was an invitation to the lurking horror beneath the surface of the ground. I wondered if it was the vibration of our footfalls which had alerted it or if it had some other method of sensing prey. Perhaps even some of the leaves which walled us in acted as eyes, ears, or similar organs for what lay beneath the surface.

Still someone had managed to get farther on, as the signs, fast being swallowed up by fresh growth, showed. And I knew that Shank-ji, at least, had won his prize from this haunted place.

Our exertions had carried us past the first of the now netted buildings and now we were offered safety for a bit, for we came out of the massed stuff unto a circle of the clean sand such as covered the land beyond the bubble.

I examined Murri's back but the suckers of the vine had not injured him beyond loosening the fur in patches. And he had stopped his heaving. My own wound was small enough and I could not see that it was poisoned in any way—or so I hoped.

"Brother—" I laid my hand on Murri's head.

"I live—but bad here—"

With that I could heartily agree. Now I set out making the round of that place of sand where apparently none of the growth could find rootage. To the right of the place we had entered, there were again signs of another's passage. To make certain this was the way, there was a nauseating odor on the air. I had been told that spoiled or rotted malon produced such. Thus the "garden" which we sought must lie in that direction.

But for this moment we were content to sit in our pool of safety and only look towards what might be the second stage of a battle, and perhaps an even more difficult one.

26

The side of the building around which we had come to find this island of safety was bare of vine, just as the other was so tightly coated with it. There had been a pattern incised there as I had seen in the city we had visited, though this had no bright color, rather stains as if vines had once clutched there but had been broken away.

I slung my staff across my shoulder and went to run my hands over that pattern. What I had suspected at first sighting was true, there were finger- and toeholds here for the climber. Slipping off my boots I began that ascent hoping so to view what might lie ahead. The top of the house had been rounded and over part of it crawled the vines. I edged around these so that I was still in the clear.

Ahead there was a bank of the tough growth, but beyond that again another stretch of sand. Through a hole in the growth I could see a line of malon vines, each trained over a trellis. On them the rounded globes of fruit hung, some already the deep purple of fully ripe.

I shared what I had learned with Murri. He was washing his face over and over, trying to rid himself of the last signs of that vine attack. With a growl which fully expressed his opinion of the whole business, he got ready to plunge into the struggle toward the garden I had sighted.

Though we went with care, we did not see any sign of those root tops wriggling out of the dank soil. And when we came to the clearing of the malons, the sand stretch there was divided into squares, every other one being earth in which one of the vines was planted.

There was a strong stench of rotted fruit. The ground around each looped-up vine was a mush of fallen malons. Of those still on the vines the ones which had turned the full color of ripeness were useless to me, for the picking must be done at almost the very moment the purple streaked the bronze fruit, entirely encircling the globes.

On the nearest of the vines I noted three such which looked promising. How long I must wait until they were ready I did not know. Even as I stood there two others fell from their stems to squash on the piles already there.

We moved out on the sand, but kept away from the mess of stinking fruit. Murri lay down, his nose covered by his paws. I wished I could do likewise, for the odor of this place, even as the haze on the fire mountains, was dense enough to sicken one.

I had my eye on a fruit well at the end of one vine which I thought I could pull down within reach with my staff and moved near as I could get to that without venturing into the mess on the ground.

It was then that I saw a shaking and quiver of the spoiled fruit. Three of the last fallen tumbled away, shaken from below, and there showed for an instant the pointed end of one of the threatening suckers. This then must be their usual food. But I was warned by the sight of them feeding.

It was the nature of the malon that the last stage of ripening came so quickly that one could actually see the spread of the darker color. I was ready, my staff out, and I angled one of its edges as a hook about the branch, pulling it down. Freed by this movement the malon took to the air and I caught it, having dropped my staff into the mush on the ground.

With my prize safe to hand I cleaned my staff in the sand and tried again with the same success. Together we turned to find our way out of this place of hidden menace.

We made it to the circle of sand by the building. The path down which we had cut our way was already being closed by a lacing of smaller vines. However, we had learned our lesson and we cut our way past those sorry remains of the one who failed, gaining the outer door and the safety of the sand dunes beyond, the malons in the fore of my jacket.

If I had expected congratulations for my feat I would have been disappointed. The commander of my escort turned the malons I delivered around and around in his hands as if seeking some flaw in the offering. However, the major stroke against me was that I came accompanied by Murri and this time I demanded what little rights a contestant had that from here on he would be my traveling companion.

There was a great deal of muttering and side-looking at me over this. Only tradition held fast. The person of the candidate between his trials was sacred and he could not be opposed unless he had failed.

Perhaps if I had been Shank-ji I would have been afforded a banquet in Twahihic's major city, presentation to the Queen, and a general flood of good wishes for my last trial to come. But I was as well pleased to take the trail back to Vapala as soon as possible.

When days later the guard which had been waiting for me at the border took over escort, I again spoke for Murri. This time the Sand Cat entered the Diamond Queendom openly and not by stealth.

I learned that I was the first to return and that news had arrived that two of the contestants had already been lost. That Shank-ji was not one of them was cheering to those around me and they openly spoke of his gaining the crown.

From the comments I heard as we traveled on towards the city, the younger members of the guard all favored the Emperor's son. Only those of some of the old and most conservative of Houses were opposed to such a break with tradition. I also gathered that he was a man of ambition and with a certain power of person which afforded that ambition a firm base. That he was one of their own countrymen made him doubly welcome, whereas the coming of an outer "barbarian" would be quickly resented.

We reached Vapala City itself shortly after mid-day, Murri trotting beside my oryxen. Oddly enough that beast accepted the Sand Cat, though otherwise they were natural hunter and prey. And he was still with me as we threaded our way through crowded streets, where the reaction of the crowd was such one might have thought I was an enemy of the state instead of the possible ruler.

The chiming of the unlatched wind chimes was near over-powering to one who had come from the quiet of the desert lands. When we entered the wide space before the palace, the resounding clamor of the great chimes overhead was almost deafening. I looked up and saw the whirl of the gem-set crown in the midst of those large plaques which the rope-tugging of a number of servants set striking one against the other.

This would be my last testing. I must thread between those swinging plaques, all of which were knife-edged, to claim the crown. Though I had survived so far, I watched the random clashing of the pieces and thought—this is impossible. There could be no possible way one could venture between such and not be slashed—cut literally to bits! Yet it had been done in the past and it was expected that it would be done now.

Shank-ji would be most familiar with the chimes, the only one who might know the way to approach them and reach the trophy within. Yet I was committed and this lay before me. With-out being truly conscious that I sought some reassurance, my hand fell on Murri's head, and, from that touch, there flooded into me a strength which at least held me outwardly strong.

The final trial would not be separate as the others. We must wait until the rest who survived returned. They would have ushered me into quarters in the palace itself but once more I stood on my right of choice. I would go to the only place in this city where I might hope to find at least a sugges-tion of friendship. Since the candidates were allowed to claim shelter from kin or friends, I asked for Ravinga, though I did not know whether the dollmaker would receive me.

The crowd shrank back, giving Murri and me an open pas-sage which did not have to be enforced by the guard, though those rode with me. At the end of the alley which gave upon the court of the dollmaker, I dismounted, turning my oryxen over to the officer. Then I went to the door which I hoped would open hospitably for me.

Ravinga had sat for many hours by her work table. But all the materials lying before her had long ago been pushed aside. She had stationed two lamps so that they gave light to a square of the age-polished and scarred board before her and her attention had been on that board. With the coming of dawn she blew out the lamps, but still she watched—what I did not know, even though as her apprentice she had granted me access to some of her secrets.

I had brought food, only to have it grow cold and left untouched, though she drank twice from the flagon of malon juice I had placed conspicuously close to one of the lamps. However, even during that taking of refreshment her eyes did not leave that stretch of wood. This was new to her, for since my coming into her household I had never seen her do so before.

It was shortly after dawn that her hand moved again, not reaching this time for the cup, but rather in blind groping among the scattered materials, for still she did not look away from that portion of wood. She dug into a tray and brought forward first a casting of gold. The form was still rough yet there was that which suggested the figure of a Sand Cat.

This she placed in the middle of that stretch of table top. For the first time she spoke:

"Bring the jewel casket." Her order was abrupt and suddenly there was a feeling which seemed to spread from her to me that there was a need of hurry for some task.

Goaded by that, I went swiftly to the far end of the room and there worked the name lock of the wall cupboard behind which such valuables as we had were stored. The jewel casket was heavy, being made of the stone of the fire mountains, polished and patterned. And that pattern clearly was of Sand Cats.

As I set it on the table before Ravinga, Wa, Wiu, and Wyna, the kottis of the household, appeared out of nowhere, jumped to the table top which was and always had been forbidden territory to them. I would have warned them off but Ravinga.

without speaking, shook her head and I took that as an order to allow them to stay.

They sat in a line, statue still, the tips of their tails curled over their forepaws, their unblinking gaze upon what Ravinga was doing.

She had chosen from her tools a slender knife and was working at the soft pure gold of the figure she had selected. Hair-thin shavings of the metal fell away from her tool. At length she had finished a perfect figure. Then she turned to the small cabinet on the table. Once more there was a finger lock to be mastered and this she did for herself, for that particular piece of her equipment had never been opened to me.

From small shelves within she took a small flask of metal and dipped one of her delicate brushes into the narrow mouth of that vessel. So she painted the golden figure with great care. The liquid she used was colorless but she gave three coatings to the Sand Cat she had created.

Now she opened the jewel case. On a square of dark cloth which she brought out first she began to lay out stones. The rich yellow of the finest citrines shone and she matched and rematched these with care until she had two which were perfect twins. These she set into the figure for eyes.

Having finished this job, she searched again among her materials and produced a plate of dingy metal, so blackened I could not have said what it was. Directly in the middle of this she put her Sand Cat and around it she poured, from another flagon out of the cupboard, a stream of dust-fine crystals, heaping these up until the mound covered the whole of the figure.

"The taper—" Another order.

I used the spark snap and lighted the taper on the table. Grasping this firmly she touched the fire to that powder. There was a glow spread from that point of contact. The kottis moved back. For the first time they gave voice—a murmur which was between a mew and a purr—almost as if they sang. There was a flare from the plate and an outward puff of smoke.

Ravinga leaned back with a sigh, her hands falling limply into her lap. Her face was haggard and I caught at her shoulder.

"You must rest—"

She smiled slowly. "We have a guest, two guests on the way, girl. Yes, I must rest for there will be much to be done."

The haze on the plate spiraled away into wisps of smoke. All the dust had vanished, only the Sand Cat sat there. The kottis' song died away. One after another they stretched their necks out, audibly sniffing at the figure head, and uttered a cry such as I had never heard before. Ravinga nodded. "So it is well done, is it? Let it be what is best needed in the days to come."

She put her hands to the board and levered herself up from her so-long-held chair as if the strength had been leached out of her.

"That," and she pointed to the golden cat. "Put it away carefully for it is now a thing to be guarded."

She staggered and I would have gone to aid her but she fended me off with one arm. "I but need rest, Allitta. Rest before our guests arrive."

Our guests came with such an escort as this quarter of the city seldom sees, unless there is some dire trouble between Houses and some assassin has chosen to flee hither. For it was a detachment of the Queen's own guard which brought Hynkkel back to our doors. Beside him openly paced Murri, the Sand Cat, whose life I would have thought would have been forfeit the moment he appeared within range of any of our proud hunters.

The warriors did not follow Hynkkel into our small court. I very much disliked the idea that they had come even to the end of the short way which opened into it.

I am free of many of Ravinga's secrets, if not all, and some of those are such one would not want to be discovered by any in authority. That she was engaged in some great plan which had many parts and reached far up into certain Houses as well as down into the company of those who seldom slunk forth in the bright light of day—that I was well aware of and had been for many seasons now. That I was part of her plan was also clear to me and I did not resent it.

There has always been a thirst in me for learning and while Ravinga was a figure of awe, she was also a ready teacher. If with her one craft overlaid another, then I was all the richer for being admitted, even if only into the fringes of her planning.

I sighted Hynkkel's arrival from our own private lookout and hurried down to open the shop door before he had a chance to knock. Mancol sat on his stool behind the counter unmoving. I wondered, as I had many times, what the old man knew, what he guessed. However, that he was devotedly loyal to Ravinga I had known from the start of my own introduction to this place.

Hynkkel entered, behind him Murri. There was a rustling past my skirt as our three kottis pushed forward. I raised hand in greeting to the man, they went to touch noses with the beast.

In the light I saw the black blot which near covered the palm of the hand he had raised in answer to me. Something had been branded there into his flesh. In other ways he was changed. There were new lines in his narrow face, a strange sense of power learned and used clung to him. I knew its like from my life with Ravinga. This one had gone in strange places and had wrought well there.

"To the House be welcome. To the hearth fire come safely. Under this roof know all are friends." I repeated the formal greeting mechanically.

He smiled and that erased from his face some of that power sign.

"To the House be all honor. I accept what is given with a heart of cheer." That return, in its last words, appeared to be more than just formal. There was a warmth in it which suggested that indeed he found comfort here.

The door was safely closed now against all prying eyes—though why that thought crossed my mind at that moment I could not have said. That we were not overlooked by any of the guard, as blandly innocent as our meeting was, seemed to be a thing to be desired.

Once more I brought him into the room prepared for him. As he laid aside his staff I saw the better that new brand on his palm—the head of a leopard. I did not know its meaning—save perhaps it signified that so far he had overcome and survived in triumph the tasks set him.

His Kifongg sat against the wall and now he stooped to take it in hand, sweeping his fingers across the strings.

"Well and skillfully tuned." He glanced at me with another smile. "I thank you for this courtesy, Allitta—"

I shrugged. As always I felt stiff and even suspicious with this man and I almost distrusted that Ravinga had woven him so tightly into her web. He was comely enough, if slight of body, certainly no match for any of the young warriors of Great Houses. But what did he matter to me? I had had my fill of those standing higher in the world, more resplendent than he—and I had found them very hollow beneath all their fine showing.

"A good instrument needs attention," I said with all the indifference I could summon. "My lady will be with us later: she labored late."

He nodded as I stepped back from the doorway to let Murri past and then I went to the kitchen, intent on preparing such a meal as would tempt Ravinga after her ordeal, as well as satisfy these guests whose purpose in our lives I could not puzzle out.

27

The lamplight lay across the table and I found it oddly welcoming. This was a room in which I felt at home—in spite of the fact that the girl by the fireplace showed me always so cold a face. But by the rest, I was cheered, experiencing a warmth which came, not from the outside, but from within.

If Allitta gave no welcome, I received it from Ravinga, and it was mainly to her I told the story of my ordeals. On the bench at the other end of the table sat the three black kottis and it was as if they listened too and understood each word I said, or perhaps they gained their knowledge in some manner through Murri, who lay at ease on the floor in that complete relaxation of his own kind.

The Kifongg rested on my knees. Now and then my fingertips brought a note or two from it. Then I realized that I was following the actions of a bard delivering a message.

The story took us well past nightfall. I had eaten of the wholesome fare the dollmaker had provided and still had a tankard of fex juice by my hand to wet down my throat as I talked. Then I became aware that Allitta had left her place by the fire and had come to the bench which she shared with the kottis.

"Thus have I won so far," I concluded.

"So far," Ravinga echoed. "There remains—the gaining of the crown."

I had tried to put that out of mind for a space, for I knew very well that this end test was indeed the trickiest and most demanding. How a man might ever gain the height to free the crown with those swinging, knife-edge plaques hung all at different lengths was something I could not understand. Now I felt chilled in spite of the welcome warmth of the room.

Each of the trials had threatened death. I thought that I had faced that fact. Now I discovered that fear still was my shadow.

I placed the harp on the table and looked down at the hands on which the guardian had set his mark. Then, as if pulled by a power beyond my conscious understanding, I reached two hands for the mask pendant at my breast.

Ravinga had arisen and without a word left me sitting there to face what I had striven for the whole evening to push away from me, that weakening fear. Shank-ji and any of the others who had survived had not yet returned. There was a stretch of time then which I must wait out, and to be companioned by fear during that time—

The dollmaker returned out of the shadows beyond the lamplight. She laid down on the table a staff, but one which bore no relation to that which had accompanied me during my journeying. This was no herdsman's weapon and companion. Now it was a symbol of power, power—

The rod length was golden and set in a curling pattern for most of its length of small jewels. The rubies of Thnossis, the topazes of Azhengir, the sapphires of my own people, the other gems which were the badges of the five nations fashioned in those whirls and spirals. At the top was the figure of a seated Sand Cat, also golden, with gem eyes which outflashed the other jewels below. It was fit for an Emperor as a rod of office—for an Emperor!

I gazed at it dazzled. This was of workmanship as fine as that from my sister's hands—heretofore I had believed that no one could surpass her craft. I put forth a hand and yet I dared not touch it—this was not meant for me.

Ravinga might have read my mind.

"It is yours in truth, Klaverel-va-Hynkkel. Or will be soon."

"Why?" I suddenly knew that chill of fear close about me a hundredfold. "Who am I to be Emperor? I am not even a warrior—but rather a herdsman and servant in my father's household." I did not want to look ahead. I dared not build upon that which I now believed would not come true.

To those of Vapala I was a barbarian. Among my own people I had been weighed and found wanting. I was—

"You are," her words carried with them something of a command, "what you believe yourself to be!

"Have you not gained brothership with the desert lords?" Her eyes flitted from to Murri and back again. "What other man for generations out of time can claim that?"

It was as if my eyes turned inward and I saw not this room and that blazing rod of office, but rather the rocks of the isle and the dancing cats. Faintly I could even hear the strange sound of their singing. Once again I witnessed their unbelievable leaps and bounds, the fact that they could even coast afloat, their fine fur fluffed, the air they swallowed holding them aloft.

At the time it had been a sight of wonder, to me now it was even more of a mystery and even delight. Those graceful forms absorbed in their own release of feeling. I remembered my own attempts to match them and take part in the joyful expression of their love of life.

"Yes," Ravinga's voice cut through that half dream jerking me back to the here and now, "remember that, brother to the furred ones. As to why you," she paused as if she might be hunting the proper words—as an adult who must explain something obtuse to a child, "do not expect me to answer that, Hynkkel. I only know that for many seasons it was set upon me to seek out a certain man. When you laid hands on that trophy of the devil knotted into the mane of my yaksen I knew that I had found he whom I had sought."

Now I arose to my feet and leaned a little across the table, my eyes striving to hold hers fast.

"Who are you, Ravinga? What purpose made you seek so?"

She hesitated and then she slipped down onto the stool where she had sat earlier and, with the gesture, ordered me back into my own place.

"I am Ravinga, a maker of dolls—" Again she paused and I interrupted her:

"And of other things. An Emperor perhaps, dollmaker? But men are not such as can be made—save through their own actions."

"We are all of the essence of our homelands, and also of the Great Essence. There stirs now that which once before strove to break the tie between people and their world. There is a Will which holds itself greater than the whole. I am one of a few who might be called Watchers, Guardians." She stretched her wrist now into the full light so I could see the scars there, so like to the ones I also bore. "I have danced with the furred ones in my time, for they have a part to play in what will come, even as they did long ago.

"I do not know when the Shadow will advance upon us— now it flits—it tests. There must be an Emperor who is of such nature that he can, in the time of need, draw upon the Essence—not only of his own country, but that of all the outlands, men, women, beasts, the land itself."

"And you believe that I can do this?"

Now she fingered the staff lying on the table. "Would this have been wrought, did I not?"

"I—I am not what you seek!" All the years behind me arose to argue that.

"You shall be what you make yourself, Hynkkel. Chew upon that thought. Get you to your rest, for the morning comes far too soon."

So abruptly she dismissed me. There was a wanness on her face as if her explanation to me had drawn out much strength. It might have been for her just such an ordeal as I had faced already. I picked up the harp and murmured a good-night, leaving her there now gazing down at the staff of power.

Chew upon her planted thought I did and sleep did not come easy that night. This time Murri did not slink away to hide but rather shared my chamber.

"Brother—" I drew my fingertips across the strings of the Kifongg, but kept the chords which arose soft, "what lies before us now?"

He had been licking a forepaw and now he raised his head to look at me.

"Much," he made short answer.

At that moment I wished with all my will that I were back in that small hut which had been my own before this whole venture had begun. I was who I was—how could such as I aspire to Emperor? I had never wanted power—to herd the beasts, harvest the algae, make a trading venture into town— that was all the life I had known and I was not fitted for more.

"Not so—" Murri rumbled.

My hand had fallen on my knee and I looked down at the brand there. Memory arose strong, vivid. I heard through the walls of the room, saw beyond the house, the city—

The Sand Cats in their grace and full beauty danced beneath the night sky. They sang their own purring, growling chants. There was such freedom, such a uniting with the Essence. Muscles twitched in that moment. I wanted to fling myself out again, to be one with them, with their world.

Then again I faced the black leopard and his jealously guarded sphere. I rubbed one hand against the other and looked again at the brands set there. There was the mountain of fire, the treacherous plain of salt pan, the tangle of vines—

I wished so much for my own old place on the dome of my house where I could look upon the stars, open mind and heart to the essences into which I had been born. By touching such I would know who I truly was.

All the stories which Kynrr had related in detail about Vapala—the court—the under struggles of one House against another so that the country was rife with intrigues. How was I to face that?

However, I could not be sure that I would be called upon to do so. I remembered Shank-ji and the fact that this land was his and so would answer first to him.

I set aside Kynrr's instrument and sought the bed mats where Murri had already settled himself. Perhaps it was the purring of my companion which brought me sleep for it speedily came, even though I had enough twisting thoughts to keep it away.

Wa, Wiu, and Wyna sat by the fire which had died down to coals. As I stirred the pannikin in which I had steeped the drink for Ravinga, they watched me with round green eyes. My thoughts were such that I dug my spoon deeply and hard into the mixture. For fear gnawed at me.

Suppose that Ravinga spoke the truth and this herdsman out of a barbarian land would triumph in the end. Thereafter he would face a maze trap worse than any he had known. He might be Emperor but he would speedily learn that there were powers which would stand stubbornly against him. And, with the Shadow spreading, we did not need dissension at court.

Shank-ji had a strong following; even those elders who would not welcome a break with tradition would back him if he won. His mother had been of the House Yuran, one of the oldest and most powerful. Those now bearing that name would be only too ready to support their kinsman. And if he failed, their anger would be great—

I bit my lip. They had eyes and ears in plenty in Vapala, did those of Yuran. There could be no long concealment of Ravinga's connection with this outlander. Once their suspicions were aroused—then what would follow?

Death could be the least and most desired end. Ravinga had powers, yes. I had seen them at work—but their success depended mainly on the point that she had never been questioned. That this Hynkkel had chosen to come to us—that he had been escorted hither by the guard—that he had dared to bring that beast which was the terror of legend—all this was enough to turn the wrong eyes in our direction.

Was I a coward? No, but I was one who had learned a dire lesson in the past. Where was my House now? Yet once our colors had shown proudly in the feast hall of the Emperor. Not to think of that. Yet it nagged me until, unable to sleep, I went into the shop. The grey of early daylight had become as full as it ever reached in this court. I unbarred the latch door and stepped out for a moment. Mancol had not yet come, nor had the kottis followed me. I was alone and in that moment I heard the chiming of the mobiles begin as those in the major thoroughfares were released from their night latching. Above them all sounded the louder clang of the Emperor's.

Today—tomorrow—when would they come, those others who survived the trials elsewhere? While he who slept beneath our roof—

"Bright day."

I turned swiftly. The man in my thoughts stood there, his head a little atilt as if he were listening to the incessant chimes, striving to separate one set from the other.

"Bright day," I answered him mechanically.

Then he spoke with the directness of his countrymen, so different from the courtesy-encased words of we of Vapala—

"You are no friend to me, are you, Allitta?"

"I do not know you—" I responded.

"You may know as much as Ravinga but it is not enough—"

Why he sought to tax me with this, I could not understand. Did he believe that I strove to turn my mistress against him? Yes, that I would have done long since had I been able. But my judgment had no weight for her in this matter.

"I fear you," I answered before I thought.

"You fear *me?*" He accented that last word as if he were incredulous. "Why?"

"Because of what might happen." Then all I had been thinking by the fire spilled out of me—that through him my mistress courted the danger of attracting the adverse notice of those who could and would act against her.

"I see," he said slowly. "Kynrr spoke of such things as the jealousy of the Great Houses and their secret ways of dealing with those who gained their ill favor. You think then that such might be turned upon her whom you care for, if by some unusual range of favor I do gain the crown? The Emperor has all power, does he not?"

"Subject to the advice of the Chancellor," I corrected him.

"But he can take under his protection whomever he wishes—"

"If he may desire to do so."

"So." I had him frowning now. He favored me with a hint of wry smile. "I think you may see only shadowed future, Allitta. I have yet to claim the crown. Nor do I think that my chances are so fair. But this much I say to you: Your mistress is one who knows more than either of us. I would back her against a war band, without even a spear to hand, and yet see her a victor. She is far more than she seems."

28

Ravinga did not share our morning meal nor did Allitta do me such a favor. Murri and I ate alone, and it was not an easy meal, for I waited for the summons and waiting has never been easy for me. It never is for one who can reckon in his mind all the evils which may lurk ahead. How long that wait would be I had no way of telling.

Allitta packed two large baskets with lesser products of Ravinga's skill, or perhaps her own, and I loaded these on a hand cart for her. I would have taken my place at the push bar of that and seen her to the market but she told me plainly that it was my place to stay under cover as I had already flaunted custom by choosing to shelter with the dollmaker. My appearance as co-vendor of wares in the marketplace would only draw such attention as I must not court.

Thus I faced a long day with nothing to do. After the activity of the last period of travel and effort, that seemed a burden. The old man took over the shop and fussed about, moving Ravinga's doll people here and there on shelves and muttering under his breath, now and then peering at me from under his eyebrows as if he found me a disturbing sight. So at last I was driven into the long room which was Ravinga's workshop.

I moved about that, as careful not to touch as a child who had been sternly forbidden to do so, eyeing her work from its beginnings to the near finished figure at hand, marveling at how no two of the small faces were alike. It was as if she looked upon her art even as did my sister and had no desire to repeat any design.

There was one shelf before which I paused to give longer study to what stood there. Within me was a chill I could not account for as I looked upon the likeness of two women and a man, and beside them—the snarling figure of a rat! Why Ravinga would wish to use her talent to fashion such a creature I could not imagine.

The women had the silver hair of Vapala, but their skin was a darker shade than that of those I had seen on the streets. Their garb was not ordinary robes or even court finery, but rather the scanty covering of cat dancers. Their faces were painted, and the fingers of their tiny, well-fashioned hands had the nails elongated into claws. Also they were posed as if prepared to leap forward in one of the intricate twirls of the hunt dance.

Their companion was a much more somber figure. His head was covered by a tight-fitting hood, so drawn on his skull as to suggest that no hair sprouted under it, not even the common top lock. He had been dressed in a sleeved robe which fell open on his breast and the body portion so displayed there was patterned with a device which was etched into the skin itself or so it would seem.

For the rest he had the full breeches of a Kahulawen and below those, boots fringed about the tops with black oryxen mane hair. There was no sword belt with ready weapon, no spear to hand. Rather his carven fingers were looped about the shaft of a staff of honor and that was topped by the likeness of a creature I had never seen nor heard described—but something which suggested great malignity.

The rat—it was a rat—but in scale with the three figures beside it, it was overlarge—more like one of the monsters which had been recently appearing, the like of which I had myself slain among the rock isles.

"You are interested in my people, Hynkkel?"

I was so unaware of all save the dolls that I started. Ravinga stood by my side.

"The cat dancers—I once saw a small company of those. But the man—and the rat—?"

"The man you could never have seen, nor even have heard of—not in your far outlands. There are no keepers of old knowledge there—"

"We have our Rememberers 'for the feasts," I protested. This implied judgment that we were indeed barbarous pricked me more than it ever had.

"Yes, and they are well trained—in the history of your people. But there were others before you, and of those none of your lore makes mention. He," she pointed to the man, "was a seeker of strange knowledge who once crossed the Plain of Desolation—before the first Emperor was crowned."

"But no man—nor beast—can dare the inner heart of the Plain!"

"The rats do," she returned. "There is much lost knowledge, Hynkkel. Some of it purposefully lost. There is also a belief that to think on things of darkness in curiosity may awaken more than one wishes. Yes—that one was a master of much power which had nothing to do with spear or sword. And the rat was his symbol!"

That any living person might use one of those loathsome creatures to stand as his House badge sickened me. Yet now I could see truly that the sign etched on what was meant to be a bare breast was the outline of a rat head, even as I wore that of the leopard on my palms.

"How do you know of him?" Perhaps the question was an impertinence but it was one I could not forgo.

"I am a Guardian, Hynkkel. From generation to generation, from reign to reign, certain women have carried the old knowledge. Perhaps not without taint or misunderstanding, for knowledge passed from mind to mind may sometimes be unconsciously altered by the very personality of he or she who holds it. I cannot be sure how true is that I myself now hold— but it is enough to warn me.

"That is Ylantilyn, once of the House of Borse." Again she indicated the figure. "His very name was a curse in its time. He reached for much, gained some, and sundered House from House, land from land, to try for more. Even the beasts, except those horrors he herded as his own, were caught up in his warring. As a result, they, too, suffered change.

"Hynkkel," now her attention moved from the figure to me and there was that about her which was like unto my father's stance when he spoke about some fault of mine, "the lives of all of us move in circles. We are born, we labor to our wills, or our needs, we come again to death. The Great Essence takes us up and once more molds us and sets the pattern afresh. Only we do not carry with us the memory of what lies behind, thus often the same mistakes are ours. Just so is the life of our queendoms; we follow patterns and in times those patterns become twisted.

"For long now have we lived in a semblance of peace. We train warriors but they have naught to raise spear against, save outlaws or the animals they hunt. We have the hardship of our lands, the sandstorms, the mountain fires, the treachery of the salt pans. Yes, all these represent danger, and many of us die of the very nature of our surroundings.

"But in the past were greater wars, and our lives were shaped by those. Such will come again, and if we are not prepared we shall be as yaksen at the coming of Murri's clan— near helpless."

That she fully believed this I could see. But from where would this danger come? Would the jealousy of the Great Houses warp and tear apart a long-held peace? Or would some danger, such as she hinted of, come from outside? And what had I, who was no warrior, to do with war?

Allitta returned home at the noon closing of the market. Her baskets of wares were depleted to be sure, but what she had brought was news and I realized that that had been her main reason in the market.

"Those of the House of Trelek have ridden out." She cupped her bowl of stew with one hand but made no attempt as yet to taste it. "Word has come that Shank-ji has completed those trials set him."

"Others?" inquired Ravinga as Allitta raised a spoon.

The girl shook her head. "No others—nor are they now expected. A courier has come to say that and the market hums with his news."

I was suddenly uninterested in my portion of the meal. No others? Two of us only for the final trial?

"They were trying to place wagers at Hawiff's booth. There were no takers—all believe that Shank-ji need only reach forth his hand to take up the Emperor's staff and it is his." Now she looked straight at me and there was plainly a challenge in her tone. "The warriors have been gathering these five days—four more House troops rode in this morning, as well as some from the outer lands. Among such is Klaverel-va-Kalikku." She repeated that name with deliberation as if to make very sure that I heard and understood.

That my brother had returned did not surprise me—this was an event which would draw many from every one of the five queendoms. All the Queens had made the journey to Vapala, ready to swear homage to the new Emperor, and in their trains there would be many of those from the principal Houses of their queendoms.

"There is talk—" Allitta paused to take up another spoonful of stew and swallow.

"Talk," Ravinga said. "Of what kind and by whom?"

"Of interference with the Customs—"

"Shank-ji must answer that then?"

Allitta shook her head. "No, the interference is said to be his." She nodded at me. "They say that his own brother has already sworn that he was not able to win so far without aid, that he consorts with beasts more than with his own kind, that he is already outcast from his House—"

I deliberately spooned up what was before me. Could I have expected less? But what aid were they able to claim was mine? I had been escorted by the troops. In each case my coming and going had been under their surveillance. That I consorted with beasts—yes. That I was outcast—perhaps so—I had not returned to my father's dwelling after my solo, but then the manner of my setting forth for that was enough to warn me off. Could such talk keep me from the final trial, leave Shank-ji a very clear field? Though he must still face bringing out the crown from among those ever-turning, knife-edged plaques.

"And this talk," Ravinga pursued the subject, "how is it slanted?"

Allitta let her spoon splash down into the bowl and held up her fingers to count off points on those one by one.

"Firstly, there are the merchants. They want uninterrupted trade most of all—and a strong hand with the Houses. Haban-ji was of Vapala and so could muster enough good will of the Houses. The barbarians do not count for much, for the greater merchants do not trade directly with them. And they believe that an Emperor from the outer lands cannot hold a steady rein on the Houses, any more than a child upon an untrained oryxen.

"Then," she turned down a second finger, "there are the Houses themselves. They will give homage, if grudgingly, to an outlander—and intrigue behind his back. One of their own kind they believe might be influenced outwardly and quickly to understand them and their ways. They might even foresee a bending of a custom in which only the senior son of a House would be thought of for selection of Emperor trials. Shank-ji has a big following among the younger members of many Houses—he is open-handed to his friends while Haban-ji humored him and gave him much.

"Thirdly," another finger went down, "there are the people as a whole. As the merchants, they want peace and that means a strong Emperor. They do not take kindly to an outsider, especially one suspected of strange powers. That you," now she addressed me directly, "have your tie with the Sand Cats is a strong theme of gossip and certainly not in your favor.

"Fourth, the people of the other queendoms—there is other gossip concerning you, Hynkkel, and from those whom all would expect to wish you well rather than ill. Your brother has attached himself to Shank-ji's following. He has spoken hard and long against you and none of your own clan has answered in your defense. We have heard that only your sister Kura has kept silent and seems to have some feeling for you. However, she is but one against many and is thought to have too soft a heart."

I winced. What else could I expect from my father? If I had gone back from my solo—no, I was sure he would never have welcomed me as a full son of his.

"They talk much," Ravinga commented. "Which is only to be expected. There are always rumors upon rumors in the marketplace. When does Shank-ji arrive?"

"Perhaps two days from now." Allitta took up her spoon again and set to work on the stew.

I pushed aside my own bowl. Though I had somehow won through the other tests, I could now only hold in my mind the picture of the slash-edged mobile swinging in answer to the full arm pull of the guard, the crown resting at its very heart. Still there was nothing left for me but to face it.

"Is there a way I can see the likeness of the mobile without going into the palace square?" I asked then.

"Certainly." Ravinga raised her voice to carry into the shop. "Mancol, bring hither one of the crown mobiles. We make them in miniature," she informed me. "They are selling very well during this time. Outlanders buy them as they come here for witnessing the last test. There will be many for that, each of the Queens will bring her guards, and many of her household, while others will travel for themselves. It is perhaps only once in a generation that this happens."

The old man brought in the flashing, twisting set of plates. Ravinga stood to hook it on one of those cords, meant to hold dried fruit and meat, which hung from the ceiling. I leaned back in my seat to watch it as she set it going well with a touch of finger. At the trial time there would be steady twirling by the control ropes.

There was even a tiny crown within the blades and I regarded that without any wish to lay hands upon it. Did not death most always result from entering the mobile? I knew that it was that which was reserved for criminals whose crimes were considered the blackest. However, those unfortunates were forced in and from the start believed themselves that they had no chance.

There was a dancing light flickering on the plates as they turned. And the musical tinkle was loud in the room, though not as loud as the sound of the thing it so fully represented.

Dancing—I watched the in-and-out weave of the blades. Those real ones were knife sharp, diamond-edged, enough to slit an unfortunate into ribbons. Yet men had survived. For countless generations there had been Emperors and each of them had won his crown by passing among those blades. So it *had* been done.

Dancing—I closed my eyes against the flicker of the light and again was aware of another time and place, of dancers who were furred of hide and not slick-skinned. Behind me there was a rumble of sound—Murri had come in to lie at length at my back.

"That house in which Murri sheltered on our first visits, it is a ruin, but does not it have a great hall?"

Ravinga nodded. Allitta had returned to her dinner as if she had played her full part in the matter. She did not even seem to be listening.

"Have I your leave to go there?" I continued. "There is a need for thinking—"

"It is yours. None shall disturb you there," the dollmaker returned. Nor did she show any curiosity about what I wished. Perhaps she believed that I was about to seek out the Essence in silent meditation. Which also I was minded to do—but later.

With Murri I made my way into the ruin. It was more promising on the inside than the out. Perhaps it had once been the headquarters of a minor House. I kicked the refuse from the center floor and hung on a panel I half pulled from the wall— where I could watch it—the mobile.

I began to hum deep in my throat and a moment later heard the purring response from my companion. Though my singing in cat speech was a sorry thing, I could well recall some of the rhythm to which that tribe had danced on the isle.

Murri began the dance. He had his people's ability to gulp in air, fluff out his fur, and take to glides as long and as high as those of the sand ships of Twahihic. That advantage I lacked but I was able to leap and twist, and I found that with practice that ability grew. We wove patterns—he as graceful as all his people, I awkwardly and far behind. Yet I persisted, and as I did I continued to sing, for it seemed somehow that the sounds I made possessed a beat which inspired my feet for each leap and turn.

When I tired I dropped cross-legged on the floor and strove to empty my mind, think only of the cats as I had seen them at their festival, and I strove to somehow tap the essence of that memory and make it mine.

I spent a second day so in the hall, striving with all my energy to master as much as I could of the dance. Whether this effort would benefit me or not I had no idea but it was all which I might summon in support.

That night there was a clatter of the door mobile and Allitta let in an officer of the Chancellor's own guard. He looked at me stolidly as he said:

"Two signals before mid-day tomorrow—those who are chosen will face the task."

There was certainly nothing encouraging about that bald statement. I fancied even that he resented having to deliver it to me. However, that was the summoning and there was no drawing back.

Once he had gone I spoke first to Murri. It was only the fact that I was a candidate which protected him here—a very fragile truce which would be broken in an instant at my failure.

"You go safe, brother. Now—I cannot spread claw for you soon."

I looked to Ravinga. "Is there anything I can do to make sure that Murri does not suffer?"

Her eyes when she turned an answering gaze on me seemed cold. "Do you then doubt yourself so much, Hynkkel? Such are not the thoughts you should hold now."

"Chance really favors no man," I answered. "If chance fails me, I would have Murri safe."

She pursed her lips. "There are ties which can be called upon, yes."

I drew a deep breath. My hand went out and my fingers were buried deep in the fur on Murri's head.

"So be it. That much I ask of you."

29

As there had been at the selecting of the candidates, the square before the palace was crowded—though the guard kept back the throng for a space about the mobile. On the steps behind it was the throne of the Emperor while the Grand Chancellor stood a step below that holding the staff of office, and at her feet lounged the Blue Leopard.

The mobile had been lowered closer to the ground and already those who were to keep it in motion had set those pendants clanging back and forth, the sun striking vivid colors from the plates' ever-moving surfaces. While, at the core, the crown of diamonds with its cat heads set with ruby, topaz, emerald, sapphire, those stones signifying the Outer Regions, formed a blaze of fire.

The crown hung on a chain. He who won that far must also be able to free it, then issue forth again unharmed. To pass those ever-swinging plates, the clangor of which alone was enough to deafen one, would require such agility of body that even to think of such action was daunting.

Yet we stood there ready to attempt that feat, one on either side of the mobile. Shank-ji had drawn the lot which would send him first into the whirling, cutting swing.

Stripped to breech clout he made a fine figure, surely such a one as we could want seated on the throne awaiting the winner. I knew that his body had been exercised for years in all the actions of a swordsman and a spearman of note. And he wore now the guise of one who was utterly sure of himself.

Nor were those who had escorted him hither and now behind him any less assuring. Sons and Heads of Great Houses, daughters of famous clans, they stood by custom to back him who had become their champion. Among that throng I caught sight of my brother, at the same time he was eyeing me, and there was nothing of support in the glare and sneering twist of lip he showed.

Behind me—yes, there were those showing the badges of some of the out-clans, and, closer, Murri. The people had come not because I was their choice. But Murri was there because of good will. They gave him room as he sat, his poise erect, his tail up quivering with excitement, watching the clatter of the plates in the wind as he might have eyed the scuttling of a sand lizard.

Farther back must be both Ravinga and Allitta though they were making no parade of their presence. However, I thought that Murri's good wishes were shared by the dollmaker, if not by Allitta—of whose good will I was hardly sure.

The high priest of the Vapala temple turned a fraction. One of his followers held a gong and the high priest himself had his short rod of office ready. He swung that. The gong note was loud even through the clamor of the mobile. I saw Shank-ji's body tense.

A second time the priest signaled. The warrior sprang. He twisted and turned, once nearly caught by the unexpected whirl of a plate which might have taken off his head had he not ducked in time. He had won within the inner circle, raised his hands to the crown. Then—

The mobile notes were broken by a louder sound. One of the plates turned as if it had been struck by a rod such as the priest held. There came a scream. Shank-ji rolled on the ground in a mist of spouting blood, his left hand clutching at a wrist from which the other hand had just been shorn as neatly as if the blow had indeed been delivered to prevent his taking of the crown.

There were shouts then, men of his war band surged forward. But the Chancellor had already signaled and the mobile swung upward enough to allow two of her own guards to crawl in and bring out the wounded man.

He was carried down an aisle quickly made in the crowd who had come to support him, and, from the limpness of his body, I thought that he had lapsed into unconsciousness. On the stone pavement where he had fallen there was a pool of blood and—the hand. Looking upon that I fought the sickness rising in my throat. Better death than to be maimed.

Three, wearing the jeweled robes of the nobles of the first rank, had pushed forward to the foot of the steps below the Chancellor. And he who seemed the leader spoke vehemently, though the clamor of the crowd and the chimes of the mobile obscured his speech as far as the rest of us were concerned. He turned and pointed to the bloodied pavement.

Just beyond that hand there lay something else which had no place there, what appeared to be an arrow, one without any paticluar markings. And certainly that had not been there earlier, for the ground beneath had been most carefully inspected before the mobile had been lowered.

An arrow, now half in the pool of blood—and that pendant of the mobile which had jerked just as Shank-ji had reached for the crown. Those added up to—

Interference—a foul! Yet that was none of my doing and certainly I had no friends, even of my countrymen here, who would try such a trick. Whoever had shot that arrow had skill— the skill of an expert archer perhaps.

The mobile arose higher by jerks and, when it was well up, the nobles who had lodged that protest and the Chancellor herself went to the site. At a gesture from the Chancellor one of her guard picked up that arrow and turned it slowly about under her close inspection.

Now one of the nobles, his face a mask of ugly malice, pointed to me. I felt rather than saw the movement of the crowd behind me. There were certainly those there who would be only too glad to drag me down as one who was unfit, who had broken the honor of the outland peoples.

The Chancellor gave an order and her guard moved in behind me, forming a wall between me and the crowd. Or was it that they were prepared to take me prisoner as a traitor to custom and a perhaps would-be murderer? Murri! They would move against my fur brother also, only the thin line of a promise keeping them from already sending spear heads into his hide.

However, now the Chancellor was pointing to the plate swinging well above her and then outward at an angle into the crowd on the opposite side of the square—that from which Shank-ji himself had come. At first the nobles seemed in no mind to accept her suggestion. They still glared in my direction. Then her own staff of office swung in imperious order and I saw some of her guards begin to thread through the crowd on the other side. Though how they might discover the culprit there I could not guess.

The intrigues of the Great Houses were so well known that this could have been aimed at Shank-ji out of jealousy or spite. Doubtless he had, as we all do, those who would wish him ill. The Essence knew that there were enough gathered here this day who had no kind thought for me. Someone must have feared Shank-ji's ascent to supreme power and what it might mean to himself or to his House. I could see no other answer.

Though my mind did go back to those points Allitta had made of those who saw in my winning trouble to come. Was there a mind behind all this which courted trouble? A picture flashed through my mind then of the figure in Ravinga's house—he who wore the stinking rat for a badge. But that one was long dead. No, this must be the result of some House intrigue.

Those under the mobile withdrew to the steps and the Chancellor gave a second wave of her staff. Once more the mobile creaked downward. I ran my tongue across lips suddenly dry. So it would go forward and now the trial was mine. It would be difficult enough to keep my mind strictly on what I was doing.

I did not hear it, I could not have with the continual chime of the mobile and the uproar of the crowd about me, but I sensed it—that song which came from behind me—Murri's song. It moved me to answer, and it was with that humming through my whole body, possessing me, that I moved forward.

The flicker of the panels before me was near blinding. My right hand sought, without any conscious order, that pendant mask upon my breast and I made my first move. There were no true paths there and no planes; rather I faced the twisting, turning bodies of cat people rapt in their own mystery into which they had drawn me.

In—out—to the left—to the right—I leaped and turned, twisted, stooped, to leap again. And in my mind I held tight to that picture of cats, dimly knowing that that was my only hope now.

How long did that dance take me? There was no reckoning for me now. Only a blaze of light before me and that was what I must secure. Suddenly that illusion of the dancers was gone. I had reached the core of the mobile while overhead swung the crown, the glitter of the gems in it enough to blind one who looked directly at it.

I stood so for a breath and then I sprang. The treasure I would hold was attached to a chain. My left hand closed about the chain and I swung, feet off the ground, as with my right fingers I strove to unhook my trophy, only too aware now of the menacing sway of the panels about. None of them had yet crashed against the chain to which I so desperately clung, though one spun perilously close.

The crown was mine—at least it was in my hold, free from the hook which had held it. I dropped to the pavement, one foot slipped, and I went belly down on the stone, an outflung hand being no help as it, too, slid along a sticky surface. With the scent of blood about me I realized that I had fallen into the spot where Shank-ji had finished.

There was a vicious swing near my head and I ducked forward. I was sure now that the wind had truly risen and that my present position was near fatal. Nor could I wriggle on my belly, for at least two of the panels were only finger heights above the pavement and swung back and forth in threat of slicing open anybody striving to pass beneath them.

I could no longer summon up again that vision of the dancing cats which had led me here. There were only those knife-edged panels a-swing. Yet the crown lay heavy within the crook of my arm and I dared to raise my head a fraction to view all I could of the swinging death about me.

Now I got to a crouch, having taking the chance that the two nearest of those panels, no matter how far they swung, had a space between them. From that crouch I reached my feet. Before me directly now was another panel helping to form the ring just before the innermost one which now imprisoned me. To clear that I must spring and twist at the same time. I tensed and moved.

Then the wind of one panel passing nearly sent me sprawling straight into the last and most vicious outer line. My head jerked at a pull upon my up-knotted hair. I could not remain where I was to be cut down on the next swing. Once more I leaped, having only seconds to judge the wheel of body to carry me past.

I sprawled face down on the pavement, the noise of the mobile near deafening me. Or was it altogether that? There was something else, voices raised in such an uproar as to drown out the metal's clamor. Jagged locks of hair whipped at my face as I crawled forward a space, fearing any movement to feel the knife edge of a panel slitting across my body. Then, hardly believing it, I knew I was free of that devilish thing and I rose unsteadily to my feet, stooping to pick up the crown I had brought with me.

There was softness of fur against my body, a rough tongue lapped across my ribs. I gripped Murri's heavy shoulder hair and held that as if the touch alone would make me believe I had really won.

At last I turned, in time to see the mobile rise again. Beyond it waited the Chancellor and the priest, beside them the Blue Leopard of rulership. Yet I did not yet go forward; rather I rubbed my hand across Murri's broad head. And I said:

"Only by your favor, brother," knowing well that I spoke the truth. There were none here—unless Ravinga was somewhere in the crowd behind me—who had wished this finish— none save Murri.

"By your will—" he made me answer.

I loosed my hold on him to turn the crown around in my hands, perhaps to assure myself once more that I indeed held it. The gems made a flashing show which were in contrast to my blood-stained body. Though by the greatest of favors none of the red painting came from my own veins.

The mobile was well up. I could cross that stretch of pavement to the steps without fear now. The end of strain had left me weak, light of head, so that the figures of Chancellor and priest wavered in my sight.

However, I set one foot before the other, until I realized suddenly that Murri was no longer by me. Some stubbornness within me would not allow me to advance without him. The roar of the crowd was even louder. Were they trying to howl down in anger my triumph, or were they cheering me for my success? I did not know.

When I looked around for Murri I saw only open mouths and waving arms, the guards with spears lowered across their bodies to form a barrier to keep this bit of pavement clear.

I could not linger, though my concern for Murri—if the crowd was truly united against me his danger was very great. Still if I was Emperor, then let me claim my victory and show these that a "barbarian" took what he had fought for without awkwardness of bearing.

I came to the steps. To the priest I offered the crown. Though I had truly and honestly won it, it would not be mine until the official coronation. Even so, at this moment I was indeed Emperor—something I found very hard to adjust to.

The Chancellor held forth the royal staff of office, the leopard crouched and rumbled something not far from a purr. I knew that I must now turn to face this unruly mass of my subjects, that rod in hand.

I climbed a step and then two. The high throne was still empty at my back but I made no move to seat myself there. Somewhere, perhaps on the roofs about, was that slinger who had accounted for Shank-ji. It could well be that some bitter House intrigue would see fit to dispose of one they considered an upstart to allow another trial—with new candidates—such was not beyond reason.

Then I saw the crowd waver, draw apart. Over one of those spear barriers leaped Murri, soaring as he had in the dance. He carried in his mouth a rod the end of which glittered in the sun.

The priest stumbled back, clutching the crown, his face showing his fear. However, the Grand Chancellor stood her ground, her hand going to the Sword of Presence at her belt, even though that weapon of ceremony might be as nothing against this raider from the outlands.

In a single bound Murri reached me and I took from his jaw hold the Sand Cat-topped staff Ravinga had wrought. I did not relinquish the other which bore the leopard symbol.

On my left side the Blue Leopard, belly down, ears flat to skull, sounded a hiss. At my right Murri stood tall, his yellow eyes round on the beast who disputed his coming, showing no fear, no sign of warning of battle to come.

With the two beasts and the two staffs, I faced the people, whose shouts had died away, and who were staring back at me as if amazement had struck them dumb. An age had ended, a new one begun. In one hand I held the ancient symbol of the past, in the other I gripped that which had come to me by my own efforts. What the Essence would demand of me in the future I had no way of foreseeing, but it was true that I must be my own man, that much I had learned. At that thought, near bare of body, stained with blood, the hair released from my shorn topknot tossed by the wind, I claimed what was mine and what I would hold, even as my fur brothers claimed and held what they had won.

Epilogue

Ravinga had lit only one of the lamps, but by that I could see well her face, and I recognized the strength of purpose in her expression.

"He has won," I said. That that win had astounded me was a simple way of expressing how I felt. This Hynkkel, what had he in him anyway? To be made to twist my thoughts of him in another pattern was difficult to accept.

"He but begins," Ravinga corrected me.

"They must accept him—it is custom—" I caught part of her hint.

"You speak so, knowing what you know, what you yourself have endured, girl? Do not play the simpleton. Shank-ji may have lost a hand, he has not lost a head. There is a slinger to be accounted for—that need is immediate. Beyond lies much more—"

Her gaze swept beyond me to that shelf on which stood the figure of Ylantilyn.

"Therefore," now she spoke briskly as one who had finished one task only to turn to another, "we move again. You, Allitta, have now the right to claim your heritage. Custom decrees that what one Emperor has done, a new one may undo. The last of your House shall do homage with all her peers, shall claim all rights and privileges due her line—all rights." She repeated that as one who could not be crossed.

Past bitterness arose in me so strong I could almost taste it. "No!" Still—a second thought—was this not what I had once dreamed of? If strange circumstances brought it about, why should I throw it away?

"Yes!"

I could not stand against her. I could not even stand against that part of me which wanted what she took so easily as a fact. A new life—a dangerous one—but I had lived with danger for many seasons—it would not be new or daunting for me.

"We move," Ravinga continued. "Even as the mobile swings, we begin to move."

Year of the Rat

The author's deepest thanks are offered to:

Caroline Fike for her computer "whiz"ardry, and to Rose Wolf, for keeping the resident Sand Cats at bay while the *Rat* was at play.

Without their assistance, the second part of this fantasy might never have appeared.

Chapter 1

Hynkkel-ji,
Newly enthroned Emperor of the Outer Regions:

I stood staring into the large mirror. Never before had I seen my full length so. But nothing in my life, I thought now, with an inner uneasiness I was fighting to control, had prepared one who was a servant and near outcast of one's House to view himself in the stiff and heavy court robes of the Emperor—Emperor Hynkkel-ji—that now was.

Another reflection moved into place beside mine, half hidden by the outflow of my diamond studded outer robe, which lay in a train for some length behind me. The tawny fur of Murri shown brightly red against the sweeping folds. If I saw, in myself, one who had come to a strange position, then Murri was my equal, a Sand Cat at utter ease in the center hold of those who had long hunted his kind.

An Emperor had, as I had discovered in the past few days, little if any privacy. However for this limited time I was free of servants and guards, though those waited just beyond the curtain door behind me. And ringing ever in my ears were the musical chimes of the diamond mobiles, large and small, which were in every palace chamber I had seen.

Only, the longer I stared at the stranger in the mirror, the less at ease I was. The heavy fur collar about my shoulders, cascading down to form half my train, was—yes, it was weighting me, both mind and body, the glitter of the gems netting the blue of the robe, the elaborate state crown which concealed the loss of my high hair knot, shorn away during that last fateful testing; my body did not welcome these.

Nothing had prepared me for this hour. And I had no companion to back me save Murri. I loosed my grip on that heavy, unfamiliar robe to rest a hand on the soft furred head of the one I could fully trust.

And that I needed him I never forgot. My ordeal within the whirling, deadly blades of the huge mobile of justice had been successful. But the belief was ever with me: the cause of my success was that archer on the roof of one of the buildings, who had loosed a shaft bringing down Shank-ji who had shared the testing. No trace of the would-be assassin had been discovered by the royal guards, but I was sure that the attack had not been made in my favor.

I had questioned within myself, sought an answer. At least I believed I had found one I could accept. Someone, as yet undetected, had wanted an unknown from one of the lesser Queendoms to assume the crown I was wearing now. Those of Valapa, with their strong belief in their own superiority, would think an outlander would be stupid and naïve, turn readily to others, allowing himself to be controlled by their advice. The nobility of Valapa were well known to be ever intriguing amongst themselves, snatching at power, bringing a weaker House to annihilation.

Haban-ji, whose death had in a roundabout way brought me before this mirror, had been well known to have played these treacherous games with much success during his reign. Who would believe that a simple herd boy out of Kahulawe could defend himself against such intrigue? Therefore any that I met within this palace, who outwardly paid me allegiance, might very well be the one to watch the closest.

Nor, if it became obvious to me that I was destined prey, could I keep Murri with me. He must return to his own kin in the stark outer lands.

I was facing now the first public duty—greeting the five Queens plus the leading nobles of Valapa and the outer Queendoms.

Turning away from the mirror, I looked at a company which I could not be sure I would ever join. On a long shelf at the far end of the chamber was set a line of figures, the height of my forearm, seeming so aware, and staring so intently at me, that they might be alive. The past emperors—some twenty of them, each in his own way deserving respect.

Murri pressed closer to my side, bringing with him inner warmth. For now at least my blood brother, whose wary talents were far beyond those of any men, would be alert to any peril to come.

There suddenly came a soaring series of chimes, exceeding all others I had heard, a summons. Reluctantly I moved to the door, using all my strength of will to assume an outward guise of complete ease and power, which I must ever fight to hold in the sight of the world as well as I could.

Allitta,
Sometime apprentice to the Doll Maker Ravinga:

I stood under the light of Ravinga's strong lamps, doll-stiff, as my mistress slowly encircled me, using the same intense stare as would be turned on any work of her hands before it was allowed to go out into the world. After some years of freedom of dress, I had again been bound, laced, latched into heavy court robes until I wondered if I could ever manage to walk freely again.

At last Ravinga gave a sharp nod. Her three Kottis, who had been sitting watching us both with the measuring eyes of their kind, arose and stretched. I wished I might have a like relief from my present ordeal. Now I actually dared to ask the first of the questions, which were haunting me.

"Mistress," I paused to favor a throat dry with foreboding, "it has been a long time since the House of Vurope has appeared at court. It was banished from among the Six Families and struck from the rolls by the Emperor's own hand. How dare I come before this new ruler and demand recognition?"

She frowned, in a way which had been a form of rebuke I had early learned to dread. "I should not have to tell you this again, Allitta. This is the Law from the beginning—Those who were reduced, their House disgraced, can, on the first throne day of a new Emperor, ask to be restored. You are also

lucky in this—your reinstatement will not make any new enemies, for the fortune of Vurope was not given to another
House, but has remained in the hand of the Emperor and can
be restored easily on his recognizing your House. Therefore,
you are the one to claim back your rightful destiny."

"And if I do not want to tread again into the tangled
nets of their intrigues, can I not choose to remain as I am,
your apprentice? You have fostered me beyond my hopes,
Mistress—I am content. I will be doubly satisfied to remain as I am."

The set of her mouth, the blaze of her dark eyes, gave me
her answer even before she spoke.

"The Essence ever rules. There is the Power of the Outer
Regions, our native Power. We do not question as to the why
of action, but face what we must. The Circle of the Six has
been broken these many years. It is your duty, Allitta, to mend
what you can.

"You are not lacking in curiosity, and in basic understanding. You guessed long ago that there is another purpose to the
making of these dolls. Life for all of us does not remain ever
the same. There are ends—and beginnings. We are facing
both now in the Outlands. You will take up the duties to
which you were born and await what comes."

She turned away to take up a polished and carven box
from one of the shelves behind her. I could not translate the
carvings—such learning had not been mine—but I knew that
they had meaning, perhaps a dire one. Several such boxes
were in the inner, secure cupboard, treated as one might treat
a treasure beyond price.

Ravinga took from that chest two dolls. One was clearly
meant to be Allitta, as I now stood, wrapped about by a rich
robe, the color of the last gleam of sunlight—a pale rose fading into gray, lit with a diamond star here and there.

The other, which companioned this, was—I do not know
why I suddenly shivered; I am not one, or thought so then,
to strive to peer into the future. Only, to study now this
man clad in the splendor of a coronation robe—no. That

gem-bound, wide-skirted sweep of blue did somehow become him! He was a puzzle to me now. When I had first met Hynkkel I could dismiss him as a servant. It had been well known that even his family found in him no cause for their pride.

Yet—everyone also knew that one who could survive the five trials had strength and courage beyond ordinary reckoning. Also he was one with a Sand Cat that all who had sense avoided. Yet it had been hard to regard him as more than an untried youth, less than those who rode as warriors.

"Why—?" I raised an arm heavy with the gemmed bracelets Ravinga had placed there, to indicate, first, the image of myself and then that of the man who was Hynkkel-ji, the new Emperor.

Ravinga laid her hands upon the heads of the figures.

"Listen, girl. These came to my mind to make in secret. None shall know of them save we two. But all such drives to create are sent to us by the will of the Essence, which formed us, enfolds us and our land. You may be sure that I speak the truth when I say that a new life faces both of you—not because of what has happened already, but which will come."

I remained uneasy but I realized that I would have no real answers, that I could only await what would face me. I had learned early that one might not foresee in honesty what lay ahead and I must accept that burden—though I could not do it with serenity.

Thus I obediently followed Ravinga, not into the shop where I had been at peace, but by a way which we had seldom used, coming to a court behind the familiar rooms. There were those who arose and made obeisance when we came, first to Ravinga, and then, a fraction more deeply, to me.

Since I was about to claim headship of a House, those who waited were not the usual escort. Instead of guardsmen, these were women—though they were dressed as warriors. They moved to a decorated carry chair, four of them taking their places, one to each of the corner poles. Four others stood waiting to provide a guard and the last held in one hand a small diamond mobile and in the other the staff to which was fastened the bannered device, which had been erased from all record more than ten years earlier.

She, who led our procession of pomp and pride out of the dull courtyard into the street, brought us to the court and perhaps a future I would find difficult to handle. Before me the mobile chimed. I could hear it, in spite of the clamor of others like it, which were placed before each building. And the House banner was held high while the bearer called with a carrying voice, "Vurope!"

The more we advanced toward the palace the more crowded the streets became. One could readily believe that the entire population had turned out. Yet there was a way opened for us in answer to that cry from our leader. Nor was mine the only chair to be seen, or the call of my house the only one to be heard.

Since my curiosity had been awakened by the scene, which had never before in my lifetime been enacted, I stared around me, wondering if any one noted that the banner of a blighted House was being boldly displayed. Slowly I became aware that indeed my passage was noted, several times by young mounted nobles, one or two of whom pushed their way closer, to stare in a rude intrusive fashion.

I have never come into heat nor have I desired to do so. Those youths and men I have met were lesser in my eyes than such women as Ravinga and others with talents they resolutely apply.

On my many market trips to the farther Queendoms I had met with those I admired for what they had developed. It had always seemed to me that those whose lives had been altered by mating, had lost an important part of themselves by that change in body and employment.

Thus I now was irritated by the notice from these bold and pushing warriors; I was glad that, by custom, my immediate household would be of my own sex.

The First Court of an Emperor is held always in the huge amphitheater, which is the very center of the palace, walled in on four sides by a three-story rise of the building.

An expansive flight of stairs at the far end served to support the wide seat of the throne. Two steps below this exalted position there were the lesser thrones of the five Queendoms. And, farther down, the backless stools of the court officials and higher nobility, mainly representative of the Five Families now in existence.

These were already filled, with those in robes of blazing colors and many gem badges of their rank, while the lowest area was nearly filled with the carry chairs and dismounted warriors, their pa-oryxen having been left without. I began to doubt, seeing that crowd, that I could ever get close enough to mount the steps when time came to make my plea. However the leader of my small party seemed adroit at accomplishing this and I was brought to within a short distance of the throne steps.

We had only reached that position when there arose such a clash of diamond chimes as drowned out all other sounds.

Hynkkel-ji:

Murri stood close, his attention partly for my other assigned companion—the great blue leopard who, in other reigns, had been the closest to the Emperor, his lip lifted to show the points of fangs as regarded Murri. That also was a difficulty to be solved. But I had no intention of bidding my cat-brother to depart.

Before me, curtains heavy with gems and metallic embroidery parted and I found myself standing, half concealed by the high back of the throne itself, while the chancellor held up a hand and the clamor of the chimes died away. Silence followed. Three times the Grand Chancellor of the Outer Regions lifted her staff to bring it down on the step of the throne. Then her voice, somehow heightened and strengthened to reach across the packed space, carried the invocation, which would formally begin my reign.

"By the Will of the Essence shall Hynkkel-ji of the House Kaverel of the Queendom of Kahulawe comes now to the Throne of the Outer Regions. Be it so!" Once more she brought the butt of the staff down against the stone of the steps.

Having been so proclaimed, I rounded the throne and seated myself there, Murri to my right and the Blue Leopard to my left. Unlike the rulers before me, I carried two rods of office—against the will of most of the court. But none could dare to question an Emperor's choice. In my right hand was the staff Ravinga had wrought for me and which, oddly, felt lighter and more my own than the Imperial, which bore the likeness of the Blue Leopard, whereas my own was crowned by a Sand Cat.

Now it was my turn to speak and I hoped that my words would carry as well as those of Giarribari.

"By the Will of the Essence do I sit here. Only by such favor may I rule; to It I shall ever listen, and I do swear that I shall ever be guided by It. Thus do I proclaim that at this hour and day I welcome all pleas and will aid that which is best for our people and lands."

It had sounded loud enough as did all the other vows of Queens, Lords, great families and court officials. The words were old and formal. But when it came time for those in the arena to add to them, there was a kind of roar as if great cats had raised voice.

Allitta:

He made an impressive appearance, did Hynkkel-ji; certainly one looking upon him now would not see the wanderer I had known. When there came an end to the ritual he arose, and he brought down both of the staffs he carried.

"From this day the Essence abide strongly in me," he said. "Now do I call on any who wishes for justice by the Law."

I had already slipped out from the carry chair and now I moved forward. As those standing close to me discovered what I would do, they opened a path for me, which led to the foot of the stairs.

He moved in turn and the Queens had arisen, now clustering behind him as he passed their lesser thrones, the great cats matching their pace to his.

"Who calls upon Justice—" I saw his eyes widen, as he must now know me.

"I do—in the name of the Essence—for the return of the House of Vurope of the Queendom of Valapa. I be Vurope-va-Allitta, Head of that House by rightful birth. Thus I ask that this House be fully restored to the rolls and recognized." There was still a shadow of surprise on his face. But he raised both wands as he answered:

"May the Essence be evoked. Vurope-va-Allitta, your House is reborn."

With his staffs he pointed to me. His feline attendants flowed down the steps and came to stand on either side of me. Ravinga had coached me well. I reached out hands, right to Murri, left to Blue Leopard, resting on their high held heads. I bowed my head in curtsey and said:

"By the Essence, I Vurope-va-Allitta, do swear my loyalty to Hynkkel-ji. My House, to the August One, shall take up its duties, being once more alive."

Thus I sealed myself to a future, which I still gravely mistrusted.

Chapter 2

Hynkkel-ji:

Though dusk was a curtain outside the window before me, my duties were not over. There was still the feasting. The Queens, the major lords of each land who had appeared before me this day, would be the honored guests.

Honored guests—for one reason that had the sour taste of wilting algae for me. I had, after a goodly space of time, seen my father this day. Indeed he had been forced to the duty of swearing loyalty to me. He had worn his old uniform of a Commander of an army—an army long since disbanded—perhaps to impress on me the belief that I was not fit to meet him so. A son who was weakling by his measure—one who was no warrior—I must still be unfit.

We might never have met, by his attitude, the cold reserve with which he looked at me. I could only trust that at our short meeting I had displayed none of my own feelings.

My brother had not appeared, or else not chosen to swear faith to me. But I had seen Melora-Kura, my sister, and had arranged that she would come with my father for this feast.

The bubble lamps about the room were responding to the lessening light from without, their jeweled colors growing stronger. Somewhere one began to play a kifongg—a soft melody such as would lead a weary one to sleep.

My time now would be, I was sure, steadily occupied. However, I fully intended to follow my own path whenever I could. I thought about my needs. This, and this and this to be done now. It had been my intention to check upon Ravinga—and perhaps Allitta. But she was now well provided for. I had been startled by her appearance, for she seemed so remote, as if the rich garments she wore walled her from the Allitta I had known in the past, an apprentice to a doll maker.

I would somehow make my sister known to both Allitta and her former mistress. Melora-Kura; my hand went to my right wrist. When I had assumed this Imperial splendor early this day, I had been presented with a soft hide bag, one on the side of which was painted the symbol of our House. It had contained a wide armband with an intricate design using of the gems of all the Queendoms—the emerald of Twahihic, the sapphire of Kahulawe, the diamond of Valapa, the topaz of Azhengir, and the ruby of Thnossis. It seemed to me as I slipped it on that its touch held the warmth such as my sister alone had shown me. And the work was truly her best. This was my own; no other ruler had worn it before me and I intended to let Melora know just what her gift meant to me.

The chiming of the mobiles was growing louder. I shrugged to settle the weight of my outer robe firmly and strove to manage my train. Murri arose and blinked. At the other side of the room Akeea, the leopard, was already moving towards me. That was another problem I must deal with. Some kind of acceptance must be made between Murri and this proud royal guard. I must meet with the Sand Cat and all the leopard guards as soon as I could.

Allitta:

We of the Outer Regions were always wedded more to the cool of night than the blaze of day. As the cat people our eyes adjusted well to darkness. But all the buildings were lit by the bobbing lamps, some of which floated free, perhaps accompanying some inhabitant. Often they had the appearance of great feline eyes. I passed under a cluster now on my way to a duty I would happily resign if I could. But with the return of Vurope to join the Six Families, I must take my place calmly in a society for which I had no taste, one I might even fear. Now I must eat and drink, and be on guard for some difficulty which could indeed come from a poorly chosen word. There was no one under this roof now to whom I could look for companionship. I blinked as one of the eye lamps swung noiselessly by. It might have been taken from the skull of some giant Sand Cat. Murri! Hynkkel-ji at least had his brother-in-fur and was not all alone.

The door of the feasting chamber stood open, crowned with bubble lights in rainbow colors. And the guests were gathering. I slowed my pace—I had no wish to attract attention by being an early arrival. The woman before me also walked alone without escort. She did not take the small steps of a court lady but rather strode with the certainty of one used to trails and freedom of the outer world. Her robes were rich, but they looked less bundlessome than those near stifling me. Sapphire blue—Kahulawe. She turned her head a little, apparently admiring the tall cat figure of golden stone, diamond collars flashing under the lights. She—but! I knew her and, of course, she would be here this night. This was Hynkkel's sister, a gem worker of high repute. Her creations were well known and were treasured by those lucky enough to have them. I had an impulse to speak with her but stifled it, though I had a sudden feeling that this was one with whom I would feel at ease. There was long table facing us within. A finely worked cover of those special yarns spun from the wool of the small yaksen, the softest possible, patterned with a scatter of diamond stars, was nearly hidden from sight by the many plates, bowls and goblets of highly polished silver. Chairs were in place along both sides. However at mid-table, facing the door through which I had come, was a high backed seat, raised a little above its neighbors—that was for the giver of the feast. Many of the chairs were now occupied but one of the seated women, to my surprise, raised her hand in a beckoning gesture to me: Yuikala, the Diamond Queen, she to whose secondary court I would be attached. I could not understand her interest in me save it must have something to do with the recovery of the House of Vurope, and she wished to find out what manner of woman had taken over that once disgraced clan line. There was nothing to do but obey.

The establishment of Ravinga, the Doll Maker:

Ravinga put a second lamp to one side, and between that and its fellow she stood two dolls with steadied care. Then she sat and considered them for several long moments, before bringing out a second protective case. From this she took a third carefully wrought figure, one of the special ones—Yuikala, the Diamond Queen.

Again she sat in deep study, before she leaned forward and lightly tapped each of her choices, Hynkkel-ji, Allitta, and the Queen, on the forehead as if she were demanding their strict attention.

In the Royal Palace at the Feast:

At the feast in the palace, halfway across the city, the Queen smiled with carefully practiced charm at Allitta and held out her hand. The girl curtseyed and bent her head to kiss the massive diamond ring on the woman's hand.

"Good indeed is the day," the Queen said, "when an injustice is righted. To welcome back Vurope adds to the brightness of this occasion. Sit beside me child..."

There was no way of avoiding it, though Allitta was well aware that, in the past, Vurope was rumored to have been brought down by some action of Yuikala. She murmured dutifully and took the proffered place.

She concentrated upon the light conversation the other began, striving not to miss any word. For she was back where no word could be fully trusted, having not been schooled in the finest nuances of intrigue, and she knew the weaknesses of her own position.

So—this girl—this unseasoned girl, thought the Queen, has chosen to evoke power, which she certainly cannot successfully use. What had the latest whisper been? The child—she had indeed been a child when Vurope had fallen—overlooked at the clearing out of a rebellious lot—Where had she taken refuge? With that maker of dolls, as an apprentice—untrained in any courtly fashion—if she tried to get satisfaction for the past, she would fail even before she started. However it might be well to keep an eye on her.

Her thoughts turned now to a ploy of her own. The unwritten but never questioned Law of Custom presented her a chance to use her own Power to extend it—to become a most substantial shadow behind the throne. The Emperor could not formally mate. But that did not deny him a female Companion. She glanced at the figure who had taken his place facing her across the table. Sooner or later this also untaught, near barbarian outlander would be tempted to taste favors early spread before him.

Only, who was as beautiful as Berneen? And who in this court was as beautiful as Berneen? The Queen shifted the angle of her gaze to note that the dear child did make a splendid show tonight. Unlike most of the feminine company who glittered with jewels and near raw color, Berneen was dressed with a simplicity which was the perfect framing for her flawless features, the startling appearance of what could only be any man's ideal. And she was suitably stupid, also. The girl had never had a complete thought in her life. But she had been carefully drilled to deliver the appearance of one well aware of any court need.

This Hynkkel-ji—he was, of course, an unknown problem she must solve. Again the Queen looked at him. However, he must be ignorant of all that would make his situation easier. He was used to a much more simple life and he could not help but make mistakes, perhaps grave ones. But let her establish Berneen as his close Companion and naturally he would welcome her grandmother and then—The Queen smiled—all she knew would be at his service. Yes, the future was most interesting. Queen Yuikala smiled, raised her goblet and drank a silent toast to the future.

In the Doll Maker's Shop:
Ravinga studied the figure swathed in court robes, and also swathed in plans. Perfectly logical those plans were, only to be expected under the circumstance. However, that woman

so steeped in courtly intrigue did not know the quality of those two she believed to hold no higher rank than game stones to be moved at her will. Only, there was the matter of time. Ravinga was well aware that the Dark One was speeding up his preparations—there was a hint that Hynkkel's brother had joined with the gathering band of young, restless warriors who had gravitated to Shank-ji in the desert outlands. Also these new rats—there were many strange tales about them. The doll maker arose to return the figures to their cases. Time—it was settling on her like a burden growing heavier every moment. She must urge forward plans of her own.

Hynkkel-ji:

This was my first official feast and there was enough about me to distract attention. However there was the feeling that I was under observation. I was not sure. Murri was not here or I could have checked with him. The great cats have keener senses then men.

I looked down the line of faces of those before me—not really knowing what I was seeking. There was my father in his long-preserved dress uniform, which had been his constant wear in the past. And my sister smiled in a greeting I was swift to answer. There was Allitta, still somewhat of a surprise. And beyond her by several places—for once my eyes did not sweep on. I had already noticed, as what man could not—that there were many beauties from the five courts. But this one was indeed rare and I wondered who she was. She wore the diamond insignia of Valapa but no House order. Certainly she was very young and shy, hardly raising her eyes from her plate. I had an odd feeling that she needed support in this place—and in that way we were akin. Somehow—yes, I would like to meet her and discover what lay behind those down-turned eyes.

However such social aspirations were of no matter now. At times, in spite of the company about me and the need to be ever gracious and show interest in my neighbors, uneasiness clouded my thoughts. Tomorrow, as Chancellor Giarribari suggested, I would meet with the Queens in close conference.

One of the most important needs was for me to learn all I could about the depredations of the new species of rats that were now ravishing the outer lands. Already caravans were being almost constantly harried, making the depended upon trade difficult.

Rats—the worst curse of our land—now this new kind, larger, stronger, and, though it was hard to believe—apparently having some mind power unusual for such vermin.

Almost I was thinking too much of this and was not as aware as I should be of what was going on around me, for I suddenly caught Giarribari's eye and realized that time for Queen toasts had come, to honor the heads of the lands.

I gripped my goblet and arose, the rest of the company rising with me.

Allitta:

I gave a sigh of relief when I saw Hynkkel-ji move. This tedious festival was at an end. Throughout the feast I had been ever on guard. The more graciously Queen Yuikala noticed me, the more wary I had become. So far I could not guess her motive. Certainly she was not so engaged by my person that I should expect such interest from her. In regaining my inheritance, I wondered, into what web might I be walking? The royal toasts having been given and acknowledged; we were going to be free at last. I had determined that, when I was able to leave here, I would not go to the High House of Vurope but instead to Ravinga, in spite of the late hour. Upon her quick thought, her deep knowledge of Valapa and its people, I thought I could depend.

I managed to get away from the Queen at long last. She had abruptly shifted her attention to another lady. This one was also encased in courtly style but she was quite young. I myself do not claim to have many years behind me but also I have lived a life far removed from those now about me. (Suddenly I realized that my own lack of polish must be shared alone by Hynkkel-ji out of this company.) This girl curtseying before Yuikala was almost childlike in her action and appearance, wearing innocence like a crown. And—she was the greatest beauty I had ever seen.

Only I had no time for the strangers now—Ravinga—I must see her as soon as possible. There were still crowds in the street, late as it was. My escort made good time. I watched the officer leading and signaling a path free. As soon as possible I must make myself acquainted with those who dwelt under my new roof. We went to the back entrance of Ravinga's shop. On the doorstep awaited three Kottis. One does not *get* a Kotti, as one might buy a mount. They, and they alone, choose whom they wish to honor with their presence. I wondered if ever one such would come to my house. Now they flitted ahead of me as Ravinga appeared from the shadows. I had eaten and drunk too well and so declined what lay on the plate and in the goblet she had set out when she indicated a stool on the opposite side of the now bare worktable. Seating herself across from me she did not speak for a long moment, but rather studied me as if I were only a half finished doll. Then she nodded—as if in response to some private thought— and began.

"There is a problem arising, one which was not foreseen."

"That being?"

"Ambition and desire for power are potent evils. An Emperor without strong House ties, one nearly unknown to those he would rule, untrained to his position; such is strong meat to lure any hunting cat. What think you of Yuikala?"

"Rather what does she think of me?" I countered, somehow knowing that my uneasiness must be plain.

"She plans. I believe that she is so set on those plans that she seeks from the beginning to note any threat to them. Did you mark Berneen, who is her granddaughter and her prized possession?"

I was sure she spoke now of that fresh young beauty and nodded.

"Such as could be a noted Companion—" she paused.

Our Emperors do not lawfully mate any woman, no matter how beautiful and worthy of that position one might be.

But they do not go unaccompanied throughout their reigns. To be so close to the throne is considered an honor. I knew enough of courtly custom to understand at once Ravinga's suggestion.

"This Berneen will be set to catch Hynkkel-ji's eye? Is she in heat?"

"Not yet. However there are ways," Ravinga did not explain, rather she continued with what was a near order of her own. "Guile can be met by guile. I would have you aware of what this might mean but I shall leave to you what could be your coming role."

I was already shaking my head. "I—it is not for me to play such a game. He—he is not what I want. As you know I am not in heat, nor do I want to be. My freedom of such ties is dear to me."

She smiled suddenly. "As I say, choices are always ahead of us and our needs may change. This I do want you to do— be with him when you can and watch—there is a darkness spreading over the land and we may none of us do what we want to do, but rather, what is right and needful."

I sighed. There had been a note in her voice—Ravinga was not one to fear rumors; somehow she believed in this danger before us and that it might curse us all.

Chapter 3

Hynkkel-ji:

Our council—Queens and Emperor—was duly held. I felt as I had when I fearfully walked through the saltpans during the trials—one false move and I would be in trouble. Thus I listened with care. Behind me Murri sat, intent upon us. How much he understood without direct contact between the two of us I did not know. However his presence was, in itself, something that erected a wall for my support.

Untangled from all the formality of a court conference the news was certainly not what one could welcome.

"Those of the caravans, August One," Alompra, Queen of my own Kahulawe, flipped through a report of her own with slender sapphire laden fingers, "are protesting to the throne. The caravans are the life's blood of the Outer Regions—without the linking they offer, no Queendom could stand and prosper. Here I have," again she fingered those sheets of scraped thin oryxen hide, "the latest complaints. Trail Leader Kahlaeween, one whose words must be taken as true even as they are dour, has had one encounter which lost her not only several yaksen loads but even one of her people." She pushed her report towards Giarribari.

Should that not have been offered to me, I wondered. Or was I so uncertain that I read sly disparagement into that simple action?

"There are the way guards," I returned. "To aid the caravans is their first duty."

It was not Alompra who answered that, rather Pamirra of Azhengir. "The guards are riding trails about each of our Queendoms, August One. But there are only so many trained men and the land is wide. In the past we had many valiant warriors but their numbers have dwindled—" She paused, as if waiting some comment from me. I had no idea of what to say.

So it went and I came to feel that between me and the five resplendent women before me there was indeed a barrier, which must be pierced. At length, having heard their reports, I turned to the Chancellor who had gathered all together.

"Let all the knowledge possible on this subject, past and present, be gathered for my consideration."

Giarribari bowed, her expression impassive. I once more addressed the company.

"Crowned Ones, soon it is my duty to visit each of your holdings. Then decisions can be made and well understood."

Each bowed her head and arose, facing me for a step or two as they retreated backwards, and I answered their curt-seys by standing to watch them out, well aware that there was a very good chance that I had perhaps displayed an awkward handling of what might be now one of the most important problems facing me.

Allitta:

The hour was very early when I was borne into the courtyard of Vurope House. What occupied my mind was Ravinga's reading of the future. Why had I ever listened to her from the beginning? I was going to tread a trail for which I had no guidance. No stone cat marked direction. However—As I descended from the carry chair, making sure to thank all those of my house following for their service, I was suddenly aware of another voice.

The carved door of the house was opened by two uni-formed servants, bowing. However, before them was another on the fore step. For a moment I did not move—Then I knelt on the pavement and held out my hands.

"Welcome, Wise One!"

The Kotti came to me as if we had long been friends. It looked up at me with great golden eyes, somehow reassuring me that the day now dawning would be better than the night just past. Fur was soft and silken beneath my hands, a hue so gray it might be blue. The little one purred, rubbed its head against me, allowing me to continue to hold its soft body as I arose.

I looked closely into those gem like eyes turned up to me. "What is the name you bear, beautiful one?"

What I had often been told would happen at such an initial meeting came to me. A name suddenly occurred to my mind.

"You are Kassca—"

A strong mew answered me. Cuddling my new companion, I went on through the open door into my resurrected House.

Hynkkel:

Murri padded close beside me as I left the conference room. There was a goodly space left free for our passing. Sand Cats were the enemy—that verdict was wide spread. I wanted no trouble for one who had been my comrade during perilous times. There was a hiss—a whisper hiss—to my right and I knew without looking that the Blue Leopard must be appeased, and soon. I sent a thought to the silent one who was sitting there:

"Where be your warriors, Commander? Will you gather them so that matters can be made plain?"

We three had paused, and beyond, courtiers ringed us about. Those I did not desire to witness such a meeting. I signaled to the human captain of the inner guard. He came, keeping a respectful distance from Murri.

"Captain Yawkwee, I would give respect to the warriors in fur. Show me, by your courtesy, where is the proper gathering place."

He made sweeping salute, touching his diamond dusted white fur headdress.

"There be their own council place, August One. By your favor I can guide you so."

I looked to the rest of the gathered courtiers. And I think it was that sweeping stare alone which dispersed them. Whether I had again offended custom I did not know. The twists and turns of court etiquette might never be understood fully by me but there was no use wallowing in uneasiness and guilt. I must do my best and not concern myself with the wilderness of rules.

The captain took the lead and we traveled through a maze of hallways and rooms. This palace was in many ways a puzzle and one must surely have a trail map or guide to reach any goal. I was so ushered into a chamber, which appeared apart from the rooms in which men and women gathered. This had much more the seeming of a cave in one of those rock islands, which formed the abiding places of the outer Queendoms. There was no highly polished floor, no windows—rather a gloom much like that of early night. Slightly to one side of the entrance, stones, which actually looked rough, had been built into a low platform.

The dusk curtained the other side of this cave room. Out of those shadows leopards now padded. For the most part they were black, hard to distinguish in this half-light. But there were other blues, matching their leader, who stood still to my right. I guessed that he had used some mind call to summon them. They continued to come and I marveled at this army, which, by custom, I could command to battle if I wished.

At last no more emerged from the shadows. It was notable that those close enough for me to see clearly, eyed Murri with no welcome. But the Sand Cat remained impassive. Those before him might have been a collection of carved beasts, which were to be seen in any occupied part of the Outer Regions.

I have always met animals with friendship. In my boyhood I had tended the herds. These beautiful cats—how could I justly answer their inborn suspicion of Murri?

Mind speech with such had developed when I was first taken in by the Sand Cats. So, that I employed now.

"Warriors in fur, mighty are your deeds, ever to be praised your loyalty." I saluted the company with a gesture from my small rod of office, which I had used at the conference of Queens.

I made a sudden decision. "Noble ones, there approaches an evil which strives to pull us down. You are of the inner guard. Thus you shall be called upon for aid. I am not aware of your customs; what I shall say may not agree with those. But I give you now the truth. There stands," I indicated Murri, "one you deem enemy. He has saved me from death, and..." I shook back the sleeve of my heavy court robe, slipping off the wide wristlet my sister had made. The scar of my blood brothering was plain. "...those of his pride call me brother. To me this is so, though I am smooth skinned and he is furred.

"News has been brought to me that a new enemy has arisen, and this is an enemy for both you and him.

"When such is to be faced it is well for all those of good will to stand together fronting evil. The Sand Cats do not and will not threaten you, nor those you are sworn to; their eyes and powers are turned elsewhere."

Murri moved, coming forward to face the Blue Leopard. They stood so, eye to eye for what seemed to me a time I could not measure. Then they moved even closer. There came no deep growling, rise of fur or lash of tail. Instead, to my relief, the two great beasts touched noses.

Those who watched stirred but made no sound. I believed that they had their own mind touch and were communicating in thoughts I could not understand. However, that this acceptance between breeds happened was an event my own species would marvel at. Part of the burden hanging about me, as a storm cloak, dropped away. A major problem had been solved.

Allitta:

My dreams had been disturbing ones; I carried fear out of them though I could not remember why. There came a soft, soothing purring; a small furred weight rested against my shoulder; now a paw touched my cheek.

"Kassca," I half whispered in return. The purring rose a note or two.

Sunlight from the window touched us and the ringing of the diamond chimes signaled a need for rising. I must have slept away the larger portion of the morning.

"I am indeed a lazy one," I informed the Kotti, trying to remember any pressing duty which lay before me. What Ravinga had told me flashed into my mind, destroying my luxurious feeling of quiet and peace.

Then time passed swiftly enough. There was the business of dressing, of eating and finally the formal meeting with those of my household. I realized when I entered the hall that I had been remiss in not summoning earlier those making up my household. But then, I was not accustomed to having a household who would look to me for direction. There was, I thought unhappily now, too great a number gathered here. I searched for a moment or two trying to recall any of the countenances now turned to me. But ten years of a very different life, one which had made me free of bond, lay between. And none of my own blood had survived the fall of Vurope. They had gone down with of the house, not to be revived. Who stood here now were guards, servants, and the heads of lesser houses who owed fealty to Vurope.

I raised hands in salute.

"The House has been reborn. Kinsmen and those who support Vurope, you are welcome once more." I guessed that the rather formidable woman standing to my right was the steward. Now I spoke to her.

"Let there be a naming of names, a true meeting of House kin." (For by custom those who paid allegiance were kin of different degrees.)

She bowed her head. "Steward am I, House Head of Vurope. I am Hardi. These be the kin."

Those in the fore were the spokeswomen of lesser Houses, five of them. Then came the guardswomen, followed by servants. At the edge of this assembly, farthest from me, there were five men, introduced in their turn as grooms and messengers.

I tried to match names to faces, thinking in despair I would never remember them correctly, perhaps offending those I must treat with. I was inwardly glad that I *did* recall the formal words for such an occasion. Now a dim memory had awakened. Once I had stood in just such an assembly, as a child behind a tall man who had been engaged in this same role I now had. Asleter, my much older half brother, had been a stranger to me, for then I was yet a child of the inner ways.

At last the end came; those of the assembly bowed and I made the expected gesture of House respect in return. They filed away save for two guards, the steward, and a maidservant. I realized that now I would always be accompanied.

I withdrew in turn to the chamber which was the heart of the house. There were wall cases there, or there should be, holding the past rolls of the house. To study these as much as I could was a duty, for so I could better serve those now depending on me.

Yes, I discovered the cases remained unlooted of their contents. Ravinga had said that Vurope had remained in the care of the Emperor, so the contents had not fallen into the hands of any jealous enemy—perhaps the very one who had brought it down. I decided that I would begin with the latest of those records. It was needful to learn all I could of the intrigues and intriguers (if possible) who had attacked Vurope.

However I had not had time to unroll the first scroll before a visitor arrived. And it was one I was ready to welcome— Melora-Kura, the sister of the Emperor. She was the only member of his House who had ever supported him and he had spoken proudly of her talents.

I had seen her only twice, once at the great market of her own Queendom, when she had come to look at Ravinga's doll display and speak with my Mistress. At the time I was at the far back of the stall unpacking and was not to be noticed. Second, at the feasting—and somehow I had wanted to speak with her, because she had been alone, even as I was.

She came in now, with that easy stride which made it clear that the outer world and not the tight ways of the city claimed her. Smiling she touched her forehead and I repeated that greeting and drew forward one of the comfortably padded stools, seating myself on its neighbor.

"Lady of the House," she leaned forward a little. "The August One," she was serious now, "has told me of you and of Ravinga to whom he owes so much. He is now in such a position as to perhaps be open to attack and he cannot be sure of his defenses."

Maybe she had read something in my expression, which disturbed her, for she continued: "No, he is not one to lean upon others; he never was. You well know what his life has been. Now my father comes to court, not to support Hynkkel, but because his pride of duty demands it. My brother," she hesitated, "—my brother has never been close to Hynkkel. Now we are told that he favors those following Shank-ji, an open enemy. Thus he has left for the wild lands, perhaps will be led into dangerous mischief. My brother, clanless now, needs those he can trust."

"The August One," I replied in a voice sounding cold, even in my own ears, "indeed needs one well aware of Courtly life and its pitfalls. I also have to learn my way. This I can tell you—one who may be of real service to him, is Ravinga."

Melora nodded. "She also I shall seek out. Though I have been trained by my father as if I were a third son, practiced in arms and hunting, yet I have no experience of the court. It is said that here words alone can bring one down."

"As it was for Vurope. I am still ignorant of what lay behind that attack."

Was it, I wondered, now my duty to hunt out that secret enemy? Perhaps it was better to forgo a revenge, which would never bring true healing.

She answered eagerly. "Will you make me known to Ravinga? I may be here for a time and I wish to study the work of the diamond gem masters, but I know not how long I will be here."

Again she paused. "I am perhaps asking too much, but you know something of Hynkkel, as others do not. When kin are heart tied, all that can be done to help becomes a duty. That is now mine, so I try."

I wished at that moment that I too had someone such as Melora-Kura. Hynkkel had Murri, Melora, and Ravinga—A small twilight furred body jumped to the top of the table where I had dropped the scroll. There was a paw patting my arm.

There was a trusty one under my roof! I gathered Kassca to me and her purr song grew stronger.

However, though I wanted badly to tell Melora I might not be able to give any assistance, I could not dismiss her plea so. First it was Ravinga and then this other to whom I was attracted. Like it or not I was netted between them.

In the Palace—the Queen's own Tower:

The Queen's Tower of the Palace possessed a broad terrace where potted flowering plants made walls. When the high heat of the day diminished it was a rest place where Yuikala liked to sit, sipping melon wine and putting her schemes together. Though the one concerning the hunt of Hynkkel-ji was the most important now, another had pushed its way into her mind. This raw girl who had successfully claimed Vurope—was she going to search out secrets of the past? Would she attempt to carry on old quarrels? She would not be much of an opponent, but no one must be allowed to interfere with more important plans. This Allitta must be watched.

Yuikala raised her hand to touch one of the mobiles, sending it swinging at a faster pace, its chimes loud enough to summon the guard. Then, hands clasped together, she waited, ready to make her first move.

Chapter 4

Hynkkel-ji:

I had discovered that being Emperor did not release me from labor. Each morning I held a court of my own, not being fronted by courtiers outwardly eager to serve me, but the major officers who always held the lines of power for Empire and Queendom. Usually there was only a handful—Those I had quickly come to know after a fashion.

Kreed, the First Minister, was one bound by tradition, a man my father's age and of the very conservative high nobility. He was not one to venture many opinions and listened more than he spoke, though before the end of any of our meetings he attended, he generally made a statement, which I had learned to listen to carefully.

I did not feel so with Mohambra, the Imperial Cat keeper. She was of middle years but effervescent and a friend to all. During the times I was free of duty, I would often approach her quarters to discuss both the feline inhabitants of the palace and the Sand Cats of which she was eager to learn more. She was a little in awe of Murri, who was apt to preen himself in her presence.

The Grand Chancellor Giarribari appeared to have accepted me, at least outwardly. With her I often asked questions concerning the various Queendoms and some of the problems of the Outer Regions. I think that my knowledge of that impressed her a little. She always came with reports and shared with Gelanni, the Commander of the human guard, a strong running discussion of the latest news concerning any rat rumor or direct sighting.

Queen Yuikala seldom attended our meetings. Her concerns were tied only to Valapa. I was content to have it so. She was, in her own way, a formidable person. Twice I had accepted invitation to an informal meal in her tower; each time she had in attendance her granddaughter, Berneen. As custom dictated, the girl seldom spoke, usually only in answer to question. At our second meeting I guessed that she was greatly in awe of Yuikala and I would never see the real Berneen under these circumstances. I had never been included in the festivals common to those of my age and I truly did not know how to approach any maiden so sheltered by the smothering rules of the court.

This day, as I greeted my usual gathering of advisers, Yuikala was there. When Giarribari entered she did not come alone. With her was one who made his first visit, Mekkuiva-Kieuku, Minister of Balances. To all the outlands he was a symbol to be feared and usually he kept apart. I felt a coldness when I met his eyes, eyes that might wreck a House without any care because he judged it his duty. For the Ministry of Balances was a dire and forbidding organization. We born in the Outer Regions depend heavily upon water. The algae pools were necessary to life. Should any pool, through some misfortune, begin to lose water and that continue, Mekkui and his guards could actually determine who would live and who would die, sacrificed for the good of Queendom.

Such a fate had not befallen us for generations. The last time came during the Reign of Zastaff-ji several hundred years behind us. Then the Emperor himself, being well along in years had ridden into the outlands, to climb on a great rock spire. He remained, fasting, striving to plead with the Essence for his people. At length he had taken up his sword and made the ultimate personal sacrifice. We were told in our records that the Essence was moved by his act and the waters in the pools began to rise.

Mekkui made a court bow to me and I waved one of the servants to draw out a seat for him. Unfortunately that brought him face to face with me, something I could have done without—the story of Zastaff-ji very much in my mind.

However, it was the matter of the rats which was first discussed. News had come that a caravan issuing out of

Azhengir, traveling at night as usual, had been attacked. The yaksens had been quickly slain and the merchant and guards cut down, so only four were still on their feet when the patrol out of Azhengir came. Nor did the patrol itself come intact out of the ensuing battle, three lying dead when at last they had been able to pick off the larger and more intelligent rats.

"They came out of the Plain of Desolation," Commander Gelanni stated.

Mohambra, who had kept eyes on Mekkui ever since he had entered, now stared at the speaker. "Dare even rats attempt to make their burrows in such a place?"

I thought it time to show that I was aware of the problem, "We deal with rats that are more than the rats we have known—perhaps they now have the power to use even the Desolation to their purposes."

"There are others," the Commander said slowly, almost as if unsure of what he had to report, yet aware that he must share what he had learned. "Half the troop of the trail guards who were left pursued those rats which survived and ran. There was a watcher—"

"A watcher?" I prompted as he hesitated.

"One sighted at a distance in the Plain. Three of the guards reported this."

"That is impossible," Kreed said. "No one can enter the Plain and hope to live."

The commander refused to agree. "There have been tracks before leading in that direction. All the outland guards have trackers whose knowledge of the land can not be questioned."

Kreed continued to look down his long nose, but he did not continue any dispute. Only I was left with this new problem.

Men in the Plain of Desolation—and how could we check on that? I had seen months ago one of these superior rats, had seen the object it carried in its skull and how that had disappeared when exposed to the air. Was it that men could also carry such and perhaps be then immune to the deadly humors of the Plain?

Who would have the expertise to speculate on that? One alone—but I had no intention of bringing forth her name now— Ravinga. I wanted to hear first her suggestions—I only, but it would be with the two of us face to face and none other there.

Instead I turned to Queen Yuikala. "Highness, who within Valapa might have the most knowledge concerning that part of our world?"

There was a small smile curving her full lips. "Arguyia, who is of the records, August One—'Tis said that she has mastered the learning of at least five Emperor's reigns."

I nodded, "Well enough. She shall be consulted."

But I did not send for her immediately as they might have expected. Again I wanted to see this historian in private. I then tackled that which had been in my mind ever since I had seen Mekkui enter.

"Minister, have you some matter to bring before us?"

His dark eyes met mine. Again I felt an inner chill.

"August One, the measures read a difference in the Pools of Azhengir and Kahulawe. Another reading has been ordered."

Any difference which would bring a measurer out was a serious one. There was no denying that.

"Render the report at once as it arrives," I gave the order and received in return the slightest inclination of his head.

Now I spoke to the Queen. "So, you also have dark news for us, Ruler of Valapa?"

"Not so, August One." However I did not believe that was true. Was it that whatever had brought her here, she now wished to reconsider? Or did she want to deliver some message when we were alone?

I did not know and at that time I did not care. I wanted to be about my own need for learning what might descend upon us. And first of all I would visit the library.

The Doll Shop:

The doll shop was open for business but it was under the supervision of Ravinga's servant Mancol, and so far there had

not been any customers and only two orders had been turned
in. Those Mancol duly delivered to Ravinga but she paid no
attention; she was too intent on her own employment.
Stretched flat on the table before her was an old map, which
she smoothed over and over. So worn were the markings on it
that she had to use one of her enlarging glasses to pinpoint
what she was looking for.

The Plain of Desolation—that was what the people of
this day called it. Once it had been perhaps the richest and
most attractive of the outlands. Now only legends could
guide one.

With a finger tip the doll maker traced a way across the
dry lands of the Queendoms. The Plain lay beyond stark
Azhengir where the only product was salt, harvested under
perilous difficulty from the dull gray pans. Azhengir was the
bleakest of all the Queendoms and there had been odd changes
in the inhabitants, but it lay in one part touching the Plain.

Ravinga had located the point for which she searched.
Now she produced a slender rod and held it over that part
of the map. Her eyes closed, she concentrated on what
she wished to learn. There was a quiver in the lightly held
rod. She glanced down and loosened slightly more her
hold. One end dipped toward the border between the Plain
and the Queendom until it stood upright. Ravinga let it
free. The rod did not fall, rather it moved from the first
point it had indicated, out over the Plain, into the heart
of the unknown. There it halted, continued upright for a
moment or two and then collapsed. From a tray before
her Ravinga took up a brush, dipped it into a small, uncovered bowl and drew a symbol on the map where the
rod had ended its travels. Leaning back a little she regarded the drawing. She was frowning. Returning her brush
to its holder she arose quickly, pausing only a moment to
roll up the map of hide and slip it into the carry pocket
dangling from her girdle. Time—how much time was left
for them to marshal their defenses?

Allitta:

At least I could read the older script. Kassca lay at the other end of the table, now and then opening an eye to check on me—perhaps with pity—as I labored over the rolls of family history. I had been taking notes and wherever I added one, I wondered whether I would ever absorb even a fraction of what I was finding. So far, though I had finished the roll left at the destruction of the House, I discovered no clue as to who had been our enemy. The difficulty was that the later entries had, I thought, been too scant and too occupied with the general business of the household.

I had progressed backward and was now puzzling out the very crooked script of some scribe whose talent was certainly not to be commended. But then I found a passage which thoroughly aroused me. So, this unknown had also, for some reason been searching history. His or her note sent me once more to the shelves, where I flicked over the labels hanging from a time-darkened collection, which must have come into being near the day when Vurope had first claimed House standing. The labels were so dark and worn it was hard to translate them and finally I chose the second roll in line, hoping that luck was with me and that this would explain that hazy comment in the later record. Had the writer deliberately clouded it for some need of secrecy? Returning to the roll-burdened table I read once more what I had found and thought that that suggestion was possible. Then I re-rolled my first choice and carefully opened the other. The skin was cracked, spotted here and there, to the detriment of speedy reading. I sat down to explore, for that dim note excited me strangely.

Hynkkel-ji:

The only collections of history rolls I had ever known had been the very scant number of those kept by my own family. I entered the library of the Palace and came to a halt just within the curtained doorway. The room was nearly as long as the inner court, and it arose to a height about four times my own. I looked back through the doorway and snapped my fingers.

Four of the bubble lights answered and swung in to give more light. All the wall sections I could see were partitioned to hold record rolls. Each was fronted by a glass panel. But looking at that display I did not think that any living person would ever be able to absorb what was stored here. Where would one begin and was there any end?

"August one, how might I serve you?" The woman who approached me almost might have been one of those rolls given half-life. Most of the courtiers made bright displays in robes and jewelry. Her garment was a dark brown, lacking even a touch of gold or copper thread; she had no jewels nor had her pale face been painted in customary fashion, and her hair was bundled into a net. Perhaps this added to the impression she gave of age, though she was unbent and carried herself with an air of confidence.

"Lady—you are Arguyia who rules here?"

She smiled, "As much as the kapper beetles allow. We must wage war ever against those, August One."

"Beetles now! Exists there any place without enemies? I look to your aid, Lady Arguyia. Having but lately come to my position, it is my desire to learn what I can about those who have ruled before me and how were certain problems handled by them."

"Those problems being, August One?"

"Rats!" I answered at once. "Then, also the water shortage in the reign of Zastaff-Ji."

Now she stared at me. "A dire time, August One," she said slowly.

There—perhaps I had aroused curiosity, which I wanted the least. Watch ever your tongue, I told myself again.

"A dire time," I echoed her. "Was it not that when the Plain of Desolation became a menace? Our present plague of rats is reported to come from that direction."

She nodded and turned briskly, starting down the long room and I followed at her heels, still marveling at the walls of records about.

In the Palace of the Empire:

Murri lay stretched out behind the cushions of his furless brother. His eyes were closed but he did not doze, as was the custom of his kind. Rather his frustration grew. He was very tired of the way they lived now. This pile of caves had piqued his interest at first but the novelty had quickly faded. The blue furred one called Akeea and the rest of his kind never ventured beyond the walls unless the Emperor went.

Now there was no journeying across the sands of the outer world, no challenge from what might lay behind a rise of rock, no singing in the night, no—Too many nos. His whole body ached with the desire for the freedom he had known since a cub. He wanted *out!*

He raised his head from his paws and uttered a small cry. In the outer world his protest might not be heard at all, in this silent room it echoed. And his brother-one turned to him.

"What would you have?"

"Out." Murri answered with the truth born of his ever-growing impatience.

For a long moment their eyes met and they shared, in a fraction, senses. Then his brother-one answered.

"I have treated you ill indeed, my brother. You are of those who run free, who go by their own will where they please, and, because you followed me you have been in a place which is no life for you. Murri, can you forgive me this binding?"

"We are one," Murri's rough tongue now touched his brother's cheek. "There awaits danger."

Strong hands caressed his head and shoulders.

"Yes, danger. Therefore desert warrior, I ask of you a better task than lying to guard my back. This palace is a strange place—I cannot go exploring without being noted, but you— Can you be my eyes and ears? Can you venture forth during the hours of sleep and learn how that, if trouble strikes, we can move with ease?"

"This you wish? It will leave you alone—"

"There are many guards—do they not stand ever at the doors? You I trust, but what you could learn may be of great service."

His brother meant that. And should danger arise suddenly, he could answer a thought-summons—He had found few of these smooth skins to his own liking.

"Yes, that tie between us is not known to most others," his brother agreed. "Seek and learn, Murri, for from your people little can be hid. Within a few days we *shall* be out for I must, in turn, visit each of the Queendoms. Even as we went traveling before, we shall be out together."

Murri's purr rumbled and he ducked to rub his head against his brother's shoulder. "I shall seek," he agreed.

Thus at the hour of sleep he did not stretch out on cushions near his brother's resting place. Rather he padded down the hall without.

The light bubbles had largely withdrawn and the light was dim, though that did not bother Murri; his sight was better than that of any human guard who paced the halls.

He had reached a level three below that from which he had come. There he paused; there was no mistaking that scent. Somewhere before him went Akeea and another of his kind. Also, senses honed by life facing the many perils of the outland told him something else. The leopards were on the hunt.

Swiftly he padded off in their wake. Rats? Had the rats somehow invaded this land? He drew a deep breath or two but not the faintest trace of that familiar stench reached him. He broke into a lope, his uneasiness rising.

It was yet another level down before he caught up with Akeea and his companion. The leopard chief swung around, his lip half lifted in a beginning snarl. The mind touch came.

"Why do you follow, Sand one?"

"Where and why do you go?" retorted Murri, "Do rats come? " The ridge of upstanding fur on Akeea's back smoothed down. "Not rats, no rat here! But come if you will, perhaps there is something else for the hunting."

Murri accepted the invitation. Akeea broke mind touch, a warning the Sand Cat accepted. Down they went, level by level. All signs of this being a palace disappeared. The walls were barren rock and the way they traveled grew narrower. It became harder to breathe yet the leopards went on with increased speed until they fronted a wall. Water dripped here and slime formed vines. There was also a sound, one Murri could not identify. However they had halted. This wall ended the passage.

Akeea turned his head mind touched again. "There is wrongness here—there is—" He was interrupted by sound as though something had struck a blow against the wall. The leopards growled; Akeea's lieutenant sprang straight for the slick surface, struck the runnels of slime, and slipped to the floor.

As he pulled himself up they listened to the fullest extent of their senses. Another sound; Murri suddenly had a mind picture of water swishing back and forth in a basin, held by a shaking hand. Then that also died away. Meanwhile, paying no attention to the slime spreading across the floor where the other leopard had sprung, Akeea was pacing along the wall, his head turned towards its surface. Only a continuing rumble was to be heard now. The blue leopard finally returned. "It is gone—for now," he said. "But watch must be kept. Snaar will wait."

"What lies behind there?" Murri was also watching the wall.

"We do not know as yet, but we shall learn," Akeea promised.

He started toward the way down which they had come and Murri followed once more.

Chapter 5

On the caravan trail out of Kahulawe:
It was the last hour of the night and the caravan had come to
a way stop on the road to Kahulawe. One of the pillar cats
serving as a trail marker centered the collection of loaded transport carts. The caravaners were at work on the lines for yaksen
and the riding oryxen. Kottis jumped down from several of
the carts and spread out, encircling the site. Two of them
reached the foot of the rock ridge, behind the trail marker.

They halted there, heads well back so they could look up
the rise of the ridge.

Above lay two Sand Cats, their tawny bodies near flat, able
so to lurk unseen. Unseen but not unscented. One of the Kottis
turned to the camp to give warning and then stopped short.

"Younger sister," the send reached her, "We do not hunt
those you scout for. Have you not heard—your Emperor is
blood of our blood, kin does not prey on kin?"

"You hide!"

"If we did not, our hides would be speedily filled with
arrows. Your caravaners may not yet have heard of the peace."

"What do you hear?"

"We watch for that which comes from the dead country.
Your beasts, your caravaners, they may well bring forth the
evil fully armed. Warn your—"

The mind speech snapped. With a snarl the great cat was
on his feet, staring down, not at the Kotti now but rather
beyond. There was movement, as if the rocks had opened
upon caves packed with stinking bodies. Rats came, a wave
of them. The first were the rats they had always known.
However leaping among them, sometimes over the backs of
their fellows, were some ready for battle. The Kottis, yowling, ran for the camp.

Along the ridge top above, the Sand Cats leaped into action, heading in a direction which would bring them behind the attackers. The caravaners were shouting. Someone beat a belt drum while the animals bellowed, jerking at the ropes which secured them, rearing and kicking for freedom.

One of the small rats, ahead of the rest, leaped at a Kotti. They struck screeching and clawing as they rolled in the sand.

Together the Sand Cats leaped out from the ridge. Almost they appeared to float, not landing behind the rat waves as they had hoped, but just in time to meet a second wave of only larger rats. Tangled fighters rolled here and there. No matter how ready the defenders, the attackers were twice more in number. There came shrieks, the terrible cries of the caravan animals, unable to shake off the rats. Fangs clamped deep into hide and flesh, weighing frantic animals down until some strike at leg tendons sent them sprawling, to be instantly covered by the enemy. Arrows flew, some successfully sinking deep into stinking matted rat fur—only still they still came—there was no end to them.

Kottis lay, torn apart. Some of the pa-oryxen were already reduced nearly to bones. And there were more piercing screams from where the caravaners stood, back to back. Upon those the large rats now moved, with a deadly purpose—and deadly they were, dragging one of the women down away from her companions.

The Sand Cats, also facing the giants, their coats plastered with spurting blood, had retreated to the base of the ridge. Piles of rats lay along their line of withdrawal. Still they faced and fought, an unbroken force.

Suddenly there came full-throated shouts, not screams, but battle cries accompanied by the throb of charge drum. Riders came at full speed—their war trained oryxen leaping, smashing down to crush rats, swords and spears busy.

The caravaners broke their ring of defense and attacked also. Some whose supply of arrows had been exhausted were using herdsmen's slings to loose rocks and split skulls.

Farther into the open came the mounted troop. Without warning the rats broke, save for the cadre of the giants. Fleeing rats were everywhere cut down but the giants withdrew in better order. The killing ended at last. One could choke on the heavy scent of blood.

He who led the mounted force headed toward to the caravaners. There he jerked the reins of his mount with force enough to make the oryxen rear.

Along the base of the ridge came the Sand Cats. One was limping and the other lifted a head from which a great strip of fur had been torn to hide one eye.

The leader of the troop swung up his bow. One of the caravaners behind him shouted, running between bloody heaps of rats.

"No!" she shouted again. "Do not—!"

He glanced calmly at her and then back at the cats. His bow cord thrummed and the shaft of an arrow danced up and down in the throat of the limper.

"No!" The caravaner had nearly reached his side.

He paid no heed. The cat with the torn skin stood for a moment, from its clear eye the man's second shaft suddenly protruded, and the noble animal crumpled beside its companion.

"They fought for us!" The caravaner was now beside him. "Such are kin to the Emperor. What shall we tell him?"

"The Emperor?" Blazing eyes stared at her. "There is no rightful Emperor—there is a liar and a cheat, one who has no right to the power he has seized. It is well known that he was the lowest of the low, even in his own Queendom. Such is certainly not favored by the Essence, Trail Mistress. Look you upon the banner under which we ride. Soon it will be seen in Valapa and the unfit will answer to the Essence in the ancient way. Sand Cats are prey; they shall remain prey. Otherwise the balance is disturbed. I give you good advice, Trail Mistress. Do not raise voice in defense of such."

He gestured and one of his men moved forward carrying a white standard bearing the diamond of Valapa and below that an insignia she thought she had never seen. Then she remembered. So had been the standard of Shank-ji, Emperor's son, in the days before he had failed the Testing.

Allitta:

"Allitta!" As if someone had shouted my name in the sleeping chamber, that call brought me awake, pulled me up from my cushions. Kassca jumped from my side, staring towards the middle space beyond. There was no one there, but I knew who had summoned me.

Against my will I slid from under the covers. Kassca came to rub about my legs, looking up into my face and uttering soft cries. I went to the clothes chest, tossing out the heavy court robes. At the very bottom I found what I sought. The plain, short-skirted garment could be that of an underservent—though it had no house crest. I pulled it on hastily; it seemed as if that summons still rung in my ears. Bare footed and twisting my hair up in a kerchief as I moved, I went to the nearest window.

Late dawn layered the sky. My labors among the records had been long. I knelt by the sill and gathered Kassca to me. The Kottis, when they bind with one, are able to understand speech.

"Little one," I half whispered. "I must go, but stay you here. I shall return as speedily as I can."

Kassca uttered a small cry, which I interpreted as agreement. Several days before, I had studied what lay beyond the window. Once I had escaped through here when enemies had struck. Then I had been a child. It remained that within these walls even now I hunted ways about business of my own. A certain deep fear lay always dormant within me.

The glass pane swung open; I perched on the wide sill. From there I swung by my hands to a ledge of carving where I must watch my footing carefully. There was more light below, where several bubble lights drifted in the outer court.

With great care, I reached the end of the carving and was able to lower myself to the edge of the courtyard wall. This I inched along. There were guards and it was nearly time for the watch to change. I had no wish to be detected even by those owing me allegiance. At last, drawing a deep breath of relief, I stood in the street.

Back against the wall I edged my way along, dodging, as best I could, the light of the street bubbles. When I turned into another way I wondered at the ease of my exit. It was almost as if I had become invisible. This had happened twice before in my life—I had chosen to pass unnoted and so it had been.

Again, having crossed a good quarter of the city, I came to the back courtyard door of Ravinga's shop. Nor was I surprised to see one of her Kottis sitting in the crack of a half open door.

Wiu escorted me to the workroom where Ravinga was seated holding a flat tray on her knees. On this blazed a scattering of large gems: sapphire, ruby, emerald, topaz and diamond, the insignias of all the Queendoms.

I was startled by her expression. She might have aged a flight of seasons since we had last met. Though I had lived with her for ten years, she had never appeared to age. Now her eyes looked sunken and there were harsh lines bracketing her mouth.

"What has happened?" I broke the silence when she did not.

She laid fingertips on the tray near the topaz. I noted that the jewel had a reddish tinge, or rather a sullen red spot colored the tray beneath it.

"It has truly begun," her voice was steady. "Death, death and rebellion. A caravan was attacked here at first light—rats—many of the strange ones. And two Sand Cats were cruelly slain—by men."

She paused; her tongue swept over dry lips. "Men who follow a false banner, who spout lies, rebels who will fasten upon the belly of our world if they are not stopped, gnaw us into utter darkness. A great attack it was."

How she had learned of an event happening afar from Valapa, I did not know. But I had long accepted that the doll maker had talents she seldom revealed. That the rats would so attack a caravan, one could accept at once. But who were these warriors who killed rats and also Sand Cats?

It was said that Shank-ji had gone to the desert, had raised a standard of revolt—was that true? That he would kill Sand Cats—yes. More readily because Hynkkel-ji favored them. But this—

If there were more killings of the great cats, they would believe themselves betrayed and would slaughter in return. What would become of Hynkkel-ji should this occur?

Ravinga must be reading my thoughts. "So will he be between one tie and the other. I ask you, go to him. Tell him what I have told you—official reports will come too late. He must prepare to act at once!"

"I will go."

Hynkkel-ji:

I had found much to interest me in the old records. The one concerning the water shortage held me the longest. It contained, of course, the martyrdom of Zastaff-Ji. Only I noted one strange thing about that part of the roll. The ink there was darker, the surface of the skin less worn. One might believe it was added later—why? The whole report had been drawn up after the affair.

Murri had not returned by the time I bedded down. I believed him with the leopards. I felt uneasy and could not sleep. Rat attacks, shrinking algae pools, uncertainty concerning what support I might have—those wove like specters around my mind. Why had the Essence set this burden upon me? By my father's opinion I was a weakling, not to be trusted. My brother, according to rumor, had already joined with an enemy.

I had Murri—perhaps Ravinga—Allitta? Why had my mind suddenly pictured her face? She had never had any regard for me. Long ago in our market meetings she had made that plain. No—I could not count on Allitta.

Sleep came at last, and I did not dream. I awoke early— night was still dark beyond my windows. Only there was in

me a need for action, as if the storm drums of the desert had
roused me.

Who—Murri! But—danger!

I was on my feet when he slipped through between the
heavy night curtains at the door.

"Brother—" I mind sent—and met a barrier!

Never before had Murri so shut me out. His large, sun
bright eyes regarded me as from a distance, his tail beginning
to swing a little back and forth. Something had disturbed him
greatly, raising this barrier between us.

"Murri—" I took a step in his direction. His ears flattened. He did not growl, but I could see the hint of fangs.

This was indeed rejection. But what had I done?

"Brother in fur," I thought slowly, baring my arm to show
the scar of our uniting. "What lies ill between us?"

The return touch struck like a weapon. "Blood!"

Had some palace lurker tried attack? It was possible.

That thought may have reached him.

"Kill—blood—"

To my shock and surprise he turned and was gone. I
stumbled after him. The entry guard barely stepped aside in
time as I shouldered past him to stare down the hall. Murri
was moving with the speed of a desert roamer. He was already at the far end. I could not catch him now.

"You," I demanded of the guard, "was the Sand Cat injured; did you see any mark of a wound?" I had not, but perhaps such had been hidden by his stance.

"No, August One. He was unharmed. At least I saw
no mark on him. Shall I follow?" He did not look too eager
to do so. With Murri in his present mood, it was best that
none approach him but I, and he had made certain that was
not to happen.

To lose Murri—and why? Unspeakable cold clutched me.

Still, I struggled to reach him by mind touch. There was
no answer. Either he was now beyond call or he was unwilling
to answer. At last I had to accept that, but I determined, one
way or another, to find an answer.

Dawn brought the heat of the day. A servant came to announce a very early visitor—Allitta. Could Murri have gone to her—or to Ravinga? With desperate hope I had her admitted.

She also stood just within the doorway to face me, looking about the room.

"Murri?" Not his name in greeting, rather a question.

"He is gone—perhaps to Ravinga."

"Ravinga sent me," she used no formalities of speech.

I flinched—I could not believe now that any news would be good.

"What has happened?" I forced the question.

"There has been a battle," she began flatly. "Ravinga has her ways of learning. Rats, many of the large ones, attacked a caravan. There came guards to their aid—but they were no city scouts. Shank-ji was their leader, under his own standard. Sand Cats had fought to help the caravan. He killed them. Perhaps their kin will now turn full enemy again."

I clenched my hands. I was never a fighting man, but in that instant I could have joyfully crushed a certain throat. My edict concerning peace with the cats had been the first issued under my seal at the beginning of my reign. I knew that Murri had broadcast that news to the nearest of his kin. Those in turn would have picked up his sending and spread it through the rock islands where they laired.

Was the blood-bond now broken? Murri—Murri, my brother—I cast that thought as far as I could. Come to me—let me aid. No answer—I could only hope that when his first anger ebbed a little, he would in some way communicate. The tie between us—might the Essence allow it to tighten once more—let Murri come to me?

Shank-ji. He had raised his own standard, gathered warriors to him. This was open rebellion and I must face it—but not with weapons unless I was forced to. I did not want to awaken such hatred among my own kind as might come from that. No, I must show myself abroad, let all know me, learn me. The Empire was not just Valapa, but all the Queendoms.

Let me visit each in turn, answer questions and be the visible ruler that the Essence had called me to be.

"Lady of Vurope…" she still stood by the door "…this day you have rendered a great service, you and Ravinga. Her care of this land is beyond price."

Allitta bowed her head. "The August One has spoken," her voice was now cold, formal. "It shall be done as he commands." Like Murri before her, she vanished before I could speak again.

Chapter 6

On a Housetop in Valapa:

Murri crouched on the roof. He was not sure why he had taken this path out of the city. Now he paused to recall the events of the morning. Blood-bond warred with hot anger. No, it had not been his smooth-skinned brother who had slain. He could swear to that before the Elders. That men often betrayed was known to every Sand Cat—but "men" were not "man;" the killers had shared nothing with cats. Long years of hunting, of slaying and being slain lay between "men" and cats.

To judge blindly without knowing all was a peril. Wait— wait and see.

Murri arose. There was more traffic on the streets below. He did not want to be sighted. Padding across the roof he looked down. Some instinct he did not understand had led him here—for now, he would obey it.

He drew upon the breeze about him. His thick fur began to rise. The breeze was near wind strong. Murri not only yielded to the pull of it but he bounded over the edge of the roof, circling down, his fall softened by his puffed coat so he reached the courtyard below with hardly a jar. Turning he faced the entry of the building.

That was ajar and he confidently approached it, nudging the inner curtain aside to enter. The smells he encountered made his nose wrinkle: glue, hot leather and metal. With those mingled the odor of humans and, faintly, spices and herbs.

She whom he sought was at the door of a chamber ahead. In one hand she held a cup, painted with Sand Cats whirling in one of their dances. From this curled incense that brought from Murri a throaty purr of greeting.

Ravinga retreated, beckoning to the great cat. "Welcome," mind touch reached him.

She seated herself in the comfortable manner she used when working. He sat. For a very long moment their eyes met before there was communication.

"You have heard, then," she made it a statement and not a question.

"I have heard."

"Go you now to the pride?"

"I began to do so—" he hesitated.

"But—" she prodded him.

"There is a blood-bond."

She settled back a little as if some problem she had faced was solved.

"The Dark stirs," Ravinga said slowly. "All manner of acts, which can lead to distrust and confusion are weapons for him." Still she held the cat eye to eye.

"Him?" Murri demanded.

She had set the incense bowl on the table between them. Now she arose and opened one of the wall cabinets to bring out the Hynkkel doll in the robes of the Emperor, then another, which she placed to face the first. This also was the image of a man—yet there were marked differences. The face of the second lacked the customary mustache; his hair was drawn high in a single knot. The dull purple robe he wore lacked any elaboration of embroidery or gem encrustment. He had a single piece of jewelry—a large pendant of metal centered by a bluish stone.

Murri studied the doll closely. That it portrayed a living person he knew—but not one known to him.

Ravinga picked up a small rod of dull black, not much longer than her own palm and pointed it at the stranger.

"Your people have also their records. How far back those run I cannot tell, for each race keeps its history in a different fashion. Have you ever heard of Quinzell?"

Murri's lips instantly shaped a snarl.

"The Dark One—but it has been long and long since he befouled the outlands. Surely only his brittle bones exist."

"He was one who pursued power in strange places and learned much that is forbidden. If he died he has risen again—for it is he whom the rats serve. It is to him that Shank-ji and those who follow that rebel will give allegiance. Anything that weakens us serves him. No, he is not dead—some time ago he awoke. Now he holds court in Renwala—"

Murri shook his head. "A place which no longer exists." But he did not seem altogether certain of that.

Ravinga settled farther back in her seat. "Renwala has been loosed from the sand this same sorcerer called up to hide it. Within the Plain of Desolation it rules once more. The rats serve as its warriors and guardians. This must change. I say this in order that you may in turn warn the pride. If Quinzell achieves his goal then our world, our lives, will fall away from the scales of the Essence. We shall drown in the sand."

Murri uttered a small growl deep in his throat. "Do you see this for us, Woman of Far Sight?"

"If those of the Queendoms, and those wind-free among the rock isles do not make peace, yes. There is an enemy, common to us both. You are young, but because you have come hither, because you have lived with your blood-brother, you must speak to the Elders; carry them my warning."

For again a long time they locked eyes. Then Murri advanced a step or two to the table, raising his great right fore-paw with knife-sharp claws extended. Flat it went between the two dolls. Ravinga did not hesitate, but at once placed her hand over the paw, sealing their private pact, warrior fashion.

"I will tell the Elders what I have heard."

She nodded. "Across the roofs will be best. May the Essence favor you."

So he returned to his former perch on the roof and began a zigzag way from one to another, coming at last to one near the city wall where he waited to avoid the duty tours of the guards. The watch was slack and lazy—it had become mere custom. In this Queendom none had ever faced danger from without.

Though Murri was better used to sand and rock, he had adapted to this so strange land, which held greenery—some of which towered high above his head. Again he drew in strange scents, but none enticed him to explore. Then he reached the cliff edge of the giant mesa, which made up the Diamond realm.

He took a position concealed by high rising growth and sent a call—first in quest of blood kin—then to the nearest Elder.

Hynkkel-ji:

I summoned the Chancellor and the Commander of the guard before I even broke my fast. There was no Murri behind my seat and that lack I did not forget. In his place was Akeea and I sensed that the leopard was uneasy. Perhaps Murri had communicated our break to him. Though the loss of Murri was foremost in my mind I must rouse myself to deal with the acts of humans. I used no formality, but came directly to the point, speaking to Giarribari.

"What news have your private scouts garnered concerning Shank-ji?"

There was no hesitation as the Chancellor answered.

"He has raised a standard of revolt, August One. There are those who join him. It is said—proof of this can be depended upon—that he is telling foul tales. Only last night did such news come."

So, I had later news and rashly I delivered it. "He has done more than wave a banner and patter lies." I controlled the anger rising in me with all my strength. "Look you there—" I pointed to where Akeea sat in Murri's place. I did not want to bring Ravinga into this but I could shade the truth and allow them to believe that I had learned from Murri. "He who is as my right hand has gone. Why? Because, may the Essence sand-bury this Shank-ji; the rebel has slain the very Sand Cats who fought to defend a caravan. Thus he may have severed all friendship between the Empire and their Prides—as well as broken our edict."

For the first time since our initial meeting I saw the Chancellor aroused. Her mouth opened as if she wished to deny my charge, then closed with a snap, not uttering a word.

The Commander's hand went to his sword hilt.

"This Empire is faced by dire danger," I continued. "If it is rent by quarrels, action against those who are allies, then how can we meet with outside danger, armed and ready?"

Neither had an answer to that. Still I believed that they were in agreement with me.

"Because this duty has descended upon me I must learn as speedily as I can how similar trials have been met in the past. Not all reigns were as smooth and without incident as that of Haban-ji. Yes, there was intrigue within this court—and others. But before that there were ancient threats to all of the Outer Regions."

"For example the war of Quinzell—"

They both froze in startlement.

"What references I have found in the records are not direct. It is almost as if he or she who recorded that period either worked with incomplete knowledge, or else the real history was directed to be made secret. Must we take the records of all the Houses and study them in turn?"

When Giarribari answered, she looked down at her hands. "Perhaps that record was altered according to decree. There were those of high rank, one or two of great power, who, a generation after that conflict came into disfavor. There came a time of destruction of Houses. Some secrets have remained intact."

"Still," I continued, "one might seek in less known collections and find answers. But this present knowledge is ours. There is before us the matter of edict breaking. Though Shank-ji is not yet under my hand, let it be proclaimed that he has wantonly dared to kill allies of the Empire and the harshest fate is to be his—he is now an outlaw beyond outlaws." To my faint relief, both of them nodded at once.

Allitta:

There were always so many things to be done. Now I tried not to glance at the envelope of hide I had discovered only late last night among the records. My attention needed to be focused on the report my steward was making. So much revenue this quarter from the orchards, so much from the weavers Vurope employed, investments in two caravans, tax due the Queen, due the Emperor—Due Hynkkel-ji—but for how long? With a rebellion already rising in the Outer Regions? My future might well be linked with his. Should he fall, would that not leave me open to attack from the same source that had already stripped Vurope from the High House rolls once?

"House Lady?"

I pulled myself out of tangled thoughts. The steward was eyeing me, a faint trace of frown between her brows.

"My thanks to you, Hardi." I hastened to cover my lack of attention. "Yes, the foretelling of water lack is of the utmost importance."

She rewound her roll of plusses and minuses. But when she answered there was a cool note in her voice.

"Surely the Queen will call all Houses to a conference. It has been proclaimed that the Emperor will begin his formal Progress in the Outer Regions soon. Already there are rumors that at least two of the Queendoms are perhaps to be measured soon. One of them is that of the Emperor's birth—Kahulawe."

I nodded. The Progress, which was the duty of the Emperor at set times, was always made with ceremony—especially so at the beginning of a reign. At least half the court, as well as the heads of the major Houses, would make the journey with him. I had no desire to be one of his entourage, but I had no choice—one followed custom. I looked back at the days when I had been with Ravinga and had known freedom of a sort. Now I was completely locked in.

I uttered the proper phrases of praise for Hardi's efforts and she went about her daily tasks. I reached at once for the envelope. Kassca, who had been stretched at ease at the end of the table, lifted her head, then footed daintily around the mass of sheets Hardi had left for my signature.

I stroked the Kotti's head. "Little one, thank the Essence that you do not have such as this to disturb you. Clever furred one, you have chosen the better way of life."

She mewed, then her right paw shot out and tapped the envelope. How much did the Kottis know of our affairs? Did she understand my driving need to know—know what? I could not have said, save some need had pushed me for days. The folded sheets I now drew from their casing were age-brittle and I had to straighten them with care. Three bore writing— in the antique script of the far past—the fourth appeared to be blank. Yet as I spread it under better light I could now see very faint tracings. I laid this carefully aside and turned to the writing. In my childhood, before Vurope had fallen, I had been introduced to this form of script. Ravinga had added it to my training, as she needed to refer to ancient instructions. She was not the first doll maker of the Outer Regions and they were all women of secrets.

I puzzled out word and symbol, one at a time as my excitement grew. Vurope—this House had had greater power than I had ever guessed! Some of the lines I reread, making sure that they revealed what I thought they had. Kassca leaned against my arm, her small head moving slightly as if she, too, were reading the faded script.

Ravinga! I must discuss this discovery before I went any further. In all of Valapa she was the only one I fully trusted. Kassca rubbed her head against my shoulder. She uttered a small sound and I felt she was urging me into action.

Hynkkel-ji:
I had made my will plain, and in turn, because I knew that I must learn all I could through the Progress before acting with confidence, I set the date for it. The Chancellor and the Commander withdrew.

My life had become a tangle—I might be an inept harvester in a sun melon patch. Suddenly I longed so for freedom that I shrugged off my heavy robe of dignity. Akeea was on his feet and now he looked into my face.

"Yes, let us go out, High Guard."

There was a private way from the chamber, which led to an enclosed garden lying between the Imperial Chambers and the Queen's tower. Usually, as the day's heat intensified, there were few who ever walked there. I could hope to be alone. With Akeea beside me, I went.

Such a wealth of vegetation might scarcely be seen in any of the other Queendoms. It had been a pleasure for Haban-ji to order the once yearly caravan to the Inner Regions—that near fabled land—to bring back exotic plants to foster here. I found a bench overhung by giant stems thick with lacy leaves and Akeea lay across the path as if to refuse passage to any intruder.

It was not bodily that she came to me, but her forlorn sobbing broke through my self-absorption. Beyond the screen of tall plants I found her. First I thought some child curled there. Her loose hair hung like a soft black veil about her shoulders and her tiny hands masked her face as her whole body shuddered with the force of her sobs.

I hesitated. Would it not be wiser to go? Who was she who invaded this so private place? I made scarcely a sound, but her head jerked up so forcefully that it sent her hair flying so that I saw clearly her tear-stained face. It was Berneen, Queen Yuikala's granddaughter! Just as I recognized her, she saw me. He hand flew to her mouth and fear flickered through her dark, lustrous eyes. My presence had frozen her.

"First Maid, why do you grieve?" I asked awkwardly, for I was always ill at ease with young girls.

She straightened, clasped her hands before her in the proper court manner and took several shuddering breaths. Finally stifling her tears, she swallowed to answer.

"August One, it is that—" she hesitated, her head turned a fraction toward the Queen's tower, almost as if expecting some rebuke to waft thence. Her words came haltingly again.

"August One, this—" she gestured widely to encompass all around us. "I am unused to this life. There are so many ways one can make a fool of one's self and—" she shook her head. "Usually, one after another, I discover these—too late. I—I do not think I was made for palaces."

Berneen had not offered me a seat, but now I boldly joined her on the bench and—greatly daring for me—reached out to clasp one of her hands.

"It is hard to step from one life to another," I said. "That I know well. But life often presents us with such changes. One has to go slowly and watch others, learn as fast as one can."

She now looked straight into my eyes. A child, not yet entirely a maid, she had been plunged into this whirl of intrigue and curious customs, with no Murri or other caring one at her back. Pain, which must be swiftly walled, struck now at me.

"We are both strangers," I told her. "Perhaps in some way we can reach helping hands to each other."

She nodded. "She," Berneen again looked toward the tower, "says I must go on the Progress with her. I have never even been out of this Queendom, let alone the outer ones."

"Then you will have much to see. There are many things there to interest one."

The tall plants rippled as from them stepped an older woman who halted the moment she glimpsed me. Berneen leaped to her feet, turned toward me and executed a graceful court salute.

"I must go."

I nodded and waved assent as she and the one who summoned her withdrew. I was left with a feeling of deep sympathy for the girl. She was far too young to have to find her way at court.

A sudden movement from Akeea broke into my musings. He half crouched as if waiting attack. Only—Murri, his fur fluffed (he might have been taking part in one of the exquisite aerial dances of his kind) came from roof to ground before me.

Without thinking my arms went out. He rose to his powerful hind legs and rested his great paws, claws carefully sheathed, on my shoulders. We embraced as might battle comrades. Relief swelled joyfully up in me. All would certainly now be well; the darkness between us was no more.

Chapter 7

Allitta:

Ravinga held the timeworn parchment, which I had thrust upon her.

"Among the House records?" She was smoothing it out. I produced the other, which bore the puzzle writing.

"With this."

"What have you learned from these?" She ran a fingertip lightly over the blank page, then picked up a small rod from the table.

"Hints, suggestions which lead to guesses. Nothing to be sworn to."

She began to run the rod across the parchment. Now a faint shadowing appeared. Not words—rather a tangle of lines. Could it be a map; were the hints right? What did lie under the surface of Valapa?

Three times she carefully swept the paper with rod tip. Now the lines could indeed be clearly seen.

Ravinga studied what had come to light closely before looking up to me. "It would seem that you have gone hunting in the past to good purpose. This," she touched the parchment "has passed as a very ancient legend. I wonder whether, in part, this explains the downfall of Vurope. Perhaps your House was the guardian of too great a secret. What do you believe you have found?"

My excitement was growing. "The script says that there are underground ways in which water runs. They weave a net clear across the Outer Regions. Could these underground ways be in some way tapped, there could be no failure of the algae ponds! Is this possible?"

"Many things which were possible have been forgotten," she returned. "Think this through: if we might tap this water, there could also be a way for others to do likewise."

I shivered. "An enemy could somehow drain our life pools?"

Ravinga nodded. She had brought forth the glass, which she used to make small things large, one of the most important of her tools. Through this she regarded the map lines.

"This should then be given to the Emperor—" I suggested.

"Not yet. Proof—more proof than this—must be gathered. Look," again she used the rod, standing it almost straight up above one point on the map. With her other hand she picked up the top written sheet and read it closely, her lips moving as if she recited some charm, or repeated some fact she had read.

"One of the inlets—outlets—which ever it may be—lies indeed under the main dwelling of Vurope. Try to find that, Allitta, then you will have the proof. However, remember this: if another knows this secret, perhaps having slain your kin to learn or keep it, then you are also in danger. Go with care and ever-open eyes and ears. Depend on your Kassca. Kottis can explore where our kind would not think to look. I would advise that you do this in secret and begin in the lowest cellars beneath the High House."

I returned to that house only to find a visitor just arrived, Melora-Kura.

My earlier impressions of her, that she was someone I would like as a friend, grew stronger each time we met, though I shrank still from assenting to anything, which would mean a closer acquaintance with her brother. She was quick to come to the purpose of her visit.

"You know the Outer Regions well. Will you be one of that Imperial Progress which they are shaping?"

"I think not," I returned at once. "Though I now represent one of the Six Families I am not obliged to join the court except when summoned formally."

She sipped at the cup of melon wine I had ordered served. "I wish that you were going. He needs at least one who knows him—"

I gathered at once what she meant. "But I do not know him. We met at the markets, yes. He asked Ravinga for lodging when he came here for the last trail. But I cannot claim any friendship with Hynkkel-ji."

She had been watching me intently and her face was very sober. "He is like a yaksen calf ringed by rats. I have listened—rumors gather as storm sand to choke all reason. Our brother has joined the rebels. His act adds credence to this story that Hynkkel-ji won the crown by some trickery."

"There were reputable witnesses at each of the trials; they have sworn to his winning of each." I replied.

"When has truth ever triumphed over rumor spread viciously? On this progress there will be many chances to attack. Hynkkel never had warrior training. He has fought only the rats to defend our herds. And he is a desert survivor. But it is his own kin who threatens now. I will do what I can in protection—already with Ravinga's help I am working on something which may be an aid." She arose. "I can not ask more of you than you may give."

There was that in her voice which made me say, "This I promise, what I can do I will."

She looked at me steadily. "Very well, let it be so."

Her departure was abrupt and I knew she was displeased, however there was truly nothing I could do. Should concrete information of some act on the part of the rebels or any of their sympathizers here reach me, I would, of course, as soon as I could, report such. But I had no such information, which could be trusted. At present I had a different task. I brought out the map Ravinga had restored with her power and set to studying those twisting lines upon it.

Hynkkel-ji:

I could leave the preparations for the Progress to those who had access to the rules for such and I was glad to do so. Now I had a matter of my own to consider. Before me was Murri, beside him Akeea and both of them had a report, perhaps a dire one. Murri had put his exploration of the palace to good

use and Akeea supplied what the leopards of many generations had known.

There were depths beneath the palace. Now that that was
made clear I could remember some hints I had come across in
my researching the rolls of history. The leopard Akeea had for
uncounted years made periodic patrols of certain passages,
obeying commands issued by the long dead. Now they were
sure that some peril existed, even though it had not showed
itself for centuries.

"Tonight," I mind sent. "If there is some danger in the
very heart of Valapa, we must know. They would have me
on this Progress. To go ignorant of what lies here cannot be
thought of."

Thus Murri did not go alone this time when he went roaming. I had stripped off the bulky robes, laid aside the coronet,
which I must by custom always appear in. Among the clothing stored in the chests which near filled one of the rooms of
my suite there was tunic and breeches of hide, meant I believed to be worn under the armor of warfare, but giving far
more freedom to the wearer than what I laid aside.

There was a rack in the shadowed curve of wall beyond
my bed. Here to hand hung the equipment of a warrior. There
were three spears, varying in length, from a short one light in
the hand, intended to be thrown, to a long one used from oryxen
back. There were two swords: one brightly jeweled for state
occasions and the other plain of hilt but probably far more
effective in combat. These two types of weapon I had known
in my own home. The various other armaments hanging here
were ones seldom seen in the Outer Regions. One, consisting
of a chain connecting two weighty metal balls, intrigued me.
This was an adaptation of something used by herdsmen to
bring to submission a feral oryxen. Twirled through the air
and flung, it entangled the animal.

I was no swordsman; a spear I could and had used against
rats. But this balls and chain weapon appealed to me. My
usual defense was not represented—apparently the sling of
the herdsman did not appeal to a trained warrior. I gathered

up the curious pieces of armament, and also slid the short
spear from its hooks.

I had no wish to let the guardsman at my outer curtain
learn of this deep night exploit. Thus I slipped from the larger
window of the outer reception chamber onto the balcony from
which it was easy, for one used to climbing the rock isles, to
reach a twin below.

My footwear was soft soled and I made no more noise
than did the great cats. We had to watch for any guard or
servant but save for one narrow escape from being noticed,
we succeeded. Down we went; I counted levels and strove to
remember landmarks of one kind or another. At last we came
to where another leopard greeted us. One could indeed hear
sounds from beyond a slimed curtain wall. I had drawn two
bubble lamps from the last level above. Now I waved them
closer to the wall. The glistening slime proved such a covering of the stone that it was impossible to see if there was any
entrance to what lay behind. Using my spear, I swept the slime
away, choking now and then because of the foul odor my effort raised. But I had my reward. One could sight the outline
of an opening. I waved the airborne lamps even closer and
fitted the point of the spear into that crack, tracing it until I
reached a point halfway down the side from where I started.
The point went in faster; there came a harsh sound, and the
wall portion within that outline began to move, swinging back.
It did not open on darkness. A strange green light beamed
from beyond. What we could see was another wall some distance ahead, and a lapping sound was loud.

Allitta:

Outside the window the night was dark; over the city lights
shone or floated. Kassca watched it as I finished snapping the
last clasp of the plain tunic I had chosen. The map of the
fabled waterways I slipped within the breast of my garment.
Still I hesitated. To venture bare handed into the unknown
was the act of a fool. In the private chamber of the head of
any House there was always a cache of weapons. Though I

had not before examined these, I did so now. Spears, two swords. Spears I had carried and used against rats to good purpose, so spear it would be. I chose one. Kassca was already waiting by the door curtain. I had dismissed the servants early and the passages in this part of the house should be clear. Still I must go with care. Thus we began the descent within. I was glad now that I had made an exploration of the building soon after I had come. There were rooms for kin and company, those of entertaining, all on different levels. Then came the quarters of the servants. There I went slowly. I knew that Kassca's senses were far better than mine and I depended upon the Kotti as I would upon the advance scout of a caravan.

Below the level of the household offices came the storage rooms. I had summoned a bubble light to accompany us and now I paused to examine the map. However I found myself totally lost. Ravinga had said to depend upon Kassca and now I thought-sent such a request.

She trotted confidently onward, threading a way between towering stacks of chests. I had to quicken pace to keep her in sight. Another door—then a curving ramp leading down. At the foot of that was another small chamber which had three doors along the wall. These were not curtained as the ones above, but rather closed with solid barriers which were barred.

Kassca stopped at each door to sniff at the floor level. Her selection was the one farthest from me. I slid up the bar, pushed the barrier inward; it brought thick sweeps of dust with it. Plainly a long period had passed since this was last opened.

Kassca suddenly crowed before me. I took warning and pointed my spear, waving the float light before me. Then—I came to an instant halt as the bubble proceeded. What darkness had once ruled here in Vurope? Against a far wall lay bones. A skull stared meaningfully at me, an arm bone, still encircled by rusted metal, hung above the rest of the bones. Each House had its secrets—that was understood. But who had died here in chains and why?

Kassca stood before the bones. She looked back at me. "Here," she thought.

Behind the bones? Beneath them? I did not want to get any nearer to this proof that someone of my blood had been able to do this. Still I forced myself forward. The lamp swung closer. I could see no mark on the wall to suggest that there was another opening there.

Kassca delicately pushed at the bone and I understood. The remains of that long ago prisoner must be moved so that I could find what I hunted. Touch, lift, shift aside—I was on my knees. There was a sour taste in my mouth; the hands I was forcing to this task were shaking. Only I knew that I could not retreat still ignorant of what must be below. This gave me the power to clear the floor.

There was left an unsavory mass of what might be clothing or even the dried remains of flesh. I used my spear to scrape that away, gagging as I worked.

The bubble had swung lower to reveal, when I had scraped the last of that mess clear, a ring set in the stone. It was a struggle, but I managed to raise a stone block to clear a space through which a body might be squeezed. I took the precaution of wedging the stone so it might not fall back and seal us in, using part of the chain which had held the unfortunate dead.

Kassca slipped through the opening with confidence and I followed. The bubble light revealed that there was an inclined ramp down which one slid. Could one get up again? Yes, there was a series of depressions in the wall, which could be used for handholds to climb.

The descent was not an easy one, but I could now sight below a green glimmer to one side and the dampness of water was to be felt.

At foot of the ramp was a very small landing, but to the left another opening broke the wall. It was from there that the green light issued. With Kassca I at last found myself on a ledge of rock, which bordered a stream of flowing water, moving from right to left into a misty distance. I chose the right and started on, shivering in the cold damp which permeated this rocky tunnel.

Water in such a quantity was startling even to one who was accustomed to Valapa's many pools, it being considered the most fruitful and favored of the Queendoms. The fitful greenish light appeared to emit from the curtains of slime along the further wall and I had to watch my footing, as there were many trails of the same growth across this way.

Kassca shook one foot after another and spat until I gathered her up in one arm. The dank moisture continued to cloak us, but I was determined to see where this walk led. I was sure that we were well below the level of the city streets and I watched carefully along the wall to my right for any hint of another exit.

"Ahead," Kassca's thought came in warning.

There was a stronger light there but the sound of the river drowned out all else. My pace slowed even more but I came on. Then I was startled by a wild ululating howl. The river beside me took a turn, which the walkway followed.

I was startled even more by the cries of raging cats. Kassca's ears flattened and she hissed, her tail beating against my ribs.

Some distance ahead broad steps descended to the river. One of the bubble lights had brought greater illumination to the scene. At the top of the steps two great cats rolled, roaring in rage, biting at green strands that bound them as strongly as ropes. Murri and Akeea!

On the lowest step was Hynkkel-ji, a hunting spear in one hand and two heavy weights connected by a chain in the other.

Chapter 8

Allitta:

Rising breast-high out of the water was a creature from some foul dream. Its skin was the same greenish gray of the water, pitted with great ulcers. It raised one arm and pointed a long, taloned finger at the invaders. From the arm depended a stringy fringe of thick grayish hair, matching the rough mass that covered the head. Eyes, like white balls, protruded blindly. There wafted from it a putrid stench, strong enough to reach me. Stronger still was the sense of utter malignancy it projected.

It screamed and threw a ball dripping slime. Hynkkel-ji struck it aside with his spear, cutting it in half. Lines of glowing green reached out of it for him. The tip of one touched his calf and instantly plastered itself around his leg. He cried out and nearly stumbled into the water, but righted himself in time.

He was able to dodge a second ball, which struck against the stone and loosed more streamers. One of these reached the cats, bringing cries of pain and fury from them.

Hynkkel-ji whirled the chain-hung ball weapon about his head and launched it at the creature. There was a singing note as it caught the arm of the monster, slamming that back against its head and neck.

Now Hynkkel-ji raised his spear. The creature was rocking back and forth beyond his touch. Loud yowls came from the cats.

I could not just stand by and watch. Putting Kassca down I ran as fast as I could along the slippery walk. The screams of the creature, the roars of the cats echoed and reechoed in the confined passage, deafening one.

The thing was pulled forward by the weight of the balls, their uniting chain cutting into its flesh. With its one free hand it held another huge glob of slime. It was plain that the band scoring Hynkkel-ji's leg hindered his movements, but he crouched and again raised his spear. With the speed and skill of an outlands hunter he struck just as I reached the cats.

Hynkkel-ji:

My spear struck true; blackish blood fountained towards me and I slipped forward, unable to free my weapon. One foot touched the water churned up as the monster weaved back and forth. Those baleful eyes were fixed on me. Over my shoulder came a spear point.

In my need I clutched at its shaft and steadied myself until I was able to draw myself back on the step. My enemy had staggered nearly to my perch. From it came a mind thrust massively stronger than any I had ever met. I staggered again. The creature might be dying but was still intent on me—to make the coming death a double one.

I ventured a quick glance behind—who had come to my rescue? Allitta! I had kept my hold on her spear and now I jerked it out of her grasp. Claws caught at my leg, burning still from the wrap of slime. I steadied myself to thrust even as I had once done at a crazed yaksen threatening our herd.

Perhaps the water thing trod on some uncertain footing; perhaps it was too intent upon getting at me. The tip of the spear penetrated its nearest eye. Weighted by the chain and balls, it went down and the turgid water closed over it. My borrowed spear ready, I waited but it did not appear.

Now that I had time to inspect it, I realized that the slime had eaten through my boot and I felt as if my skin had been torched. Getting groggily to my feet I managed my way up the steps to stand once more on the ledge where I held out the spear to Allitta.

"Well met, Lady of Vurope."

She accepted her weapon, then gestured to where the water thing has sunk out of sight.

"Well fought, August One."

"We have much to discuss," I returned. "But first I must deal with my loyal ones—"

Murri and Akeea were panting, tearing at their fur where the slime had tightened. They must be seen to as soon as possible. Allitta came with me and the Kotti followed as we stood over the poor cats.

The shop of the Doll Maker in Valapa:

Ravinga was not to be seen. Her salesman, a small fellow who walked with a limp, was showing two women a doll at the far end of the room. Melora gave her attention to the cases and wall displays near the door. As ever when she visited Ravinga she was speedily lost in wonder at the workmanship which had produced the dolls in the glass-fronted cases on the walls and in the standing ones which sectioned the room. She moved slowly, viewing the wall display.

The floor cases reached above her head and she went unobserved by the other customers. It was at the sound of her brother's name that she halted to listen.

"—Hynkkel-ji—She believes he will meekly submit to her ordering of his life." There was a sneer coloring the words.

Melora was not ignorant of those courtiers who watched her brother closely, intent upon catching him in some gauche blunder. That he was very aware himself of that contemptuous appraisal of his every appearance, she had guessed. Anger possessed her each time she heard the belittling gossip, though she made no sign.

"The girl is very young," a second voice commented.

"But attractive in a childish way." Returned the other. "And this nobody out of nowhere could not have hoped to speak to her had he not been so oddly elevated to a position he can never hope to fill rightfully."

Melora's hand curled into a fist. She had always fought to control her temper—the Essence knew that that temper was part of the inheritance of her House. Except for Hynkkel. He never lost control, no matter how they had ill-used him. However he had survived the testing for the crown, which meant he possessed all the courage her father and Kalikku had always denied him.

"The Queen is clever; no one can deny that. But will the girl come in heat? She is so young and is of a retiring nature."

"You have said it; Yuikala is clever. It is whispered—very softly, of course, that heat can be manipulated to appear—using certain methods—"

"But—that is against the Law of the Essence!" broke in the other.

"If it is done with the kind of secrecy the Queen can command, her meddling with custom will never be known."

"I would not like to assume such a debt before the Essence—it can well bring disaster."

"We shall see. The Emperor is to go on Progress. I think that Yuikala will see he has the Companion of her choice when he does that, that Berneen will be so hailed in each Queendom. Ah," the voice was raised, "thank you for suggesting that coffer, Mancol."

The shopkeeper must have gone and now returned. Melora was sure they would not have talked so openly had he been there. She stood very still. Let them leave soon and might the Essence help her to keep her presence here a secret.

They went indeed. Unfortunately, without moving into a position where she would be seen, she could not in turn see them. But she was certain that they were of the Diamond Court.

"Hail, sister of the Emperor." Ravinga came into view at the end of the case-walled way.

"Hail, Mistress of arts," Melora waved towards the displays. "Such a wealth of beauty I have never seen except here."

She followed Ravinga into the back room. Then she halted not far from the door. On the worktable stood three figures. One—it was perfect—Hynkkel might have been reduced by some power. And that one was Allitta—between them the great Sand Cat Murri.

As she stared words came to her mind, as if one of the figures had somehow whispered in her ear.

"Water—'ware the slime—the spear—use it well!"

Misty half shadows—Hynkkel, Allitta, Murri—writhing in bonds—and before them a creature, which was not of Melora's world—and she had hunted far across the Outer Regions.

The mist faded. She thought she saw a spear raised and then all was gone.

Melora still gazed at the dolls. These words she had heard—she could not connect them with anything she knew. Water—much water—and a thing coming from it to attack—Allitta—Hynkkel facing it—Hynkkel bringing it down.

At last she raised her head to look to the doll maker.

"You have great power—these things," she gestured to the dolls, "spoke of a thing that was—or will be."

Melora turned one of her jeweled wristbands around. Now she slipped it off, placing it near the Hynkkel doll. "Is it that only dolls may report to you so? Is the power within them?"

Ravinga picked up the wristband, held it for a moment as if weighing it.

"This is your work?" At Melora's nod she continued. "You made one such for Hynkkel. Very well, this I have not tried before but perhaps it can be done. You may work here—I have the tools and the materials. Fashion another such and it may keep you in touch with your brother when he goes on Progress. There are those in Valapa who will hold to their oaths of allegiance; they might be rallied. But it is well to make use of any device we can think of.

"All of the Outer Regions will be hard tested very soon."

Hynkkel-ji:

With the edge of Allita's spear and both our personal knives we worked to free the cats. As the slime ribbons fell away they pulled patches of fur with them. And the skin beneath showed raw and bloody. We had to work carefully making sure we did not touch the slime. Allitta had carefully freed me from the one wrapped about my leg. I bit my lip and did all I could not to show pain. The leather of my boot was soggy, and, as the cats' fur it came away. My flesh looked as if I had been branded.

As we worked we talked, sharing knowledge. I learned of her discovery of these lower ways and she learned of mine. She was certain that some enemy knew of the passage to the water from her home and that had led to extinction of most of her family. I suggested that this secret flow of water was somehow allied to the great Dry of the past when some of our people had been ruthlessly harvested that others might survive.

"I must go on Progress," I plied my knife on a last patch of Murri's fur, having warned both cats not to lick their hurts after their usual manner, promising healing ointments once we were aloft again. "It would be well, since we share this secret, that you be one of our party."

"It will depend up on the Queen's will."

"No! It depends on mine. What does it mean to be called 'August One' if I can not have my will now and then?"

She had lowered her head as if to view more closely one of the bloody seams on Akeea's body. "Will it not be a matter for remark if I am so singled out?"

"It is customary for an Emperor to have a Companion—" I began, seeing only the value of such a cover for continued close relationship.

She sat back on her heels, slamming her knife back into its sheath.

"It is customary for the Emperor to have a Companion," she repeated. She might have summoned the curtain of a sand storm to fall between us.

I realized than how my thoughtless statement may have sounded to her. Without being conscious of it I put out my hand. My fingers barely touched her arm before she jerked further away.

"Please believe," I felt as awkward as I had always been in my father's house, "I meant no disrespect—" It was difficult to find words which might soften my arrogant suggestion.

"There is this—consider, please, what I say—You have shown me the map of the waterways—or such we believe it to be. It is necessary to discover whether access to these might be found in each Queendom. Perhaps in the past each had more water—or less. If the supply can be controlled, it must be discovered how and who would do it. Can you face the Lord of Measurement to again cull the old and the very young as mercilessly as was done in the past? I do not want the secret to be made public until I can trust—and trusting comes hard.

"This demands trust from us both. If you travel with the Progress, it would be best that we share the outward seeming of a relationship until our purpose is complete. Then all shall know the reason for what we have done. I ask of you no intimacy, only that we be as battle comrades even as we have been this night."

"I am not in heat," she replied sharply. "How then can I claim such a relationship?"

Being largely ignorant of the ways of women I could not indeed answer that. I remembered my younger sister's mating feast when she had come into heat. Being her sibling I had not been attracted to her, yet a number of young males appeared and vied for her attention until she made her choice. Perhaps Allitta was right, if there were no signs of her status she could not be selected as Companion.

Now she stood, looking coldly at me. At last she spoke, "You have given me much to think on, now give me time to do so."

She left me, carrying her Kotti. There was nothing I could do but agree.

In the outlands at the outlaw camp:

They had found this rock isle uninhabited though there was a healthy pool with a fine stock of algae. Shank-ji took this discovery as a sign that the Essence was indeed favoring him. And reinforcements continued to ride in.

So far not even the rats had found them. They had ample supplies, given by the people of Kahulawe when they had escorted in the remnant of the caravan to that Queendom. That had indeed established them as guardians of the trails. He sipped at a cup of melon-wine. It had been very easy to blacken this jumped-up servant there—it was the fellow's own home and he certainly had not gained any supporters— they knew him for what he was.

Sooner or later this upstart would have to make the Progress. Of course he would travel with guards, perhaps even the leopards, if they would serve one who outwardly supported Sand Cats. But there should be chances to get at him, there surely would!

"Commander!"

Shank-ji looked around. It was that brash youngster Kalikku, brother to the imposter. He had his uses but certainly he would *not* be included in the inner council of the next emperor.

"Yes?" he acknowledged lazily.

"There comes a rider—from the north."

"Another who wishes to serve the right—they come now as they should."

"Captain, this one is different—"

The boy seemed excited. Had he recognized some one of rank who should be greeted formally? Shank-ji set aside his cup and got to his feet.

Chapter 9

A messenger from Desolation:
A shrill whistle sounded—the outer sentry was alert. This
newcomer was strange. Shank-ji swung up to a higher point
of rock, where he could view the new arrival for himself.

The rider did not wear the puffed wig-helm of a warrior.
Instead he was hooded and cloaked by folds of gray, dabbed
here and there with splotches of black. If this was meant to
bewilder the eye it did not work here, for it stood out boldly
against the yellows and browns of the desert.

Shank-ji held up his hand, clicked two fingers together—
the sound would not carry far but was an order. He heard a
scrambling sound and knew that a guard was forming at the
rock incline by which one could reach the ragged crest of
the isle.

Now their leader was able to sight differences in the rider's
mount. It was like a oryxen, yes. However it was larger and
three instead of two horns burdened its head. The stranger
had swung towards the incline as if he well knew where their
camp was and felt no uneasiness in approaching it.

Shank-ji watched. His command were crouched behind
outcrops of rock, concealed from sight.

That bundling of cloak did indeed serve as a mask. Still
the stranger moved with ease, or perhaps he left it to his mount
to pick a way.

Several lengths from where the hidden warriors lay the
oryxen came to a halt. The masked rider did not urge it on; he
merely sat waiting. Shank-ji was suddenly sure that somehow
this visitor knew very well that he was within weapon distance of hidden men.

When both mount and rider continued to wait, Shank-ji
decided that boldness was the answer. He could not see any
weapon in the other's hold, though what could be concealed
under that cloak was a matter for guessing.

Arising from his own hiding place, Shank-ji came into the open, facing the rider. He held up his single hand, palm outward, in traditional sign of peace. There came no answer, either with gesture or voice, from the other. Playing games! Shank-ji was irritated. Did this one out of the desert believe that he would be awed so? Yet to speak first might well belittle the speaker and that was not to be thought of. If this was to be a trial of patience he would display his own stock of such virtue.

A sharp whistle again from a sentry—was this rider only the scout of a larger force? Movement at the foot of the climb—rats!

Shank-ji surrendered any advantage continued silence might give.

The wrapped lump of the rider's head turned. Then came a high-pitched squealing. The rats halted their advance. Again the stranger uttered that cry. Now the furred ones drew together, their heads all held high to watch the rider.

No squeal this time, rather a sing-song of words totally strange to Shank-ji. As if he commanded a war party of men, the rider continued. The rats drew back, retreating with their heads still turned to the stranger. Then they broke and raced down into the sand, fleeing at a surprising speed.

Shank-Ji felt the same desire to—run! So, this stranger was able to command the rats. Therefore that could be done. With such power at his own command he could easily conquer the Outer Regions!

"Well met!" He gave that greeting in the same tone he might to one of his own party.

"You come to war." A flat answer, cold as if one of the Dark Season winds carried it.

"We come to protect this land."

The rider slipped from his saddle, his drapery loosed by the movement, yet no sign of his body was visible. He did not grip the reins of the oryxen to lead it, but the animal responded as if he had.

"How may we serve you?" Shank-ji took no step backward though the other headed straight towards him.

"That is not the question. Rather it is how can those of the Desolation aid you? We shall speak on that."

Shank-ji gestured toward a seat on the rock. Not one of his troop showed himself. As he took his own opposite the stranger he said nothing. Let the other explain himself and his mission.

The stranger might have caught his thought. He shifted and his cloak loosened to fall away. Shank-ji closed his eyes then opened them again. He could hardly believe what sat before him now.

No body protection was apparent, no gleam of jewels, such as the speaker for a House might wear, nor was there any weapon in those hands—hand possessing fingers of abnormal length tipped by claws as long and strong as those of a Sand Cat. His body was bare to the waist, but the skin over the breast was covered with a growth of dark fur. The head—that was the least human—nose and mouth combined and jutting out, large furred ears flaring from a fur-covered skull. The eyes burned like sparks of red fire in their sockets.

Rat! Man-rat—if such a thing be.

"I am the voice of the August One. No, I do not mean the weakling who thinks he rules this land and will learn in due time that he is no more than flesh for the table. The August One knows all, man. You reached for the crown. Now you would reach the High Seat of your people. That will be the gift of the August One, but gifts must be matched. He has ways of learning what is done, what must not be done, and what will come. He can summon such ills as will blast all the Outer-Regions. Yet he can be merciful to those who lend their strength to his use.

"This he says to you: 'there is a force gathering which might rip this land apart; Queendom after Queendom will fall leaving nothing but ruins.' However, he can lend a part of this force to you, Shank-ji, Emperor who longs to be. The August One will remain apart as he always has. You may have the throne and all the power you wish over the Outer Regions. In turn you will listen to the August One and help to carry out his will."

"And if such bargain is not made?" Somehow Shank-ji summoned the will to ask that. The eyes of this man-rat bored into his own. The stranger might be reading every thought. Still—the offer—he must have time to weigh it. Again the other followed his thoughts.

"Yes, the August one will grant you time. The weakling goes on his Progress soon. This is the time to strike at him. Do not hesitate too long, for the August One has little patience with those such as you who can gain by his favor and yet waver over the asking for it."

Hynkkel-ji:

I relied on the skill of the two cats to get us to Mohambra's chambers without being sighted. Somehow we did this though it was well into morning and the hallways were in use. Their ability to make every bit of cover serve was a lesson to benefit any scout.

As we went I attempted to think of some explanation for our wounds. Perhaps this was one time when only the truth would serve. For if there had been one monster in the waterways there undoubtedly were more. Whether those would attempt to invade us I could not know. Somehow I still hesitated over letting our discovery be widely known.

Mohambra was startled, aroused to instant questions, even as she brought out salves and nostrums. Murri and Akeea had collapsed and I saw that their blood now gathered in those stripes from which Allitta and I had cut and pulled slime bonds.

I dropped down on a pile of cushions stretching out my leg. Blood dripped from it also and the burning was worse. Was the slime poisoned? One could well believe that.

"August One," the care keeper of the cats looked over her shoulder, "what has caused such wounds?"

Truth or tale? I choose truth.

"This must be kept secret for now, Mohambra. You are one who has the skill and learning we must use. But what I tell you must remain a secret."

Her greasy hand went to her lips and, not touching her skin, she signed agreement. I made my tale short as she continued her work. At times she looked up to me in amazement. When I had finished she said:

"Old tales are sometimes true then?"

I pounced upon that, as Murri would take a rat. "Tales? What tales?"

"August One, my mother and her mother before her served the cats, even as I do. There is a coffer among our supplies that has been sealed for a long time. Ah—what am I thinking of?" She interrupted herself, was on her feet and across the room to fling open another cupboard, standing then on tip toe to fetch down from the top shelf a dark box she brought back to show me.

"See, August One?"

There was indeed a line of red characters interlaid on the lid of the coffer. Writing changes over the years; some words are forgot and new one take their place. I puzzled for a moment before I could read:

"Water Ones' Bane."

She stooped and picked up one of the thin, blunt edged knives she had used to spread liniment. Using this she pried off a second lid. Within were two smaller boxes. She selected one and opened that in turn. How long that had been closed might not even be guessed but again she had work to force it open. Mohambra's treatment room was always a battlefield of odors but now such scent issued forth as seemed to clear one's head. She took a bit of yellow paste on a fingertip and held it close to her nose.

"It is so old—"

"So old it is of no use now?" I asked.

"That may be so—we can only try it."

Both of the cats had their heads up, looking more alert. "It is good!" Murri's thought reached me.

Could I depend upon his judgment? I had no wish to see the cats suffer from a mistake.

Reaching up I pressed one of my fingers into the paste, gouged out a ball of it, to smear across my own hurt. There followed a burning, stronger, more of a torment than that the slime had left. Then it was gone, to be followed by a soothing coolness. Murri was right, I was now sure of that.

Mohambra and I went to work, covering those plucked bare lines of skin with the paste. When we had finished both cats were on their feet.

As I wiped my hands on the towel Mohambra tossed to me, I nodded toward the box. She had lidded it again and was inserting it into the coffer.

"Where did that come from?"

"It is not of my making—" she answered.

I knew from our past conversations about cats and their care that part of her duties was concocting herbal remedies.

"As I said, this is old, old."

Yet it signified by the name on the cover that at one time the water creatures had been known well enough that this had been prepared to counter their slime.

"Take good care of that," I was on my feet. "We may need it if we go exploring again."

"Be sure I will!" she answered.

I hesitated, remembering Allita's map with the far spread of lines we believed marked waterways.

"The Progress is near at hand; can you give me a store of this paste to take with me?"

Mohambra looked from the casket to me. "You believe that these creatures may be found elsewhere?"

"It is always well to be prepared when a menace is discovered." I did not explain that one of my reasons for visiting the Queendoms was to prove our guess either true or false.

"I shall do more," she said slowly. "I shall test this and try to find what ingredients went into it that we may make more if needed."

I nodded. "Yes, that would be well. Let Murri and Akeea stay here. It is best that their hurts not be seen as yet."

She had again taken the paste from the larger box and was weighing it in her hand. "It shall be as you say, August One."

On the desert isle of the Outlaws:

Shank-ji had climbed past the uppermost sentry post to crouch high on a precarious knob. The messenger was on his way, riding as if he followed a trail clearly marked with the tall stone cats of the Queendoms. Only none such led any way into the Plain of Desolation. Shank-ji could sight black dots escorting the rider—rats.

He was aware of his own men waiting. None had over-heard the offer. Had it been an offer—or was it a warning? What was plain was that the unknown leader had resources, perhaps greater than any available to him. But how might he himself learn the extent of those? He was sure that there was no possible way for any scout to get into the Plain of Desolation.

There was no way of telling either how much that "August One" knew of Shank-ji's own defenses. He dropped down from his perch; the rolling sand dunes had hidden the rider now. It was time to do what he could to strengthen his own hand—His hand? He looked down to his handless right wrist. That must be paid for.

He came into camp. Most of his followers were gathered there—only the sentries missing. He must choose his words carefully.

He did. That the visitor had been a messenger, yes, it was well to admit. That there had been an offer of an alliance—that could be hinted at. However, he must make clear that no decision had been made. Now he would need messengers of his own.

Choosing his words with care Shank-ji started his action. This troop had been drawn from all the Queendoms; that was an advantage. He named names and then signaled that the general meeting was over. Left with him were those he had selected. One after another they were dispatched, each to their own home to gather the news, to recruit, to trade for arms, oryxen and supplies.

At last, only Valatan from Valapa and Kalikku of Kahulawe remained. It was not necessary to give Valatan any orders, he had long been a follower and supporter and he well knew the contacts Shank-ji could depend upon.

He had his own sources in the very heart of the court. He needed only be told it was time to put their network into action. And in a moment he was on his way to ride out.

Kalikku remained and Shank-ji surveyed him critically. He was well trained; any son of a one-time commander of forces would be. And—he *was* close to the usurper. But how good was he at dissembling?

"There is a special task for you, Kalikku, something only you can accomplish. It will mean that you must change outwardly. Your brother preens himself with crown and court— he is not aware how unsteady both of those may be. Were you to go to him, make him believe that the call of House is so strong you cannot resist it, that you are now willing to swear loyalty to him and that you have come to think what I do and say is not of the Essence, would he not be willing to accept you?"

Kalikku was scowling now as he burst out: "In what way have I failed you that you could think I would do this?"

"You have not failed, no. You will be serving our cause as no other does. We need one within the close company of the usurper—who better can we find? For, Hynkkel is of your blood, you have long known him, his weaknesses, those he depends upon. Thus you can learn much of his plans."

Kalikku shook his head vigorously. "He will not believe that I have changed so. If I know him, he also knows me."

"But I do not think that he does," Shank-ji set himself to the task of influencing this youngling. He must control his temper and exert himself to this task.

Kalikku continued to shake his head. His hands were knotted into fists.

"You are a key, Kalikku, and you have it in you to do a great service to our cause. Yes, you will have to play a part, which you dislike. But I say to you it is worth it. You come from a House of great warriors—look to your father. Has he not sworn allegiance? But to the office and not to the man—or he may now recognize some hidden talent in Hynkkel—"

"Not so!" Kalikku burst out. "It may be right that my father honors the office—he would never honor Hynkkel."

"Then would you not be honoring your father? And it would be very good to have close contact with him. As time passes he may realize that he is wrong. If you went to him and agreed to be at peace with your brother, he may be pleased with you. Your father has a high standing among those of Kahulawe; his example and beliefs could influence many. If he could be brought to see the justice of our cause it will be greatly to our advantage. Your brother is about to start his Progress. He will go first to Kahulawe, since he is born of that Queendom and will follow custom. This is an excellent time for you to ask for peace. No—" he held up his hand to silence the other's continued protest. "If you can serve us best this way, it is what you must do. Make your peace, then use your eyes and ears with ability. Who are his real supporters? What guards are in his train and for what purpose? What kind of reception awaits him in the Queendom? Has he any marked enemies now in his train?"

Kalikku did not answer for a long moment. Was he going to remain stubborn?

"You believe that this will be of service?"

"If I did not, why would I ask you to do this? Wars are often fought with other weapons than you are trained to."

"Wars?"

"Wars—we may have to sweep all the Outer Regions. We must be prepared for that."

"What I can do, I will. I will go to my father." Kalikku voiced no other farewell but headed for the pool valley where the oryxen grazed.

Shank-ji stared at the rock where the man-rat had sat in all his arrogance. He raised his arm and regarded the stump of his wrist. Payment—there must be that. Could the price be too high?

Chapter 10

Hynkkel-ji:

There were four report rolls waiting for me. And Giarribari was impatient for my choice of the date for the Progress. Many of the preparations were made, guards selected. But I was waiting for the recovery of Murri. I would not leave Valapa until the Sand Cat could accompany me.

"The season of storms is not too far distant." There was irritation in the Chancellor's voice. Perhaps she was right and I had waited too long.

"You are right. Shall we say five days from now?"

I knew from her expression she would have chosen an earlier departure. If it had been her will we might be setting off this very evening.

"There needs to be the Leave Taking," she reminded me.

Here was another court festival I could do without but could not dispense with.

"Make what arrangements are necessary. I leave such in your hands."

Having received the answer she had been long waiting for, she made the formal gesture of withdrawal. Once she had gone I pulled aside the heavy spread of my court robe and rolled up the inner one to examine the wound on my leg. Mohambra's ancient treatment had worked. There were some reddish patches on my skin but no other sign. Could I hope that the medication worked as well for the cats? I pointed to one of the chime mobiles and at its sound, the waiting messenger came from the outer chamber.

"There is one asking audience," he said. "The August One's sister, High Maid Melora Kura."

"Bid her enter. And do you go to the Imperial Cat Keeper and ask her to attend upon me."

He saluted and vanished. I rose to greet Melora as she entered and placed my hands on her shoulders to signify our closeness, avoiding formal courtesy.

"What brings that frown, heart held one?"

It was plain that she was indeed disturbed and I was instantly alert, knowing that under the surface of the court there was much which threatened. I drew her with me to the cushion seat by the wide window, hoping that I could in some manner reassure her.

"You go on Progress," she began.

"In five days. I can not put it off any longer."

"Have you selected your company, one perhaps to be your companion?"

I was startled. Had Allitta talked? I had not heard from her though I knew I must very soon.

"A companion?" I asked.

"Yes. Oh, Hynkkel, this I have heard—perhaps it is gossip only, but it was spoken as fact. It is said that Queen Yuikala's granddaughter Berneen will be our chosen one."

"But she is only a child. If she is in heat it is not apparent."

My sister was turning a small packet around and around.

"It is also said that there is a potion which can bring one to heat—"

"But that is meddling with the Law of the Essence! Who dares to do that?"

"The Queen—but she will not, she cannot, go against the Essence! Brother," she dropped the packet, "what has happened that one could break one of the Inner Laws? Would there not follow some great ill? A woman comes to heat at the time the Essence foresees—this has always been so. Yuikala is a Queen, answering to the Essence for this Queendom. She is accountable to her people, for the safety of Valapa. If she herself breaks the bond will not the whole of Valapa suffer?"

That was certainly the belief I had held all my life.

"Who carried this tale?" I demanded. "We must learn the truth!"

"I—I heard it as gossip. One who spoke so appeared to have some connection with the court. But I cannot not name her!" She burst out with the story of a visit to Ravinga's shop and there overhearing this nasty tale.

"Such could not be spread without some truth behind it. However, I do not know how we could learn more. There is none whom I can truly trust within the Queen's court. As it is, I must test each person who comes to me as well as I can. To make such an accusation without full proof would bring the wrath of the Essence."

"There is the High Maid Allitta," Melora said. "She has a place with the Queen if she claims it. Certainly she is apart from their schemes."

I thought of Allitta, of my own brash plan to bring closer one I could trust. Dare I approach her again and ask for help? It was like being entangled in slime ribbons, save that these could not be seen and cut away.

"Why do you not consult with Ravinga?" my sister asked. "She holds wisdom. This I made with her teaching." Melora unwrapped the packet.

What she revealed was another wristband. A line of very old inscription ran around it—silver on gold—the ancient words separated by gems—not diamonds, but the sapphires of my own home.

Melora took my hand and slipped it on. "Look you," she gave it a tug and it loosed to slide forward and rest now about my knuckles. "Thus!" She lifted my hand higher and I caught her meaning. I wore now a weapon of sorts and one not to raise suspicion.

"This is of Ravinga's learning and my work. Both of us labored under the Essence. Let it be your shield against all harm."

Her arms opened to me and I drew her close. Nor did I want her to leave. Like Murri she was warmth and good will, something to hold to amid the murk of the court.

"May the Essence be ever with you," she said when I released her. "You are far more than they believe, Hynkkel. I think that some will discover this to their sorrow."

As she went out Mohambra entered, flanked by Murri and Akeea. Their fur was still patched with stripes but bare skin was no longer to be seen and they were fully themselves again.

Allitta:

I had much to consider and no one at hand to whom I could appeal for advice. Ravinga's interest was not mine—she favored Hynkkel from the first. I thought of our meeting in the under ways and his abrupt, shaming suggestion. It would seem practical to him, yes. It was a blow in the face to me.

Yet, since we shared knowledge of the waterways and it was his hope to learn if the Queendoms were so linked, his idea was realistic. But how could he claim me as a Companion when I was not in heat? That would be apparent to all. Such pretence might even be against the will of the Essence.

I held Kassca close as the Kotti sang a song of comfort, which vibrated through her warm body. Cuddling her I went to that private place where, by custom, none might intrude.

Once settled on the cushions there I turned to the time-worn appeals I had known from early childhood, calling upon the Strength of the Essence. Kassca was a part of me; this room was a part. I opened wider invisible gates. The city was full of other lives, which, in turn enfolded—one with me—with the Essence. The rocks beneath, the air above, all of the Outer Regions: I was carried aloft—my eyes closed—yet I could see, I could feel—This was true life—not separate—but part of the whole. I was cushioned, held by greater arms, even as I held Kassca. There were questions to be asked but I did not ask. I was part of the whole. Allitta as one alone ceased to be. Never had I gone so deeply into the hold of the Essence. The peace that filled me now was all I could ever desire and I wanted to remain one with it.

Yet the comfort of it was not with me for long. There came a troubling through that which held me. My content was gone. I saw again the Outer Regions below. From the north arose a shadow, even as the slaying force of a sand storm. For

several breaths I saw it so, and then was again in my small
room with Kassca's small body vibrating, not with soothing
purrs, but deep chested growls.

"A warning, little one?"

There were stories of favored ones who had so closely
communicated with the Essence. But I was not a Seeker. I
had not sought, yet I had gained an answer. It was our belief
that only as we were aware of the Essence would our inner
lives be safe.

"Kassca, what is asked of me?" But I knew.

To go openly to Hynkkel, to boldly tell him that I would
agree to his plan: I just could not face that. A message—
then—

So I wrote some terse words on a strip of parchment, which
I twisted around a chain about Kassca's throat. At the last
moment I had to resist tearing that away and denying what I
must do.

In Queen Yuikala's private Garden:

The Diamond Queen had chosen the inner garden for this
meeting. It gave her confidence, which she hardly needed, to
glance up now and then at the windows of the Emperor's chambers. So—it had finally been decided. She looked to her in-
formant, one of her quarry's body servants. Pulling out a bag
from the swirl of her robes she tossed it to the elderly man.
An excellent tool—he had been a confidant of Haban-ji and
was resentful of the outlander who had taken the late Emperor's
place. He bowed deeply and withdrew, having pushed the bag
into the breast of his tunic.

When he was out of sight, and she hoped out of hearing,
Yuikala rang the mobile near to hand. It was Luvania, her
trusted First Lady who answered the summons.

"She has come?"

"Yes, Highness. I do not think that she is pleased."

Yuikala laughed. "She must learn she is under orders."

"Highness, she—she is said to have strange power. Perhaps if she is provoked too much—"

The Queen smiled. "Do not listen to childish babble, Luvania. People talk and raise common acts to the level of things mysterious. This one has great knowledge of growing things—but she has no invisible powers. Now bring her and then make sure that you stand as guard. I do not wish this meeting to be talked of—"

Luvania brought out a woman harshly treated by age. Years had weighed down her upper back, throwing her head forward. In contrast her face was unwrinkled, smooth, though the large eyes were sunken into pockets of flesh. Hair was untouched by any gray and gem-pinned into elaborate coils, as a much younger woman would wear it. She wore a false mask of youth above shrunken flesh and creaking bones.

As she joined the Queen, she offered no gesture of respect.

"You have sent for me, Highness," her voice was a rusty rasp.

"I have sent for you." The Queen pointed to a cushion such as inferior would use. "Be seated, Gornar. There is an important matter to be discussed."

The woman scowled but she did lower herself slowly, as if such action pained her, onto the cushion.

"You are said to have a vast knowledge of the uses of plants. I have heard of the First Maid of Verdit." Yuikala eyed the woman closely as she spoke.

Gornar needed to hold her head at an angle to meet the Queen eye to eye. She showed no surprise to hear very secret matter spoken of so openly. Nor did she make any comment, though Yuikala waited for a space. Finally the Queen continued.

"That such a thing is possible is difficult to believe."

"That First Maid is dead. Those who tend the ill have sworn it was sand fever that killed her. The silly wench went hunting a guardsman who caught her eye."

"So we are told," the Queen agreed. "There is another and more truthful tale, is there not?"

"Of that I know—" Gornar began.

"A great deal! Come, come, Learned One! I tell you that I have read the full report sent from Thnossis. Also a later one— the case of the daughter of Rasmussion, the dealer in gems. And that occurred in Valapa. That case was more successful. I believe she mated with her cousin, thus keeping a fortune safely within the control of her House."

The woman made no reply to that. Yuikala continued.

"It is said that you are in search of a certain plant which does not grow in the Outer Regions." Now she reached again into the folds of her robe to produce a box of metal, its cover and sides patterned with symbols of blood red.

Gornar's hand was out in a flash but the box was held out of her reach. The Queen laughed again.

"Everyone has a price, Learned One. It only remains that it must be found. Yes, this shall be yours—in return for that you have used twice before."

Gornar's eyes were still on the box. "The potion may kill if it is given to the wrong person."

"So. But that will lie on you, Gornar. You must help to make a certain maiden very happy. She will look high and if she succeeds, she will bring power to this court. You have other products for sale—have you not one which can keep certain aspects of age at bay—one you yourself are using? Would not the good will and needs of one at court be worth much to you?"

Gomar replied with just one word. "When?"

"Within a day," Yuikala answered promptly.

"I may not have enough to hand."

"Oh, I think that you do. I shall expect you to return before nightfall tomorrow. We have very little time. Go now and let me see you again before the tenth hour."

Hynkkel-ji:

I straightened the ribbon of parchment I had unwound from Kassca's throat chain. The writing was very small but clear. Reading it I gave a sigh of relief. She would do as I had suggested, but she demanded a promise in return, one that I would cheerfully give. I reached for a pen and used the last scrap of unmarked surface to tell her so.

Kassca was gone, a small gray shadow disappearing into other shadows. Murri looked at me.

"Take mate?" his thought reached me.

"Not so. But those about must think so."

If there could be a thought expressing laughter, I caught it then.

"Ho, brother, you do now follow a twisting trail," the Sand Cat returned.

Allitta:

I held Kassca close but the message she had carried lay crumpled on the floor. What had I done? I still lacked, and would at the crucial time, what I needed. How could any one possibly counterfeit going into heat? One certainly never did it by wishing—many women never had the experience at all. I had never wanted it. To allow one's self to be tied to some man, to have to consult with another over the needs of everyday living, to relinquish freedom? No!

Our coming together would not mean such a surrender, he had sworn to that. But all males within any company I joined would know that the situation was a false one. It remained the one barrier against carrying out his plan.

There were those well practiced in dealing with ills of the body. Each House had at least one such on the rolls. Here it was—I searched for the name—Ulvira. I had seen her only at the first gathering of the household. I knew nothing of her trustworthiness. No, I could not share my quest for knowledge with a stranger.

I thought of my openness to the Essence—surely what I had experienced had been sent by that. Therefore somewhere there must be the help I needed.

Kassca mewed. In my mind there was a picture, rather distorted but not enough that I did not recognize it. Ravinga. She did not deal with healing but she had power—far greater probably than I could envision.

Thus I made ready to visit her, taking with me—for I went openly—one of my guard and of course Kassca. I spoke idly of dolls and that I wanted an image of the Great Lady Assansi, who had been my grandmother.

I left the guard in the outer room where she could browse the many treasures on display and followed Ravinga into greater privacy.

Once there I made haste to state my problem. To my surprise, for I thought she would be shocked at such a thing, she laughed.

"So, girl, he has made an excellent choice. As for what troubles you—there is an answer."

She went to one of those concealed drawers, which only she knew how to open and pressed the proper spot. From the interior she scooped up a box the size of her palm and brought it to the table.

"Press here and here—" I watched her carefully. "No one who does not know its secret can open this. And here," the box opened and she took out a fabulous necklace of alternate beads of silver and rock crystal. The pendant it supported was also of crystal and hollow, the contents within a swirling mist. As it swung from her hand a fragrance floated to me. I had known many perfumes but nothing such as this. My heart seemed to beat faster; in me an inner heat began to rise.

"Wear this when you must show yourself in company. No one will say that you are not ready for a relationship."

She placed the necklace back in the box and handed it to me. Then she laughed again.

"Be warned that when you wear this you will indeed be noticed—and by every man within sniffing distance."

I made a face and determined that I would wait until the last minute to prove her right or wrong. But I was sure that, being Ravinga, she was right.

Chapter 11

At the House of Kaverel in the Queendom of Kahulawe:
"So," Kaverel-va-Meguliel sat at ease, "my dutiful son has at
last come to his senses."

He had not indicated that Kalikku was to seat himself.

"And just what has brought you here now?" Meguliel continued. On the small table at his side there rested an impressive array of battle honors. Kalikku thought his father must
be preparing for some very formal occasion.

"The honor of the House!" He could not summon any
other answer.

"Honor of the House? You appear to have forgotten that.
Was this House honored when you did not pledge your duty to
our new ruler?"

"To Hynkkel?" In spite of his attempt at control, Kalikku's
anger flared.

His father leaned forward. "Selected by the Essence, a
man faces the Five Ordeals—he who finishes is Emperor.
Kaverel is a loyal House, accepting without question the will
of the Essence. Our Emperor earned the throne by the ancient custom—no man can question that. Have you so forgotten what our House stands for—loyalty to the chosen?"

It was and yet it was not his father—Meguliel was again
the commander of Kahulawe's forces.

"What must I do?" Kalikku knew the answer to that, but
his pride was like a spear point in his breast.

"What you should have done from the first, as you very
well know. Are you also lacking in wits these days? You may
remain under this roof for the present. The Emperor is to
make the Progress. He will come here first. Then, if you are
true son of this House, you will give allegiance. What ties you
to the rebels? An oath to an outlaw is treason. You say you

have seen your mistake and return to your duty—can any of those lurkers claim that you have already lost your honor?"

"No!" Kalikku said. He was not honor broke—yet. Rather he was here to serve the leader he had chosen.

He braced himself under his father's searching stare.

"While you are waiting," Meguliel said, with the deliberation of one giving a order. "You will assume the guardianship of the herds."

Hynkkel's labor in the past. Kalikku swallowed. He could taste the sour anger he had to subdue.

"You have my leave to begin your duties."

That was the way that a servant was dismissed. Kalikku swallowed again and somehow got himself away from his father's presence without losing rein on his temper. On the other side of the door curtain he brought his fists together with force—could he last out this humiliation? He must.

Hynkkel-ji:

I had nothing to do in preparing for the Progress. This was governed entirely by tradition. However there was one thing to be done. I sent a message to Ravinga, desiring her attendance at court.

It was the custom of the ruler when visiting the Queendoms, to present each of the Queens with some lavish and unusual gift. I had a sudden idea what mine would be, if, of course, I had not left the matter too late for Ravinga to be able to supply what I wanted.

When she came I had her ushered into my private quarters, for once not caring if I were breaking custom, and I dismissed the servant. Murri lay down before the door and I was sure that he could detect any would-be listener.

I again shattered custom by rising at her entrance and escorting her to a seat.

"High Lady—" certainly her support raised her in my eyes to nobility "—for all you have done, I thank you. Those are but words—I cannot truly put what I feel into them. I am one who walks a dangerous trail. Therefore I cling to those I can trust."

"Thus you consider me?" she asked quietly. "Now what would you have me do?"

I flushed. Had I again spoken brashly? Could she believe that my true gratitude was only expressed because I wanted a new service?

"Please, my tongue sometimes does not aid me as I wish. Yes, it is true I need help. Only—" I threw up my hands, "I ever make myself a fool when I mean to speak the truth! I never wanted to be emperor and certainly my ineptitude is visible. I do not know why the Essence has brought me here—"

"Because you are the one who can keep the balance," Ravinga replied and I did not know what she meant. But now she continued and I listened, first eagerly and then with growing concern.

"The Darkness rises again. There is one who, long ago, strove to warp and twist our land, remold our people to serve his own purposes. He was beaten before—now he returns refreshed, determined to succeed.

"Our lives rest on factors which other nations—those of the Inner regions—do not have to fear. Water is our first, our abiding need. All now living have heard the heart-tearing tales of what happened before when the algae pools shrank and died. The Master of Balance had then more power than any ruler. There was a closely guarded secret which was bought by the sacrifice of him who was then Emperor. Several of the Great Houses learned it."

"In each Queendom do the rivers run?" I demanded as she paused.

"Just so. But this was also known by the Dark One. He used his power. Those who knew this secret of water were targeted and died. Sometimes the secret was relearned by those descended from the victims."

"Was this the fate of the House of Vurope?" I asked.

"Just so."

"But who in Valapa served this enemy by bringing down that House?" I wanted to know.

"The Dark Lord is able to spread his concealing cloak over those who obey him. Yet there was a Companion of the Emperor at that time who had much power. She died suddenly—after Vurope was erased. Had the House fallen for the reasons voiced at that time, then all its resources, as was the custom, would have gone to the accuser. Rather the holdings all went to Haban-ji."

"Then," I said slowly, "when I returned the holdings to Allitta—did I put her at risk?"

This I did not want to believe. Ravinga shrugged.

"Who knows? So far no shadow has reached towards her."

I studied her calm face. As ever, when in her presence, I felt that she was far more than she appeared. Though she ever wore merchant robes and very little jewelry, still, in any courtly assembly, she would be at ease with the nobility, even with the Queens.

"No shadow shall!"

Murri raised his head; there was a growl from him. As ever he had caught my thought. But, almost as I finished speaking, I knew that my promise might be a vain one. If I might not even be able to protect myself, how could I promise safety for another?

"The Progress will be a test perhaps as great as the Ordeals. And those I faced successfully. Has Allitta not already been drawn into part of this danger? She must have your protection."

"This is why you have summoned me?" She was abrupt as if she were preparing to leave.

"Yes—but now there is a far more important reason. Will you join the Progress?" I did not know how I would explain adding Ravinga to our company but I was sure that if she agreed, her advice would mean more to me than any weapon.

Ravinga did not reply at once, rather she continued to view me as if I were a doll over which she had labored and she was not certain I was complete.

"Do not judge yourself so poorly." Thought reading? Was I so poor in self-confidence that I displayed it openly? "There is this, Hynkkel: any one of us can rise to a challenge if we believe that we can. You are Emperor with the Essence's blessing or you would not be here. So—be Emperor in truth!"

"The Wise One is right," Murri had risen to his feet.

"But," I kept to my need, "will you ride with us?"

For the first time she smiled and I saw the Ravinga I had always respected.

"It was in my mind when I came here. Yes, I shall come. Now, is there any other need?"

"Dolls!" I settled back among my cushions with some of the same relief I had known when one of the ordeals was behind me. "Gifts for the Queens. However, I have another purpose—I wish all to understand that the Sand Cats can be friends, that they are no longer to be hunted. I can utter decrees. I have already done so, but these are only words. We know the Kottis to be more than friends. Sand Cats may not share our homes but they have loyalty and their thoughts can reach those they accept as friends."

Ravinga leaned a little forward, her face alight with interest. "Yes, oh, yes," she said softly. "For each Queen a subtle gift, unlike any given before. A cubling, life size, wearing a collar to match the Queendom to which it will go. It will enchant—"

"Will you have time?" I asked.

She laughed. "Oh, August One, this has been anticipated. The cublings already wait within one of my safe cupboards. The Essence seems to have given me foresight. They will be ready—as shall I."

Two promises, and I was sure she would keep them both.

The Outlaw camp:

The rock island on which the rebels had established their camp had been thoroughly explored before Shank-ji had made his decision to hold it as a fortress of sorts. From the volcanic realm of Azhengir several recruits had been drawn. Two were expert workers in metal and now they were inspecting weapons, making sure all were in battle condition. Algae had been harvested from one end of the pool and pats of it were being dried. There was much drawing of trails on rock surfaces, each warrior who could adding sections of the Outer Regions over which he himself had hunted.

Shank-ji spent much of his time on one sentry peak. There had been no more messengers from the Plain of Desolation. None of his scouts sent to the Queendoms had yet returned. Waiting made him irritable and then uneasy. He still had not made up his mind about the offer from the mysterious Dark One the man-rat served. There was in him a foreboding concerning this new player in the game. Though the rats had not been seen since the monster had ridden away, the four-footer killers could have brought down any of the scouts.

Valapa was the end goal of any campaign. If that were in his hands—hand—he rubbed his wrist stub—he could rest secure. The guards there—very few of them had ever faced rats. They had grown slack over the years—that he knew from his own observations. There were also ones there who would openly welcome his House banner.

The usurper was in control of the resources of the Empire. That did not mean much outside of Valapa. The false Emperor could demand services and supplies from any Queendom. However with the distance between each nation and Valapa, his orders could be easily delayed. There had come news that the Queendoms were building up their own armies, needing more protection against the new rats—New rats—He rubbed the scar tissue braceleting his wrist. It might be where there was one man-rat there would be others, an army of them to control the four legged ones?

Already the recruitment in the Queendoms attracted warriors with a taste for battle away from the trail guards. Sooner or later the caravaners would demand a service few could supply. With the Caravans unable to tie the Queendoms together there would rise anger against the Emperor.

The barbarian could not even swing a sword properly. Surely he had planted that double damned archer who had been the cause of this! Once more he rubbed the scar.

The Outlander could not know the secret Haban-ji held. Too bad his father had never had the guts to really explore the Vurope holdings. Or had that tale just been another rumor? There were always enough of those floating around the court.

Well, if Haban-ji had not had the fortitude to uncover secrets, his son seemed to lack courage to make up his mind— sooner or later he must decide.

Close to sunset—time for the night patrol to ride. This time he was going to take command. They could not reach the Plain in one night, but uneasiness rode him. He wanted to see if any trace could be found of the trail the Man-rat must have used.

In the great palace of Valapa:

Queen Yuikala signaled the maid to close her massive jewel chest. She had been inspecting every one of its crowded trays, choosing from them with particular care. No, the child must not be overloaded with glitter; that was for an older woman who desired to attract attention. Simple, but of course, rich as was only fitting for her granddaughter.

Diamonds discreetly set—those would be necessary for one from Valapa. However there was a triple necklace of rainbow moonstones—very rare in the Outer Regions. Also clear crystal hairpins, cut in the form of stars, set in silver— very proper for a maid just come into heat.

She looked the girl who sitting not far away. "Very suitable. You will wear the robes you have been shown. Most of the guests will appear in colors—silver and white will make you more visible. What is the matter with you, girl? You have shown little interest in this. Have you no gratitude? Any maid should be dazzled at such jewels and robes."

Berneen's hands were tightly clasped as if she did not want to touch clothing or jewels. She shivered though she wore the usual heavy court robe, one into which she had drawn as if it were a sheltering cave.

"Yes, Grandmother," her voice was hardly above a whisper, "You have been most generous—"

"Girl, sit up! Stop acting as if you were being scolded! I have been most patient, full aware that your raising has been against you. Your foster mother is noble, certainly, but she is not aware of court procedure. I blame myself that I left you too long in that place which is hardly better than a produce farm."

But it was safe, Berneen thought, and House Mistress Faterine had been kind, even when she had been so busy with the management of the estate that she never seemed to have time for Berneen. There had not always been strangers about watching her, as she was sure they did here, thinking her clumsy and ignorant.

Now Grandmother had put on her expression of exasperation again. She would talk and talk until Berneen's head ached. They would bring out all those stiff robes and bundle her into them and string the jewels on her, Grandmother making critical remarks all the time the maids were busy.

However Grandmother had stopped speaking and was just staring at her. Berneen did not want to raise her head and look back, but something made her do it.

The Queen picked up the large mirror by its handle and thrust it at the girl. Somehow Berneen caught it safely before it slipped through her fingers.

"Look!" The Queen demanded. "Screw up your face in that fashion and no one will find you attractive. Look, I say. You must will a smile on your face when it is necessary."

There was a threat implied in that. Berneen shivered and tried for a weak quirk of lip which she hoped would satisfy her grandmother.

Yuikala threw up her hands. "You have a fine future before you; more than half the court will envy you. Oh, go to Hanlika and practice your steps for the ball!"

Berneen made her curtsey and thankfully left. She was not going to be freed, of that she was sure. Indeed she would be at the frightening ball. But she did not understand yet what was expected of her and there was no one she could ask.

The Queen expected that some surprising event was going to place her, a shadow of a proper court lady, into some high position. But what—and how?

She did not return to her own chamber nor did she seek out the stately court advisor as she had been ordered. Instead she slipped out into the private garden. Once more she reached the bench where the Emperor had found her. He had seemed to understand. She remembered clearly his admission that he also felt ill at ease here. If she only had a brother like him, or some close House relative. To dance with a person who was not critical but wished her well—that would take away much of her fear. Only wishes very seldom came true—at least Berneen had found it so.

Chapter 12

At the Outlaw camp:
The night was clear—for now. Each day the time of storms grew closer. That fool on the throne is risking his Progress. Was he doing it deliberately, hoping to buy time before he had to visit the Queendoms, in which he would face trouble? Shank-ji led the troop part way along the caravan trail but when that angled away in the direction of Kahulawe he kept them riding ahead.

This was open territory with none of the slickrock islands showing, though here and there were lone, sand worn peaks. If they kept on they would reach the edge of the Plain of Desolation. The puzzle of how any living thing could use that as a base teased him.

This talk of an August Other who ruled there—He had never been one to go stirring up dust in any record room. If there had been such a one troubling the past of the Outer Regions surely there should be some memory of him. Yalan— his thought brought a picture of the age-touched face of that capable warrior who had taught him skill with arms and had always been his shadow since he had become a man.

Shank-ji slowed the pace of his oryxen and spoke to the rider behind him. "Pass the word for Yalan."

In all this band the veteran was the one he could trust the most, yet he certainly would not allow even Yalan to know of the Dark One's offer—not yet.

"Yalan reporting," the other rider had come up before they had advanced further.

"Ride with me. There is something I would know." He was choosing his approach with care. "You rode in the Emperor's army when it still was an army—" he accented that, well aware that Yalan was contemptuous of the so-called warriors of this day. "Was there talk in the early days concerning a Dark Lord who threatened the Outer Regions?"

"Talk, yes. But it was forbidden. Haban-ji decreed that it was not to be mentioned. But that was when he first won to the throne many years ago." The veteran answered promptly.

Shank-ji was startled. That his father had given such an order was strange. The reign of Haban-ji had been a quiet one. Of course there had been the usual feuding among the Great Houses—Vurope, for example, had been stamped out. But such struggles among themselves had gone on for centuries. War—a war which would threaten all of the Queendoms—it was surely waged before Haban-ji had passed the ordeals and won to the throne. His father's family had been of Valapa and the interests of the Emperor had been mostly engaged in the affairs of the Diamond Queendom.

"That must have been very long ago?"

"True, Commander. It was just before the great drought when balances had to be made."

That was something Shank-ji did know. It was a time when the Outer Regions suffered greatly. The old and the weak young were put to sleep. Most of the Houses, great and small had a quiet private place, a plaque listing names that were honored on certain dates but otherwise were not mentioned. It could be that a war would be wiped out of mind by the later horrors of water failure.

"Was this dark lord given any name? From which Queendom did he rise?"

"No name. That too must have been forbidden. Tradition has it that my father's father's grandsire fought then. The Lord was said not to be of the our land; he came out of nowhere and perhaps went to nowhere. Commander, that strange one who came to us—" Yalan was quiet; he might have overstepped some bounds and Shank-ji would be angry.

His leader did not answer at once. His indecision still gnawed at him. Finally he did the best he could to explain in part, not wanting Yalan to believe that he would be angry with him for daring to mention the messenger.

"There are bits and pieces—I must learn what I may before I can be certain. But your memory has helped greatly and I am indebted to you."

The dunes, which had made their path a weaving one at first, were subsiding. Though they had not suffered a storm near their own isle, there must have been one here, one hard enough to sweep the ground level. The flat feet of his mount, intended for traveling the ever-shifting sand, were thudding on a harder surface. Shank-ji tried to see what was causing the difference. Rock—rock over which sand shifted.

In his tracking over the sand lands before, he had never come across its like. It stretched ahead almost in the form of one of the roads of Valapa, a far more enduring one than those. He drew Yalan's attention to it but the veteran did not show surprise.

"Many times storms clear such. There was a company of keepers of old knowledge which my squad once guarded as they went about hunting remnants of the past. It was the opinion of one of them, a dried up, wooly witted one from Twahihic, that such were roads of a very ancient time. Most of his fellows laughed at him behind his back."

They continued to follow the trace until Yalan said suddenly, "Commander, this leads in the direction of the Plain of Desolation."

Shank-ji pulled his mount to a halt. "Which is a way not to be taken—at least not now."

At his command they angled east, coming again to where dunes made one more comfortable by their familiarity.

Allitta:

I had not held my House Rule so long that I had a large wardrobe. And I could not see riding forth in court robes. So I viewed all the garments maids pulled from chests and tried to foresee what demands might be made during the coming journey. I could only believe that the role of Companion might make such choices difficult. Time and time again I questioned my agreement to this wild venture. We were going against all which was considered correct.

I must prepare myself to face what was nearly immediately before me. Of course I could not share with any of my household what lay ahead—only that I would make one riding forth on the Progress. As Head of the House of Vurope, that could be expected. My Steward listed the supplies for such a trip as well as what must be done to assure the smooth running of the estate while I was away. I retired to my cushion couch at night very glad that now only Kassca shared my chamber.

Ravinga had sent a message by her kotti Wiu that she also would be with us. I sighed with relief. To have her near was a blessing from the Essence.

Most of the day of the Farewell Feast was spent in preparation for that event. I slept late, lulled by Kassca's purrs, and ate food a maid brought, the fruit that was a treasure of Valapa and an algae cake spread with shaved meat.

There was a bath of perfumed water. My hair was washed likewise, to be dried with scented towels. I had never completely surrendered myself to the skills of the maids before and now they were eager to show what could be done to render one into the semblance of a high noble woman.

I had chosen to wear an outer robe of cream, one somewhat lighter in weight, as I well knew how the heat would render any heavier one a burden as the night progressed. The jewelry I chose had the customary diamonds of Valapa. However those were small, set in the eyes, and in frames around miniatures of Sand Cats rendered in fine enamels so matching in color the fur of the real cats that one could believe that was real fur stiffened by some skill. I added a wide necklace, earrings heavy enough to pull rather painfully on my ears, broad wristbands and a girdle.

My hair was dressed in coils, held by pins, each bearing a Sand Cat's head. However I dismissed the contents of the many jars and bottles made to enhance one's lips, paint longer one's brows, and produce the proper mask for a courtly occasion. I also waved aside the perfumes which were offered, much to the dismay of the two maids. At last I sent them to order my carry chair and was safely alone.

Hurriedly I got out the small box Ravinga had given me. When I opened it fragrance wafted out stronger than the perfumes I had refused. I sat with the crystal charm in my hands and then, with an effort, managed to put the chain about my neck and work the whole under my clothing into complete hiding. The empty box was dropped into a painted bowl on the window shelf.

"House Lady—" The summons came from outside the door curtain just as Kassca leaped up to the shelf and curved her body in protection for the bowl.

The maid Ruffine stood outside. Her eyes widened as I came out. She drew back, raising her hands in a new salute.

"House Lady—what joy! The Essence is with you!"

"I trust so," I replied. Above all I would need all the Essence could give me this night. Ravinga' s charm was well awork, though I had not suffered any of the forwarding pain and excitement which was often discussed among women themselves.

Ruffine appeared a little taken back by my calm. But I did not know just how I would properly appear under the circumstances and thought I should modestly keep silent and as withdrawn as possible. I must indeed make sure that I would *not* be the center of attention for only males. Luckily custom would come to my aid. Would-be mates must not approach a possible bride unless she signified interest, though that did not rescue her from their regard.

I dropped the curtains of the carry chair once I was inside. Already the news must be current in the house, to be followed very soon by speculation over which noble I might favor. Sometimes such choosing went on for days, the maiden coy and the unwed warriors and courtiers present. At least I did not face that—my supposed fate would be made plain tonight.

In the Chambers of the Queen:
Berneen held the goblet in her hand. The contents had an odd metallic scent. She wanted nothing more than to hurl

the whole thing away from her. Now she had to steady it with both hands lest she let their shaking dribble the contents on her feast finery.

"Drink!" There was no softness in that order.

Queen Yuikala stood clad in the new splendor of a diamond frosted robe of winter snow-white. Her crown was a fan of white fur, combed and stiffened about the head-hugging portion of a diamond-studded cap which covered all her hair. A prisoning collar of silver and diamonds flowed over her breast, glittering white to her waist. To Berneen's eyes she was a presence one could never hope to disobey.

The goblet still shook in spite of the girl's effort to control her hands as she raised it.

The Queen raised one hand a little as if intending to grasp that cup and press it firmly to Berneen's lips, forcing it into her mouth.

Berneen uttered a little moan but then she drank. She might have stuffed fire into her mouth, a terrible heat which burned her throat and then settled into her middle as she swayed. Yuikala caught her by the shoulder in punishing grip and kept her standing.

The girl gasped. "Please—"

Suddenly she no longer felt so weak. There was no more pain, though the heat still filled her. Oddly that was fast banishing her fears. What had she to fear? By the moment she gained strength. She jerked herself free of the Queen's hold. Her grandmother had also lost the tension of a moment before. Yuikala nodded.

"Well done. But remember well what has been told to you."

Berneen's head was held high. For the first time since she had been summoned to court she did not wish to hide herself. Why should she—for this night she would become what her grandmother promised—First Lady of the Empire, the chosen Companion.

"I remember," even her voice had taken on a new strong note. "I am to stay always with you, I am not to notice if any lord pays me attention. There is only one man who will count."

The queen stepped back and viewed her critically from head to foot.

"Well enough. It is time to go."

Hynkkel-ji:

Murri sat before me and I felt his critical appraisal. As usual I was imprisoned in a heavy robe, the back skirting of which trained for some distance across the floor. Its presence was not only irritating but had always to be kept in mind. It was of a green-blue, patterned in ovals which suggested feline eyes, each centered by a pupil of a gem as pale as a diamond but still with a hint of the green-blue—a new stone found in the lava from Azhengir's fiery outbreaks. The outer robe was edged by fluffed and treated oryxen mane. The roll of fur stood tall behind my head, its two lengths open to the waist where a wide belt of the gems drew it together. My crown was a circle of several rings of the gems, set in silver, fastened to a tight cap.

I could see in the mirror this puppet of an Emperor half hidden by these trappings, and not for the first time I thought of decrees to change court dress. Not that the finery-loving courtiers would obey, any more than the outlaws had the decree concerning peace with the Sand Cats.

In my mind I again felt Murri's amusement.

"Excellent for traveling," he commented. "What passes in the minds of those gathered here, Brother, that they must so wrap themselves? Certainly they cannot hope to dance in the proper fashion."

I well remembered the air borne graceful leaps and floatings which formed dancing for my brother's kind, and I laughed.

"No, I do not dance so, Murri—We do not know the freedom of your kind. No matter; there will be other things to consider tonight."

"Your mate, brother?"

I shook my head so hard, I suddenly worried if I had loosened the crown.

"Not so. Yes, these of the court will think her so. She will be safer with us than if she was left behind. When we set out, do you be on guard for her also."

He yawned, arose, and moved towards the door. "I hear and obey," he returned in mockery of courtly language.

Allitta:

I left the carry chair in the outer courtyard, crowded near to the walls with just such equipage as had brought me here. Since I was alone, I had made arrangements that the captain of my guard accompany me to the assembly room. We had not taken more than a few steps before I became well aware that I could not hope to pass unnoted. But I kept my eyes straight ahead and held to my chosen avoidance of those around me. Luckily I had not been returned to my rank long enough to have made acquaintances of any of the noble families. In fact I had been avoided in turn by them, which had suited me well.

At the door curtain, held aside by servants, I dismissed the Captain with my thanks and went forward. It was my hope that outwardly I did not display what churned within me. What I was to do this night was so alien to my wishes and the life I had marked out for myself that I had to force every step I took.

I was announced in the flattering terms used on such occasions. Heads turned—far more interest was being shown in me now than since I had mounted the throne steps and Hynkkel-ji had reinstated me in my heritage. As Head of one of the Six Houses I had my ordained place and I headed straight for that.

The rising din of voices near drowned out the sweet music of the kifonggs, but now and then came a short roll of drums which did reach one's ears. Such came even as I reached the line between the House Heads of Orsmer and Raferhok. There was a stir by the other entrance to the larger chamber, that which connected with the inner Palace. Into the clash of colors of gems and fine materials, the two leading newcomers advanced hand in hand. It was the Queen of Diamonds and her granddaughter.

I knew instantly, as did all those nearby, that Berneen had indeed fulfilled Yuikala's hopes—the girl was in heat. There was a difference in her—she, for the first time I had seen her in company, was confident. There was even a faint shadow of the Queen's ever present arrogance to be detected in the way she carried herself—no sign now of any shrinking from company.

They proceeded to the throne of Valapa' s queen where Berneen had been provided with stacked cushions slightly behind her grandmother's place. Behind her where the male courtiers were gathered—there was movement, almost like a sand dune under the thrusting of the wind, though it did not advance far. Berneen had a court of her own, though she did not steal any glances towards those eager noblemen.

Whether I, also, had a gathering behind me I did not want to know. Only let this begin and be as quickly over. I clasped my hands and kept my head high, my gaze away from my neighbors—neither of them had given me any greeting.

Once again the drums rolled. Between the upheld curtains Hynkkel-ji entered. Though he was tall and, as I knew, well muscled, his ornate robe seemed to burden him, turning him into more of a doll than the image Ravinga had made.

On either side of the Emperor paced Murri and Akeea. Thus the courtiers must part a wide path for the trio. We had risen to our feet at his entrance. The Queen and her candidate for his notice were standing nearer to his path. But Murri turned his head a little and those great golden eyes met mine. A moment later Hynkkel glanced in my direction and I knew that Murri had passed the message to his blood brother.

Chapter 13

Hynkkel-ji:

I was aware of the tension about me. How many of these here, I wondered, knew of Yuikala's plan? As I approached the Queen to whom I must first render greeting I sensed something else, an inner excitement being fed from a source new to me. So—she *had* tampered with matters controlled by the Essence. Berneen had come into heat.

The girl who had seemed little more than a child to me had changed. Her soft face looked as if the mask of a woman several years older covered it. There was a curl of lip that made very plain her heritage; so much was it like the Queen's.

And—Murri's thought reached me. "Think, Brother, this one is ripe for the taking."

There was no amusement in that comment.

Yuikala was bending knee slightly in the obeisance proper for the occasion. I kept my eyes on her, though I was only too conscious of the white-clad figure moving forward, probably in answer to some gesture from her grandmother.

I had never been subjected to the full power of enticement a maid in heat could project, since in my homeland I had been considered too lowly to notice. Now warmth which was not the result of my weighty robe, flushed my face. My body was answering to a strange compulsion.

"August One," the Queen said. "I beg your favor for the one new to our court."

Berneen was sinking in a very low curtsey. However Yuikala's confidence had led her astray. No untitled one, no matter of how high a House, could be greeted before the Six who were standing a short distance away. It was from them that future Queens would be drawn, and each House had given in turn a woman to hold that title.

I grasped quickly at Yuikala's mistake. Looking at last directly at the girl I did not even grant her a nod. I heard a faint sound from Yuikala as I moved toward the House Heads. The men drew themselves up, their right arms across their breasts in salute, Allitta giving the prescribed curtsey.

Again I sensed something of the same attraction. Surely she had NOT come into heat at will. I was sure that Ravinga could not break the ancient laws. I was also certain that Allitta would not allow herself to act against custom. However it was true that there now arose from her the same enticement with which Berneen had threatened my senses. Only now I need not practice the control to hold me safe.

Even hampered as I was by my robe I took an eager step towards her. For our plan was working and my interest would not be suspect. All knew that we had met when she was in exile and I was the least of my clan.

My hand went out and I drew her up from her curtsey.

"High Lady," I used the proper greeting, "Our court is indeed graced by your presence."

I could hear gasps, some muttered words not too far away. Never before in any public place had I so unbent before a woman.

"August One," she replied in a clear and carrying voice, "you pay me great honor."

I carried the hand I still held to my lips, and pressed it. Now the sounds from the audience were louder gasps. I was granting Allitta—in public—the treatment of a Companion.

However such a choice was always staged in public, as I had learned when researching the history of earlier reigns. And usually with no more courting than this. There might be a lot of speculation—there would be. But no one would ask questions. Unlike the customary ritual when a maid could choose her mate, the Emperor need only signify his choice and all other nobles would immediately withdraw.

I must move on, reach the throne. But still I did not release Allitta. Holding her hand high in mine, I drew her along, Murri moving in on her other side.

At that moment I longed to look back at the Queen. That I had ruined all her plans would not defeat her—I was sure of that. Murri's thought came.

"She is raging, brother. A she-one so used nurses wrath over her defeat."

"And the girl?" I thought back, for I remembered her youth and how she had disliked the court. Whatever Yuikala had done she had aroused Berneen and in such a state she was dangerously vulnerable.

"She is running, brother. Already she is through the curtains—gone."

I had blundered, perhaps badly. To those who had been aware of the Queen's plotting, my turning to Allitta would be an unforgettable insult. And what could I do to make sure Berneen would not now be sneered out of a life of her own?

In the feast chamber—Feast of Farewell:

Queen Yuikala paid no attention to the wild retreat of her granddaughter. She stood, drawing on her inner power as if the girl had never accompanied her. There was the hiss of whispers—they were like death-lizards, the full lot of them! Rage choked her and she fought to keep it from bursting forth in curses.

The insolence of that creature out of Kahulawe! A barbarian nothing! And that green girl he thought to honor—Vurope had vanished once before—it could again. This slut—she had traveled the trade routes, been apprenticed to a workwoman. Everyone knew how they lived. Yes, she was fit to match with a stupid outlander. Bring them both down. Already there were those oathed to do that. Berneen—the Queen had carefully kept control of her features—allowing no scowl, no sign of her anger to show. Berneen might still be a weapon to be put to good use. But she could not withdraw from this assembly until the end. No one must be allowed think that the barbarian and his slut had banished her—

Berneen's sandaled foot caught in the trailing skirt of her over robe. She felt it tear, but she gathered up the skirt and ran on. They were laughing; everyone would laugh. He had not even really looked at her! Yes, they would laugh and Grandmother would be really angry. She might even have Berneen beaten as she had ordered her maid to be yesterday. Away—just let her get away from this awful place. Where could she go?

Pain pierced her body and she staggered, clutching the door curtain of a room opening off the hall. She halted; cried out in pain. It was gone and then it came again. Her hands pressed on her lower body as she tried to ease her misery.

"Lady—are you ill?"

Another pain. She flung out her left hand trying to find a hold to steady her. Her fingers were caught in a warm, strong clasp, and then she was leaning back against the support of a sturdy body.

"Ahhhhh—" That pain!

She found herself swept up. She was being carried into the room before which she had stopped. With tears running down her cheeks, she turned her head to look up.

The face under the fluffed, diamond-dusted warrior's head-dress was young. He was looking at her with open concern.

"It hurts," she said simply, as if she were indeed a child.

The room was dim after the well-lighted hallway. Only one of the bubble lights swayed there. It swung down to-wards Berneen and him who carried her. There was a pile of lounging cushions and he carefully lowered her to rest, even as the lash of pain again curled about her.

"Nooooo!" She cried out. Her body twisted; she sunk her hands into the cushions at her sides.

"Lady—I will bring help—"

Frantically she reached out and grabbed at the hem of his short uniform. "No," she panted, her body arching under an-other attack. "Do—do not leave—Please—!"

"But you need tending—" he began.

"She—I do not want her—there is no one—ohhhh!" She released her hold and stiffened on the cushions. Black terror had her now. What they had done—what had Grandmother done and she herself been persuaded to do? They had broken the Law of the Essence! How could she hope for help? Was she dying?

"Lady!" He was on his knees beside her, had slipped an arm behind her shoulders and was bracing her shuddering body. "You must have help!"

"There is—no—help—" Berneen choked out.

There came a last vicious stab, a spear might have been thrust through her. She was left limp and shaking; only his hold supported her.

Weakly she turned her head to look at him. There was open concern in his expression. "When—when the Essence takes me," somehow she got out the words. "Do you leave me quickly. She must not know that you have been with me. She is—is the Queen. I am Berneen, her granddaughter and I have failed her. She will have no pity for me, and her rage will spread to you. Please go now—they will come seeking—"

The pain did not strike again but she felt that she had no control over her body. It was now an effort to breathe.

"Hush." The low-pitched word came as a command.

He settled himself farther back in the cushion nest and drew her closer to him, cradling her in his arms. The comforting warmth of him fought the chill that had sent her into shuddering.

"So—"

"Hush!" he again ordered her.

She could not urge him again. There was no way she could force him from her—save him. A creeping shadow began to enfold her. She sighed and closed her eyes and let the dark take her.

Allitta:

It had all happened so swiftly that I was like one of Ravinga's dolls being placed in view by another's will. By the time we had reached the throne from which Hynkkel-ji was to view this festival, servants had readied a lower seat heaped with scarlet cushions. To this he led me with the same ceremony by which he had acknowledged me. Luckily custom demanded nothing from me at this point. I had only to be seated and leave all to him. Murri took his place at my left side as Akeea was to the right of the Emperor.

"Queen-one."

I was startled, but not so much as to look to the Sand Cat. It was true that Hynkkelji could easily communicate with Murri, but that the great cat could thought-speak to others I had not known. However, the words had been directed to me. There was only one Queen within this crowded chamber and her place was now directly facing the Emperor's throne.

That Murri's thought had been a warning of sorts I was sure. Thus I did look to her. The crowd of courtiers was forming into line—they must each come in turn and speak to me of my new rank and congratulate Hynkkel-ji, wishing us both joy—though we certainly would not experience much of that.

Yuikala still stood, not yet moving. Her face under that elaborate crown bore no expression. She was not one to allow any here to be sure that this was a defeat. It would, however be a scandal as would birth bitter rumors. That both Hynkkel-ji and I had now made an implacable enemy could not be denied. And—it would be towards me that the earliest and fiercest arrow of her rage would strike. The fault in our plan was very obvious now.

"Be ready—" Murri's thought came again and this time I was able to answer.

"Be sure that I shall."

Then Yuikala did start across towards me, all clearing a way for her. She was followed by her major courtiers, then the House Lords. She was smiling, the rigid curve of her lips covering a very different and darker emotion.

Hynkkel-ji:

Now that I had seen my plan at work I was in no way proud of my action. The thought of Berneen pricked me. The girl, I believed, had been the victim of her grandmother's intrigue. I

must, in honor, make some attempt to see that she was not
hurt by what expediency had required of me.

For the moment I could think of only one thing that
might be done. Even as the Queen had nearly reached me
I thought sent:

"Murri, the girl—"

He assented at once. Before the advancing Queen and
her court reached us he slipped away. For the time being I
must trust him—but I was impatient to get this ceremony
behind us.

Outside the Hall of Festivity:

The Sand Cat knew he would be seen but he took what pre-
cautions he could, for cover using the wall tapestries and the
movement of the courtiers eager to view those who had made
such an unexpected addition to the general festivities.

The guards were well used to his coming and going by now
and he had learned all he could, concerning their stations and
how those might be avoided. At length he slipped through the
parting of the great door curtain. One or two testings of scents
told him he was on the right path and in very little time he was
able to push his way through another door curtain, that of a
small side room.

The girl was there, right enough, but also there was someone with her. Murri had moved with his customary silence, so
he had a time to assess that other before the young man noticed him. Fear shown in the warrior's eyes. He shifted the girl
to the pillows behind him and was on his feet, sword in hand.
Murri came no further into the room but stood silently as they
eyed one another.

Murri had never tried mind touch except with the few humans who were close to his brother. He had long ago discovered that, for the most part, the general clan of men did not
possess this talent. He could only suggest by some action of
his own that he had no designs on these two young creatures.
Sitting down, he might be one of the many decorative figures
to be found everywhere in the palace.

The man watched him but made no move. This would bring no needful result, the Sand Cat decided. Not for the first time he wished that these men *did* have speech one could understand—if they did not have mind talent for communication.

On the cushions Berneen stirred. Her hand went out. She might be in search of something. The warrior gave her a quick side-glance and then his attention returned to Murri.

Though the cat did not recognize him, this cubling might be a regular of the palace guard. If so, he should know Murri, and also he should be aware that the Sand Cat was no enemy, though ever ready to defend himself.

Yes, that appeared to be getting through. The guard's sword was back in sheath.

Berneen had dragged herself up to a sitting position. She stared at Murri and then spoke to the man beside her:

"Are you mated, young lord?"

He gave a start and his steady scrutiny of the cat was broken.

"Why—" he began. Then he added swiftly. "Forgive me, High Maid, I must make myself known to you. I am Valapan-va-Jaclan, Second son of the House of Orsmer, Leader of Twenty in the Palace Guard. And, no, I have no mate."

They wasted time, decided Murri—and they might not have much of that. He stood, and instantly Jaclan was again on watch. Murri uttered a purr, a singsong of good will. The man's hand had reached for his sword, but now he dropped it again. Slowly, still purring, Murri approached the two.

Berneen made her choice. One of her hands went again the to the hem of Jaclan's uniform and the other she held out to Murri. Jaclan raised his right hand as if to stop her but Murri was already within reach and her fingers were stroking his head.

"You are his brother," she said. "And—and Grandmother was wrong. The Essence did not wish what she did. He sent you, did he not?"

Murri bowed his head.

"I must be away from this place," Berneen continued. "I have not the courage to face her rage. But where can I go, Desert Warrior?"

Murri knew, but whether she could reach that refuge he was not sure. His kind had talents—more than Hynkkel-ji was aware of—some, which he himself had yet to grow into. The lack of straight communication with the girl would make this difficult.

"You are ill, Lady; you must have help—" Jaclan protested.

She was weak, yes, but the thrusting pain was gone now. This feeling of safety was strange. For the first time since she had left the country home she loved, she was nearly at peace.

Loosing her hold on Jaclan's uniform she took the great cat's head between her hands, looking deeply into his eyes.

Faint as the song of a witmoth, she met him mind-to-mind.

"—Away—"

Murri touched her with a tongue tip. "Away—" he thought the same word in turn.

Her head came down until his fur brushed her hair.

"Lady—" there was protest in Jaclan' s voice.

Berneen looked up at him. "The Emperor's cat brother will aid. I must go—it is needful. If I remain, I shall be found and dragged into darkness, for her will is stronger than mine. If you will it as I do, Valapan-va-Jaclan, Second son of the House of Orsmer, Leader of Twenty, I say this to you: this day the Essence has called me to the mate choosing and—I choose. Is it also for you?"

Jaclan stooped and gathered her into his arms. "With me you shall be held in honor; you shall be safe—I swear this oath to you!"

"No, neither of us shall be safe. You do not know the Queen as I do." She raised her hand and stroked his cheek. "Even though we may never stand before the Essence and say the binding words, I have been in heat—I have made my choice and that I shall ever abide by. You must let me go, for neither of us is safe if I remain. Murri will see me into hiding. And if better times come—I shall stand again with your arms about me."

Chapter 14

Hynkkel-ji:
It was my will that the Progress make the earliest start possible. If Yuikala still desired to accompany us, as was her right, I did not wish her a part of my entourage, but rather that she keep to her own court, with a space between my people and hers.

Murri joined me when I arose and we had a short time of privacy. He had news. Berneen had, by some Grace of the Essence, found a champion, but she had refused his company for fear the Queen would at once get rid of him, trying again to control her granddaughter.

The Sand Cat had no more than reported this fact, when he swung around with a growl to face the window. Luckily I had already shucked my robe of state. I grabbed a short spear such as I had used against the water creature.

There was no reason to give Murri any order. He was moving soundlessly toward the window. The curtain swayed.

A guardsman swept the light barrier aside. I was sure I had never seen him before. He wore the puffed headgear of a junior officer. But his tunic and leggings were the black of the Imperial Army. He had his sword naked in his hand but when he saw me, he knelt and laid the sword on the floor, the point toward him, and the hilt to me.

He was thus asking boldly for an audience in private and I understood that whatever had brought him here was, in his eyes, of major importance.

"This one," Murri thought, "was with the young she."

"August One," the guard's head was up. "Look upon this one with mercy. There is that which must be made known to you—"

I dropped the spear; Murri sat up from his crouch.

"You have served a lady well. She is now safe."

There was an instant expression of relief on his young face.

"August One, it is for her that I have dared to come thus. Your promise is an Oath before the Essence—"

"It is so. And you are?"

"Valapan-va-Jaclan, August One, Leader of Twenty in the Palace Guard."

"You have proved yourself worthy of your House and Rank, Leader. What has happened to the lady must remain known only to us," I nodded to Murri who uttered a fraction of sound he meant for approval.

"That I have already sworn to, by the Essence. I am on the roster to be on the Progress—I had to be sure—" he hesitated.

"That the Lady was safe. Yes, that would be the thought of any honorable man. She is safe. Be sure of that. The one she fears will travel also on the Progress and perhaps by the time we return matters will be resolved. Now—I shall order that one, Valapan-va-Jaclan, be assigned to my personal guard."

My need of those I could trust was great. This guardsman's actions had proved him a man of honor. He was now in my debt. From the beginning of my reign I had been wary of the high nobility. Now I was doubly so, for many of them were in some manner related to the Queen's House. This youth was of the minor nobility. It was plain that Berneen was important to him, therefore I would be appeasing my conscience concerning her as well as adding to my personal staff one I could trust—at least in part.

It was plain from his expression that he had not expected anything—perhaps he thought he would suffer some punishment for his intrusion. He stood staring as I stooped, picked up his sword and handed it back to him.

"A good blade, Leader. Use it well."

"August One—it will be used ever in your service—" He backed towards the window and then was gone. I looked to Murri.

"I trust Brother, that I spoke the truth; the she-cub is safe?"

Murri yawned. "After great effort on my part, Brother. Now she is with the Wise One."

"Ravinga!" I identified. But Ravinga was going to join us. Certainly she would not add Berneen to our company. I could see nothing but trouble in that.

Again Murri read my thoughts. "The she of your own pride, will serve the Wise One, keeping the shop when we go."

My sister. I was surprised that the doll maker was leaving Melora in charge, though I should not have been. It was true that they were both craftswomen of the top rank and had much in common. Yes, I believed that with Melora in charge and the chief enemy gone, things would go well for Berneen.

Allitta:

I must continue to wear Ravinga's amulet, I knew. But the news had already spread through my household that my rank had suddenly changed. I was addressed, by those I called in to check on last minute details, with the same ceremony that they would use for Yuikala. My rise in rank would only be temporary—no Companion ever held that position continuously through the reign of any Emperor. And I would last the shortest of terms.

I had named five of my servants to accompany me. Two of the guards—utterly trustworthy—they had been far-traveled caravan leaders, well trained in weapons, and used to handling difficulties. The eldest of my maids was a necessary choice. And to complete my small party, two of the grooms to look after the care of our beasts and to oversee the baggage train. These were men who had served my family and both of them remembered me as a child.

For Kassca I had made a riding tote lined in fur. Her dishes and other needs were packed together. I could carry her bag on my shoulder, or fit it to my saddle, as was common for Kottis traveling—so we would continue to be together.

I was overseeing the packing of the baggage, having inspected the pa-oryxen I would ride turn and turn about. Ravinga appeared at the front gate, heading a following of her own. Her mount was of the same fine breeding as those from Vurope's stables and she had a second oryxen as well as three pack animals under the care of Salcana, the guide and guard who had ever traveled with us during our caravan days.

Mounting, I joined Ravinga, my guards and maid on well-trained beasts behind, and the grooms with the pack animals at the rear. The doll maker also had a Kotti bag and the black head of Wiu was well above its edge, yellow eyes intent on what lay about us.

It had been given out that our place of assembly for the entire of the Progress would be well outside the walls and we found a number of personal parties as we rode in. I saw no reason for separating myself from Ravinga.

Everyone who knew my story was also aware that for a number of years we two had traveled together along the trails. Also, as the Companion, I had more freedom in choosing associates. There would be a number now, jostling each other, who sooner or later, would aspire to be noticed. Opportunities to be more closely known to the Emperor often followed the favor of the Companion, though certainly none would come through me.

Hynkkel-ji and his followers—a guard of some size, Murri, several servants and a long baggage train—arrived. He did not wear those robes which always seemed to diminish him, but rather high boots, form fitting trews, and a jerkin with loose sleeves over a tight shirt. A wide sword belt of gold with pale greenish stones supported a weapon I had never seen before and which I suspected he did not know how to use. Trews and jerkin were green; the jerkin edged with fluffs of white fur.

As with his robe he had discarded his crown for a helmet, meant I supposed to conceal the loss of his hair knot in the final ordeal which had put him on the throne. His guardsmen did not wear the elaborate uniforms of the court but rather those meant to be used for the field. Their bushy head coverings had been changed for helmets. One of them carried the personal standard of the ruler, and pacing along beside Hynkkel's mount was Murri. The blue leopards did not serve away from Valapa.

I made no move to attract his attention but he must have early sighted me, for he cut directly across the crowded field, followed by his guards, to where Ravinga and I waited. Urging his mount close to mine he bowed his head. I stretched out my hand. He caught and kissed it, watched by Kassca and everyone else in sight range.

On the Progress trail:

The relative cool of the night closed about the long train. In the beginning the nobles and higher courtiers pressed to the fore. Two musicians rode with saddle drums and they set up a beat to which most of the travelers kept time. Only the end of the baggage train was still visible when the Diamond Queen and her following arrived at the assembly field. Through the night she stifled all outward signs of anger. None of her immediate following had yet been treated to the results of such suppression of her smoldering rage.

However messengers had gone out secretly to certain sections of the city. There were ones who rode ahead of her now who had come, under cover, to listen to her orders. Elsewhere others were assembling arms and meeting privately.

That she had not been able to discover the whereabouts of Berneen remained a minor frustration. The search she had started would find the stupid girl sooner or later. She dismissed that matter from the fore of her mind and was busy laying out lines to be spun into a new web.

Shank-ji was as schooled in intrigue as she was. They would have a common cause. One of those in her party was his own chosen man, who would drop out of the Progress before they arrived at Kahulawe. When he reached his leader he would report such news as would interest Shank-ji.

At that moment, listing in her mind what she had set in motion during these past few hours, she felt more alert and assured of herself than she had for many years. The intrigues, which had amused her in the past, were nothing compared to this tangle from which she was determined to emerge the winner.

Battle in the desert:

Twice Shank-ji had led out scouts at night. Each time he had angled towards the Plain of Desolation, though he had never attempted to go too far. The man-rat had not shown himself again but, on this third journey, the quiet of the night was broken by the distant roll of an alarm drum. It was not the such as heralded the rise of a storm, but rather a beat such as might be begging help for a caravan. Instinctively Shank-ji led his men to answer the plea.

It was not long before they could sight the blaze of a large fire ahead. There sounded the bellows of animals, now and then war cries of guards.

Shank-ji sent his mount into a run. From what he could see a caravan had been attacked. Luckily the firelight also revealed a wave of rats. The outlaws swept upon them, weapons ready. Several figures fed the fire with the reed blocks they carried, having also torn apart bales of goods to add their contents to the flames. Arrows were thick in the air and Shank-ji shouted encouragement.

The rats were mad in their leaps, tearing at flesh, stripping cloth with teeth that showed cold green fire. As far as Shank-ji could see it was only rats, rats which seemed to have no fear, rats which closed jaws on both humans and animals, even though the attackers' bodies were masses of bloody fur.

Such ferocity was seldom seen but there was no time to wonder about that. Slash—stab. Some of their mounts shrieked in pain, rats dangling from their legs. The oryxen plunged, snapped, while some of their riders had to forgo attack to keep their saddles.

Most of the animals of the caravan were down, heaving under masses of rats. Though their dead carpeted the sand, still the vermin continued to burst out of the dark. Bellows of torment shattered ears as the animals were eaten alive.

For the first time Shank-ji knew a flash of fear. His well-trained mount had gone totally mad, was plunging and screaming, while he, himself, slashed first to one side and then to the other, cutting at the rats that had fastened jaws in the oryxen's legs. They appeared to be leaping to reach the rider.

Kill! The oryxen reared to smash down, stamping on rats, catching one in its teeth and tossing the eviscerated body away. Shank-ji cried out, dropping his sword to swing from its wrist knot, as he caught an enemy that had sunk teeth in his leg. It did not turn on him as his hand closed on its throat. In spite of such pain as he had never felt before, he tore the thing loose and hurled it away.

Then, somehow rising above the constant beat of the drum, there sounded the eerie whistling, which the man-rat had used. The devil things out of the night loosed their holds, surged back and away from the battlefield.

Then they were gone entirely except for the piles of bodies, which the caravaners began to throw into the fire, making sure that there would be no survivors.

The whistle—Not looking to see how badly his leg had been torn, Shank-ji realized that this encounter might well have be a trap—or a sharp lesson. He who held the Plain of Desolation was no longer ready to wait.

This army of rats could well be turned on their own camp. Had such not appeared in company with the man-rat? Not since the night when he had nursed his wrist and faced the fact of his lost hand had he known such a loss of confidence. But there was always a way out for a man with courage and belief in his cause. If he could turn such a disaster as this upon his enemy—perhaps during the Progress—However to do so he at least must seem to accept the terms of whoever skulked now in the midst of that dangerous stretch of country.

Camp of the Progress:

Ravinga sat in her tent at the end of their first night of journeying. Marching by moonlight instead of by day was the way to travel the desert at this time of the year. But the storm

season was close. They were still at least four days from
Kahulawe, though this was a well-traveled way and there had
been refuges hollowed in rock isles along the way. The storm
watchers were also on constant duty now. Still, a company as
large as this might well overflow any refuge intended for a
caravan. From a hidden space beneath the false bottom in
Wiu's carrying tote she brought out the doll she had named
"Quinzell." Placing this with care so it stood upright she studied it. Though it did not contain what would make it a spy—
she had nothing from Quinzell's body to tie him to it—yet
there was one ritual which might aid.

No, not yet. They must be closer—which would mean
waiting yet a while—until they reached Azhengir. Yuikala and
her escort had come into camp. There had been a staged welcoming on the part of the Emperor, and the Queen had offered only the most formal of greetings.

However, Ravinga had sighted one of those standing behind Yuikala at that meeting. That one was ill met indeed.
Perhaps even a storm might be welcomed over this brewing
evil. Reluctantly she put the doll into hiding once more. All
she could do at present was let Allitta know of the presence
of that courtier. To be forewarned was always best. Wiu rose
out of the pile of sleeping cushions and touched nose to her
arm. Ravinga nodded.

"Yes, little one. That we shall do."

From a script pocket she brought a scrap of parchment
and paint stick. In letters almost too small to read she printed
out a message in her business code, one long ago Allitta had
learned to use.

Allitta:

To be a member of the Progress was indeed a different form
of travel than I had known as one of a trader's caravan. For
one thing we went at a slower pace—something which was
not to Hynkkel's liking but there seemed to be little he could
do about it. It was true that some of the nobles and their
ladies were well along in years and probably had not braved

such a trip since Haban-ji had made a Progress. Such were every five years, so that the Emperor could hold court in each Queendom and learn how fared the people.

Valapa was so different from the other Queendoms; its inhabitants having a much easier life, that any trip across the Outer Regions would be a trial to the nobility of the Diamond country.

I rode beside Hynkkel at his wish and ate our midnight meal from the supplies his servants produced. Though these were not the many viands of a state banquet, the number of dishes filled with fruit, and various well-cooked servings was again more than any ordinary traveler could dream of. The fruit would not last long and we would not see its like again until we returned to Valapa. Thus I indulged myself—I hope not greedily—on lanonbemes and slices of the vapears.

At first I found myself at odds with my new rank. But Hynkkel-ji set himself to amuse me. During his own wanderings he had gathered some of the old legends of the wayfarers and we traded tales as we might have bargained for goods.

I relaxed; he did not in any way over step the bounds. His companionship was like that of a brother rather than a suitor, such a brother as I had never had. That I had been wrong in my past opinion of him, I realized before we went into camp at dawn. It did not bother me that my own belongings were brought to his private tent.

Our second meal on the road was eaten and most of the train had gone to their sleeping cushions when Hynkkel-ji dismissed the last of the servants. Murri was pacing back and forth impatiently.

"There are those waiting, you should meet," Hynkkel said. "Come!"

With no more explanation than that, he took my hand even as he had at the festival and led me to the tent curtain, looping that up to usher me out into the day. A young officer snapped to alert as we passed him.

"Heart-one," for the first time Hynkkel used one of the customary endearments—and loud enough for the officer to hear, "we do not have far to go." Then he spoke directly to the officer. "Leader Jaclan, we do not go into any danger and we wish not to be accompanied."

I believe that the officer would have made some objection but Murri pushed forward and he stepped aside for the great cat. We struck out into the desert in the light of dawn as we rounded a dune. Facing us was a pair of the carven cats the height of a man, flanking a spur of rock. Murri was well in advance and, with my hand still in Hynkkel's, we followed him as the sky lightened even more and the day was born.

Chapter 15

Hynkkel-ji:

Those whose greeting had come to me were waiting. Though Murri had appeared to have his full growth, when confronted by Myrourr, his huge sire, and Maraya, whose cub he had been, suddenly he appeared less impressive. He crouched before Maraya as she welcomed him with a lick on his head. Now as we came closer, he turned to Myrourr who also acknowledged him.

As he moved to one side I brought Allitta forward until we were in touching distance of the majestic pair. I saw no sign of fear in my Companion. Instead she loosened my hold on her hand and went to her knees, bending her head in a gesture far more humble than was used at court.

Her Kotti, who had followed us without my notice, moved in front of her as if in protection, though she was smaller than a Sand Cat cubling at birth.

Now I also went to my knees. I had shed the wristband, which covered the scar of my brotherhood, and I gave greeting, well knowing that these two were indeed more powerful than any Queen or Emperor.

"By the Blessing of the Essence we come, oh, Rulers of the sands. I won to leadership among the smoothskins, but only by the aid of Murri. That you sent him to be my battlemate is a grace for which I ever give thanks. Now I wish you to look upon this she whom I have brought to you. Courage is hers, and good will. There may be danger for her and I plea you to look upon her and accept her—"

Maraya advanced. The fur of the Kotti bushed up, as did her tail, and she hissed. It was easy to read the humor in Maraya's thought then. She regarded Kassca intently and the Kotti's warning subsided.

"The smoothskin she is well served by this one," the female Sand Cat commented. "That this she is accepted by the little ones, speaks well for her. I say let her be made free of the Pride."

Maraya glanced at her mate. After what seemed a long time he answered. "Does the she ask this," he inquired, "or is it your thought brother?"

To my vast surprise his answer came not from me but haltingly from Allitta.

"If I am believed worthy, Great Ones of the desert, then grant me this honor." She held out her arm, stripped off a wide bracelet and pulled back both outer and inner sleeves.

As it had been with me, Maraya took her wrist into her well fanged mouth and the teeth closed on flesh so that blood appeared. Upon loosing her hold, the Sand Cat licked the oozing blood.

I was ready with a short scarf and drew it tightly about the wound, believing it was as deep as the one I had taken in my adoption, and I trusted that Allitta would suffer no ill effects.

"To the Great One," Allitta was plainly addressing Maraya, "do I give thanks, for such kinship as honors all of my kind. The Sword of the House of Vurope shall be also the Sword of your Pride from this hour forth."

She was adding part of the oath of allegiance, such as is sometimes given between one noble house and another.

I bowed my own head. "Brother and sister, deep are our thanks for your favor. There is evil—"

Myrourr's thought interrupted mine. "Brother and Sister— you go into dark—not that of night—but evil. There is one who leads others to bring you death—behind him is a greater one who once tore apart the Outer Regions in his rage.

"I say to you that both smoothskins and furred ones must unite. All deaths, which lay between us in the past, must be set aside, for this is our land and we shall not again see it laid waste. Therefore, should there come a time, when you and yours and I and mine must stand so fronting evil, we shall come."

Murri had moved beside me and I sensed that some un-heard order had passed to him from the older cats.

"Be it so," I replied. This offer was more than I had dared hope for.

Once more I bowed my head. Allitta reached out, did not quite touch Maraya, but the Sand Cat's tongue licked her fingers.

The full of sun blasted in the day. Now the two cats van-ished at a speed my kind could never equal. With my arm about Allitta, we returned to the encampment.

Allitta:

I had tasted a way of power, not one known to most humans. Awe possessed me. It seemed that I came from that meeting as a long-hungry woman might have come from a feast. Some new thing had become mine. The thought speech of Myrourr was a clear voice in my mind. My wrist burned and I stumbled. Hynkkel steadied me at once. Though a wound draws blood and strength from the body, this wound healed an inner part of me, aroused feelings I did not know I possessed—inputting rather than draining.

The young officer was still on guard at the tent. He stared; I knew he had sighted the bloody scarf. But he said nothing as we passed. Servants had heaped a double bed of cushions to which Hynkkel led me. He brought out clean bindings from a chest and a small pot filled with paste, and poured a measure of water into a basin.

Washing my wrist he concentrated on what he was doing, saying nothing. Paste was patted into the tear in my wrist and he rebandaged it. Only then did he sit back on his heels and look up at me.

"If there is any more pain, say so at once."

"Was this done for my safety?"

He did not answer straightly. "You are as free of the Outer Regions as any of our kind may be. But trouble travels with us, not coming out of the sands to meet us—"

Almost in answer to that Kassca mewed sharply from the cushion beside me and a black Kotti, larger than she, squeezed under the door curtain to come directly to me: Wiu, Ravinga's companion. Around her neck was tied a strip of parchment. Speedily I freed its knot.

"What is it?" Hynkkel asked.

I smoothed it out carefully with my left hand, but I had to hold it much closer to make out the characters. Every caravan merchant has her own code. This one was well known to me from the days when I had followed Ravinga from Queendom to Queendom.

"Do you know one Kalikur of the House of Zahant?"

He frowned as if he were trying to recall someone. "The House of Zahant—that House is sept to the Queen's own, is it not?"

I too was searching memory. My return to the ranks of Valapa's nobility had been so recent that the name meant nothing. I did recall that I had met on one occasion the First Maiden of that family. She was a silly youngster who had companioned Berneen. I said as much and then added:

"But she is not this Kalikur. Ravinga would have you know that he has accompanied Yuikala. Since she thinks it important, perhaps we should learn more about him."

I was not at first aware that I had said "we" but he was smiling. "Battlemates?" he asked with an amused quirk of eyebrow.

I smiled, "Perhaps, August One."

Outlaws on Scout:

Shank-ji and what was left of his company escorted the remaining members of the caravan within sight of Kahulawe. He would go no further, though those he had rescued begged him to, that they might replace his slain mounts and have his and his men's wounds treated by healers.

Slain mounts and men not withstanding, they must return through the territory of the attack. However he wanted no chance of being challenged by Imperial troops scouting for the Progress.

Those unwounded shared mounts, turn and about, so they were kept to a slow pace that the unmounted might match. The sun was well above the horizon and soon the heat would present another problem.

Shank-ji soon realized they must split their troop, risky as that would be, and send ahead the few well mounted at a pace they could command. He chose to remain with the dismounted. Ahead and to the east they sighted a rise of spire rocks. The tallest of these bore the flapping banner, marking a storm station. There they could find aid, for these were always manned.

Shank-ji chose that for the goal of those following him, but ordered that they must represent themselves as trail guards who had survived a most vicious attack.

Barely before the heat became too burdensome, they reached the base of one of the spires and a drum roll from above announced their arrival had been noted. However not only those of the storm station had noticed them, for taking advantage of every possible bit of concealment, two other guardians of the Outer Regions had trailed them.

The ears of one Sand Cat were erect. She no longer watched Shank-ji's force; rather faced north. Her lips shaped a snarl and deep in her throat sounded the rumble of a challenge. There was no sound from her companion; rather he crept, his belly to sand, heading north as if to attack. His mate remained in place, dividing her attention between those they had tracked and the direction into which her mate had disappeared.

Shank-ji found himself and his men eagerly received by the watchers on duty. He told the tale he had hastily prepared. Food was provided, their wounds tended, and quarters offered in a cavernous crevice inside one the spires. In return Shank-ji gave carefully edited news of the questioning of Hynkkel's right to the throne, and the fact that he was headed on his initial Progress.

At that news the Head Watcher shook his head, frowning.

"He must be ill advised. The great storms will be upon us soon and the Progress can be in great danger, or else confined to one of the Queendoms, unable to finish the ritual."

Shank-ji, sober faced, nodded. "Thus it appears that not only is he ignorant of the land, but also he would risk the lives of others to unlawfully retain the throne. Meanwhile the rats grow bolder and caravans may stop. What then will the Outer Regions do?"

"Yes—and we have heard another tale," the Head Watcher replied. "The Master Of Balance is said to be preparing a journey of his own."

There was utter silence. Shank-ji found it as sharp a rat wound. If this were true he must indeed change his plans, move before he was entirely ready. The Progress—yes, there would be guards, perhaps enough to stand off any attack he could now launch. What if a rat attack could meld with one by men? That messenger had been able to control the rats. He served the Dark One. The offer—perhaps he had no other choice. The Dark Ones knew his camp—they could wipe him out with such an attack as his company had just survived.

But—that he had not been already wiped out meant that the mysterious ruler saw some use for him. If it were true, he still possessed bargaining power. It was time to forget shadow fears and strike out for what he wanted.

"When the measurement fell upon us before, there were very few Houses which did not lose kin. What ill has come upon us that the Essence would desert us thus again?"

At length, for it seemed that no one wished to explore this memory, Shank-ji limped to join his men. Then, as loud as the warn drums overhead, came a summons. It was to him only, for the trooper tending the wounds of the man near him showed no sign of hearing it. Shank-ji turned abruptly left and struggled along the side of the watcher's spur.

He was sure he knew what awaited him—there was no more time left him now. As he reached the back of the spur, hidden from the Watchers' perch, he saw he was right. The messenger from Desolation was there.

The Sand Cat, who had trailed the newcomer for some distance, flattened himself on a dune, and then slowly slipped down its side. He settled himself in sand the color of his fur and opened his mind.

As Shank-ji approached, the man-rat did not dismount. The beast lowered its three horned head, shook it as any trained war oryxen would do before charging. Its red eyes gleamed.

"It seems you have suffered something of a mishap," the man-rat commented as Shankji came up. "Our warriors have sharp teeth and know well how to use them."

"What do you want?" Shank-ji replied tersely.

"Why—what has been wanted for far too long, an answer to the August One's offer. It shall not be made again. What you have just seen is but a small skirmish compared to what will happen when patience comes to an end."

The man-rat's tone was almost jocular but Shank-ji was instantly aware of the threat within that sneering speech.

"Such decision should be between your master and me, face to face."

"Do you then say that the August One should wait upon you?"

"Does he say that I should come to him?" countered Shank-ji.

The man-rat yawned. "You will come..." now there was the snap of an order in his voice "...to the border of Twahihic at the point of the be-headed cats. There you will learn what the August One will have of you. The storm time comes soon; I advise no delay."

His mount swung around, presenting its rider's back. Shank-ji knew that was meant as an insult—one he dared not show he resented. Within him rage sparked. To be treated so—and he was of a princely House, one that did not bear insults lightly.

He did not see the rider out of sight but returned to his men. The Sand Cat lay in hiding until they were both gone. At first he watched in the direction in which the Messenger had taken. Then he waited behind a dune until his mate joined him. They touched noses and conferred for a moment. Leaving the female he went on, heading in the wake of the Messenger—but a good distance behind, all senses alert.

His mate padded to the spire and using her strong claws began to climb, until she was at last able to pull herself to a perch well above the cave of the watchers. Facing south she sent forward her report and, far away, Myrourr and Maraya listened to what the thought waves brought.

With the Diamond Queen on Progress:

Though she had not had a good day's rest, Queen Yuikala paced back and forth over one of the carpets within her tent. She stopped to stare at the disordered cushions of her bed place, but not as if she really saw them.

Her maid called softly from the other side of the curtain and she gave permission for Luvania to enter.

"Your Highness, they bring your breakfast. And—" she hesitated before adding: "they are already taking down the Emperor's tent."

Yuikala's smile was hardly a pleasant one. "So, the August One again thinks it well to move out early. His restlessness is marked. We shall go more at leisure. It is not well to face an hour of sun. Bring me the skin cover. I do not court dryness and wrinkles—I need not go looking like a caravaner."

"Your Highness need only look to your mirror—your beauty is undimmed."

Always flattery—but her court must believe, at least in seeming, she was as when she was first crowned. She was never vain of her body, but that she thought quickly and clearly, was adept at planning—of that she was proud.

So they were afraid of her—wanting no close contact with her now. Their fear could be used to serve her purpose. The barbarian oryxen herder had publicly insulted her. The slut he had taken into his arms and bed would be quick to see how the sands drifted and take her lead from that. She came of a cursed House; that was a known fact.

The Queen greeted the arrival of food with pleasure and chatted with the two ladies who shared her repast. None alluded to recent happenings.

It was when she went to mount her sleek oryxen that she saw who was standing ready to assist her. A trace of frown appeared between the sweep of her eyebrows. What did Kalikur here? He was one of her guards, but not the one she expected. Where was young Jaclan? She asked that as she faced this substitute.

"The August One summoned him to be of his private guard, Highness. It was a surprise—"

His voice was very low as if he did not want to be overheard. Still he must have no reason to approach her *in public*. To have him do so jarred her earlier complacency. Why was Jaclan promoted to the Imperial guard? His being used so in the palace was only a temporary assignment. The youngling owed first service to her.

She nodded her thanks and mounted. To her surprise he still lingered by the side of the oryxen and she looked at him quickly. Was this henchman, too, seeking to advance himself in some fashion?

He made a small gesture. She glanced quickly down. There was a twist of writing parchment hidden in the mane of her mount. He turned away and Yuikala urged her beast on a little, freeing the slip with her gloved hand as she rode.

"Morning—two meet Sand Cats—give homage to cats."

The slut was now also tied to the cats? That would sharpen another weapon for those wishing to follow old customs. Well more than half the men of the kingdom based their pride on hunting Sand Cats—that the Barbarian must know—Had not his decree already been broken? It was almost too easy to gather such a profusion of mistakes to show the whole Outer Region that, if he was not mad, he was close to it.

Give homage—why? What did he believe he gained from that? It was true that Murri had changed the minds of some of the palace dwellers about his breed. She must learn more— could the beasts be really other than they seemed? Among her possessions she had a number of furs presented to her—now kept tactfully in storage and not openly displayed. But before the coming of Murri she had never known a live cat.

She beckoned to the nearest guard to draw near.

"Rurtar of Orriz is with us, is he not?"

"Yes, Your Highness."

"Summon him."

She cut the pace of her mount until the burly hunter joined her, bowing low in his saddle.

"I am at your service, Your Highness."

She smiled. "You can indeed aid me, Hunter. I would learn something of the lands between the Queendoms. Such have provided hunting territory for you and your men for many years."

"True, Highness; but no more. The August One has declared that we can no longer hunt Sand Cats."

"Many have wondered why he has done this. Do you know?"

Rurtar shook his head. "No, Highness. Murri shares favor with Akeea. That the Great Leopard does this is also a puzzle."

"Are the stories told about Sand Cats true? That they gather on rock isles of their own—that they appear to patrol the desert as do scouts for an army?"

"I have heard such tales, Highness. I have never seen proof of either story. It seems that men have ever hated Sand Cats, and the Cats, men. If the cause is not just fear, it lies hidden in the past. The leopards are as great and dangerous as they, yet leopards have formed a royal guard for unnumbered years and we know them well."

There was another question but she hesitated to ask it. Had the Sand Cats some strange power which men did not possess? If the barbarian paid the cats homage, was it because he understood this? A hunter, she thought, could not answer that—too many deaths lay between. However when she reached Kahulawe—There were many hunters there; their fame had reached to Valapa—she would set Kalikur to locate such and she would summon him.

The dusk had faded and night enclosed them. She had all the dark hours ahead in which to plan the right questions.

Chapter 16

Allitta:

When we halted for food and rest at midnight, I noted that our neighbors regrouped, some dropping behind and others coming to the fore. Among those now in view was Ravinga and I took her coming as a summons. Night shadows offered me concealment. I had informed Hynkkel of what I would do and he agreed.

Thus I slipped away on the pretext of a nature need, and, carrying Kassca, made my way to the doll maker's campsite. Her guide was bringing out food. She raised a hand in greeting and I settled down beside her I though I did not throw back my cape hood.

She passed me an algae cake spread with yaksen milk cheese. I broke off a portion for Kassca.

"Was this Kalikur known to him?" she asked at once.

"No. Nor to me either. I know very few of the courtiers. There was a First Maid of that House who was with Berneen for a space—her I met once or twice."

"Another tie with the Queen," Ravinga commented; "however, the one to be watched is Kalikur. He is a noted archer but perhaps not a truly intelligent man."

"Archer? One who might perch on roof tops?"

"Just so—but that is only guess and there is no proof."

"But if he is Hynkkel's enemy why would he wish to remove the opponent in the Ordeal?"

"Hynkkel learned well from Murri—he followed no regular pattern in his leaps and bounds to escape the cutting edges of the swinging blades. Even a good archer can be defeated when he is faced by something new. But Kalikur went out of sight then and reappeared only when summoned to the Progress by the Queen. By rights his House does not stand so high that it is worthy of such a summons. Yuikala, at times, fancies handsome young officers and he is well to look upon."

Another coil of intrigue reaching from Valapa in threat. I was impatient—was my life never to be free of such?

Then, as suddenly as a Kotti would reach for an oose fly, her hand caught mine, drawing wrist and arm out from the folds of my cape so that the bandage I wore was clearly visible. I did not try to twist loose from hold she released a moment later.

"So—they have made you free of the Pride?"

"Early this morning," I admitted. "Hynkkel greeted two Great Ones—those whose cub Murri is—they honored me."

Ravinga nodded. "Indeed they honored you, Allitta. Once they lived in high respect with those of the Queendoms. That ended in blood and hate fostered by the Dark One. Hynkkel has within him a power of friendship with animals which few possess any more, even surrounded as we are by our beloved Kottis. At least so far the poison has not touched the little ones."

Kassca gave a small mew in assent to that.

Seeing that many around us were finishing their meal, I bade Ravinga farewell and slipped back to where the Emperor was dining with some company. I threw off my cloak and settled down in the empty space at his right hand. He did not glance in my direction but continued to speak with the Commander of the Progress now in charge of our safety.

Hynkkel-ji:

Vorsun-va-Ortaga had asked for my attention just after Allitta left. I noted also that where I had settled was apart, though whether he had arranged that, I did not know. The news he brought was dire. One of the scouts sent ahead had picked up a warn drum, not for a storm but an attack on a caravan, one of such fury that it had near wiped out all the caravaners as well as troops who had gone to their aid. That this troop was Shank-ji's, I guessed. And the attack had occurred within a short distance of Kahulawe.

When I mentioned that to Commander Ortaga he showed no surprise and I suspected that perhaps warriors within my own guard knew better than the rest of us what was happening.

"We must close up, August One. There are those who drop behind on each half night's travel. I shall send out extra scouts, but it is best that as a whole our company tightens."

I agreed. Allitta had returned. She reported what she had learned from Ravinga. Murri drew closer. I heard the rumble of a growl. His head was high as he stared at a squad of warriors jogging just within sight. They had passed behind a line of the baggage beasts before I had more than a glimpse of them.

"Who goes?" I thought-sent.

The Sand Cat looked to me. "One I shall find again," and since he had not to wanted to elaborate I asked no more.

There came a drum note and our temporary camp was astir. As I escorted Allitta to her oryxen, Murri remained close company. He matched his pace to that of our mounts, remaining with us. We rode in silence; each of us burdened by our thoughts. However we were startled as a small party joined us.

Captain Ortaga was carrying out his plan. I was far from wanting these fellow travelers but I had no choice. Welcoming the Queen formally, I managed to ride between her and Allitta, alert with eyes and ears.

Arrival at Kahulawe:

The following few days of travel were felt by those of the Progress to be an uneasy time. The third night before they broke the day's camp a detachment of the Sapphire Guards joined them, bringing more ill news of rat strikes. Apart from the company, yet riding with them, was one in full dress of a General of the Sapphire Elite Royal Guard. Though that office had long been one of honor only, he carried across his saddle the Leopard Headed staff which had once been used to give orders in battle. Several lengths behind him was a younger man in wardress, but not that of a guard. As they approached the Progress and exchanged greetings with the Imperial Guards, the younger man dropped even further behind, until the General, without looking back, lifted the staff gesturing him forward. It was plain to Leader Jaclan he was scowling as if riding against his will.

The General addressed Commander Ortaga: "We crave speech with the August One. I am Kaverel-va-Meguliel and this is my son, Kaverel-va-Kalikku."

The younger man stared straight ahead. Ortaga was well aware of court gossip. So these were the August One's father and brother. He gave a salute and beckoned to Jaclan.

When the request was delivered to Hynkkel-Ji it was not one he wanted, but one he had expected. Allitta and the Queen reined in their oryxens as he rode on with only Murri pacing beside him. Behind him the travelers broke ranks to establish camp; however, he was sure that most eyes would be on this meeting.

Once he would have been standing to accept his father's orders, holding back resentment when Kalikku used words to belabor him. Now they must dismount and approach *him* for recognition. It was never good to nurse resentment. These two were faithful to their caste; he had never wanted what they sought. To accept them as he would other nobles of the Queendoms was his duty here and now. Nearer company of the Progress spread out to give some privacy. On sudden impulse Hynkkel-ji swung from the saddle and stood waiting by his well-trained mount. He was not keeping to custom, but custom keeping often brought new difficulties. This was his father and in spite of their differences, he would show him this respect.

Hynkkel-ji:

My last meeting with my father might have been taken from one of those puppet shows children delight in. He was the much-praised leader from the latter wars of the Queendoms, giving his oath to a new Emperor. To me then the ceremony had lacked reality. This was real. He saluted and I inclined my head.

"Welcome to you, General of the Sapphire. We are well met indeed. I have heard dire things of the open lands and with your skill you can supply me needed counsel."

There, I had given him an opening. We probably would never have any close relationship. I knew him for what he was, a hard man bound to the past by many memories. I wished at that moment that I might indeed spread before him all the trouble arising. Not perhaps those which threatened me personally but certainly what hung darkly over the Outer Regions.

"I have given my oath, August One. Ever have I served Kahulawe with all the strength the Essence granted me. My sword is at the August One's command. Now I bring one who also wishes to serve, my son Kalikku. He is schooled in arms and knows the Outer Regions well."

My son—not your brother. He was keeping the barrier and I accepted that.

"We have need for valiant warriors." I looked to my brother. "The Empire welcomes you, Kaverel-va-Kalikku." I made no attempt to establish any more than a formal relationship; for I was very certain that my brother did not want that. He was not scowling. However I knew his humors well enough from the past to guess that this meeting was none of his seeking.

He had been reported among Shank-ji's following. Was it my father's will that had separated him from those?

I freed the scepter staff which bore the representation of a Sand Cat from my saddle, and held it out in his direction. I saw his upper lip lift a fraction as if he were about to exchange snarls with the cat. Both he and my father had kept their eyes away from Murri. After all, they were known as formidable hunters.

Reluctantly Kalikku brought his right hand away from close proximity to his sword hilt. He stared at the staff but not at me. Then he raised that hand to touch the Sand Cat head with fingertips.

"This one swears service to the August Crown." His words came as harsh as if he were offering a challenge.

So he gave an oath that tied him to my cause—if a grudging one. His honor would be broken, were he to make any move against me, though he had sworn to the Crown and not to me personally.

Once more I spoke to my father. "Ride with us, General. Have you fresh news of the rat pestilence which is turning the Outer Regions into a battlefield?"

He accepted that invitation, matching his mount's pace to mine. Without further urging he supplied me with more recent and exact information about the latest caravan massacre as we rode. Commander Ortaga was summoned to listen.

"There is this:" my father continued, "The Storm Watcher drummed that those who came to save the still living were not regular trail guards, rather they were not united to any Queendom."

"There have been reports of such a troop," the Commander answered when I said nothing.

I spoke then, a single name: "Shank-ji."

Neither my father nor Ortaga made any comment. After a short pause my father continued:

"Kahulawe is recruiting. There are objections now from the Caravaners, for the young warriors are joining the armies of the Queendoms rather than becoming route guards."

"And," I returned, "the caravans cannot continue without efficient guards. From what has happened we must conclude that rat attacks will grow more frequent and undoubtedly more vicious. The Queendoms' own forces will only serve on their own lands, and not on the trails. The caravans will cease."

My father looked at me. I thought he was wondering if I had any answer to such a problem. Because of my present rank, he would not ask openly.

I had one solution—one which might be only last for a short time, but which could hold long enough so the Dark Lord would be met with an equal force.

"We have allies, ones which marched with us a very long time ago, or so have I been told."

I heard a sound from my father's direction as if he cleared his throat to settle what might be an instant protest.

"Murri has been my battle comrade." I continued. "Those of his pride have far better knowledge of the desert than any scout has ever gathered. Their hatred of rats is equal to our own."

"You speak of a pride," said my father, "as if you rate these cats as noble as men."

"I do."

"His hate of us still abides. He sees us as only a source of carpets for his nesting, providing hunting for the cubs of his kind." Murri's thought came. "Such as he, so mind set, will not be easily changed, brother."

We all fell silent. Ortaga excused himself to inspect the guard. A short time later my father withdrew, followed by Kalikku who had been riding at a little distance, to join the Sapphire force.

Into the Unknown with the outlaws:

His wound still troubled him. Shank-ji shifted in his saddle. However he knew he must ride. And it would be a long journey as they had to avoid the shorter trails, striking out into empty territory to pass unseen. Twice the outriders reported sighting Sand Cats perhaps watching them.

For the first time there had been questions from his followers. His answer was not easy to shape. He continued to explain that they were to spy out trails which could be used to go from Queendom to Queendom unobserved. Also they must watch for evidence of any flood of rats—discover, once and for all, from where they issued. They rode and camped away the heat of day to ride again. Several times the carven cat trail markers were sighted, but all wore their heads firmly on their shoulders.

If they were still followed by Sand Cats they ceased to sight them. Yet all were uneasy. Heads turned and eyes searched. The third night wind-borne sand made them remain in the rocks where they had camped. It was not the force of one of the great storms, which would set them to unroll the wide hide blankets which every wise traveler of the Outer Regions carried. However there was turbulence severe enough that they and their mounts crouched against the stone to weather its fury. Shank-ji shut his eyes against the drive of the sharp grains which rasped the skin, and, breathed in, causing racking coughs.

If the Progress met this type of assault they might end their journey at Kahulawe and try to wait out the storm season. One could not measure time when fronting a great storm. Some had been known to last for days.

There was only one advantage he might win from such an interrupted journey and that would be gaining more time to spread rumors of the Barbarian who had stupidly waited too late for a proper Progress.

When at last the wind and sand subsided they were, as always, presented with an altered landscape. Dunes had been carried away, to be rebuilt in other directions. Only the outcropping of mesas and the much smaller spires might remain as landmarks.

Shank-ji would have climbed one of the outcrops which had sheltered them but he could not trust his wounded leg. There had certainly been the bite of salt in the heaving sand. He could taste it as he strove to brush the grit from his face. They could not be too far from their goal which lay so close to the salt beds. One of the youths of the party volunteered to go aloft and see if fortune favored them by revealing the headless cats which were the promised guides.

Shank-ji chaffed at the wait. From the bottle on his saddle he tipped a very small measure of water onto the end of the scarf with which earlier he had tried to protect his face. The wet fabric he used to wipe out the nostrils of his oryxen. His men did likewise for their beasts. As it was still damp when he had finished, he used it to clean the skin about his mount's eyes.

The scout returned, sliding part of the way. By his muffled exclamation he had felt the bite of the rough stone on flesh.

"A cat without a head can be sighted in that direction." He announced loudly as he pointed.

Shank-ji drew a breath of relief. For the first time since setting out on this quest he believed fortune favored him. Then only too quickly his thoughts skipped to what might await him. He had no real wish to go on, but he was left with no power of retreat. The messenger had made him certain of that.

They rode on. Here the dunes were in such a tangle they could proceed no faster than a walk.

"They go—there are those who wait."

The Sand Cats, one a warrior of many seasons and the other a youngling of three, climbed to the rock ledge between two spurs where the men had sheltered. Both dipped noses, drawing in the personal scent of those who had been here. From this time on the cats would be able to follow traces only a great storm could scour away.

"Those who wait—" the cub was circumspect, however he had the curiosity of his kind.

His elder snarled. "We do not follow now. Those are of the Dark—they do not follow the Essence. The time is not yet."

The cats settled themselves on the rock. The party they had trailed might well return. If so they would again follow, as ordered. The elder started out over the dunes. Perhaps in this matter the Essence would indeed honor the prides with Its presence, grant his kind the use of the Forgotten Powers. It was true they faced again the Great Dark.

Chapter 17

The Progress at Kahulawe:
The rugged limits of the rock island, which was Kahulawe, at last came into sight. Waiting at the foot of the upward winding road to the mesa top was Alompra-va-Kanna, the Sapphire Queen, and most notable members of her court.

Cheers sounded from the crowd higher up as she moved forward to greet the August One who had dismounted to meet her. Her greeting was all correctness. There was no hint of his former rank as her subject, nor was there any warmth of friendship.

The Progress had completed the first quarter of the journey, much to the relief of many of the travelers. Before the sun was into the broiling daytime heat of the season they were settled in the guesting apartments.

Hynkkel-ji:
So at long last I had returned. However, looking out over my homeland from the luxurious chambers of the highest Nobility, there was a strangeness to Kahulawe. From this height I could sight a stretch of the upland. Below that a yaksen herd loitered on its way to one of the five algae pools upon which all life here depended.

Water—or the lack of it. At this moment that, more than rats or outlaws, was the worst of the problems riding with me nearly every pace of this journey. The Queen—dared I reveal to her even a hint of the possible existence of such a hidden river as we had discovered in Valapa?

The map Allitta had discovered suggested one. It had been her proposal that she learn what she could from the court women. Yuikala would be housed in the palace, sharing Kanna's suite. However her courtiers would be scattered elsewhere.

I had no doubt that court gossip would be shared and any word from the Diamond Queen would be entirely to my discredit. Also I was concerned lest she employ such means to stir up trouble for Allitta. We must depend for a time on the formality of the court to serve us.

My father's attitude, if I accepted it as a warning—I was in mid-thought when Murri joined me at the lookout. "News, Brother. The warriors of the Pride are out." Fear touched me then. "In defense?" I demanded.

"Not against those gathered here," he replied. "They watch the outlaws."

"And there the reason?"

"Darkness beyond darkness. He who leads them has ridden to the edge of the Plain." Swiftly he added what was serious indeed. Shank-ji was meeting with some force out of the Plain.

"Man-rat!" A foul addition to those fast raising ranks against us. Had my father heard of this? I thought not, or during our conversation dealing with a possible need for allies he would certainly have mentioned it.

"Ravinga—?"

"The Wise One knows much, Brother. Perhaps more than she has shared."

"Will you act as messenger, Murri? She has a good pretext for coming here—to bring the Queen's gift."

When the doll maker did arrive, she carried a wrapped package. However she did not come alone; accompanying her was one who had once given me shelter and aid when I was a wander in desert—Elwene Karafa, Caravan Leader. I welcomed them both. Murri, without explanation, slipped again from the room.

Elwene Karafa was known in all the Queendoms. She had gathered great wealth by trading; still she kept to her chosen life. Often she had been called upon by both Queens and Haban-ji for up-to-date information concerning the trails and the Outer Regions.

I set aside custom and addressed her at once, even as I waved both of them to pillow seats.

"Trail Mistress, you have news?"

"Ill news, August One. Caravan Leaders now speak much together. We cannot hire more guards. Perhaps these days each caravan would need such an army as marched to battle, Queendom against Queendom in the old days. Already near half of those experienced in our work speak of withdrawing from the journeys.

"August One, I mean no disrespect, but you have known something of our life yourself. Should the caravaners no longer follow the trails, the Queendoms will suffer."

I nodded. "It is so. Have you and your companions anything to suggest—except a full army, that is? At this time it would be difficult to recruit or train new warriors, to gather supplies, to be able to hunt down rats which may emerge anywhere without warning."

She looked at me for a long moment and then down at her sun darkened, capable hands which curled and recurled, making fists. I was sure she would love to use them to clear the situation.

"There is no hope that the Queendoms will unite to march against these devils of the sands? The Plain of Desolation—do they not come out of that?"

"So we believe. And all the Queendoms must unite, as also the caravaners, any venturing into the Outer Regions, or we will achieve nothing but our own deaths. This I say—the Progress will urge every Queendom of the necessity for standing together.

"And I ask you, Caravan Mistress, raise your voice and ask your trading companions that they join in this. It is a charge upon us all."

Allitta:

Against my will I was, in a fashion, holding a small court of my own. Was any of this politeness false? Two of the Sapphire Queen's attendants were sharing melon wine with me.

One was near to me in age, and familiar. She had been one of those who had visited Ravinga's stall in the market. She was the Lady Siggura-Meu, now mated into the House of Koolkan—and Hynkkel's younger sister! I no longer wondered that she had arrived here uninvited. She might well be interested in the one her brother had singled out as his Companion.

The one with her was older, her round face sleek with that oil from Azhengir, which was thought by many to keep the skin supple and youthful. Her name was Tassgar-va-Almira, united to Siggura-Meu by the House binding.

I summoned all the veneer of courtesy I had learned and showed them a friendly face. As we seated ourselves Kassca poured herself into my lap. She did not relax as she usually did but watched them as if she were on guard duty.

Siggura-Meu offered trifles of gossip, compliments and bits of information about the court. She lacked Melora's stately beauty, being plump and round of face, far too elaborately dressed, in colors which clashed and did not become her figure. Oddly enough she did not mention her brother. Instead it was Almira who watched me carefully over the sweetmeat she had been sucking and then addressed me boldly on the subject Siggura-Meu had avoided.

"You are blessed by the Essence, High Lady. He is handsome, our August One."

Now they both eyed me intently. What sort of a game did they play? That they in any way wished to pay me compliments, I doubted.

"The August One," I replied in as sweet tone as I could muster, "is indeed above all men, having been granted great gifts by the Essence, whom he serves with all his will."

They continued their now irritating stare. Somehow I was compelled to add to my praise of Hynkkel. I did not think that any flattery of mine was out of place.

"The August One—you must be very proud that he is your brother, High Lady. Do you not miss him since he now is of Valapa?"

I never understood why the question aroused such an answer in her. Almira made a small movement; she might have wanted to stop her friend's swift reply.

"The Essence has raised him high. He was a herdsman and a servant in the House when I came into heat and found Koolkan-va-Kastern." Pure spite underlay her speech. Her mouth twisted over her words.

"Yes," I returned calmly, "the Essence has indeed favored him. And rightly, for now he has come to serve the Outer Regions with all his strength." Though I would not have said that some moons before, I now knew that it was true. Siggura-Meu tittered. To her my defense of her brother must have displayed some stupidity. Almira refilled her glass with wine and gulped a mouthful.

"How right you are, High One," Siggura-Meu refilled her glass also. "One must ever see the best in one's mate. It is only that we who knew him here in Kahulawe remember him as one who made very little mark in the Queendom. But, of course as a man grows older he may change."

I felt the tension in Kassca. She did not hiss but I was sure she wanted to.

Almira abruptly change the subject with a comment concerning the large market-fair, the last given before the Great Storms would blast the rock isles. For then the caravans would not come again until that season passed. I mentioned some of the wonders, which might be brought from Valapa—some even from the Inner Regions about which we knew so little.

Shortly thereafter they made formal farewells and left. I could only brood over the real reason for their coming and why Siggura-Meu so brazenly misspoke her brother.

The Royal Barracks—Kahulawe:

The barracks were crowded. Officers had little privacy, being shown into rooms in pairs, once the Sapphire Queen had officially inspected the guards. Jaclan dropped his saddlebags on the nearest cushion bed.

He did not know how roommates had been selected, but he had little liking for the one he had drawn. They were known to each other well enough but were not friends, though they had served in Queen Yuikala's personal guard for several seasons before Jaclan had been reassigned by the August One. Kalikur had a taste for gambling and before the Imperial Test he had been one of those who had trailed after Shank-ji.

Now the fellow stood by the window gazing out over the clusters of rock bubble houses of the Queendom.

"Very different from Valapa!" he laughed. "We should be glad we are not stationed here for good."

His hand went to a pouch at his belt. Loosing its tie he shook out six round silver disks into the palm of his hand. They shone bright against his dark skin, having glittering centers—some set in diamonds and some with rubies. Kalfkur tossed them into the air and caught them deftly.

"What say you, Leader? Do you think these local sons of herders will be interested in a game or two?"

Jaclan shrugged. "I do not think it will take you long to find out." He had no intention of playing gambling comrade to a man he had disliked from the first moment he met him.

Kalikur laughed, "Like that, is it? You don't take to wagering, I remember. Well, to each his choosing. I have a liking for these little toys."

He dropped the discs back into the bag and replaced that at his belt. With a flick of his hand, meant to be a farewell of sorts, he left his unpacked saddlebags on the floor, and was gone.

Jaclan dealt with his own baggage. He had heard talk of the Market-Fair. A Fairing now, his mouth softened into a smile as his thoughts lifted to a certain heart-held one. A Fairing for a friend, no one could say that was unacceptable. Yet, she was far more than a friend. Had she not chosen him to be her mate? When this Progress was over he would again go boldly to the August One and ask where that place of safety was.

Allitta:

Since the August One was still cloistered in conference with the Queens it was time to be about my own task. I had carefully copied the ancient map onto fresh parchment and I drew out now the bag containing it, which I wore against my skin. As I pulled up the cord that held it, I touched that talisman Ravinga had given me. There was no reason to wear it any longer. The purpose it had been used for had been a success. Also its force would surely have been drained by now.

However no one must learn of this. I lived always in the shadow of suspicion. That my possessions might attract attention—I was forced to laugh. To think that any spy would inspect my wardrobe was indeed seeking for specters where they did not exist.

Still what I held now would cause instant scandal at court, gifting Hynkkel's enemies with another weapon. This must not be suspected. I restored it to its former hiding place. At least its cloying scent was gone.

I must now concentrate on the map. I spread it out on the surface of a tray table and snapped my fingers at the nearest bubble light, which swiftly obeyed my summons.

The lines that formed the outer strands of the web—I began to trace them with one of the long pins from my hair. Copying had made it quite clear that they did weave the Queendoms together. Also—I retraced one line twice. On the original drawing it had been so faint that I had needed an enlarging glass to finish the copy. But, that line did strike into the Plain of Desolation. Did it mark an underground way to Valapa? Now I must determine if any line led here.

In Valapa, the secret had at least been known to the House of Vurope. Was the same true—an entrance through some House in each Queendom? Hynkkel intended to bring up the matter of water shortage. Did the Sapphire Queen know of such an underground stream and if she did, would she admit it?

I needed entrance into some of the First Houses of Kahulawe. In my visits here as Ravinga's apprentice I had undoubtedly served many of the upper nobility. And there was Siggura-Meu and Almira. But I must find just the right person, one who would be proud and flattered by my attention, eager to gain a deeper tie. I could not believe that

Siggura-Meu was such a possibility. Yuikala would have me under surveillance; that I could believe.

To approach strangers openly was not to be thought of— any contacts I made must appear to be by chance.

There was the fair. This was the last day as the caravaners must be on their way before the storms. I dare not make myself conspicuous by going alone. An escort? Hynkkel was out of the question. Ravinga? She was too well known. However, according to my rank I should have a guardsman in attendance.

Who?

The young leader of twenty! Hynkkel-ji had told of his interest in Berneen, also that he himself had been impressed by Jaclan. I folded away and concealed the map before I summoned the guardsman beyond my curtain door.

Chapter 18

At the edge of the Plain of Desolation:

He must go to this meeting alone. Shank-ji wanted no witnesses if the dweller in the Desolation did show. When they had nearly reached the headless cats he gave an order that might be unfortunate, one that could raise questioning and suspicion. No one would dare to question him openly but what they might say among themselves was the problem.

Pushing the pace now—he wanted to get this behind him as soon as possible—Shank-ji circled out around the bases of the cats. Two more spires rose before him but he could see no one waiting. He ordered the men to stay.

On the other side of the first spire, well out of the sight of the waiting company, dark figures arose as if they had been buried in the sand. Four of the man-rats! Shank-ji limped more slowly. There was no human with them. Was it then that the August One of the messenger's speech was one of these disgusting creatures?

They were separating, two in each side, though still spaced evenly. Shank-ji could see that they were carrying a square sheet between them. It was slick of surface and emitted a greenish light, the color of rotting algae.

He halted; they came briskly on. About five feet away they stopped and the pairs facing each other, and planted the square firmly in the sand. There was a constant flickering across its surface, and now it showed red.

One of the man-rats—it might have been the messenger, but they all resembled each other so closely he could not be sure—came on a pace or two.

"The August One has come," he pronounced as formally as a Chancellor on court day.

Shank-ji hid his uneasiness as he pointed to the mirror-like artifact on the surface of which light was now whirling as might sand in a forceful wind.

"That—" he nodded toward the display, "is the August One?"

The man-rat swung partly around. In his hand was a short rod, which appeared as if it had suddenly been called into existence. The night was dark about them and the rod was black; yet, by some quirk, it was fully visible.

It was aimed for the center of the red swirls. They slowly coalesced into a solid figure at which Shank-ji stared, unable to look away.

The figure, gathering substance steadily, had the likeness to one of the Outer Regions, but no resemblance to the monsters about it. Moments later it was not only brightly clear but appeared somehow to step away from the surface where it had materialized. Very real eyes met and held Shank-ji's. He tried vainly to break that contact but discovered he could not.

Now the menacing stranger grew taller until it fairly towered over him. A robe, which lacked any of the rich embroidery or gem embellishment common in the Outer Regions, cloaked the newcomer from throat to the sand underfoot. No decorated belt, no sign of wealth or position, could be seen. The features of the face on which thin lips curved in a taunting smile were narrow and easy to view, for there was no mustache, while black hair was drawn tightly up in a double knot.

The man-rats were on their knees, their heads bowed. Their master spoke. His voice was rich, warm; Shank-ji might be meeting with a well-regarded friend.

"Greetings, August One, who should be."

Yes, a warm voice, yet something in that greeting carried the sting of a lash laid across the Shank-ji's face. He swallowed the insult but something silenced his answering.

"You have at last made up your mind, it appears. I am not one of prolonged patience. My offer still stands, however. I possess powers unknown to your kind, as the Outer Regions will discover. And I am owed a blood debt that must be paid. This I say—we shall join forces. The warriors of the Queendoms have become soft—you yourself have remarked upon that. There is little real unity. Do you believe that this new August One can draw all together to act in accord?"

"He is a nothing!"

The other smiled. "Quite sure of that? But of course. However it might be well that he have no longer any chance to be otherwise. He will proceed from Kahulawe to Azhengir, or so he believes. You will have new warriors to swell your force. It is left to you to see he does not finish the Progress."

Shank-ji, drawing heavily on his will to break the other's hold for a breath or two, spoke:

"No aid goes unpaid for—in one form or another. What is the price?"

"Wise, oh, wise indeed! Yes, there will be a price. I cede future rule of the Queendoms to you. Be enthroned as the August One. I shall claim the desert lands and for them I have plans. There my rule will hold. Also—There is a certain one from Valapa with whom I wish to settle an old matter. When the time comes you will seek out and send to me the doll maker."

During their meeting Shank-ji had come to accept the reality of this solid figure before him. Now he started, fear clutching him as the nearest man-rat raised the rod. The figure vanished in an inky cloud. The rising wind scattered a few wisps of blackness leaving nothing but sand to be seen.

Tricks—he had heard of such tricks, which twisted a man's sight leading him to report the impossible. Undoubtedly this had been staged to confuse and frighten him. Still uneasiness gnawed him. Had he taken a step he would regret?

The sky was growing lighter and his leg ached. Before him was the need to plan. He was hailed a warrior, command capable, foreseeing danger and preparing for it to ensure himself ultimate advancement. This was the task at hand.

Allitta:

The young Leader Jaclan stood at the door of my chamber when I had no more than draped my shoulder shawl to form a riding place for Kassca.

He saluted me as he might a superior officer and suggested that he summon a carry chair. I refused; I did not wish any undue notice. Many noble House Mates and daughters took a guard with them if they went into the crowded sections of the cities. I had seen that custom in my earlier visits to Kahulawe, thus Jaclan's escort would be common.

Here time had been reversed; there was more faring forth by day and the streets between the round domed houses were crowded. This was no city to be compared with that which was the core of Valapa. The bubble-like dwellings common to the lesser Queendoms were designed to be storm resistant and situated some distance from one another. They looked very insignificant for there were no guardians to give them color.

However, much carving on the outer walls was common and I was aware that only a few rooms existed above their foundations in the more pretentious homes. Carvings of Kottis and cats covered the visible walls and there was a name standard in place by each outer door.

No one rode in any of the crowded slits leading to the open market place. Nor did I see any carry-chairs. We were kept to a slow walking pace, so great were the crowds, but I believed we went unnoticed.

We emerged at last into a large oval space that was walled and divided with merchants' booths. Apprentices cried wares and some, such as the makers of weapons, beat small belt drums.

Those selling food were already besieged and we slipped past their booths as quickly as we could, though beguiling smells beckoned. Those I sought, however, would not dishonor their rank by eating so in public.

"Leader Jaclan," He had offered his arm and, as well as was possible, he kept the press from me; "I wish the jewelry, the scents, the fine material for robes—" I laughed, "as is ever so, for a woman."

He lifted his head high to see as far ahead as possible. "High One, I do not think that such traders are in position near here. But there is a crossway near. Do you wish to try elsewhere?"

I heartily agreed and found that he had chosen well, for I began to distinguish acquaintances known in my own trading days. Those were not whom I sought—but rather their customers.

I came to a halt a little to one side of Vaslonga's booth. Three women elaborately robed and jeweled, their hair piled and pinned under fanciful headdresses, shopped there. They examined scarves stretched high on a line to display their involved patterns properly. I recognized the eldest had been one of Ravinga's best clients. Each time we had come to Kahulawe she plied us with new orders. The frenzy of an obsessed collector possessed her. Her dwelling must be entirely walled with figures and noted Queens and major warriors of the past. She had a love of history and legends and often discussed rare finds with the doll maker.

I moved close to the stall, reaching out to touch the silver fringed border of a green scarf on which sported gold and silver furred Kottis engaged in play. Kassca reared half way out of my shawl and sounded a demanding mew.

Vaslonga looked up, her eyes alight, and she would have welcomed me. However, I made that touch to my chin in a well-known trade signal. The collector asked a question and she turned to answer. Five scarves had been selected and the buyer passed a laterpay coin to be redeemed at her home. When they were gone Vaslonga smiled and reached for the green scarf. "No storm for you, Allitta. By the grace of the Essence you have indeed climbed high!" There was warm affection in her hail.

"You are well engaged also, Vaslonga. I saw the price symbol on one scarf and notice it was adjusted—upward—a few moments ago."

"Hrangle-van-Jessley does not worry over prices—" She paused, "I wonder if she will continue long so uncaring. Hrangle House founded its prosperity on the fur trade—Sand Cat furs. I do not wonder at the new decree. This August One has always been a friend of animals, more friend to animals than most men."

Again she hesitated and then continued, "His brother is here. It is said that he has made his peace and entered Imperial service. Why, not long ago I myself saw him at Placky's knife table along with one of the Diamond Guard, the two of them chatting away like shield mates."

Interesting—but I wanted information of another kind. When I left Vaslonga I had made a small beginning—a name, some scraps of gossip and a direction to the House of Hrangle.

I was ready to make my next contact.

At the Fair of Kahulawe:

This was the first trading fair Jaclan had seen. There were no fairs in Valapa, only streets of shops wall-to-wall, open for business all year long. However he saw some wares new to him and the richness of many along this lane surprised him. There were guards—not drawn from the Sapphire regiments but hired by the merchants. What impressed him was their official bearing and quickness to spot a thief. Even while the Companion spoke with the merchant she seemed to know, he had witnessed two arrests.

They were at a stall now displaying a number of small favors: carved animals, beasts out of old legends, rings and wristbands. Some necklaces lay upon a dark cloth to better show fine workmanship. He longed to buy a carving of two Kottis wrestling. It was quite small, but he was sure that at this booth the price would equal a month's pay. He was still intent upon it when he heard a hail.

"Jaclan! If you haven't parted with what's left of the last pay, we're bound for the Hissing Cat—they serve good wine there."

Kalikur wavered closer to the young warrior who was with him; it was clear that both had been wine tasting. Jaclan was somewhat surprised to see the August One's brother, the subject of much recent barracks gossip. He still wore a hint of a sullen frown and his glance dismissed Jaclan, though he made a small raise of hand.

Kalikur shortened introductions: "—Kalikku—who has taken Imperial Service—Jaclan of the August One's personal guard. So you be sword brothers after a fashion."

Jaclan was sure that Kalikku was no more pleased at this introduction than he was.

"To the wine shop, warriors!"

"I am on duty—" Jaclan glanced at the Companion who was listening to an elderly trader explain a new game played on a painted board with carved inch high figures.

Kalikur looked around. He dropped his voice somewhat. "And a very pleasant duty it must be. She, Kalikku, is the August One's chosen Companion."

Jaclan's hand dropped to sword belt. "The High Lady is not to be spoken of so—" He snapped.

Allitta had nodded and the trader was wrapping the game in a thin mat of split reeds. Jaclan hurried to join her, snapping his fingers to one of the bearer boys he had hired to carry purchases.

He was angry. Kalikur's speech was certainly not acceptable. Yes, the whole court by now was well aware of the Queen's rage. He had not missed the fact that their wanderings this day had been watched. At least two members of the crowd had entirely too great an interest in them. There was the stout woman in the too revealing yellow robe, and before her a hunter. His belt supported so many tools of his trade, skinning knives and the like, that it was near dragged out of shape.

Jaclan made careful note of each of the followers, to be able to report them to the captain. That officer might also be interested in Kalikur's new associate.

"I think, Leader, that I have seen enough. We shall return to the palace."

As she turned back he looked hastily at the crowd. Kalikur and Kalikku were gone. And he could see nothing of the blowsy woman draped in that poisonous yellow robe. Nor was there any well-armed hunter.

Chapter 19

Allitta:

Kassca graciously accepted a bite of algae cake rolled about dried meat. I was trying to be patient. No word had come from Hynkkel-ji; he must still be in council. Also the message I sent to Ravinga had brought no answer. It was beyond my power just to sit here.

I had not summoned the Captain of my personal guard to go to the fair, as that was against court etiquette. Now I wished both to repair any ill feeling this might have caused and obtain an escort I could trust. Not that I believed that Jaclan would play me false.

However I had not missed his meeting with Kalikku and the dubious Kalikur. If Jaclan was unaware of our suspicions of the Queen's guard, he could innocently make some remark which would serve us ill.

When Captain Sanspar arrived she faced me with all the stiffness of a military servant obeying orders. That she was resentful of my choice of the morning's escort was plain.

"Is it possible to obtain a carry chair bearing the insignia of some local family? I would pay a visit in the city and pass unknown."

"It can be done, High One," she returned curtly.

To take her somewhat into my confidence now was my best move. I waved her to a cushion seat.

"The August One has asked that I make certain enquires on his behalf. Rumor is always ripe in the court. We travel now with some who believe that they have reason to do him ill."

To my surprise she nodded. But then the affair of the Queen and Berneen must have been widely gossiped.

"This morning I abode by custom," I admitted openly. "Now I can choose my own way—"

Again she surprised me. Leaning forward as if to decease the space between us, and speaking in a much lower voice she said: "This day you were followed. The Leader knows his duties well, as does his Captain. I was summoned to hear his report."

"Followed!" I chewed on that and it was sour. "By a certain Kalikur of the Queen's guard—or perhaps the August One's brother?"

"Not so. There were two, yes, but not those you name. One was a woman of the Daughters of the Night," she fairly hissed that. "At least she was so robed. The other was a hunter. They were never together, yet neither lost sight of you, House Heart." She had returned to my family title.

"A hunter?" There would be little liking for Hynkkel-ji among hunters now. Most of their prey had been Sand Cats. Theirs was a dangerous trade of which they were very proud and they would resent having to hunt wild oryxen or other game, most of it being harder to find.

Captain Sanspar's thought marched with mine. "There are a number such here. They cannot find employment. They are bold and dangerous men."

"Which is all we need." I sighed. It seemed that the Outer Regions supplied more trials with the coming of each day. However I was not to be turned from my own quest by things that were still shadows.

"That you and the Captain of the Progress know is a support. However, what I would do has importance for the here and now. Who will carry the chair?"

"I shall select with care," she replied. Her resentment had melted.

"I go to the House of one Hrangle, a dealer in furs. Those of his clan may not be friends. Or on the other hand they may welcome me, believing I can influence the August One to withdraw his decree. She whom I would see is the House Mate, Hrangle-van-Jessley. I must see her, if I can, before night."

"It is said; it will be done." She arose, saluted and was gone.

In the Tavern of the Dark Dune, Kahulawe:

Kalikku yielded to the urging of his companion to be introduced to a tavern which seemed a favorite of warriors, not the place any of a noble house would use. They had to push their way through a door that was almost corked, into a room where any newly come nose was assaulted by a mixture of odors, none of them pleasant. Kalikur pushed past one table where a tune was beat out, empty bottles for sticks to drum. Voices were raised in a new version of raucous songs known to caravaners.

"The Rats, oh, the rats, they use their teeth.

They take their prey with ease.

Why does he not draw sword from sheath?

But the blade above or the blade—beneath—

No man or woman sees!"

Kalikur continued to urge Kalikku toward a table not far from that of the would-be bards. So even this trash could so mis-say his brother and no one cared. Well, why should he? Except that he wanted nothing so much as to choke the singer with his own teeth—He drooped down on a stool as Kalikur pulled at his arm. The song continued, growing louder, stressing further shortcomings of the "he."

"They express themselves most valiantly," the Queen's guard observed. "But their caterwauling gives us good cover. You have indeed done well for yourself, joining the August One's service. Our leader will be pleased. What you can learn and pass along will be worth even more than another's sword."

One of the servants slid two murky glasses and a red bottle before them. Kalikur poured for both. He was quick to swallow his own portion.

"To the captain!" he gave a husky toast.

Kalikku did not drink, nor even glance at his companion. He had known this meeting would have to come; still he did not feel ready for it.

"Snow Cat scooped out your tongue? Do you have anything now for our leader?"

Kalikku gave the glass a slight push. "I am no longer in that one's service—" he began when Kalikur's hand shot forward and imprisoned his wrist in a hold he knew that he would have trouble breaking.

"You try to tease, eh? One does not lightly leave service."

Kalikku faced the other directly. "I am of the house of Kaverel. We stand by our oaths. I did not give one to your leader, but I have to the August One as my father before me. Therefore I do not spy—"

Kalikur's lips flattened against his teeth. Kalikku tensed.

"There are fangs for the flesh of a traitor, you of the House of Kaverel! So your father still rules you as if you never made the solo and gained true manhood. Look well behind you, Nothing One, payment awaits you from our leader."

Kalikku was already on his feet. Perhaps he should have prepared better for this encounter. But he stood by his sworn oath. Turning he made for the door, weaving a path through the crowd to avoid any immediate attack. He was almost sure Kalikur would not try that here—unless he called formally for a duel.

He himself could besmear his name by betraying Kalikur to his father. However it would be his word against one said to be Queen Yuikala's favorite. Also he must hold to what honor he had; without honor no man could claim warriorhood.

Allitta:

The carry chair met few pedestrians as we headed away from the fair. At last we reached a narrower way leading directly to our goal.

Suddenly Kassca, who had been lazing upon my lap, sat up. Her head pointed to the dwelling ahead. Her ears flattened and the fur on her back and tail puffed up. I could feel and hear a deep growl within her.

We reached the entrance door. The bearers the Captain had found were laborers but I knew she had chosen with care.

They set down the chair as Kassca leaped to the wide stoop. She voiced a battle cry. I took a second look and saw what had aroused her so.

The typical outer door slab was open. On the very threshold lay a pitiful bundle of torn fur in a spreading pool of blood.

"No!" I cried out.

The Captain was down on her knees by the sadly twisted body. I head oaths from the chair bearers. To kill a Kotti was one of the great crimes, for which there was a single answer—death!

Kassca sounded another battle cry. Before I could reach her she was into the house. Was the murderer still inside?

Captain Sanspar drew her sword. "Go you," she snapped a quick order to one of the bearers, "for the city guards; bring the first one you sight—or if you come upon any of the Progress warriors, call upon them."

He was already on his way. I drew my sleeve dagger. That Kassca might be in danger too sent me after her in spite of the Captain trying to keep me from the house.

I stumbled into an entrance hall where the walls were alive with carvings. It was somewhat dim, since only two bubble lights hovered there, one by the entrance and the other at the far end. There a door curtain hung half off its rod. The captain pushed past me to halt at the torn curtain, then used the point of her drawn sword to push it fully back.

Another yowl from Kassca sent me past Sanspar. The room's circular wall was not only carved but glittered with gems. On the floor a rug of Sand Cat skins had been kicked into a tangle. Half covered by it lay the body of a woman, face down.

With the Captain's aid, I rolled the inert body over. The flesh was still warm. The House Mate Jessely stared up at me open eyed. Heavy bruises were darkening her upper arms where her robe had been nearly torn from her body. Two deep cuts, one slanting across her right eye, had produced a mask of blood. Her mouth was open as if she had died screaming and from it her swollen tongue protruded. Around her neck was a cord twisted from one of the scarves I had seen her buy at the fair, puffed flesh nearly concealing it. She must have fought; her fingers were curled, broken nails red with blood.

This was not the first time I had seen death. No one who has caravanned escapes such sights. But most of those had come from rat attacks, or some force of nature. This had struck the woman in her own home where she must have felt safe. Even when House raged against House in some private quarrel I had never heard of such savagery as this.

Kassca drew back from the body. Her head high, she faced the door but did not yet move. Then I heard what had alerted her—a faint mewing cry for help. Kassca leaped—then she was on her hind feet clawing at a carven cat which was part of the wall. The whisper of a mew sounded again. As Kassca scratched at the wood, she turned her head to me and uttered a full voice demand.

"In!" a thought not as distinct as Murri's, but understandable.

I went to the wall and knelt down to run my hands over the strip of paneling below the carving. Nothing was to be seen or felt. Stroking higher toward the cat I felt a line a fraction higher than the rest of the surface.

There were voices, the sound of boots outside and the Captain was by the torn curtain.

Hynkkel-ji:

It seemed that we had been seated around this conference table for more than a day. There was a drift of parchment sheets at hand but I no longer needed to reach for any, having reached the point I believed I could recite by rote every word written there. I could only trust I had impressed upon my audience the seriousness of what we faced.

My main subject had been the threat of water failure. And that had instantly caught their attention. Making a decision, which might indeed defeat me even before we were pushed to battle, I had disclosed the existence of the underground river in Valapa and the chance that it might be part of a wide system.

It was my father, together with Alompra's chancellor, who seized upon that. Yuikala was not far behind.

"August One, you say that this lies beneath Valapa. Yet we are not in Valapa and only now you speak of it."

She was plainly hostile. Her heavily ringed fingers caught up a page of a report and twisted it.

"There may be those in Valapa, Highness, who have had knowledge of this for long and kept it secret." I met her eye to eye and I could feel her malice as plainly as if she cursed me openly. "If this net of water lines touches all the Queendoms then it must be uncovered. Our time is short and there are other dangers."

"I propose that we unite our forces, prepare for a coming attack. Once the warriors of each Queendom did march under a single banner. There was such a war as we still remember racked this land. Dark is once more arising. There are these great rats, more evil than any we have fought. They are fostered somewhere within the Plain of Desolation."

"There is proof of this?" My father asked.

I indicated the pile of reports. "You have the latest news beneath your hand."

I had never been one able to influence others with words and I seemed to be failing now. However, I continued to assert that we must unite to face danger or be lost. No one Queendom could stand alone.

As the hours passed servants brought hand food and melon wine. However, little was eaten or drunk. My father had been scrawling on the back of one of the reports, a series of notes as to what must be done to assemble such a force as I bespoke. More hours wasted away.

Perhaps we might have kept on through the night. Only, when dusk gathered a shadow appeared behind the curtain of the large window and Murri slipped in.

I was instantly alert as his warning reached me. "Trouble!" He came to my side.

My father half arose. "What does this beast here?" He scowled at the cat.

"One who aids us." Never had I spoken so to him before.

My back was toward him as I looked into Murri's eyes. I had seen the great cat in many moods but never had I sensed such strong emotion in him before.

Thought speech came swiftly. There had been a meeting between the outlaws and that which abode in Plain of Desolation. Also new enemies—monsters—man rats! The thought speech came so rapidly I found I must open my mind completely, no longer conscious of those around me.

Murri had entered without any warning—now excited voices broke my concentration. The curtain was swept aside and two high officers of the Sapphire Guard came in.

We were all on our feet. The newcomers awaited no formal permission to speak.

"August One," the elder reported, "the High One has discovered a murder!"

I was not even aware I had moved until my hand clamped about his arm and I actually shook him.

"Murder—The High One—?"

"August One, she wished to visit House Mate of Hrangle. We found her dead—strangled. Also one of the Kottis dead. The guards were summoned."

I did not even look at the others.

"This conference is over." With Murri several paces before me I was already on my way.

Allitta:

With the point of my sleeve knife I pried at the small fault, paying no attention to anything else. That piteous mewing grew louder. Some catch gave way and a small section of the paneling opened. Beyond was darkness and the pleading intensified.

"Give me light!" I did not look around. One of the bubbles had been captured and was now held above my shoulder.

I saw well enough to cautiously slip in my hand until my fingers closed upon fur. As gently as possible I worked to lift a small body and draw it to freedom. Then the full light showed me another Kotti. Plainly it was injured, though I could see no open wound.

Kassca put forepaws on my knee so she could reach to lick the wounded one on the head. She made a strong effort to touch mind to mind. "Hurt—inside." She reported.

I handled the Kotti as gently as I could. "Where is the nearest healer?" I demanded of one in uniform beside me.

He spoke to one in a Kahulawen uniform, sending him off at a run.

"High One," he asked—I judged him to be an officer of the city guard. "What has chanced here?"

I was trying to hold the Kotti as still as possible. It had stopped mewing, and nestled its head against my breast.

"I wished to see the House Mate of Hrangle," I returned curtly. "We came to find a Kotti dead at the door. Then we entered to discover Death had been here also."

"Perhaps it was a thief who was surprised."

Perhaps yes. Still I was inclined to believe this had been a planned crime. Though I did not suggest this.

The guard surveyed the richly furnished room. "You met with no guards or servants, High One?"

"None. We came no farther than this room. My Captain was with me, and the chair men also, for upon finding the dead Kotti we feared evil might still be here."

There was another stir in the hall without. A stout man richly robed, his upstanding fur headgear askew, burst in, panting, his jowled face flushed. He stopped short, his eyes going from one to the other of us, then to the floor. Someone had flung a covering over the body but there was no mistaking that one lay there.

"Who—"

The guard stooped and drew away the cover to disclose the swollen and torn mask of what had once been a face.

"Noooooo—" The newcomer's voice became a scream as he clutched the robe at his chest and tottered, to fall on his knees beside the body and then collapse utterly.

"Is he House Head Hrangle?" I asked.

Again there came the sound of boots almost at a run. This time a woman in the gold-braided green robe of a healer joined us. She headed straight for the motionless man, went down beside him feeling for a pulse. Then she snapped open the bag she had brought with her. I smelled the invigorating scent of baylo as she waved a vial under his nose until he coughed and aroused.

It was her turn to give orders. "To bed with him! I have warned him that his heart needs treatment. Perhaps he will now believe me."

She noticed the shrouded body and snatched away its covering. "What is here?"

I heard her give a small gasp—"Jessye! How—?"

"Please," I raised my voice and she looked around. "This little one is badly injured."

The Kotti reinforced that with a small mew, which Kassca echoed. At once the healer was at my side holding out gentle hands for my burden.

"What's this?" The guard, who was in command, stood at the wall where the Kotti had been imprisoned. He knelt, thrusting his hand into the opening.

"Kassca, my Kotti, heard the little one crying and guided me to that. It must be a place of safekeeping. But how the Kotti got into it I do not know."

He leaned forward pushing his arm within to the shoulder. When he drew it out he held in a tight grasp an oblong of what could only be gold. On its surface series of gems had been scattered—emerald, sapphire, diamond, topaz, and ruby—The five Queendoms.

He regarded it with a puzzled look and put it on a nearby table. It was plainly a treasure, yet I had a suspicion that it might be more than just gold and jewels.

Chapter 20

Hynkkel-ji:
This was no time for any ceremony. Paying no heed to anyone save Murri, I took to the street. If a tail of guards and court-iers were following me I paid no heed to them.

Dusk was upon us and visitors to and from the fair crowded the streets. There were screams at the appearance of Murri and shortly I saw that I was flanked by the Commander of the Progress and Jaclan.

Bubble lights had been released ahead and we pounded at a run to a dwelling where city guards were gathered. Even they scattered before Murri. I dashed in after him. The Sand Cat was already half through drifting rags of a door curtain.

"Hynkkel!"

Murri was already beside Allitta, his nose against her hand. But he was only a moment before me. I caught my foot in a tangled rug and more fell against her than embraced her. She steadied herself against my weight as my arms went about her.

Nor did she try to deny me. Her hold on me was as tight as mine on her. I quite forgot in the moment that we were in company.

"What has happened?" I finally caught my breath enough to demand. Turning a fraction in my hold but not enough to free herself, she pointed to a covered bundle on the floor. By that knelt a man in bright robes, his round face beslobbered by what only could be tears. A tall woman in healer's garb was trying with the help of a guard to get him on his feet. Three other city guards stood by while the Commander and Jaclan were just inside the door.

"The House Mate Hrangle-van-Jessely," Allitta said, "has been killed. One of the Kottis also, and a second imprisoned in a wall."

"A thief?"

"We are not yet sure, August One."   The nearest guard answered.   At the use of my title Allitta slipped away from me.

"I want to—" I began when the healer interrupted.

"August One, the House Head is ill.   He must be put to rest and treated at once."

"Let it be so."

I gestured to the guard assisting him to stand.   It was plain the Healer could not handle him alone.   His head wobbled from side to side and he seemed able only to whimper.   With the aid of a second guard, both of them having trouble keeping him on his feet, they lurched toward the door.

They had not supported him more than a couple of steps when the whimper became a loud cry.   Showing unexpected strength, he twisted free, took another weaving step to snatch an object from the top of small table.

Hugging it against his chest he turned.   Now his face was a mask of rage as he began to back towards the door.

"Essence blast you—murders—blasphemers—may rats gnaw on your bones!" his voice arose to a screech.   Then he crumpled to the floor and lay very still.

The Healer was instantly on her knees beside him.   After a quick examination she raised her head.

"He has suffered a severe attack.   He must be tended *now!*"

The force of her speech brought the two guards back to her aid and now together they carried him after her out of the chamber.   At that final moment of collapse he had dropped the object from the table.   Jaclan retrieved it and handed it to me.

It was heavy for its size; it must have been solid gold.   On the surface, not set in a pattern, were five large gems.   I stared down at it and then understood.   This was a map of the Outer Regions.   I held it closer to the bubble light at the wall.   Allitta was once more with me.   Almost together we recognized a record we had studied before.

"The waterways!"   She clutched my arm.

I looked up.   "Since the House Head is in no state to answer questions—who is there to speak for the house?"

The city guard answered, "The House Head has no children, August One. There is a son to his elder brother; the brother is also dead. The son rides with the caravan guards and is on Trail at present."

I gripped the map tightly. If this were what we believed it to be, it had long been a secret. How did it then come to be lying openly here?

"It was in the wall," Allitta might have caught that thought even as Murri could do. "The second Kotti was trapped beside it. So it was discovered when we hunted for the little."

A secret of Hrangle House, however perhaps one known to the Sapphire Queen. Her guards would take charge now—she might come to claim what I held. But for the present I would keep this discovery.

In a guest chamber at the Palace at Kahulawe.

Yuikala lay on cushions while her personal attendant unlatched her slippers. The room was shadowed and she would rest before having to don court robes for the feast prepared to honor the Progress.

Still her thoughts did not allow her the rest she wanted. This matter of waterways beneath Valapa—She waved the maid away and her lips twisted in a grimace. So, not only the barbarian meddled but also his slut shared the discovery. All those who had inherited that knowledge had been wiped out save the few who were accepted as safe. Haban-ji had believed all leads had been erased.

He thought it was his chance to be more than a somewhat impotent Emperor. Maybe he wished to be a hero, should another water failure develop—as seemed to threaten now. That detestable Sand Cat! There was no getting at the barbarian as long as the beast was near. And by stupidly blurting out in company that there were possible hidden waterways—There would be those who would believe that this secret had been hers—and that she had kept it to increase her own power.

The barbarian must be removed—but first—that cat. She had already sent for those eyes and ears that had so well served her over the past months.

Pulling herself up from the cushion nest she went to the great round of the window, set to look out to the stars and the Outer Regions now so far below. Sweeping aside the curtains she examined the frame, finding at last a hidden catch.

The windowpane, huge as it was, gave a fraction more and then stuck. Yuikala pushed and it swung out a fraction. Sounds of traffic, music and life broke the peace in the chamber.

She stood for a long moment. To have to depend on another was something she never relished. But now there was no other answer. Returning to the lounging cushions she pulled at one until she could force her hand within a seam and bring out an oddly shaped container the length of her middle finger, carved from the point of a yaksen horn.

A cork was set in place, sealed with a gum that had dried as hard as the horn. She inspected that stopper carefully, then held the horn to her ear and shook it. Yes, the contents were intact.

Relaxing again on the cushions she sat slipping the vial back and forth in her fingers staring at the curtain now billowing towards her as the rising night wind swept through the chamber.

She did not have long to wait. The curtain shifted even more as a man in a plain jacket, void of badges, came through, landing on the floor and raising a hand in salute.

"There is something I must know?" Yuikala gave him no greeting, only a question.

"There is much. First—one that our leader was depending upon has betrayed him, left his service to take oath with the Emperor—his brother whom he has always so damned. Whether that one has talked we do not yet know."

She dug the point of the horn into her hand. How much had the Barbarian learned from that turncoat?

"The one of Vurope found the House Mate of Hrangle dead."

Yuikala slammed the point of the horn into the edge of the cushion beside her. But perhaps that could be twisted to bring the slut into suspicion.

"And—" she prompted when he did not continue.

"That which was stored there was found by her and given to the barbarian."

The Queen was on her feet. "And by what ill did that occur?"

Her visitor took a step back towards the window. That question had been delivered as sharply as a spear thrust.

"I ask you—how came such a stupid act?"

"The House Mate believed—at first—the story you told her. But—" He licked his lips, tried not to look at her directly, yet was held by her furious gaze. "The Kottis—they attacked. One was killed. She had opened a hiding place before the Kottis warned her. She fought; one of the Kottis went in the storage place. I tried to reach what must have been within. The Kotti there—" He held out his right arm. Around his wrist and right arm was wound a thick white bandage, a splotch of red across it.

"The Kotti would not come out. What lay behind it could not be reached. There were sounds outside. It was necessary to get away as soon as we could. With a dead Kotti, and perhaps another soon to die—as well as the House Mate—we slammed the secret place that no comer might find it and fled."

"So the Barbarian—may the Essence curse him—living and dead—has what will profit him most. You are a broken sword, Kalikur. Get out of my sight lest I, too, wish to deal with a tongue which might wag too much. Think of what you must do to climb out of the pit you have dug for yourself."

He left in no small haste. Rage darkened her face. That she might indeed kill him she did not doubt. The horn vial— she could not risk another bungler—care—always care.

Allitta:

I sat watching Hynkkel-ji pace up and down the room. And I was remembering—not the horror which had been wrought here, but something else. Hynkkel's coming, the strength of his arms about me—and how I had not wanted him to let me go. But such feelings were against all I had ever known. One might be a friend, a co-worker at some action, with a man. I shut my eyes so I could not see him, shed of his over robe, frowning, treading heavily as if on a trail. I had *not* come into heat—I could not have. Had Ravinga's gem bought me to this?

And Hynkkel—I slid my hands up my arms. Almost I could feel his grip. What—what would it be like to—He stopped directly before me.

"There are too many secrets. But this I know must be done. It is my duty to hold our find, to discover its meaning. Also, we cannot keep to the slow pace of the Progress. All that baggage we must carry, all the courtiers to be nursed along—I must make the rounds of the Queendoms as quickly as I can. Messages do not have the power that my appearance will have. Therefore we shall leave behind both courtiers and much of the baggage. I shall announce this tonight."

"There are many who will be angry," I said. *"We"*—*did* he intend that I was not to be left behind?

Hynkkel-ji:

I dispatched messengers. Twice Allitta reminded me of those we must be sure would travel with us. But the formation of the Progress within a Progress gave me an odd sense of some burden lifted. That round of ceremony which had nettled me from my crowning faded a little. The fact that I had forced into the open a secret which might be the salvation of the Outer Regions gave me some of the satisfaction I had known in the past when I had worked with a yearling pa-oryxen until the mount would answer to the lightest touch of the reins.

Those I had summoned to the Palace came and I stated my will. It might be that inwardly they cursed me, resented my orders, but they listened. They left understanding there would be no changes in the new plan.

Always I was aware of Allitta, Kassca dozing in her lap. I resolutely pushed away the teasing memory of her in my arms. How could that seem so right? We were playing a game; there was no possible reason that it would become a reality. Our bodies would not—should not respond. Allitta was not in heat—my response to her must be aroused by the talisman Ravinga had given her to start this.

My father was the last to come to me. When I outlined what was necessary, he nodded. "This is no time for ceremonies," he agreed. "Travel light—travel fast. And time must serve us and not we it. Though there is this also—they speak of you as a barbarian; this will give them more to gabble about."

"They will always do that. But what must be done I shall do despite them."

He was studying me oddly. "Do not be sure that you stand so alone. However, let the gabblers repeat their tales. This I can do and shall. Give me back my general's standard. I shall build such an army as we have not seen for tens of tens of seasons."

That he could do this I was very sure. The army had been his life and he had suffered when it had been disbanded, the remnants coming to be trail guards.

Suddenly Allitta stepped nearly between us. She held out a sheet of parchment from the stacks on the table behind us. There were only a few lines but they had been hand printed very darkly to catch the eye at once. That she had been able to produce it so quickly was one of her own secrets.

I showed it to my father. At his nod I went to the table. Taking up one of the tiny balls of malleable clay I pressed it hard against the page and used a roller to make it stick. The brilliant red splotch was in turn pressed by my ring, leaving stamped on the clay my device. Having written my name below, I handed the commission to my father.

All men are never equal in talents. I was not warrior born, though at need I could handle some weapons. However my talents were otherwise—I was not yet certain what they were.

What I had given my father was what he had built his life upon, and trust was what we now exchanged.

In the Palace at Kahulawe:

The Diamond Queen consulted the mirror. "Tis well done, Luvania." She no longer studied her reflection but turned her head to observe the waiting Lady who had just anchored the high, fan shaped crown firmly.

"Highness, as always, you shall be envied."

Yuikala laughed. "A nice speech to sustain one, Luvania. We have been many seasons together. Your skills have served me well. I trust you now as I do no one else. How many of my secrets have you locked in your mind?"

"Highness, how many have you shared with me?"

Yuikala turned entirely away from the mirror. "Many past counting. This night I share one more."

From the table before her she picked up the sealed horn. "Luvania, there is one who has disputed the Will of the Essence, who has wounded me, not in body, but in my spirit. He must have the guards about him weakened so that he may be dealt with. Was not your mate slain by the Sand Cats? Is the Essence now pleased that wild beasts be made free of our cities, dwell in our houses?"

The lady, first in Yuikala's service, was very still. There was no change in the blankness of her features. Yet that very stillness answered the Queen.

"You are very deft, Luvania. I know how well you can act upon occasion. This beast, now in favor, will be at the feast. There is ever a bowl of water within its reach." She held out her hand palm up, the horn lying across it.

"Can you be deft enough at the farewell feast? Cleanse the court of this filth which has been forced upon us."

The woman said nothing as she stared down at the vial on the Queen's hand.

Then she whispered a name. "Nitaota."

"A warrior of great bravery, a hunter of great skill. It is for you to collect his blood price."

Luvania still looked only at what the Queen held. Then she moved slowly—it was at last in the hand she pressed against her breast, as if she clutched some amulet of power.

Chapter 21

Allitta:

The feast was no time for rejoicing. I was sure most of those attending were wishing to be elsewhere. Hynkkel-ji' s choice of those to ride out on the greatly reduced Progress at dusk on the following day had been very arbitrary. Many of the original company were grievously hurt by their omission or seething with indignation. Certainly among the latter were both the Queens who had every right to be considered of first importance. The Sapphire Queen sat at Hynkkel-ji's right and Yuikala to his left. By my own choice I was beyond Alompra. Behind Hynkkel Murri had taken his place. Standing a little apart were various servants. As usual on the Progress Yuikala was so attended, by a woman I knew had been long in her service.

As one of the servants bearing trays of food passed, she shifted her position to allow more room. So doing she somehow tipped Murri's water bowl. The Waiting Woman went down on her knees at once using one of her own floating scarves to dab at the spilled water. The Diamond Queen scowled at her as a refilled bowl was brought.

Yuikala's woman seized the bowl hunched forward a little on her knees to present it humbly to Murri. The Sand Cat sniffed at the water.

His head snapped up, he was on his feet, a rumble of growl sounding. At the same time Hynkkel slammed his seat back, was out of it to stand by Murri, one hand on the cat's head.

"What would you do?" he demanded of the woman.

Her face was darkly flushed. Spittle sprayed from her distorted mouth as she screamed. "False one! Blasphemer! To bond with that creature of the dark! The Essence never intended man to aid beast. Blood—let blood wipe out blood debt. May the Dark swallow you both!"

She now brandished a sleeve knife. As she aimed it at Murri, Hynkkel deftly brought down his staff of state on her wrist. She screamed as the knife fell from her hold.

I alone, save Murri himself, caught Hynkkel's plea.

"Brother, do not take battle price from this she—"

"The she calls for death. But this is not the place or time. Remove her lest I be forced to—"

The woman continued screaming, calling on all about to aid her in slaying this bloodthirsty beast. Guards moved in. She fought wildly against all those who would lay hands on her.

Yuikala suddenly stood before her servant. She raised her staff of office and brought it down viciously on the other's head. Then there was sudden quiet as the woman collapsed. Hynkkel gestured, and the guards half carried, half dragged her toward the nearest door. Most of the guests were on their feet. Yuikala spoke to the Emperor.

"I appeal to you on behalf of one who has always faithfully served Valapa. At this time two seasons ago, her mate was torn apart by a Sand Cat. She saw what was left of his body and the horror shadowed her mind for a space. Her assault this night is my fault. She had seemed to recover so well that I believed she was herself again. I will see that she is cared for, carefully watched until we return to Valapa where she can have treatment—away from the court."

"If, Highness, you assume responsibility for her and take her back with you, no more will be said," he answered.

Yuikala's face lost all animation. In spite of the heavy mask of powder, paint, and her wealth of jewelry, she might been one of the weathered desert trail markers, sometimes found in the oldest traveled parts of the Outer Regions.

"You are compassionate, August One." The words were as hard as her face.

Her sister Queen hastened to sooth the feasters; reassemble the courtly façade to cover memory of the wild scene.

However, that any could settle back into silence, no matter how practiced in etiquette they were, I did not believe.

The wild ranting of the servant had carried another message. Such an accusation must have fermented a long time. Without the death Yuikala had mentioned there had been many other slayings caused by the now forbidden hunting.

The feasting did not last long and I was eager to be able to discover just what had been attempted.

Within the Chamber assigned to Ravinga:

Ravinga was repacking her luggage. It might well cause trouble that she had been one selected to accompany the shrunken Progress Company. When she had mentioned this, Hynkkel had quickly disagreed. He was insistent that he needed her knowledge. She was also sure that her talents might well be needed in the days to come. Having discarded all she reasonably could, the rest was repacked to be sent back with those returning to Valapa.

She had no sooner finished when Murri entered with his usual silent tread. As he reached her side he opened his mouth to drop something before her. A vial only, finger length and carefully stoppered though the age-darkened wax bore signs of recent opening. She studied it as she might a written message.

"It has been resealed—" she commented, "but still dangerous as you carried it. Whence came it?"

"From the hand of a waiting woman out of Valapa."

She ran her finger across the seal, which did not move at her touch. Murri continued with his account of what happened.

"Stupid and clumsy," she commented. "Yuikala can not be pleased."

The doll maker rummaged in the small pack, which held her most private possessions, drawing out a short rod of crystal. Using it as she might a pen she drew the sharp point slowly around the edge of the stopper.

A thin mist arose. First it was gray and then a watery red—a tinge that suggested blood, finally a deeper hue, as if the heart of a fire. The color flickered, swirling along the rod.

Murri watched with deep concentration matching hers. That flickering now fell into a pattern. Ravinga's lips moved, though she did not speak aloud. Then she jerked the rod away, and raised her head to look at the Sand Cat.

"This we must keep between us, Desert Lord." She did not lay finger on the vial but drew out a bag of woven fiber. Again she reached into her pack and withdrew a box, snapping it open. From this she pinched some powder, so strong in odor that it overpowered the customary fragrance of the chamber. Into the amulet bag went the vial and then the powder. These she tightly fastened with strands of her own hair to form a safe packet.

"It is sass."

Ravinga agreed. "Even so. They were indeed stupid if they overlooked that you could identify it at the first sniff. At least when we leave we shall use eyes and nose well. Sass requires time and rare ingredients. However, Murri, watch every shadow, for any one willing to risk the use of this is not easily defeated."

She stowed the packet away in one of the side pockets of the large bag.

Hynkkel-ji:

At least, since it had been made plain that we marched at sunset, we were allowed privacy to rest during the day. Allitta withdrew into a small alcove at the side of the chamber, having put her baggage together without summoning a maid, and curled up with Kassca on the cushion lounge.

I also prepared for rest, dismissing all servants. But sleep was elusive. Murri had informed me that what had been added to his water was a potent poison and we must be watchful for fresh attack of one kind or another.

As I lay in the darkly curtained room, I was drawn into another state of consciousness. All who live in the Outer Regions are taught from birth that when one is faced with burdens more of spirit than of body, there is a way of seeking aid from a source outside ourselves.

Striving to put all that had happened out of my inner mind I invoked that power which, if my need were a rightful one, would give me an answer.

We never stand alone—for we are all woven into one—land, sky, rock, sand, animals—man is only a part of the whole. Thus, shutting my eyes, and seeing only darkness, I made my call. The Will of the Essence had brought me into this rulership. With humility and patience I stated my need, waiting for any answer that might come.

The darkness I had drawn in about me began to lighten into a kind of grayish veiling. Within that moved darker shadows.

The shadows never entirely became clear, though they indeed wore faces, a few of which I knew. Allitta passed and behind her Ravinga. My father and another appeared for the space of a breath—my brother. All of them gazed at me, but none of them spoke. Allitta again—and Ravinga—and Murri.

Now the mist changed—sand—sand filled the air, hiding the shadows then suddenly disclosing them, only to hide them once more. Storm—Sand—I struggled to deny the threat of sand.

Except for the clouded scene I was denied any further answer from the All-knowing. Outer Regions—I concentrated on a single problem. The mist cleared; I looked upon the golden plaque, now faded—the gems dulled—what I had held fresh and untouched only a short time ago.

The Outer Regions—I had given solemn oath that I would serve the people, the land, and all living things. As I lay there I repeated my oath. Under the Essence I would hold—even at high cost to myself.

The veiling was gone; I believe that I slept. Now I must accept and deal with matters as best I could in trials yet to come.

In the guest chamber given to Yuikala:

Yuikala stood looking out upon the sand set ablaze by the full sun. Her window faced north, not upon the city. Many seasons behind her were full of private triumphs. She had been cautious and slow in the beginning, had damped down all impatience. Perhaps she had come to believe too much in the power she had built upon.

She had had her defeats then also. Haban-ji—she had thought herself necessary. How long had that lasted—three seasons—no, four. She had not allowed her anger at his betrayal to be guessed—nor discourage her. One resolutely climbed a stair—leaving behind the cracked step—seeking the strength in the next.

This Hynkkel—he was a nothing—how else could he be rated? Yet Fortune favored him. Her thoughts shied away from that path—the Essence.

She shook her head. The fault was hers—she had underrated him. What did he have that her plans should turn to sand when she had been so careful in forming them?

There was a still another chance—one he was stupid enough to provide her, with this cutting of the Progress. Valapa was hers. She had many strands twisted, prepared for the weaving. Perhaps the land itself would serve her. Storm season was very close. In Valapa she would not have to face that. But if he were stubborn and persisted—She savored the thought.

Yes, the storm season, the underground water, Shank-ji and his rebels, the many Houses in Valapa she could bend to her will—There were many weapons still to her hand.

The renewal of the Progress:

The much smaller company had made no elaborate camp two sunrises later. There was no erecting of tents, only the simplest of structures. Hynkkel saw the silhouette of Murri against the dawning sky. The Sand Cat had climbed a dune of formidable size, facing north, his head well up as if he were testing a wash of air, which rippled the sand about his feet.

He had given no warning, but Hynkkel was uneasy, waiting for a thought-sending of alarm. The caravaners and guards seemed unusually alert, concerned with both mounts and draft animals. The Commander had dispatched a pair of scouts ahead, with orders to seek out any isle of rock, no matter how small, which could be used for shelter if need arose.

There was still a three-night journey to the harsh rock island of Azhengir where the throat stinging of sulpher, the never-dormant core of volcanoes, smoked the land. Hynkkel faced in the same direction as Murri, recalling the journey they had taken together into the fireland where the cat had briefly lost his sight and only their bond had saved them both.

Allitta:

How different was this journey. Where there had been singing and the rousing rattle of small drums, voices raised in laughter, now we moved without encouragement. I had sought out Ravinga—wanting reassurance. Kassca clung close to me, sharing my uneasiness. I only wanted to keep on going—vainly hoping to make haste this desert land forbade.

Hynkkel was speaking now to the commander. Murri had vanished from his perch atop the dune. My maid came to say that food was ready. I wanted none of it but I must keep up my strength. I think that all of our company shared that uneasiness, though none spoke of it. It had been folly to wait so long—storms might hit at any time.

Here the dunes were high and if the winds struck to set them moving—

I was at the curtain door of our shelter when I saw Ravinga. Caring nothing now for the silly rules of the court I beckoned to her vigorously.

"Storm?" I asked as she settled beside me, the black furred coat of Wiu sharp against her dun travel cloak.

"Perhaps—"

Ravinga had spent many seasons along caravan routes. She had often suffered the fury of the Great Storms and once wondered aloud if her luck had served her so often, as to indeed be exhausted. Now she set about eating, as might a wild Yaksen gorge itself on available food, knowing at any time it could face near starvation rations.

She did not instruct me, simply pushed platters closer. I discovered that if I were not hungry at least I could swallow.

Then—I heard at last what I had been only half consciously expecting—the roll of distant storm drums. As yet they were far away. Still we would have so little time—time for what? There was not even the smallest isle near—no real shelter.

We were on our feet at once. Ravinga whipped off a sun veil and emptied into it all that was left of the dried food. Kassca fitted herself across my shoulders as I tipped one of the carafes of water back into its travel jug, thumbed in the stopper as tight as I could.

Hynkkel burst in upon us. "OUT!" He took my arm and dragged me towards the door curtain, catching at Ravinga also to give her a hard push.

Our camp was in an uproar. And always the drums thundered closer, filling the air with warning. Hynkkel pushed ahead as Jaclan fought to bring us three mounts, the animals rearing and squealing protest.

Hynkkel bundled us up on the beasts. Once we were in the saddles they became somewhat less fearful. But Hynkkel did not mount the third oryxen, though the young Leader urged it.

"Murri!" I caught the sharp thought call.

Then Hynkkel spoke to us. "There is a small rock isle ahead. Murri was with the scout who sighted it. Murri!" he switched from speech to thought.

The Sand Cat bounded toward us in great leaps, almost as if he had taken to the air, his thick coat widely fluffed.

"GO!" Hynkkel slapped both oryxen across the hindquarters. Instantly Ravinga and I were struggling to keep our seats as the beasts leaped forward following Murri.

"Hynkkel!" I cried out, not daring even to turn my head to see if he followed, so perilous was my hold on my bounding mount.

Hynkkel-ji:

Once, during my ordeal of the Solo, I had been caught in one of the great storms. But then I had been on one of the small rock isles with some shelter. These storms were usually not of short duration—some had been known to last many days. Here was no rock protection—protection—The wagons, which carried our supplies and luggage, were in line ready to be loaded.

They were here by my reckless desire to travel.

As the leading edge of the storm reached for us, I caught at the shoulder of Jaclan. "The wagons!" My voice approached a scream just to reach above the shrieks and cries of those about us. I was not sure he understood, but he did follow me as I threw myself towards the nearest transport. I slashed the harness to free the bellowing beasts. Jaclan's sword flashed down to shear the tough hide lines. Commander Ortaga seemed to materialize out of the thickening wind borne sand. Others joined us in our frenzied efforts. Together we manhandled the carts into a circle. The rising sand mist made each moment an agony as we fought to drag boxes and casks of supplies within the circle. The animals stampeded from the pitiful encampment, driven by the scouring blast.

We strove to account for all our party, urging them into the cart circle. Supply boxes, when shoved against the inner side of the carts, helped to form a makeshift barrier. Lastly the huge, many layered hide shelter quilts were drawn and anchored to hooks on the carts to provide what shelter they could—poor as it was.

By some quirk of nature—or favor from the Essence—the dunes were not yet on the march. Rather the main, airborne rivers of sand began their inexorable eastward flow.

And watching that I caught a glimpse of movement—Murri! He no longer moved in the long floating bounds. I could barely see him, but I caught his thought. "Ones—in storm—"

He made no mention of a wound—that I could feel for myself, through the mind link. I grabbed up the smallest storm hide and, before the man nearest me could move, I vaulted up and over a cart. Panicked shouts followed me but I paid no heed.

The sand scoured and burnt my skin but I focused all my being in that mind link that was my only guide. Murri was still on his feet as I reached him, but he wavered where he stood. I became aware of a guard at my shoulder. I put out hands to Murri and shouted as loud as I could.

"Under him, then pull!"

Strong hands joined mine to jerk at the hide. Our combined strength at length managed to cover the sand crusted body with the length of storm cover. I could smell blood— how grave was Murri's injury? That he came back alone, hurt, could only mean disaster.

Having covered him and shifted his body, we began the laborious pull back to our makeshift shelter.

"Come on! We can make it. Pull!" I jerked my head towards my companion and he met me eye to eye. His helmet was gone and I could see him for the first time clearly. It was my brother.

Chapter 22

Allitta:

Our wild race into the unknown did not slow pace. I knew however, the oryxen in this footing could not keep up with Murri. The great cat must be holding back so that we might not lose sight of him. Blasts of wind driven sand were but a promise of what they would become. I had twisted a travel veil about my face when I had left the camp shelter. Now this clouded my vision as sand began to cake its fibers. Kassca, inside my cloak, rubbed against my body. She was as sheltered as could be.

Luckily we did not appear to be riding into the wind, but rather along the edge of the fury. Limited as my sight had become I could not see movement of any dune.

How long we rode so I could not guess; it seemed our race had occupied hours. However, as we went, the force of the wind, the grit of the sand lessened. Our push westward—if Murri still led us in that direction—was taking us away from the storm lash.

Hynkkel! That he would follow us could not be. He was simply accepting the duties of his office—those the imperial crown had thrust down on him when it had first been placed upon his head. What was the duty that weighted the crown? The six fold virtues all of the Outer Regions knew—courage, confidence, commitment, empathy, trustworthiness, imagination. In truth he was himself the very heart of this land. And if that heart ceased to beat—Yet he must see first to those of the Progress.

I wrestled with pain—not from my sand scoured body— but with an emotion born of fear—the dread of loss that gnawed at me. I was so caught by that nameless emotion that I was far from ready for what came now against us.

The haze of wind and sand had cleared and, holding the reins in one hand, I tried with the other to scrape sand from my veil. The frenzied gallop of my mount had eased to a stumbling walk. Now the oryxen was gasping as its strength had near been drained. Yes, shadows were rising—the spurs we sought were just ahead.

The roaring of the wind was muted—enough so I heard a piercing whistle. Light—a brilliant eye searing light, burst from one of the spires before us. It struck at Murri! He reared with a squawl of pain, twisted as if he would throw himself out of the path of some weapon, fell into the sand and lay unmoving.

I urged my oryxen on and struggled to mind touch Murri. But I reached Ravinga instead.

"They come!"

Muffled figures burst from the ground at the base of one spire, heading at us. I tried to pull my mount to the left, but the beast near tore the reins from my hold and kept stubbornly on. Then it halted, so abruptly I was almost thrown from the saddle, for one of the figures detached himself from his fellows to ride straight at us. I had no weapon—nor did I think that he intended rescue. Rather such a wave of fear shook me that I was helpless as an arm emerged from his hooded cloak and long fingers caught at my reins. My arms fell leadenly to my sides. The light, shrunken a good deal, now encircled me and the stranger.

I could still breathe but otherwise my body refused to obey my will. While I could not move, my oryxen followed my captor's will (for captor he assuredly was) as the cloaked and hooded one pulled at the reins.

The rider's mount was strange to me. Well muscled and larger than any oryxen or even a yaksen, it sprouted three horns rather than two. Within my cloak, I could feel the trembling of Kassca. Her fear only fueled my own.

Ravinga, I saw, had been as easily taken in the same fashion and was being drawn before me by another rider. We passed the body of Murri over which the sand was already drifting. He would soon be buried. My inner terror was fed by grief.

Suddenly we burst through what seemed an unseen curtain. Instantly flying sand and wind both vanished. Looming before us only a few feet ahead was an arch of light tall enough to admit our mounted party. On the far side of that I could see whirling lines of color weaving back and forth. To look at them made my eyes sting and I was forced to close them. But my mount continued on through that strange gate which had nothing of the honest desert land about it.

The Land by the Spires:

Murri stirred, awaking slowly. He realized just in time, that only his head still rested above a drift of sand. His struggles to free himself were weak at first until, fed by the fear all desert dwellers knew, he wrenched himself free. The wind subsided as he tried to discover the extent of his injury. One of his shoulders was near consumed with scorching pain. He remembered the sudden warning of his senses, which had caused him to dodge the shaft of light. Most likely it had been aimed for his skull—to put an end to him.

What did trigger a different kind of fear now was a scent, not part of any wind. Undeadened by the sand, a loathsome stench—strong enough to make him gag—intensified. Rat yet not rat. Evil—as evil as that water thing in the underground ways.

He lurched up and forward, not in retreat but to follow that odor. They were gone—the she of his brother, the wise one who knew so much! Rats—As he made himself move he fought the fiery pain. Then—he sank down again and put one of his big forepaws over his nose. The stink in itself added to the fire. He might be lying across a caravan blaze with his body fueling it.

Ahead was a faint light. He could see it formed the tracing of an arch that faded even as he watched it.

Evil and Black Power. He had failed to guard his charges. Murri growled. His brother must know as soon as possible. Painfully he edged around. He could see the sand whirls. Must he venture into the edge of the storm yet again? He had no choice; summoning all the strength he could, Murri staggered on, intent upon reaching the camp.

Allitta:

Kassca crawled up me and bumped her head against my chin. Though my eyes still burned I forced them open. I drew a deep breath, for now I rode in the center of a party of warriors. On the fringes of the company were men such as one might see in any Queendom, but around me were others of a different breed. They wore body and head concealing hooded cloaks, but the one who still led my oryxen was—What does one do upon meeting a monster out of nightmare? This—this *Thing* displayed no normal head—Rather a rat's red eyes regarded me, a rat's ears twitched alertly, a rat's jaws spread slightly apart to display great yellowish teeth.

I must not, I was sure, show disgust or fear. Long ago I had learned that one must keep a closed face, and fight any sound or shiver of fear if possible.

"Bad! Bad!"

Kassca's thought speech only underlined what I already felt. She had fastened herself flat against me. My arms were still unnaturally heavy; I could not raise them. And for some odd reason I believed that I dared not try to use mind touch again. Nor did I allow myself another glance at the creature leading my mount.

All my life I had known of the rats. Warnings of them had been as common as speech itself among the dwellers in the Outer Regions. I had met them in battle when I traveled with the caravans and had killed my share of the noisome things. But this *Thing* was a horror of horrors. To see that which was a monster feigning the ways of a man—I tried to look only ahead as if, though my eyes were open, I rode in sleep.

Because I must needs keep myself under control I studied the land directly in front of us. There was a measure of sand, but it was more drably gray than any I had seen. There were also places where the sand was swept away to show a pavement of darker stones, laid smoothly.

Now there was a change in the land itself. No sand now but patches of very dark soil showed. As we advanced, these began to support growing things such as should only have been possible in the sealed gardens of Twahihic or in Valapa.

Though there was still not more than the hint of dawn, shapes of the strange vegetation were visible, for each stem and leaf bore an outline of greenish light. While above these weird growths there fluttered flying things whose wings at each beat sprinkled what lay below with a sparkling dust.

There were scents, too, growing ever stronger as the tightly filled earth patches spread larger and larger until they became one verdant carpet ending at the edges of the pavement over which we rode. Though one was well able to see what was immediately about, that ahead appeared to lurk behind some great curtain, which retreated at the same pace that we advanced.

Suddenly there came a stir among our captors. One of the human warriors was purposefully edging between his hooded companions. His uniform was plainly that of a Queendom. There had been no attempt to discard the badge of Valapa. The bushy fur of his war helm formed a shadowy mask across his features in the limited light.

At first it appeared that those about Ravinga (toward whom he pushed) were set to deny him. However at length one of them pulled up a little and he reached the doll maker's side.

"Greeting, oh, Foreseer," There was a distinct sneering note in that hail. "You have been eagerly awaited."

He paused—she made no answer. There was, I believed, a threat behind his words.

"An old acquaintance I am," he continued when she still did not reply. "Once you foreread for me, Ravinga—" He pushed his thick headdress up a fraction and now I could see him better. His face was vaguely familiar but I could not put name to him.

"Yes, you foreread—" now he uttered a grating laugh. "But your farseeing was not true, was it Doll Maker? No more true than this."

He was holding out a doll, though I could not see it clearly. To free his hands he caught his reins between his teeth. In his twisting grasp the doll came apart and he leaned as far as he could towards Ravinga shaking in her face both its parts.

Our party halted. The monster that had been towing my oryxen dropped the reins and pushed his three-horned mount towards Ravinga. She gave no sign of either hearing or seeing the warrior who had spoken.

Suddenly I felt those invisible bonds, which had held me, were gone. I swiftly caught up my dangling reins but the troop was so close about us I could see no possible escape. Nor could I have taken one, if it had existed, without Ravinga.

Now the warrior threw the broken doll at her face. Still she did not move though she swayed a little as part of it stuck against her shoulder.

The man-rat who had led me squealed (there was no other way to describe the sound he made) and another hooded one dismounted to gather up the pieces of the doll while he faced the warrior directly.

"The August One has decreed," he used understandable speech now. "These are his." For a long moment they confronted one another. I could sense the rage of the man— anger, yes—and disgust. He might ride in this company but not in comradeship.

He gave first, turning his mount away. They withdrew, leaving him space to reach the edge of the troop again. The man-rat glanced back at me but he did not return to take my reins once more, rather remained in a position near to Ravinga as we started on again.

We had gone but a little farther when the curtain disappeared giving clear sight ahead. There we saw, not too far away, the spread of a city. It was walled and around those walls arose tall vegetation, which formed patterns. Towards this we headed.

Hynkkel-ji:

Somehow, with Kalikku's aid, we made it back to the carts. There others joined us and we were able to get Murri over the barrier and into the crowded circle. When he was under the shelter of a storm hide I was at last able to care for him.

As I pulled aside the covering, which had been about him, Commander Ortaga came, a healing box in his hands,

"Brother?" I sent my thought call with all the energy I could summon. Murri's great luminous eyes opened.

"Evil—" his thought came slowly and faintly. "Out of sand—burning light—your she—Wise One—taken—"

I shivered. So the menace had struck—who—or what? I did not know enough. I must go. Only the storm was raging. First Murri must be tended. His eyes were closed again and there came no answer when I strove with the touch.

The wound was not a cut, such as one would bear from a sword or spear, but rather a long streak from which charred fur sifted, showing badly burned skin. Burns were common enough caused by campfires, wind stirred. I knew I could find the answer in the healing box. I worked with all the care I could summon to treat this one.

When Murri was bandaged and asleep, I held council with those sharing our shelter. We had only Murri's few words and our suspicions to guide us and we could not guess how long the storm would hold. I had to grind my hands together to conceal their shaking. Imagination was only too quick to suggest what might be happening to Allitta and Ravinga. I hoped that they had been taken as hostages and so, safe for the moment.

Allitta:

This city was nothing like the major ones of the Queendoms. Such odd buildings, many of them three and four stories high with here and there a tower reaching even higher, were unknown where the storms came. Had that gate transported us in some fashion from the Outer Regions to a strange site, perhaps to the inner lands about which we knew so little?

Kassca's head bumped against my chin again as she edged around within the folds of my cloak to face outwards and view the spread of buildings along the street, which had met us beyond the wall.

There was no sign of life in the streets. No one watched from any window. Save for the sounds of our own company there was heavy silence. We might be riding through some long deserted ruin, save there was no crumbling of any of the structures.

The walls were bright, to be seen directly now, for the sun was well up. Colored stones had been set in the duller rock to make patterns. Many of those I recognized as designs which recalled House badges. They were not all of one Queendom. Diamonds shone brightly next to sapphires or rubies.

We passed by a number of structures so enhanced until we came out in a square not unlike that of Valapa where an Emperor, having passed the Five Tests, was proclaimed. Hynkkel-ji—almost I could close my eyes and see him as he stood, his well-muscled body bare save for loincloth, to face the world. In his one hand was the Leopard Staff and in the other the one bearing a Sand Cat, which Ravinga had made.

We came to a halt and those about were dismounting. The man-rat who appeared to be in command—at least of Ravinga and me—assisted her to dismount and then turned in my direction. Though I loathed the touch of his hand I prudently allowed him to help me down.

I was startled, for Kassca, as soon as my feet touched the pavement, uttered the piercing scream which could only be a battle cry. The man-rat started back as the Kotti's head pushed out of my cloak, teeth bared, following that first challenge with another.

There appeared the gleam of a knife blade. He had drawn the weapon so quickly that he might have formed it by some gesture in the air. I retreated so that swing connected only with the edge of the cloak. The fact that a fragment of that garment was slashed free testified to the sharpness of the blade. As I held Kassca tightly with one hand, I jerked at the scarf that had served me during the storm. It billowed forth, so that my captor met it head on. I had not intended what followed, acting from instinct only, but it draped about his arm, covering the knife.

He looked at it and then at me. The mindless rage of a desert rat in attack flared in his red eyes. He lowered his muzzle for a moment and tore at the flimsy cloth. Behind him one of his hooded people appeared, then another; they sprang not for me but at their own leader. They caught and held him fast in spite of his struggles, chittering and squealing in their own language. The struggling stopped; he had regained control. His underlings quickly released him and retreated hurriedly, but not before he loosed a fierce sound.

I had continued to edge away. If those buildings around us were deserted, perhaps Ravinga and I had a slim chance. Free for only a few moments from those who had brought us here, escape into such a city proper might require the full military force of a whole Queendom to hunt us down.

Kassca fought against my hold as the man-rat leader suddenly snapped his fingers and pointed to me. Again two of his force moved forward and one swung from a hand a short rod that ended in a small noose. That they were intent on taking Kassca I did not doubt.

I risked a mind touch order: "Run—hide" and loosened my grip. She disappeared back under my cloak and I felt the thorn sharpness of her claws as she descended my body. Within the protection from sight that covering offered, she moved around to my back. Her movements under the cloak must indeed have been concealed, as the warrior continued to move in my direction.

"Go—" the mind touch was like a swift pain within my head. I did not turn to watch but I knew that she left me, even as the first attacker grabbed a handful of the cloak, jerking it with force enough to bring me to my knees.

Chapter 23

In Kahulawe:

The Diamond Queen stood looking out over the open land below. So far the storm had not reached the city, but there was no way the Progress could have escaped its full force, or so the weatherwise insisted.

However, travelers had managed to survive in the past. That the Progress bore with them every possible aid against such fury was also true. Still—Yuikala crumpled the small square of parchment so that her painted and pointed nails cut into it. The messenger had arrived when they had been gone only one turn of the time wheel. There was a chance that what had been promised could not be carried through. Let the dolt ride now straight to his fate. The preparations she had started might not be needed.

Impatience gnawed at her. There was so much to be done—she was needed in Valapa. Yet she would not dare to leave this provincial Queendom and the stupid pile they called their chief city until the storm was over.

Someone scratched discreetly on the wall outside the curtained door. She turned to face that. Her hand hovered near her sleeve knife as she called: "Come!"

The woman who had failed her at the feasting slipped within, twitching the curtain straight behind her. She was silent, looking at her mistress, her fear plain to see. Yuikala's low laugh carried a hint of warning.

"What would you now?"

The woman appeared to pull courage about her as a cloak. "What ever you will, Highness," she answered. "He who brought that," she nodded at what the Queen held, "says he must return at once. He waits only for an answer."

"So. Let me hope that they are more efficient than others I have trusted."

Her maid tensed visibly but she said nothing.

"Well, perhaps I can still call upon some loyalty, even at a distance." She had taken two strides and was now within touching distance. "Forget not; there is that between us which must be settled."

The woman made no attempt to retreat. Instead she bowed her head and waited in silence. Sparing her no more attention Yuikala moved on to a small desk and dropped into a cushion seat before it. Smoothing out the note, she reached for a colored writing stick. It did not take her long to scrape the tip of it across the parchment. As the point touched the surface, heavy black words appeared. Once more Yuikala took up a small knife and slashed back and forth, leaving only thin strips. Twisting them together, she tossed them to the maid.

"Fit only for a fire," she commented. "Let them burn well. But give them to him who waits. Say that we pack to ride out as soon as we may."

As the woman left she settled back among the cushions. Her lips moved soundlessly as she counted. Though her eyes were turned to the wall she saw a scene her thoughts summoned. One, two, three—full-strength regiments, equipped with weapons carefully stored half a generation before. Shank-ji would be moving according to the plan they had discussed—the ploy that they had decided upon if he did not win the trials.

Hynkkel-ji:

I fought for control. To plunge out into the storm was the same as drawing my sword to fall upon it after the fashion of the heroes of old when deserted by fortune. To calm my raging impatience I demanded from Commander Ortaga—and my brother, whose far roving of the land as a hunter must have supplied him with a better knowledge than mine—to tell me all they could of the Plain of Desolation. Though both of them had ridden on caravan patrols against outlaws and rats, there was little they could say that I did not already know.

We still awaited the heaviest blows of the storm, wondering how long it would be until floods of sand burst our flimsy shelter to bury us in fatal waves. So far we had survived but there was nothing more we could do to ensure that we would come out of this sane and whole.

Murri still slept and I would not disturb him. I longed for a more detailed account of what had happened. This "burning light"—which certainly must have caused the wound I had dressed—"out of the sand"—what did it mean? Ortaga, my brother, and Jaclan who shared our shelter, had all advanced guesses. But my brother had ended:

"They rode in the direction of the Plain when they left," he said slowly. "No man has walked or ridden into that and returned. We cannot know what really exists there."

"Only," Ortaga said, "any life which abides within that dead land will not be like that around us. These larger rats that have suddenly appeared must come from there. Yet it is a place of vile threat and dread memory. Those legends set down after the shadow war were wrung free, I have heard it said, of certain truths the survivors chose to forget." Bleak words indeed but they would not keep me, once the Storm died, from heading into that forbidding country.

It was very late in the day before the wind began to die. That the storm was shorter than most was a blessing from the Essence. We had not exchanged any more speculations on what might lie ahead. But I had made plans.

We would again divide our force. Those in duty with the Progress must return to Valapa. Emperor or no, I would strike out to search for Allitta and Ravinga. Perhaps Murri, when he roused again, could give me the directions I needed. I refused to consider that my resources were much less than his and I had no clear trail to be followed.

In the Forgotten City:
Shank-ji rested his handless arm on the sill of the window as he stared down at the gathering below. Two women captives—they had not yet moved to a position where he could see more

than the crowns of their heads. The rich embroidery on the travel cloak of the slender one spoke of a connection with some noble House. He watched her confrontation with Zhan and was perhaps the only one to mark that small Kotti dashing from behind her into the doorway of the nearest building where the shadow swallowed it up.

Kotti! With his left hand he tugged the mouth-bracketing hairs of his carefully tended mustache. There was plenty to be known about Kottis and at the top of that list was their unbreakable loyalty to any human they chose to join. Such a one loosed in this maze of nearly deserted city must be reckoned with.

Now Zhan clicked an order and a trio of guards—all man-rats—urged the women towards the steps leading to a raised entrance of the largest building. Though the crowd in the square scattered, Shank-ji remained where he was, still gazing after the captives. His thoughts again fastened on his main problem. His lips twisted as if pronouncing some curse he dared not speak aloud.

His initial wariness, the inner warning he had ignored, had been true. Here indeed was an overlord who had his own plans and ability, with strange and secret weapons to carry those out. Beside what that one could do, Shank-ji stood no better than a green, untrained recruit. His pride was threatened, but still his stubborn will held. The Kotti would be a way to reach the new captives and from them he might learn—

One of Zhan's followers came out of the Palace of Inutis (he had learned what he could about the city, trying to fit scraps of information together). The man-rat strode on in the open, heading for the door of the building where Shank-ji remained two stories above.

Shank-ji moved away from the window. Following habit he hid his maimed arm under the edge of his riding cloak. He was not surprised when Gorgoal, one of his first and most loyal followers, shortly pushed aside the improvised curtain and ushered in the man-rat.

As the creature raised a hand in salute, the man of the Outer Regions swallowed with all his might the bile that rose to his throat. He fought to hold control. To be sought out so awakened the ultimate fear. No—there was even something beyond that—that emotion itself would utterly destroy him.

He remained silent. After a pause the man-rat—he who had been—NO! He would not think of that! A man's brain might twist out of his skull to—The man-rat broke the silence.

"The August One awaits—"

He turned and Shank-ji perforce followed him.

Allitta:

I was able to join Ravinga as we entered a vast hall. Valapa's Imperial palace was the standard against which all other buildings in the Queendoms were measured. There could be no thought of measurement here. Valapa's glory and might, its pride, was no more than a herder's cot when one viewed this. Walls towered up for four stories. Along each of these were latticed balconies. The carvings on the screens were inset with burnished metal and jewels. Under our feet, covering the entire floor was a mosaic of polished blocks set in intricate design. I noticed that the one we appeared to be following contained a pattern like that of a roadway.

On the wall level of those passing here were slabs of grayish rock, the uneven surface of which was incised with markings I was sure was writing of a sort, but in no language known to me. Though I could not help staring about, Ravinga strode along the same way she might have with a caravan, looking neither to right nor left. One could almost believe she was familiar with her surroundings.

We reached the other side of this entrance chamber to be fronted by a staircase. It was wide enough to allow, in marching order, a squad of five guards to pass. Yet there was no one else to be seen now save the man-rat leader who kept ahead of us, and two of his command who came behind.

The rails on each side of the stair were thick and heavily carved with patterns, which baffled the eye. I blinked and looked up ahead. The stair led past the balcony at the second floor where the rails swung up to form an arch on each side, but our guide continued to climb.

Step by step we passed two more floors, then the stair ended and the rat thing turned right onto a balcony. Our captor-guide did not turn or issue any order; however the two behind us now remained at the end of the staircase. Only their leader continued. The other guards no longer focused any strict attention on us. I let my hand swing down, moved it until I touched a fold of Ravinga's cloak. She did not glance at me.

There was a black furred head rising with caution to the level of her chin. Wiu was still with her. A twitch of my fingers and my touch failed. I thought I understood. It might well be that our enemies had some method of communication which could pick up even thought casting.

Almost immediately our journey came to an end. To our left was a doorway framed by two of the inscribed stones. The man-rat stood aside but waved us forward, jerked the door curtain open and commanded, "In!"

Ravinga preceded me, but I was very close to her as we fronted the ruler of this dead city. To my eyes he was very tall, perhaps there was a head's difference between him and his guards. He was without doubt the leader here but he wore none of the richly trimmed garments that marked our nobles. A robe, loosely girdled and heavily wrinkled, hung about his shoulders and upper body. He might have been wearing clothing intended for a much larger man—it was a colored a dull purple, completely unadorned. Unlike the men of the Queendoms he was closely shaven, lacking face hair. The strands on his head were drawn tightly back and up, held aloft by a ring of copper. That metal also formed the large beads of a necklace from which depended a disc, also copper, and centered by a blue-green stone. His only other ornaments were wide copper bracelets fitted on each arm from wrist to elbow, as might sleeves of metal.

His features were very sharp and his eyes alive. We had time to view him in such detail for he said nothing, though his thin lips were curved in what might be a welcome. Those gleaming eyes surveyed us with the same intensity as we regarded him.

"Well met," to my surprise he spoke in the rich tones of one who sang to a Kifongg at some imperial feast.

I would be guided by Ravinga. Since she made no answer I remained silent instead of demanding an explanation. Also he showed very little interest in me; his attention was for my companion. When she did not reply his quirk of half smile deepened.

"It has been a goodly number of seasons but time has favored you. Have you discovered a Power which grants you such boons?" He still did not address her by name but I was sure that once they had been well known to each other.

"Faugh!" His lips lost that half smile. "You never used to be at a loss for words."

"Shakasse, Quinzell." She spoke mildly as if greeting some customer in her shop.

A frown creased his slender brows. "You dare—"

His emotion began to erupt. The music was gone from his voice; sharpness was displayed, as might be a weapon. "That is gone—there is no one left to say that to me—but you!"

"Shakasse, Quinzell." she repeated

He tensed. "So be it." There was a shading of finality in that. Now he turned his attention to me and smiled. I was aware of the sneer that lay behind.

"You at least are not going to mouth ancient curses. Those are not suitable for Allitta, the Companion to the Emperor. Well." His stare dropped to my feet and traced up my body slowly.

It was if those eyes were hands, pulling at my clothing, baring my body. We of the Outer Regions in the heat of summer half seasons have no shame of body—clothing is shed piece by piece for comfort. But this slow gaze turned on me was that of one buying an oryxen. I could expect him next to

demand that I open my mouth so he might inspect the sound-
ness of my teeth. His eyes were suddenly on my breast when
he laughed.

"Ho, that is the way of it?" He spoke again, not to me
but Ravinga. "I thought that which you serve forbids such
meddling."

Before I realized what he would do, he took a sudden
stride bringing him very close, and directly before me. His
hand swung up and his fingers shaped some gesture mean-
ingless to me.

Only—as it had been before I could not stir, my breath
came shallower. As I fought for breath his hand now reached
for me, thrusting aside my cloak, to tear roughly at the fastening of my riding tunic, then at the silk shirt beneath.

A moment later he held before my eyes the chain warm
from my body, at the end of it the amulet Ravinga had given
me. He swung the chain yet further, until the pendant cut
through the air.

"A trinket, which this emperor of yours should and will
see. How does he answer to betrayal and trickery, Allitta?"

I made him no answer.

"Well enough—you are of a like kind," he addressed us
both now. "However, if your ploy has failed, you are still of
some value to me."

He looked beyond us to the door curtain. Though he gave
no signal, that was drawn aside and one of the man-rats entered. His master moved towards him. Then his armlets
gleamed brightly as he indicated this monstrous guard.

"See what stands here? Ravinga, Wise One, ask him who
and what he is."

"What he is, is an abomination," there was no tremor in
her voice. "Who he *was,*" she accented the 'was', "answers to
the name of Upitan-va-Harkkel."

Quinzell nodded. "Just so. Now perhaps you understand
that it is in my power to handle those of your kind not only to
prevent any betrayal of me, but also to substantially add to my
forces."

Sickness arose in my throat. Since Ravinga did not pro-test, this must be the truth. How the evil from the past could accomplish such horror I did not understand, but the sicken-ing truth was clear.

"Think on this; think well. You will have time to con-sider." Now seeming in the best of moods, he laughed.

Exploring the city of the past:

The Kotti's head was high and now and again it halted, always making sure to remain in the shadows. Kassca's sense of smell was acute. What she picked up now was perhaps the odor of age—and emptiness. The talent of her kind was her guide. So far there was nothing to fear here. She flowed up steps, to trot down a second hall. Had these doors once been curtained, such barriers had long ago rotted way. Dust, emptiness. So it went until another flight of stairs lay behind her. Now—She flashed to her right, into one of those empty rooms. The win-dow was well above her line of sight but she leaped to crouch on its sill. Pavement was far beneath her now but there was very little space between her and a similar opening in the ad-joining building. Again she strained to catch the faintest sniff of a familiar scent.

There was movement on the sill of that other window. Crouched there was the Kotti of the Wise One.

Thought touched thought—"Come!"

In spite of another scent Kassca now picked up, that of the rat-headed thing, she understood. Calling upon all her skills, she launched herself and landed on the narrow width Wiu had just left, to face down into the chamber where he waited for her impatiently.

Again Kassca leaped, to join the black Kotti. Together they slunk into a hall, making a swift way along it until they came to another doorway, this properly curtained. Both Kottis snarled near silently. Wiu leaped—not through the curtain, but to an ornamental edge farther up the wall—and disap-peared through an opening there. Kassca followed. They came out inside the room.

Her own human! Kassca would have immediately leapt again, but Wiu stopped her. As they sat on a dust carpeted inner projection he said:

"They cannot move. Evil has been wrought. They are caged."

He spat. Kassca hissed loudly. Her human did not look up, nor did the Wise One to whom Wiu was companion.

Chapter 24

Hynkkel-ji:

Kalikku was a shadow in the faint light that reached us through the cracks between the hides.

"It lessens," he reported from where he crouched before one of the cracks.

"So soon?" Commander Ortaga demanded. "That is not natural!"

Perhaps not, I thought, unless we were favored now by some Power great enough to master wind and sand. My fingers moved in a sign of respect. At the same time Murri's head, resting against me, raised a little and the large golden eyes, which carried their own light, opened.

"How goes it with you?" I thought sent.

"Well enough," he returned. "Soon as the way is open, we go." It was not a question but a statement.

It seemed to me that I had spent most of our storm-cloistered time striving to settle one plan and then another. The fatal effect upon those daring to enter the Plain of Desolation was well known. In the land even the sand was not of the reddish shade as in the Outer Regions, but held the gray promise of ever-present death. Some element in it wore away a wayfarer's skin, blinded him, or else played upon his mind with visions, which sent him insane.

Yes, I must make that journey. But what could I do if death met me before I reached Allitta?

Murri picked up my thoughts; they had worn deep paths during our wait. Now he gave me a single word. "Waterways—"

The underground rivers, yes. But what had they to do with the Plain of Desolation?

Suddenly, as if Murri had drawn back a curtain, I thought of that house in Kahulawe, of a woman dying because she might know a secret. If it were true, as I believed, that the Queendoms were linked by those underground ways, did such also serve the Plain? Legends had hinted of a rich land swallowed up by the Dark in ages past. And there had also been that terrible drought following a war, which had ranged across the entire Outer Region—perhaps one for water control. It all fitted, but it was only one guess laid upon another.

"The Pride has its legends also," again Murri touched with thought. "In the day of Harsie Longclaw there was said to be one who went an underground way and survived, though afterwards he was slain by a hide hunter."

"What do you plan?" Kalikku continued to watch the growing brightness without.

"First," I answered, having in that very instant at last made up my mind, "we will return to Kahulawe." I discarded my earlier decision to go west straight for the Plain of Desolation. "There are those among us who must be cared for." I went no farther; I must know more before I could construct a workable plan.

So we pulled together and I went about, Jaclan at my heels, my brother several paces farther back, to see what damage had been done. There had been several deaths. All of our mounts and draft beasts were missing. Luckily the Cat spires marked the path of retreat, so we could not lose our way because of shifted dunes.

At last, with the Commander's agreement, we dispatched ahead five of the guard to summon aid. Two of the carts were righted and supplies crammed in, leaving enough space for those exhausted or suffering from sand fever. Kalikku volunteered for the scout party.

Murri was on his feet when they strode away, each bearing a pack of supplies. Had I done as I wished, I would have had him in one of those two carts. But I realized that he would never consent. He was of the desert and might well show us how best to travel through storm ploughed land.

His burn wound seemed to be already aided by our treatment and he was content to walk beside me instead of forging ahead as was his usual fashion.

My own place, in spite of all protests, was with the rear guard, except when I took my turn in the crew dragging the carts.

There began a blurred time, which led at last to the sheer determination to set one foot before the other. I had already shed most of my gala apparel. The sand clung to my partially bared body as it did to those of my companions. The water bottles were passed, skin was brushed and then coated with creams, and handfuls of dried meat and algae were shared out. Keep going we did, until at last those from Kahulawe came to our aid. I can remember very little of the last of that trek, but reach our goal we did.

On the Road Back to Valapa:

Where Yuikala rode there were few signs of the storm. They were already a night out of Kahulawe, and she had to admit to herself that the party she now commanded was indeed slow travelers. There was no possible way to speed ahead with her own guards and leave them. She wondered at the fate of the rest of the Progress. Those in Queendom behind her had pessimistically shared the belief that they had been caught in the storm and were lost.

Another Emperor—and this time certainly one of their own way of thought. There were the tests, of course, but also there were men, some among her own guard, who were trained and skillful enough for that, even to finish and hold the crown. Such tests could not be hurriedly set up—it was too short a time since that barbarian had the unbelievable luck to grasp a rule he was not entitled to. They could now, she thought with satisfaction, believe him removed from the game. And with him—her lips puckered as if she was about to vulgarly spit—that slut! So Vurope would be vacant again. This time, naturally it would remain in Imperial Hands, or perhaps be granted to a new House, bound properly to the Diamond Throne.

She had dispatched two messengers. If the barbarian had survived—and managed to reach Kahulawe—he was going to discover that his crown was about to be lifted from his head—and perhaps his head with it.

In the City of the Plain:

Kassca and Wiu used eyes, ears, and noses to the fullest extent. Finally they leaped from their perch and carefully approached the two women, each settling before the one with whom bonded.

Both Ravinga and Allitta remained silent and unmoving, only their eyes watching the Kottis. Ravinga blinked slowly and blinked again. Wiu jumped, landing on the doll maker's knees. He stood on his hind paws stretching up to put forefeet on Ravinga's breast. Higher still he reared until he was able to touch noses with the woman.

So they sat for several long moments. Then Wiu dropped to four feet again and stepped down to the ledge on which the women sat. He began to hook claws and set teeth in Ravinga's robe. When these were fully anchored he retreated, drawing the outer garment away until it spread on the ledge at the right hand corner near Ravinga. At length he crouched and began to tear with his claws at one special section of the lining. The heavy material gave way almost thread by thread. Meanwhile Kassca had gone over to the door curtain. Seating herself before it she set her senses on guard.

The material was at last in shreds, which once more Wiu nosed until he drew carefully from the rags a gleaming coil where colors rippled along each loop. The Kotti busied himself biting at a narrow piece of cloth that held the coil together. Kassca trotted over from the doorway as the string gave way. Wiu jerked his head and the loops were loops no longer, rather a length of color glinting cord.

With one paw set on this he looked intently at Kassca. The younger Kotti reared up to catch in her mouth the dangling end. Now back on the floor, with a last long glance at Wiu, she moved to the left drawing the cord with her past Ravinga. Wiu held the other end of his find before the doll maker, unmoving.

Kassca proceeded. Having passed by Allitta she dodged behind the girl's legs until she had made a circle coming back to Wiu where she dropped the cord's end, and went to sit before Allitta.

The cord suddenly flared brilliantly; one color pursued another in ripples, which came faster and faster. Wiu made no move, yet Kassca felt pain growing ever stronger until she could not subdue a protesting cry. The light was no longer a part of the cord. Rather it flowed to the sitting women, climbed their bodies, and thickened until they could not be seen—there was only brightness.

Kassca moved until she could feel Wiu's throbbing body against hers. Pain deepened and she cried out again. There came a final blast of pure agony. Then the light was gone. As it disappeared there sounded a cry, not from Kassca.

"Little one!" sound and thought touched both.

"Kassca! Wiu!" Two voices joined. Hands reached, closed about small bodies, and lifted both Kottis up. The pain was gone, there was now stroking, the warm feeling of being where one always wanted to be.

Kassca shook her head as tears wetted the fur of her head. Her file-rough tongue swept along flesh, which held the proper scent of her own tall one. She nestled closely into comforting arms.

"Dreaming can certainly have a good purpose," Ravinga cuddled Wiu closer. "Had I not had such a warning I would not have come prepared. Quinzell may have summoned new evil to do his bidding, but I have also added to my resources."

"Magic—will he not be warned when it is used within his very fortress?" asked the girl.

"It depends upon what he was doing at the moment the furred ones freed us. However it is right that we should make good use at once of this chance."

Still holding her Kotti she stood and Allitta followed her.

Allitta:

Any action of my companion no longer had the power to astound me. It would appear that she had an answer to every need. Now, supporting Wiu with one hand, she stooped and gathered up the ragged bits of cloak lining.

"I think up instead of down," she continued and my now unclouded wits translated that to mean we must scout a way into the upper floors of this pile.

Even as I had seen Murri do with Hynkkel—so did the Kottis take over the scouting for us, Wiu to the fore and my Kassca at our heels.

Twice we were warned in time to dart into a chamber as a guard passed. However after we reached the floor above that where we had been captives we were alone. At last we came to a cluster of chambers, five of them, two to a side, and one ending the hallway. Here the walls were all of the dark colored slabs, more thickly inscribed than the panels above.

Ravinga halted before the mid door. The Kottis waited by us showing no desire to proceed. From her inner robe Ravinga brought out the small rod by which she had summoned the old map to life. Her lips moved but I heard no sound.

Then, with the delicate touch she used with her finest work on the dolls, she inserted the rod into one of the graven paths of the carving, about half way down the stone. At the meeting of rod and stone, a spark flashed to light.

"Amassia fraku Sandaska," she intoned and began to draw the tip of the rod along, away from the point of contract. As it went it continued to illuminate the stone over which it passed. The carvings stood out boldly as it traveled upward. Now the design it traced was blood red.

As Ravinga at last lifted the rod the light failed and vanished. She nodded.

"Not all is gone. Come!"

I obeyed. The door opened under her hand and once more with Kassca and Wiu we went on.

The chamber into which we passed was bare—even of such a ledge seat as had served us in our prison. Nor did any windows break the gray walls. It was so dusky we moved with care.

When she reached the center Ravinga became intent on the flooring. Once more she waved the rod in the air, then held it straight before her and began to raise it slowly.

There was neither sound of a lock giving away nor any grate of stone against stone. However even in this limited light I could see a large block rising at a speed matching the movement of the rod. Now Ravinga swung the still rigidly held rod to her left and the stone, free of its bedding in the floor, swung to one side.

One could now see not only the opening left in the floor, but down in it. The dusty-musty odor, which had haunted us since we entered, vanished. We breathed air that was warm but it carried also a scent, which was so nauseating that I swallowed, and my hands flew to my nose.

Ravinga stepped before me into the black square opening and beckoned. Wiu sprang and caught claws expertly in her tattered cloak, climbing to the doll maker's shoulder. Though the stench which now enfolded us made me near unsteady, I also stepped down into the pit, catching up Kassca as I went.

"Stand steady," Ravinga ordered. She had put away the rod but now she sing-songed in that strange tongue.

Under us there was indeed firm footing but that began to sink slowly. Kassca hissed in my ear and I could easily have done likewise. This was a strange trail we followed.

Hynkkel-ji:

Having made what provision I could for my people, I called a meeting of those I had already learned to depend upon and those I must win to me. My father and Kalikku, Queen Alompra and the captain of the city guard. Behind me, still bandaged, Murri waited.

There was no time to waste in formalities. Baldly I laid it out for them, translating Murri's report of the kidnapping force— underlining the presence of the man-rat as well as the unusual weapon that had been used. And I ended with all the force I could summon—"The Plain is death, yes. However, there may be another way—the gate to it lying here in Kahulawe."

The House of Hrangle was locked securely so that the Captain of the City Guard needed the Queen's order to let us in. We entered a hallway where a deep chill and a daunting feeling of emptiness waited. This is the center of a clan, I thought, but it lacks any touch of life, as if, with the death of the House Mate, the continued illness of the Head had indeed brought an end to a line.

Murri pushed before us and he went as one knowing well the way. Down through the house offices he went. I alerted a bubble light to accompany us. The storerooms on a lower level—then another stairway, only to find ourselves in a small room without any other opening. Remembering well how what we hunted had been hidden in Valapa, I studied the wall against which Murri stood, his nose near rubbing the stone.

"Here, Brother," he thought with utter confidence.

I joined him, to run my hands across the wall, seeking any irregularity, which might mask an entrance.

My father stepped up beside me, holding his sword by the blade that he might rap on the wall with the heavy, gem studded hilt. Into place directly behind him moved the Captain.

"A tougher hammer, Sir? Or a varied beat?"

My father varied his pounded assault but kept to it. I was about to suggest a search for a hammer when a final blow of the sword hilt sent a block of stones, man-high, swinging outward, pushing me, my father and the Captain and Murri backward, loosing a blast of damp air in our faces. That air I well knew—we had indeed found the river, if not a large body of water. As I waved the bubble light on, however, there already showed the green luminescence I remembered.

The passage now revealed was still shadowed. We pushed through onto a circular platform, surrounded on three sides by water. Here those festoons of slime, which had bannered the walls in Valapa, were missing,

There was, however, a surprise. Drawn to the side of the platform where we stood, indeed fastened to it by a chain of rusted metal was a curious object. Water transport was unknown in the Outer Regions. This was near in shape to a trail wagon though it narrowed at one end. Its sides appeared seamless; it might have been fashioned in a single casting, though it showed none of the chain's rust.

Here was a hitherto unknown means of travel. But if we were to penetrate to the secret of Desolation (so I hoped) it could be by the water linkage between Queendoms, which appeared on the secret map found in this very house. Despite ignorance of its depth, or what monsters might hide in it—this water must be our road.

My father regarded first the moving water and then a disc, banded to his forearm. He caught my interest and held it out that I might also see its face where an arrow point first swung wide and then came to a halt.

"This belonged to the late Emperor, August One. He had it from an Inner Region trader, several seasons ago. He sent it that I might prove it. I did not use it in the desert lands as the roads there are well marked from Queendom to Queendom. And I have not gone on any hunting trip far enough to count. But without way markers I am certain it is what we need. It appears to register now, August One. The water does flow in the direction of the Plain."

Surely the Essence watched over us. I gave inner thanks. It remained now that I must make best use of this favor.

Chapter 25

In the Forgotten City:

It could all end here. Shank-ji edged his body along, scraping the wall as he approached a side alley. He had no idea why the restraint, which had controlled him ever since they had been brought here, was gone. However he was thinking clearly now—there were no invisible bonds to hold him in fear and obedience. There was nothing in this side way he was scouting. He made a hand gesture to those following with the same wariness. Those who were still—men! At least the fear of becoming otherwise was bringing them to the highest level of action.

The side way led them to what he had been able to discover through his own efforts—the point of departure. Another gesture brought the squad about him. He pointed to Hywel. They had been comrade bonded since boyhood; he the only one Shank-ji now trusted completely.

The answer to his unspoken question came in a barely audible whisper.

"There are guards—"

"Men or rats?"

"Men and man-rats."

This was no time to order others; Shank-ji must engage himself. He gestured to the squad again and whispered to Hywel, "If I do not return, do the best you can to save yourselves."

Hywel's protest was only a faint hiss as Shank-ji darted to the one story, windowless building, holding but a single room. He was at the wall, again pressing a shoulder to it as he moved. The entrance must exist on another side. He slunk around a corner to seek it.

The freedom with which he moved might not last; he must make the most of it. There had been five times in the past,

Shank-ji knew, when the invisible leash had been dropped, however those short intervals followed no pattern. Each time it had meant another of his men had been seized.

Yes—there was the door! Though their swords had been confiscated, the city was large and exploring had provided them with weapons. He grasped a rod tightly in his left hand. Its original purpose, he did not know, but one end had been ground into a wicked point.

He listened, shook his head. No more delays. One could not tell how many were within by sound. The door had neither curtain nor any other barrier.

Two strides brought him in. Before the device, which he had seen only briefly on his entrance to the city, stood a single man-rat. The creature spun to face him, a queer object in one hand. Shank-ji leaped, as he had once leaped for the Imperial Crown, and this time did not meet with failure. His rod swung and connected. Under that blow the guard fell sidewise to crumple against the wall.

Fortune favored; there was only one guard. Shank-ji raced out and signaled his men to come. He did not wait their arrival but returned to the room and the device that filled almost half of it. He continually feared the resumption of the restraint. Surely he who ruled here must have set alarms.

What he faced was a mystery. But it was also the only chance they had. When they had entered the city he had tried to memorize everything he saw. Also Hywel, who had been pressed into the party which seized the women, had reported watching the opening of the gate. Now he crowded forward to Shank-ji's side.

"It is thus, Brother," he pointed to a large flat plate on the side of the box-like device. "One stands here, and places his hands—so." Hywel flattened his palms against the plate. "This arm is then employed so," he clasped a bar extending outward at one side of the outsized box. "Out there," he nodded at the door, "beyond the wall, the gate appeared when they tested it—only there is something else which I did not see done."

He stood aside as Shank-ji moved into his place. He wanted to pound his fist against that plate and demand that this devilish thing serve him. To win this far and then fail—

Anger would not serve. He had studied much of the history of Valapa but there had been nothing recorded about this city and no´such strange devices in any account he had uncovered. And there was so little time. Shank-ji recalled the rows of record scrolls he had once sought out in the Palace. There were scraps of knowledge he had found there and used now and then. But—"Great One!"

He heard the shuffle of feet and turned, dropping his hand from the plate—"Great One!" Hywel jerked Shank-ji's hand, slapping it back against the plate. "Great one! The gate showed—out there—but a strange place—many shelves—records standing on them!"

"Out where?" demanded Shank-ji. "Out there!" Hywel motioned to the doorway. "You saw shelves and records?"

"Many—many!" Men were at the doorway now looking in.

He had been thinking of the library and so perhaps had produced it—or a likeness of it! Impossible! Yet in this place who dared to say that?

He might try to recapture the "impossible" and prove it true. Did not the barbarian communicate with his deadly cat by thought?

"Listen," he looked back at the plate, not turning to see who listened. "Get you out there—wait. If anything appears—another place, go—as swiftly as you can!"

He heard the sound of their going. "You also," he said to Hywel.

"I go only with you, Great One," the other returned.

There was no wasting time when Hywel had taken that stand. The library?—No! Where? His own desert hold?

He concentrated on building a mental picture of the rock isle. There was a rise there, the crevices and caves they had used as shelters. Something moved—Sreko who had been left on guard to welcome messengers.

There were cries from without. Three others appeared on the site he had visualized—they were going through!

Hywel seized his shoulder—shook him—slammed one hand on the plate. "After them—get you after them!"

Instead Shank-ji raised his single hand to cover Hywel's. He drew upon his full strength, hurled himself at the door, dragging the other with him. Was the scene fading—or once begun would it hold a while? He plunged forward, Hywel, no longer resisting. Then they were through, rough rock, instead of ancient buildings about them.

Hynkkel-ji:

We had no way of reckoning the passage of time, yet it seemed to stretch longer and longer. I was certain that already more than one day had passed. So far our voyage was undisturbed. The current carrying our craft continued the same, untroubled by the rise of any water dweller. Dividing into two squads we took turns between sentry duty and sleep, resting as we could in cramped positions. Twice we were all aroused, lying down to free our feet for kicking along the right hand wall and propelling the transport around a curve.

I hailed Murri, where he had taken his place at the fore.

"Brother, the walls seem clean; there is this water skimmer left here. Has this way been in use?"

"Not for a long time. There is only the faintest of scents." He replied.

"August One," Jaclan was near. "Look you."

He had lain next to me when we had used our push power. Now he pointed to his feet. We wore the knee-high boots of desert travelers, fashioned from more than one layer of stiff hide. Where the soles met the tops there was now a minute pitting of green. He scraped at it with the blade of a sleeve knife. Flecks of green, like sparks, arose in the air. The man next to him on the other side cried out sharply, slapping his thigh where one of the sparks had lodged.

"Don't touch!" I ordered. All were now examining their own boots.

"It eats!" That was Kalikku.

Men were moving and our transport wobbled unsteadily.

"Sit still!" commanded Ortaga.

"Ahead!" I caught a warning from Murri.

What I had feared since our small band of volunteers had set out appeared to be coming upon us. Beyond was a troubling of the waters. Something of size was moving under the surface directly on the path of the boat.

We are a desert people, living harshly with limited supplies of water. To enter the river itself had been to court unknown peril. What if that ahead would attack our craft, perhaps overturning it to throw us into the river? There were no ledges here as there had been at Valapa. One of the caravaners who had joined our party yelled and kicked out, sending sparks flying. The sole of his boot had begun to part from the uppers, eaten away by what had attacked the hide. Another peril—that which could eat through several layers of thick hide might easily strip our clothing, baring our bodies so that flesh might burn from the bones.

So far all we had seen was a movement within the water. That had drawn no closer—in fact, was keeping the same distance ahead.

I hefted the hunting spear that was part of my choice of weapons. Its barbed head was a wicked stretch of metal. I was against the left side of our transport near Murri's perch. I spoke to Jaclan.

"Steady me, Leader."

Instantly his hands were on me, and Ortaga moved to add support. I leaned forward, hands holding the spear so that its head clanged against the rock wall higher than our feet had touched, to rasp along the stones for a space. I saw no sparks of green, nor sign of any clinging to the metal, save that the point no longer shone but was dulled.

By my foot was a half empty pouch, which had held the dried rations we had been eating a short time before. I touched that with the butt of the spear.

"Empty this."

Jaclan, Kalikku moving into his place to steady me, emptied the rest of its contents into a second bag. I reversed the spear and thrust the point into the first bag. There was a stench of burning—the hide shriveled.

"Yes!" Jaclan was with me once more and Kalikku was free, his hands already on an arrow quiver. He arose cautiously and the caravaner beside him moved to steady him as he scraped arrowheads two-by-two against the stone.

"Ware!" Murri's warning.

The passage was suddenly cleared of the luminous mist to show our way ahead and the ceiling of the tunnel dipped unexpectedly. We saw not only the possible peril of being scraped off into the water, but perhaps having to fight in a very tight space. I gave the only possible order, since we could not retreat. We could only ride with the grip of the current.

Thus we huddled as flat as we could. I took one long look ahead before I settled so. The water now was churning faster. Whatever disturbed it was already passing under the low arch.

We were in the dark now. The light mist did not hold here. Weapons ready to hand, we waited—and waited. This took as much energy, it seemed to me—if not more—than fighting.

Murri growled—my hand was tightly stiff about the spear shaft. "Ahead—"

But that was too ambiguous—what lay ahead?

There was light ahead now and one could see the roof grow steadily higher. As the light increased, so did the disturbance in the water. One of those monsters such as I had fought in Valapa showed head above the surface. However, it was not facing us, but something else.

An ear-deafening shriek broke from it as it hurtled forward. Another water thing, enemy to the first?

The current would draw us on into that battle, since there was no way to halt our craft. We had come out onto a very wide space in which the water was cupped. Here once more a ledge lay to our left. Ortaga arose, his body steadied by two of the guards. In his hands he had a large double hook, such as is sometimes used in spire climbing, at the end of a thick length of rope. He whirled the hook aloft and sent it flying at the ledge.

By the favor of the Essence the hook caught. After a couple of vigorous jerks it still appeared caught. He and two others began to pull. More swiftly joined them and we moved toward the ledge.

There was indeed a battle at the other end of the pool. Scaled bodies showed dripping wounds. On the surface floated others who looked human. They too were being torn apart. None in the battle appeared to notice us, but we were quick to reach the dubious safety of the ledge.

A whistle sounded shrilly.

At the far end of the pool, there moved out on the ledge a kind of dark wave. This headed straight for the disturbance in the water, pouring over the edge. Rats—desert rats!

Allitta:

Down the stone square under us dropped. Luckily it passed so slowly that my uneasiness waned a little. Since we passed no openings, I could not even guess how far we had gone, and were going.

Only there rose about us again a ghastly odor as if a pool of clotted blood might await us. However such a horror did not face us as we stopped at last. There was a greenish mist about us, perhaps exuded by the walls. But those walls no longer held us in such a confined space. Rather, we were standing together in the center of a chamber.

Ravinga stepped from the square without a word, but I knew I was to follow. There were splotches of shadow about the walls, marking doorways. She unhesitatingly headed for one of these. No curtain was to be looped aside but—Light blazed at us and with our coming another scent covered and dispersed the sickening one. There might have been a soft breeze blowing over the private garden of the Palace. Now the light began to change. It was still as bright, but it took on beams of color that faded one into another, only to be born again.

The radiance issued from a source—a large block of stone faced us, its surface covered with endless patterns emphasized here and there by the setting of the five gems of the Queendoms. And—Ravinga went forward as I sank to my knees. Kassca wriggled out of my hold and ran straight to the stone and rubbed against it.

Words came from me unbidden. Here was the Greatest Power of the Essence I had ever touched, so great I felt that such as I had no place here. Then I understood that a choice had fallen on me, unworthy that I was. I moved toward a service that was asked of me.

Ravinga had gripped the edge of the altar. I could see a sheen of sweat on her face. Her eyes were closed and I moved behind her to steady her body. She was shaking and her flesh felt chill. She moved—to turn so we stood breast to breast. Her right hand raised and with a forefinger she traced a pattern across my forehead.

"Remember!"

Yes, who could forget? If it was ever needful, I could find my way here again.

Now she clasped hands on my upper arms.

"Out," she rasped.

With my support we made it to one of the doors in the other chamber. There both Kottis arose, growling and spitting. I hesitated. I lacked even a sleeve knife for defense. The stink from the door grew stronger with every breath I drew. Rats! The old enemy.

"Out—" Ravinga freed herself from my aid to stand alone. Before I could prevent it, she passed into the waiting shadow. I followed.

Rats indeed. The small fires of their eyes were uncountable. But they did not launch themselves at us; their advance was slow, but the unspeakable threat of being eaten alive remained. We stood, backs against the wall of a hall as they pushed nearer.

Now they began squeaking. Still with our backs to the wall, moving sidewise, we inched along, they, suiting their pace to ours, ever following. A voice sounded through the squealing.

"Guests do not leave so easily, Wise One. Come to me." That restraint; the invisible bonds were back. I was sure, without trying, that we could go nowhere other than where the voice desired. The wave of rats behind prevented retreat, even had we been free.

There was a stair. We had to turn our backs on the evil horde of vermin to climb. Up and up, holding, until fingers cramped, to a rail gritty with dust, doing what I could to steady Ravinga.

From above came a brilliant light. Ravinga went very slowly. I heard the Kottis growling, but could not see them now. My eyes smarted and I kept blinking. We had come to the head of the stair.

"Welcome—" The voice came out of the light, which was now a blaze. Having heard it once, I could never forget—we were again fronting Quinzell.

Neither of us answered. No, but a powerful hand might have dug fingers into me. I was jerked ahead by the force of that pressure that caught and held me. Now I could see the master of the forgotten city.

"Ah, the False One's play toy," he commented. A snap of fingers and guards moved in on either side of me—man-rats. They did not touch me, only stood waiting some order.

Their master spoke—slurred words I did not understand.

He laughed. "Waste no time hoping for escape. We shall provide you with other things to think on, Play Toy. We have not given these faithful ones of ours females. Now it is time to fulfill promises."

Did he think to send me to my knees with such a threat of horror, to scream a plea? His hand vanished into an inner pocket of his robe and he brought out the amulet Ravinga had given me, letting it swing on its chain.

"These loyal warriors still possess some remnant of their vanished selves." He came to me where I stood helpless, to toss the chain over my head. A faint scent had lingered about it, but when it rested again on my breast it was strong once more.

"Take her," he nodded to the man-rats.

Even speech was denied me, I discovered, as take me they did. They gripped my arms, one on either side, the restraints on my feet and legs lessened. They pulled me with them, on to what Quinzell had planned.

Chapter 26

In Valapa, Audience Chamber of the Queen:
The Diamond Queen waved the Imperial Chancellor to a seat.
By tradition this officer owed allegiance only to the Emperor.
And if, because of death of that ruler, there was no one on the
throne, it would be she who would arrange the trials to select
a new overlord. With the whole of the Outer Regions now
threatened on two sides, the rat attacks and water failure, such
a choice must be made as soon as possible.

"Your Highness," Giarribari said, "in this time of peril,
should the tests be ordered? Would any gather to risk them?
You have read the reports, which come now thick and fast.
Attacks by rats such as we have not experienced since the
days of the Great Dark." She toyed with a pile of messages
before her, chose one. "The pools of Azhengir are shrinking
fast. To have Minister Mekkui give the fatal order now—"
she did not finish that but simply regarded Yuikala somberly.
After a moment she broke the silence.

"Yesterday one Kaska-va-Klavdu was arrested by the city
guard as he forced himself into the shop of Ravinga, a re-
spectable and well regarded maker of mourning dolls. Since
she had gone with the Progress and not returned, the shop was
being kept by Kaverel-va-Melora-Kura. She is sister of the
Emperor and a woman of outstanding repute. Klavdu was
raving and demanding that some weighty secret be given openly
to the whole city."

"Was he soused in old wine?"

"One would think so from his first actions. However, by
the time he was brought to the guard house he was like another man, bewildered and denying what had happened. A
healer was called as it was thought that he might be suffering
from some head injury. He was very distraught, swearing that

he could remember nothing. Yet Melora-Kura and two other
shop keepers who had come to her aid, plus the first guard on
the scene, all swore to the same story."

"Old wine," returned Yuikala. "What has the ravings
of a drunkard to do with the troubles which have come
upon us?"

The Chancellor laid down a message and took up a
second.

"At near the same time Klavdu was engaged in this intrusion there was another such. The House of Vurope has been
under guard since the news has come that its Head may have
been storm slain. There is no heir of the Blood. Since she
was the Companion, the throne will inherit.

"Four men tried to enter the House. The servant who
tried to stop them was beaten unconscious. Another servant
was able to strike the alarm mobile. By the time the guard
arrived three of the criminals were already in the lower part of
the building—"

Yuikala's hand had knotted in a fist. "They were caught
and identified?"

"Two were killed—they resisted with force—too much
force for what seems a case of trespass, for they had taken
no loot. But the third and the fourth were indeed captured.
The name of one caught in the lower part is Rakunnan-va-
Rager. He claimed to be on a mission—then he attempted to
swallow this."

She laid beside the reports an oval, the size of a little finger joint.

The Queen stared at it. Long ago she had learned to control her emotions.

"An Imperial seal—doubtless stolen, Giarribari."

But her attention was still centered on it. Now with fingertip she flipped it over. The device, which had been carved
on the other side, was not repeated here. Rather there was
incised the head of a leopard, plainly Imperial.

"That is a counter of Haban-ji," Yuikala said. It is truly
Imperial, but of no worth now."

The Chancellor nodded. "The guard is questioning those taken. He who was the other is a guard for hire and may know nothing of importance. He is the murderer. Rakunnan-va-Rager now refuses to answer any questions. This much we do know, in the last reign he was a shield brother of the outlaw Shank-ji. Highness, I must ask you to support a search for any others who may have associated with these men. Rumors always fly about any city. For long we have kept careful count of such as might threaten the August One. When he won the crown he broke a tradition, which has held through five reigns, for he was not a man of Valapa, rather one of the desert Queendoms, an unknown. There are many who have no liking for him."

Now she was eye to eye with Yuikala, and she spoke slowly, as one who chooses words with care.

"We all have our duties, Highness. For the honor of our posts we must follow them. Now I must meet with those who search, Highness. Have I your leave to go?"

"Yes." The Queen's lips pressed closely together. She watched her go with a sweep of salute.

Who were these fools risking all? The message from Shank-ji, which she had found waiting for her on her return, had been a worrying one, but another had come only the night before. He spoke of Dark power, a need to move swiftly now before another Emperor was chosen, and this Dark One emerged to give battle. She had given her secret order to assemble. Not the Chancellor, of course; Giarribari would follow only the well established patterns. Yuikala's head had ached dully since that first message; now the pain was sharp. Events were coming to a head far too fast!

Hynkkel-ji:

The slaughter in the pond was whipping the water into a bloody soup. We had no way to escape as the fighting was at the far end of the very ledge where we had landed. There appeared to be no end to the force of rats gathered there, ready to leap into the water and engage the monsters. The enemy pulled them under when they could, but their very numbers were leading to the water ones' defeat.

Those around me held weapons ready as we waited. Return to the transport and the current would draw us straight into the conflict. I wondered how my brother's arrows and my spear would deal with rat flesh.

Murri regarded the roiling water intently. More and more torn bodies were rising. We could now see only two of the water things and a moment later one of those was pulled under the surface. Some of the rats were turning to swim for our ledge but its upper edge was out of their reach. They swam back and forth, many of them bleeding.

"Perhaps they will turn on us if we try the water trail again." Several of the squad had hands on the mooring rope.

"Not so!" The great cat was right, none of the beasts looked in our direction. Those on the ledge paid no attention either to the swimmers of their kind. More and more of them were disappearing below the surface. There was no more sign of the water monsters save sickening refuse in the river.

Murri moved. He could not go, as he would in the desert, protected by the fact his thick coat was the same color as the rocks about. Still as he took one stalking step alter another, he seemed to remain invisible to the rats. Then he paused and his thought reached me.

"Stay—beyond one watches!"

There were no crevices or hiding holes along that wall to my left. But I trusted Murri's talent highly and I signaled a halt.

Most of the rats had disappeared now either into the shadows behind them or into the depths of the pool.

Again Murri thought touched. "Watcher gone."

We went with all possible care, passing by the first of the bloody waste bobbing in the current, which was sweeping away the battle filth.

We might not be sure we had reached our goal, but we might discover how the rats had entered and perhaps gain a way to the outer world.

There was a straggle of rats still to be seen. They had turned their backs on the water, disappearing into the shadows at the probable end of the ledge. There was no rear guard watching for pursuers. It might be that the water creatures never came on land.

"New rats—" Murri's pace had outstripped ours. Then came a sharp warning. "Wait!"

I could now see a faint tracing in the air—Then—an arch of light marked on the green mist thicker and stronger than it had during our journey.

"Gate—" Murri announced.

If there were a gate we must make use of it—such an exit might be the only one. We must be ready—"Go for the light!" I passed the order to those behind me before I sprang behind Murri, who leaped up and forward.

My body was gripped by a force that held me prisoner. There was a sensation of being wrung, nearly pulled in two. Then—it was as if I was spat forth—some great creature of the Dark might have mouthed and instantly ejected me.

I sprawled on hard stone so forcibly that the air was driven from my lungs and I was left gasping.

In the Outlaw Camp of the Desert:

For a short time Shank-ji could only thankfully accept that he was indeed back in the world he knew. He ran his hands over the stone of the rock isle which held their camp, so that his touch assured him that he was out of the City—free of the Dark One.

Not only he, but the remaining men who had dared the gate, were now headed toward the camp set higher, while around them gathered those they had left on guard.

He chewed away on the reviving paste of algae, which contained those carefully mixed ingredients meant to supply energy for one who had been too long in the desert. While he did this he listened to reports.

Three of his specially dispatched messengers were back, having been successful on their missions. There were more mounts in the grazing space, new weapons, and another score of men added to their force.

However, where was the expected contingent from Kahulawe? At his question the man in charge of the camp shook his head.

"Great One—there has been a storm. Any planning to come might well have been taken by it. Also—"

He turned and called a name, which summoned a man from the group beyond.

"Great One, this is Alvertos-va-Alver, out of Azhengir, a caravaner. He joined us only yesterday and brought late news."

Shank-ji nodded to the stranger and the man spoke eagerly.

"The drums have not yet spoken, Great One, but we may hear them at any time. It is thought that the August One has been lost within the storm with his Progress."

Shank-ji stared at the speaker without truly seeing him. Matters were moving too fast; he was not prepared to meet them. If this news were true he might obtain his goal without the battle he had been preparing for—and *not* by the favor of the Dark One. Let another testing be held now—or would it be delayed because of the growing rat raids and the water shortage? He stroked the blunt end of flesh which was now his right wrist. Could he fight again through the tests? And—did the Dark One already know somehow of the empty throne? That one had many powers to serve him. Valapa might be the answer. He became aware of the caravaner again.

"You have brought news of worth, Alver. When we have won, full honor will be yours. You have rightfully come to join with those who regain the proper rule."

Then he abruptly dismissed them all and settled on his private place higher in the rise. His body was still stiff from the tension of their escape, and he did not seem able to center on any plan well enough to work it through. Valapa continued to haunt him.

Would the Dark One issue out of the Plain of Desolation to strike for his own purposes? Would that gate operate outside of the Plain? How long would it take to build an army of man-rats—unless there would be raids to capture men? Valapa, certainly Valapa held the greatest strength now of the Outer Regions, the largest army, the most knowledge and skill. If the barbarian had not been storm swept and buried, he must speedily be disposed of.

There was the Queen. Yes, she had sent several subtle messages; he had been informed of the insult Hynkkel had given when he had ignored her granddaughter. Shank-ji knew he would have her aid—because of her own purposes. One could not have lived as many years as he had in Valapa, noted and listened to rumors and curtain tales as he had carefully done, and not realize that the Diamond Queen was practiced in intrigue and possessor of no small power. She was not one to be content with a small portion in any plan or in the division of spoils after the victory. Any promises she made must be most carefully studied.

All at once, he was wearied as if he had been seriously wounded. There appeared to be a mist between his eyes and his maimed wrist where it rested against the rock. He—was—too tired. Too—tired—to—think.

Allitta:

Kassca was gone; in a small measure that gave me relief. That the creatures now pressing about me, the stench of their vile bodies thick in the air, would instantly slay her; I had no doubt. I might have been one of Ravinga's death dolls, greatly enlarged and mounted on wheels to be so dragged along. Only by extreme determination could I resist the sickness gagging me as the man-rat to the right jerked at my journey jacket. He tore it open, the undershirt with it, so the chill air of the dead city struck my breasts. Only where the amulet rested against my skin was there a palm-sized stretch of warmth. I felt the scoring of his claws on my flesh as he reached for that crystal, reached but could not touch it.

He snarled and then deliberately scratched so that I felt the pain and flow of blood, though I could not look down to see the wound. His mate to my left chittered angrily, and stopped short, bringing us all to a halt. His head flashed down and he bit, not at my exposed flesh, but at the other's hand. Though those yellowed teeth did indeed scrape me, the hold on me from my right was gone. Then I was given such a push forward that I near lost balance and stumbled ahead, while I heard the shrillness of rat battle cries behind me. They must be fighting, but I could not turn to see.

Did I have a chance? I could again walk free; the hold on my legs was gone. Weaving and staggering, I lurched on, sure that any moment those claws would again grip my limp, useless arms.

It was lighter ahead and I wavered that way, my breath coming in gasps. That I had not already been overtaken, I could scarcely believe. So, I came onto one of the balconies around the great hall, more light entering the carved apertures on the walling screens.

Then, the flooring seemed to swing slightly. At the same time I flung out my arms, my fingers catching at the pierced holes in the screen—my hands were free! The spell, which had made me prisoner in my own body, had been broken. That I had not been recaptured remained a puzzle. I could only keep going. The heat that marked the stone on my breast was rising. Though most odds were certainly against me, I must go on as long as the evil here would let me.

I dragged myself along from one handhold on the screen to the next. It was like making my way through the inside of some beast, for there was a surge in the air, a humming. Power spiraled to a fervent pitch—not too far away. Whether I was going toward the source or fleeing from it, I could not tell.

Another doorway to the balcony loomed to my left. My badly scraped hands could hardly pull me on and I felt that in spite of the screens, I was too visible. Somehow I reached the doorway, half fell within. Unable to aid myself, I landed not on stone, but rather a thick softness. I might be lying on the cushioned floor of a tent. My legs were not again invisibly bound; it was rather all the energy had been withdrawn from the muscles. So I lay, my gasps turning to rough sobs, unable to lash myself to go farther.

Murri in search:

A great wind caught him up, but it did not carry scouring sand to tear his fur. He flew, but he had not fluffed his heavy coat and danced the proper dance. Murri whined as he tried vainly to master his flight, as a warrior should. He was blind also, or the storm had blown all the light out of the world.

It was no whine he uttered now, but the blast of a great war cry. And it was a challenge that was answered. Blue light burst and then was gone. He slid, belly down, across hard stone, fighting to stop, to gain his feet. Instead he struck a surface before him with force enough to drive the air from his lungs and leave him, gasping as he lay, wincing from the shooting pain awakened in his wound.

He was—slowly he fought to remember. The water—water under the ground—His brother—Murri sent out a questing thought. Answer very faint—but definitely an answer, which acted on him like a deep drink of restoring water.

Now—yes, sight had returned to him also. He was plainly in a stone walled room. Where were those who had been with him when he had leaped through the arch of light? He tested the air—there were many scents—he snarled—rat—and other things, human, too. Again he sent forth a seeking thought call.

The answer came very faint—only a hint that someone sharing this talent was not too far away. His night sight came into full service now and there was a door immediately before him. Getting to his feet, the great cat limped toward that opening.

Chapter 27

Within the Ancient Palace:
Ravinga stood, feet planted as solidly as one among the deep carvings on the wall. He who held her prisoner lolled back in a well-cushioned chair, his lips curved in an evil shadow of a smile.

"If I gave you a voice now," he observed, "you would not use it. It has been a long time, has it not, Daughter of Light? If I know you, and I do not doubt that I do, you have been seeking knowledge in many places. Perhaps I can call forth some of that knowledge, for I also have used my time well, and have learned much. You have sought in the earth, the air, the rocks; I have followed another path, a stronger one."

The statue stood, voiceless, lids near closed over eyes, which might just betray alertness.

From out of the dusty, chilled air came a sharp sound. Quinzell was on his feet instantly. Then he was gone, a section of wall peeling to let him pass in such haste that the chair from which he had hurled himself was still a-quiver, cushions sliding to the floor.

The doll maker waited, counting in her mind. When she had reached a certain number, she loosed thought to seek thought. Her enemy had not gone far. He stood before a mass of metal wrought by pattern, the purpose of which hung about it as a thin black cloud. He was summoning—There was an indrawing of energy. Suddenly the bonds which held her loosened.

However she was not tricked into summoning her own power. That also could be sucked away, woven into whatever force he was raising. The very walls about were misting.

Old things were coming to his call. Some she knew for what they were—but those were all lesser ones, ones she might be able to face without any doubts of her own. A steady whine filled the ears now.

For the first time Ravinga moved. She was well aware that there was a guard without the door giving onto the hall. To face such down would seriously deplete her talents. She was determined to be gone before Quinzell returned.

The Kottis were gone but she wasted no time trying to contact them. Slowly the doll maker pivoted, not leaving the place where she had been held.

There was still a small force holding her. Once more she dared a seeking thought. Yes—Quinzell had disappeared through that hall. The fringes of what he fed for control would sweep in any unprotected human energy. Would it also act upon the rats? All life within reach might be drawn for such service, though she was sure he could not so take her with her defenses up.

Now she reached a window wide enough to be a door. It was dusk outside—there was no way of telling how much time had passed. A sudden thought—when had she eaten last? She could not remember—and yet she had no hunger. Was that also part of his control? Ravinga took a long stride and a stir of air managed to reach her past the stream of force.

Against the dusk she sighted lines of greenish yellow proceeding from a window not too distant, feeding into some aperture to her left. There was another window facing her but no light awoke there, only emptiness. A story below, a roof stretched over to unite with that facing wall. Ravinga pulled her cloak tightly around her, extending her arms through the sleeve slits. For a moment she stood looking down, measuring the drop. Then she settled on the sill, letting her legs and feet dangle into space.

She slipped over, her hands still anchored on the sill. Then she dropped. Anyone who traveled the Outer Regions knew that intention mated to effort might serve one well. She held that thought as she launched to the roof below, the cloak in part protecting her from the heavy jar of landing.

Above her the lengths of light disappeared. Ravinga crossed the roof to the far side as swiftly as she could. Panting, she spied a tangle of carvings protruding from the other wall. Without releasing the folds of her cloak she started to climb. The pressure of the force was gone.

Hynkkel-ji:

The greenish mist that had provided us with light was no longer around me. My eyes were blurred by the bright glare of the gate through which I had passed. Then that was gone and a body slammed against mine as I tried to regain my feet.

I rolled and gasped as a knee thudded home in the middle of my back and I heard exclamations and a scraping like metal against stone. The stench of rat was very strong—and to think of having to do battle in the dark was a proving ground for fear.

When I called out those others hidden from me answered back. By the Favor of the Essence we had all made our way through the gate to—to where? Doubtless some fortress of the enemy.

"August One, there is a way ahead." Jaclan! My hand was touched, fingers curled about my wrist to draw me slightly forward.

"Murri!" I thought called. There came no answer! Was it that the furred one had not joined our escape? Yet I was sure that the last sight I had had of him was in leaping through the gate ahead.

In the end I ordered a clasping of hands making us into a line. The clasps I held were both steady. My shoulder scraped along a stone wall. We were traveling totally blind and must use caution. I passed a second order, taken up by Ortaga and relayed in a voice hardly above a whisper. From now on we must make noses and ears serve us. Nose already warned of rat. But hearing supplied no warning as yet. We continued, having rounded a turn to the right, to scrape one shoulder against stone. We were either in a hall or a very large chamber. Jaclan stopped so quickly that I half fell against him.

"August One, I must let go my hold—there is nothing ahead that I can feel. I will search."

My fingers did not let go as his did. "Leader; toss some object ahead to see if there lies a pit before us."

I freed him then and stood waiting, hoping that Fortune still favored us. There came a ring of metal against stone. Then I sensed movement.

"There are steps, August One, leading upward."

"Very well. Carry on."

So we climbed, always in the dark, which was as thick about us as those hides we used for storm shelter. If only there were a weapon against this blackness, a small torch to carry in the hand, one that would not burn away. But such was not possible.

Light shown at last, a pale glimmer above. It spurred us to hasten our steps. At this moment our ears reported. I froze in place so that Ortaga pushed against me. Such a cry! Torment, despair, total abandonment of hope. It wracked us once, and then again.

One of the women we sought?

We reached the top of the stair and, for the first time since we had passed through the gate, were able to see distinctly. The light issued through a slit in the wall to our right. I lunged forward to see what lay on the far side.

The space, which was much lower than my lookout, was filled with objects of metal, large and small, save for one place where there was a clearing. Three constructions walled about it, but did not quite block my view.

Two low tables were ranged close to one another. One cradled a rat, much larger than most of its foul breed. On the other a man was strapped securely. One could see by the writhing of his body he was still alive. But his head was completely covered by a metal bowl.

The captive's body jerked. Again that scream echoed. He was plainly in agony. I remembered the tale of the man-rats. Was he somehow being altered to satisfy the monster ruler here? We had surely reached our goal.

To watch such torment without trying to end it—The thought of Allitta, or Ravinga undergoing such handling awoke my full rage.

Wheeling from my spy hole, I stared back at the company wedged into the space at the top of the stairs. Where we stood was not a hall—rather a long landing—darker the farther it lay from the steps. However one could catch a glimpse of a hardly visible second stairway. I gestured to that and ordered: "Up!"

Search in the Hall of the Past:

Murri halted. The rat stench now mingled with a strange scent. Time to take care. He attempted a final mind touch. And— The she his brother had chosen!

There was no more time to hold that touch as a guide. He could hear very well now, growing ever louder, the click of claws against stone—many claws.

Some sounded from behind, others ahead. Was he caught between two parties of the desert vermin? Murri made his choice and started toward the unknown. There was a wall ahead and a sharp angle to the left where the way made a sharp turn. Rat stench—strong.

Around the corner. There the she was, cowering back against the wall, before her the rats, a large company of them. They had not yet launched an attack, merely gathered in an ever thickening arc, as more of their kind arrived continuously. A wisp of luminescence hovered over them so they could be plainly seen.

Now they appeared so engrossed in whatever they proposed to do—or were doing—that they had no attention for Murri, even as their fellows had been blind to the squad by the river.

Murri launched himself in a powerful leap. As he landed to flatten a number of foul creatures under his weight, he swept out both forepaws, smashing bodies, tearing with fully extended claws. He uttered no battle cries. The shrilling of the enemy echo eerily, but the Sand Cat fought in silence. He must not bring any others hurrying to this battle.

He had cleared a way, bringing him to half crouch beside Allitta, facing the squealing rats. They closed the space he had opened, more and more surging in.

Still, they did not attack, though they kicked away torn bodies. What held them back? There were so many of them now. Were they all to attack at once—this was not the open land with with room to dodge, to summon others of his own clan.

"Brother in fur!" Allita's thought reached him. "They call in the monsters—"

He had not picked up any summons, but he had never heard of one able to catch a whisper of rat communication. Monsters—man-rats! He remembered the strange weapon in the hands of such. His shoulder still ached from that wound.

A whistle sounded, sharp and clear. The rat pack backed away a little as those they had silently summoned from the end of the hall approached, slipping from the gloom into full sight.

Man-rats—four of the creatures. Two held the tube weapons. The others were armed with sword and spear.

Allitta:

Alone in this evil hold, I fought fear with every breath. At least the stiffness had left my body, now freed from the restraint the enemy commanded. Then came a seeking touch to revive me, even as a storm survivor might be revived by water.

Thought communications differ, even as the tone of speech, from one person to another. It was not Hynkkel who had sought me so, rather Murri. But where Murri was Hynkkel could not be far behind. I was revived enough to leave the small room in which I had taken shelter and press on into the darkness of the corridor. Twice I paused and tried mind touch but even I was able to sense something here preventing me. I could only go on, energized by hope.

I shook my head and coughed. Rats—and they must be close by—ahead or behind? I did not have a weapon, even a short sleeve knife; they would be able to pull me down with ease. I feared to go any farther, nor would my fear allow me to retreat. I backed against the nearest wall.

Once more the amulet grew warmer against my breast. What had seemed to die when the man-rat had tried to take it was coming to life. Having nothing else I closed my hand as tightly around it as I might clasp a spear. Slowly fear-born tension began to relax.

They came in a dark wave, rats, yes, but not yet the Evil-spawned monsters. However they did not instantly hurl themselves at me, following their usual pattern of attack. Instead they halted some paces away, forming a curving barrier to my escape. Instinctively I knew they waited— awaited the others.

I had not long to shiver. Out of nowhere Murri hurtled with all the speed of his kind. Rat bodies streaming blood flew through the air. He trod on more, breaking bones with his weight, while his fearsome paws dealt death. But I must warn him, and with all my might I both spoke and thought my message.

He instantly faced the passage in the direction I had been heading. From where he had emerged, more rats flowed to gather strangely quiet around us. In my grasp the warmth of the amulet continued to grow.

Man-rats now. One of them stepped forward, his companions allowing him to advance alone. To my horror I believed I could read the purpose in his red eyes.

In his revolting body there must also lie the same appetites common to men—which I would never welcome, even though I held that which would and did mimic the answer my body was designed to give. The rats drew back on either hand to allow his approach.

I was aware also of the blood born rage that seethed in Murri. This enemy held a strange weapon, with powers we could not guess. My hand held a blazing coal of fire. I did not break silence, rather something within me swelled. Nor was I conscious that my hand moved.

The amulet slipped from my hold but my fingers still grasped its chain. I acted as if another will had taken control. My enemy had gone into a half crouch. Murri would have moved between us but that power, which I only half sensed (from what unknown source) now sent the blazing crystal aswing.

Time froze about me. When I moved, something held those others, even Murri, motionless. A hazing of flame arose from the pendant. It was now akin to a weapon I had used on the caravan trails, with well-remembered skill. Out flew a bail of fire. The chain wrapped about the rod.

Fire! Not from the rod—that had shattered. First it engulfed the hand that held the weapon, then became a tower encasing the man-rat. In my mind flamed an agony of pain. I had dropped my left hand on Murri's back. With all the strength of his body he pushed me away from the blaze. All the while there was utter silence.

The fire leaped upward, its living core no longer visible. A burst of scarlet shifted. Sparks scattered. The cloak of another monster guard, he who held the other rod, caught fire. Behind that double pyre the remaining two broke and ran, and with them the rats. Fire reached farther to lick up the laggards.

Heat was threatening us also. Murri pressed against me again, urging me along the wall. There was no opening here into which we might retreat as the fire continued. I choked and gagged as noisome smoke thickened the air.

With a last crackling leap the flames were no longer so solid. Only blackened lumps remained, which had been rats and guards. There was still a shining spot amid the carnage— my jewel, holding not the flames it had generated, but rather lay glittering white, as might a diamond from Yuikala's state crown.

I avoided as best I could the bodies, but I knew that the strange jewel was bonded to me and I could not leave it. There was still heat in it, but not the living flames the amulet had awakened. As I bent to retrieve it, I saw the second rod, which the other man-rat had carried. This too I gathered up. In contrast to the amulet it was cold, so cold that I nearly dropped it. Murri bent his great head and sniffed it. His thought came.

"It still lives—but not for those who carry such. We must learn its power."

I rammed it deeply into an inner pocket of my cloak. When I gathered up my jewel I once more slipped the chain over my head and tucked what it supported into hiding again.

Chapter 28

Hynkkel-ji:

We had no way of learning the extent of the forces against us. Murri might have been able to report on this. But Murri—I could only continue to hope that he had made it through that gate into the same pile of ancient masonry as enclosed us now. That the force of power to project those who dared it might have a different effect on men and on Sand Cats, was something pricking me.

It was not the desert lord who joined us—rather a small body near the same color as the massive walls leaped at me from a low opening, which might have been drilled for the use of rats. Then I stood as Kassca reared on hind legs to clutch at my leggings.

I stooped and caught her up and she hammered her head against my chin.

Murri I could thought touch. Would that talent answer me now with this much smaller representative of the feline race?

"Allitta?" three times I repeated that, hoping that I was making a true touch.

The picture that came in answer was unsteady—far from clear. One wearing a journey cloak such as all women who traveled the caravan trail favored—yes. Surely it was yes! There came into view beside her what could only be a man-rat. A long nailed hand grasped her arm, which had been jerked through one of her slit sleeves.

Only for a breath did this mind picture hold. Then it was gone, our bond of communication cut. Perhaps my hold on that small body had tightened too much; small teeth closed warningly on my finger, as I was left to a fear which wrenched me. That had been a male locked onto the table, certainly not Allitta. Yet the body was that of one of my own kind. We must do all we could to find her before she would take her place in that torture chamber.

I raised Kassca until her green eyes, widened to their greatest extent, were on a level with mine. Though Murri was missing, it might be that a Kotti could still be a guide, able to pick up traces of one who had shared a closer bond than any I had known before. At that moment I realized that Allitta aroused in me a feeling, which was strange and disturbing.

I had not yet tried to communicate again with the Kotti; however, Kassca's forepaws shot out to push against me in a way that was an order to release. She did not run but stood looking up at me and I guessed that she indeed was ready to act as a guide, though we certainly could not squeeze through that door from which she had come. My belief was right. Her gray head nodded. She turned to the main passage and trotted on, the rest of us following her.

Among the Many Roofs Aloft:

Ravinga pushed herself through an open window to which her climb had brought her. The power that had been aroused was gone. She had no way of learning what had happened but she was certain that the summons of that force, the bending of it into service, must have left Quinzell exhausted for a period. She herself was in little better cause.

Staggering over to one of the wall benches she could go no farther. Huddling against this support, she worked her cloak loose from the temporary fastening. Drawing a deep breath she continued to sit, her inner forces so centered on what must be done, she might have been transported to her workroom in Valapa, supplies for an intricate doll awaiting her.

The Doll Shop in Valapa:

Berneen threaded a needle, trying not to remember how this sanctuary had been invaded. It was her conviction that her grandmother had now traced her and she expected any moment the arrival of some servants to take her into custody. If only Ravinga were here to unleash her power! Berneen found

Melora a support, yes. However, she was sure that the Doll Maker was the only one Yuikala would hesitate to confront.

She and Melora had kept close together after the intruder. Neither of them had recognized him. There were riches enough here to attract other night runners.

Berneen took two careful stitches of gleaming silver thread before using the point of the needle to pick up a glittering gem bead, fastening it to the cloth, which was taking on the appearance of a court robe suitable for one of the dolls Ravinga had set aside to be finished.

The door curtain swayed and Melora entered. The happy look she most often showed the world was gone, replaced by a grim mask. This she had worn since the news had come that Hynkkel might have found lodging beneath a mound of sand drift. Berneen herself dreamed far too often of a dread sight—the dried hand of a man—and that wearing the seal ring she had seen three times in her life and which would be part of her memory forever. Tears had been shed, not publicly before Melora, but to dampen her pillow. She had kept her thoughts to herself and tried to control them, for she had discovered that fears must always be fought with all one's inner powers.

Melora went to a wall cabinet, which she opened. She stood there quietly, looking at the four dolls standing within. At last she touched the one, which was a portrait of Hynkkel—Hynkkel-ji—in his robes of state, but she did not lift the doll out. Instead she reached for the figure representing Ravinga, which she brought to the table. Berneen pushed back to give her room, though Melora might not have seen her; her eyes were all for the doll she carried.

The girl ran her needle into a small fold to sheath it. Though her hands were busied now with the folding of her work, her attention was caught wholly by Melora's actions. The gem dealer had placed the doll on the table, making an exact business of it.

For a second time she turned to the wall, but a different cabinet, bringing out a box of burnished copper, a flask as tall as her middle finger, and two thin brushes no thicker than a dozen fine hairs squeezed together.

Having laid these out she again stood motionless regarding all she had placed there. Berneen shifted unhappily. Yes, she had known that there were powers and talents, which could be controlled by those born to do so. However, before this time she had not believed that such had been given Melora. These strange gifts were mainly possessed by members of certain Houses. Though there were rumors that the Queens had such, nothing had been said that Hynkkel had such forces to hand.

Again she shivered. The day was as warm as any during this season, but her flesh roughened as if she were exposed to the chilled heart of the mid-storms. Twice she formed a question; neither time did she voice it aloud.

Melora ran a forefinger across the surface of the table and back again. She opened the small coffer to display dust the color of desert sand. Then, swiftly, as if she must be quick about what she did, in turn she uncorked the bottle to dip a brush within. When she again drew it forth, the hairs were a sharp sapphire blue, the color prized by Kahulawe. Melora's other hand raised to the collar of her plain work smock to draw out on a cord a very small packet glittering with beads, tiny ones cut from the gems, which stood for each of the five Queendoms.

An amulet, and one Berneen was sure was of more than ordinary power. Again Melora made a slow business of placing that directly before the Ravinga doll. Berneen stiffened again. Her companion's hands were cutting signs in the air. Some of those she knew herself. The half finished miniature robe slid from her knee and she made no attempt to fetch it. She was copying those same signs, ones meant to summon the power of the Essence.

Though there was no sound, Melora must be pleading silently for the notice of the Great Light to favor her.

Berneen continued her own shaping with her fingers, as well as an inward petition.

Wet brush touched the red sand in the box. Blue glyphs flowed across the table, glowing like lines of fire. Four swift paintings and Melora set aside the brush. She sat silent, her eyes on the doll as if she expected it to address her. Berneen believed that was happening, though she could not hear anything herself. It was not a woman but a thing crafted of cloth, hair, even though the molded face was a mirror image of Ravinga.

Within the Lost City:

Ravinga' s eyes were closed, her body so still it might have been that she no longer drew the breath of life. Her own Essence could have taken flight. Then her lips moved soundlessly. Her hands lay where her ragged cloak had fallen open on her knees. Now her fingers began to move. Were they busy with a thread, as they wove it in and out—linking that which was invisible to the outer sight?

So and so and so.

Time vanished. Thus and thus and thus. From the far past she drew substance to be wedded to the light. Pain thrust above those open eyes. She forced herself to hold pressed her need to a deeper level.

Ravinga touched, in one of those periods out of time, what was not hers, nor of the true world. The touch obeyed, thread knotting itself to thread. It vanished; she was alone. Then a second touch—a meeting with utter dark. That other remained unaware of her. Ravinga searched on. It was not the Light that she could sense in what she had called; still she remained undetected.

Her hands moved quickly, finger against finger, pressing that unseen force, locking other now more than finger—sealing, subduing, taking it in hold.

Ravinga sighed; she paid for her labor with such torment as she had never met before. Her whole inner self fought to break that tie; but she held.

The Doll Shop in Valapa:

Berneen watched. She could only guess now at the meaning of what she saw. Other dolls stood in line before Melora now—she knew them all—Hynkkel, Ravinga, Allitta, Murri. They were not a line but a circle where they moved without any touch. That circle was not completed. Out of the table surface rose a spot of viscous blackness, its ever enlarging tip weaving back and forth, gaining height and thickness of bulk.

Though it grew larger it did not develop in any other way, save over its surface netted a tangle of blood red lines.

Melora had edged back from the surface of the table; was half crouching now. She bent forward and back, uttering a sound more an expression of pain than a croon.

At length she fell silent, even as the black thing appeared to reach its chosen height. A small rod in hand, Melora touched the doll that was Ravinga before moving quickly to touch in turn Hynkkel, Allitta and Murri. Having done so, the rod dropped from her hold, struck the table and shattered. Melora's hands went to her temples and she moaned.

In the Lost City:

Ravinga wilted down on the wall bench. She was breathing heavily, struggling to draw more air into her lungs. Moisture gathered in the corners of her eyes and began tear tracks down her cheeks. But she did not allow herself to rest, rather pulled up and stood for a moment before leaving the chamber.

Hynkkel-ji:

During all our journey on the river we had not been able to keep an account of time. Hours had passed since we entered this maze of stone walls, rooms and passageways.

Twice we halted, fed on small mouthfuls of our stores (oddly none felt hunger here) and rested for a space. We must always be on guard against rat attack. Lacking Murri's talent and ability to warn well ahead of trouble, we went warily. I attempted to use touch with the Kotti, wondering how effective this would be. Kassca was not my bond mate. There were never any results to clear touch as I knew with Murri. What I did touch was another mind.

A sense of startlement was what I gained from that other when our talents met. I found myself swinging my sleeve knife as I would against an imprisoning cord. Almost, in an instant I was free. But I was left with a demanding need to meet that other. The unknown drew, and I must follow.

Ravinga? That the Doll Maker was in possession of many great powers I had come to accept. Also I was certain that she moved now to battle in a way unknown to any warrior. So sure was I that I had been summoned, I moved speedily ahead, leaving the rest of the squad.

A soft weight settled on my left shoulder. I heard voices behind, growing ever weaker. Here there was no light; I moved through utter darkness. That shadow of touch took on greater substance as I went. I fought to identify the source of the drawing, growing more and more suspicious. Then I realized that Kassca was my companion—and the drawing was not hers.

Never had I regretted my ignorance of weaponry so much. Certainly I lacked the proper warrior training. The dark continued. How large could this edifice be? Surely it must cover as much ground as a whole collection of houses would need, even in Valapa, the largest of the Queendoms.

Soft fur brushed my cheek and I understood some change lay before me; then I reeled as I struck against what could only be a barrier. I used my knife to explore. The blade grated against what could only be a solid surface. With my other hand I began to sweep fingers along gritty stone. I had made another discovery. It was not dead stone that I touched now— rather a ribbon of life pulsed and called me on.

The rhythm of that beat held me. I felt that I moved to the sound of a drum such as the caravaners danced to now and then. I could not withdraw my fingers from contact with that barrier. Thus I turned left and started on. Heat now rose from that ribbon, gathering even greater force.

Bringing myself to a halt, I closed my eyes. The heat was traveling upward until I wore, not one of the elaborate crowns of my office, but a coronet of—water—hot water! How could that possibly be? For the continued sensation did not alter from the feeling of a circle, rather whirled around and around, spilling nothing on my cheeks below.

Voices, words strange to me seemed to be connected with that wet racing, tattered pictures out of strange memory.

"Zarrinkk!" I could not have cried out that name, yet I knew I had. Standing away from the wall I went on. Who was I? Where did I walk? Another personality was settling on me, as a travel cloak. It did not bring fear but rather a new feeling of being complete.

Light, could it be dawn light? I kept blinking as my eyes adjusted. Before me stones became misty and the drum was louder. This was truly the way; I was needed! Colored ribbons swirled about, movement to the water crown I still wore.

The color tinged mist hid any walls until there burst forth at floor level a chest. Kassca jumped from my shoulder to its lid. A pillar of silver, red, green and milk-white in which glittering stars moved—became Ravinga!

No, the Star-One—Jadiza! She was—I tried hard to hold on the name that new presence within me deemed was right.

"The time is now!" She uttered those words as a commander might.

She pointed to the chest, but remained apart from it. However, the deeply carved lid was rising, seemingly by its own power. At the same time I advanced but not in answer to my own will. Then I stood looking down.

Ravinga—Jadiza lay within, but how could that be? Was she not also standing close enough that we might clasp hands?

"Zarrinkk! The time is now."

My hand opened, stretched forth. A hand and arm in turn rose from the chest, holding a rod the same hue as the milky white, color-dotted light the woman wore. Against all my wishes I accepted what she offered. As my hand closed about the warm smoothness, there came to me that this had happened once before—a memory so worn I could never understand it.

"The time is now—"

For the third time I heard those words. Forward I moved, away from the chest. Mist cleared. We stood in a chamber of size, filled to the greater part with vast bulks of metal. Some- one else was there; his hands were lifted to adjust a lever on the nearest of these, back towards me—Lord of the Ever Dark, Snuffer of Light, Granter of Pain, evil not meant to destroy the earth. Once again we were together, though I did not know how.

I pointed the rod I had been given even as he turned his head. Foulness, utter death, enfolded in a body like to mine. What I held struck at me as well as at my ancient enemy. Dark—or had I been blinded by a power? Blinded and swept on into nothingness.

Chapter 29

In the Palace of Valapa:

The Diamond Queen loosed what she held from one hand into the other. Three times she juggled the stones so, then she tossed them on to the black tray of a soothsayer. In these days such action was merely a game to most dwellers in the Outer Regions. Those who remembered old tales out of legends considered such jewels more than parts of some forgotten game. Read the glints of light; note where is the emerald, the sapphire, how the diamond relates to the other stones.

Yuikala studied the display now lying before her, her face set in a stern mask as she considered the position of sapphire to diamond. Suddenly she slapped her hand down with such force that the stones raised a fraction from the surface, returning again to form the same pattern. Her dark brows seemed to draw closer; her lips had become a thin line. So!

There had been so much forgotten. Once, it was said, Power would have answered. Had that Power drained away through the years?

Rising she touched the crystal mobile with a finger so it uttered two chiming notes. The on-duty guard drew aside the curtained door.

"Highness!" He saluted.

"There has been contact, Ibberk?"

"Just now, Highness. A scout from the desert force."

"Well enough." She rose from her seat. Yuikala still held the diamond stone; now she gave it to the Guard. "This to Commander Haldis."

He saluted and was gone. There was at least no news of the Emperor. If he lived and returned they would be ready for him. He had had no time to bind to him any of the greater Houses or the armies of the Queendoms.

Allitta:

I was tired; my body ached; I longed to rest. We were well away from the debris of the battle. Murri might be consulting some map of his own, for he went a pace or two before me without hesitation. Twice we journeyed upward, once along a sloping ramp, again by a narrow stair. When the passage branched to the left he continued, nor did he raise any warning. We met no rats. Perhaps they did not meet us in body, but their fetid stink, far from fading as we advanced farther, was still heavy.

My mouth felt dry, devoid of moisture. I began to cough, though I fought to stifle that with all the determination I could summon.

We emerged into another hallway, this barred along the right side with narrow vertical windows. Murri had padded only a short way along before he reached a doorway to the left.

The shift of his body had already alerted me to this. In we did go.

There was very little light here, only that which blazed through my torn shirt. The amulet was gathering force again. The room was not bare as were most of the other chambers. Against the far wall a series of shelves towered to the ceiling, all of them filled with pouches, boxes, bottles—supplies in abundance and confusion.

Murri delicately mouthed a pouch and brought it to me.

"Food," thought touch declared.

He scarcely needed to say that—though I had not felt hunger before, I was now instantly ravenous. However, the dryness in my throat set me to coughing. I wavered to the shelves, seeking, myself, until I chanced upon a dusty bottle. Coming back I struggled with a greased cord until I had the packet open and with a shaking hand pulled out the contents. Then I forced the cork from the bottle and sniffed the welcome fragrance of melon wine.

Murri was pawing at the cover of a tall jar and when I helped him free it, we found drinkable, though stale, water. When mixed with the wine, it tasted much better.

Soon we were at ease. I alternated bites of cured algae journey-food with careful sips from a basin I had found. Murri lapped deeply of the water until he had emptied the larger pot I had filled for him.

My needs having been satisfied, I began to wonder why I had not been hungry earlier—perhaps the Powers centered in this place too might strangely control that. Also, how did this unsuspected bounty come to be here?

"A fortunate find," I commented.

"Siege supplies," came the answer.

"What siege?" Had time so passed that the armies of the Queendoms were now on the march?

"The one which threatens," Murri was not very informative. He returned to the shelves and nosed along them, finally pawing off two pouches joined by a strap, such as could be carried on the horn of a saddle.

I longed to remain where I was, stretched out on the floor—resting—But I knew that the choice was not mine. I began to pack the bags with more food.

Murri had taken to pacing up and down restlessly, but when I tried thought touch he had established a barrier. Fastening the last latch, I was up on my knees when there struck such pain in my breast that I reeled and sank back to the floor.

Could stone writhe like an ancient tower assaulted by a fierce storm? I could see no shifting of any of the walls about me, but my body seemed to vibrate from blow after blow of raw force.

From the four corners of the supply room dust (or was it truly dust?) arose like sand blown from dune crests. Murri's shoulder steadied me. I picked up the united bags and obeyed an unvoiced order, crawling on hands and knees to the door.

The pressure increased. Murri wavered but still kept his feet and urged me along. My breath came raggedly. There was nothing in sight but sturdy walls, yet I sickened with overwhelming fear.

I was well aware that what strove here now was nothing of my world, rather far from what I had known. Roaring, wild energy. I dragged myself on with no idea of where I was. Warm breath against my cheek, jaws closed on my shoulder anchoring me as I weakened. Murri—suddenly it was as if a shout near deafened me. I pulled myself to my feet, hands still buried in Murri's fur for support. It was plain that leadership rested with the great cat. I have no memory of what remained of our journey. There had been that sound that split the air—yes, *air*. We had come out into the open: how, why, I did not know.

It was not wind pressure upon us now—I struggled and brought forth a cry—"Essence, I yield; I yield!"

Then came blackness, smothering blackness. I was nothing, nowhere, gone.

A rough wet tongue rasped my cheek. In my mind loomed the image of a great furred head. I opened my eyes. Above me arched an expanse of many colors slowly fading. For a moment I saw another towards whom I yearned. He was silent and motionless, yet I believed that we shared the same world.

I tried to call—then he was gone. His disappearance set me moving. As I struggled to rise, Murri came into my angle of sight. Again his tongue swept my cheek, arousing me to greater effort.

"Hynkkel—!"

"He lives. We must also—"

The sky was darkening; it could not be far from twilight. Murri turned and paced some distance from me. He did not again communicate, but I witnessed then something I had heard Hynkkel speak of in awe. And his awe I could now well understand.

The Sand Cat had been pacing back and forth. His movements became faster. On the sleek body the fur began to rise, to lighten in color. The big head was erect, the large golden eyes afire.

Up, fore paws, hind legs—up and up and up.

I heard also—sounds that might be words—none that I could understand. Up—Murri was now my arm's length above the surface on which I stood. In the air he was twisting and turning his body. This was the Dance—the legendary Dance of the Sand Cats.

He arose yet farther above the roof. His movements brought him not only higher but in wider circles beyond the knee-high barrier along the edge of the roof. I was still prey to the pressure, thus I crawled to the edge as he swung out so far he was well away from me. Nor did his circling continue, but now he shot forward as I watched.

He had found one of the highest points among the city buildings from which to launch himself. I peered down and jerked back from the low barrier. Below the city streets were no longer deserted. Black rivers of rats, both of the original size and the larger ones, poured out of this palace.

Under me the roof moved, recovered, to slightly move again. About me the stone was throbbing. Not being able to follow Murri treading air, I pulled myself higher, searching for some way to escape. I had an ever-growing fear of falling, as I could see sections of stone from other buildings crashing down. What was more: I saw no way to retreat.

Could rats wail in fear? The sound arising from the street was surely rooted in terror. Though the black stream grew, the vile creatures below retreated no farther. Now there came others from surrounding buildings, sometimes fighting those already there. Quickly the wide plaza before the palace became crowded.

There they were in constant movement. The greater rats tore the throats of the others, tossed their bodies into the air, blood spattering around. Still none retreated from that choked space.

A crash—I witnessed stone shiver, loosen and fall in one of the other streets leading here. What followed was, to any one born in the Outer Regions, a wild hallucination straight out of nightmare.

Dust did not rise from the site where the stone had fallen. There was a haze which should have been dust—sand—air borne. Rather, rising straight upward was a plume—not dust— Water!

Water in such a quantity as this was unknown to any Queendom. I had seen the underground river—But this! It was fountaining up and up. Now it formed a greenish water tower. A growing wind carried moisture, and snipped at the edges of the column.

That was only the first of such columns. They rose up near and far. So far none had appeared to threaten the Palace.

Murri! For the first time since this impossible eruption, I thought to search the sky for the Desert Cat. Had such a watery spear somewhere beyond my range of sight caught him?

I wiped a hand across my eyes. As the water continued to rise, with no sign of lessening, I could only hope that Murri had soared above its threat. All that remained for me was to save myself as best I could.

Was the Essence now at war—the earth rending itself to defeat evil?

My tattered clothing was wet through. I might just have crawled out of the hidden river. Runnels of water were plainly visible on the walls, forming swiftly into streams that sought the streets below.

These struck at the massing of the rats. They broke—to run, only to meet others of their kind pelting toward the Palace. With these newcomers ran man-rats. Only, I could see that they were not the same kind as the ones who had captured me. Those had been clothed as my own kind, wearing uniforms of Outer Region guards, possessing only rodent heads and clawed hands to mark them.

The man-rats below were bare of body. Human shaped as their bodies appeared, they sprouted coarse fur brindled black and gray. At center on their rat faces, between red, beastly eyes, was a symbol as red as those eyes—a crooked claw.

In place of spears and swords, their clawed hands held shafts ending in long, triple knives. Using these with cruel skill they hacked a path to the palace and finally disappeared from my sight.

Still the water fountained; streams gathered and flowed. The sky darkened no further but became a gray dome.

Hynkkel-ji:

My blindness held but I fought it now. I would *not* be held captive to it! Was there a black so intense as to be further distinguished in a place of utter darkness, or was I deceived? The pain in my head became a racking torment. Nevertheless I was again on my feet. In spite of my blindness I took one determined stride and then another toward what I thought I could distinguish.

Quinzell had commanded all that the Essence would destroy—had already blasted much of the Outer Regions, long since turning them into a waste of heat, sand and rock. Yes, a part of me drew upon a strange memory. I began to recall an earlier life in a land far different from the one I now knew.

Remembered also what I carried.

I took my stand, bracing myself as if I was facing the rage of a wild oryxen. Flipping the rod I carried, I set its butt against my breast. I must make myself a part of it, praying for what I must have.

Nor did I call upon the Essence outwardly. This was no battle of force against primeval force. It was I, all that I was, against this shadow ahead. Light against the Dark—in the shape of a man born in this land to linger by his evil arts.

I pressed the button on the side of that I had found in the tomb.

My blindness remained. There was a draining from me. Body answered with pain; my will held. I heard what might have been a chittering of a giant rat. The sucking of my life force increased. That power drew back from my opposition suddenly. I rocked, to nearly fall when it failed.

Not in my ears but in my pain filled head it sounded:

"The wheel has turned; the time has come at last!"

The Power against me suddenly lessened. I staggered, nearly fell, then somehow achieved steadiness and continued, for that shadow within the dark had not retreated.

Yet suddenly it vanished. I again pressed the stud, which controlled my ancient weapon.

There came an answer that near defeated me. I was now blinded in another fashion by a blaze of light. Where we stood must still be within this Palace of another time and people. Since I had come here I believed more and more this was a place apart—almost as the storm winds shift a dune from one place to another.

No shadow confronted me now. This was Quinzell! His face was like the sharp point of a spear turned towards me; his mouth stretched as might a rat displaying fangs before it struck.

"The time is now!" This time it was I who shouted the words. Once again I pressed with all my strength against the control of my weapon.

He hurled at me a ball of flames. It flared into reaching tongues of fire. Instead, though my skin knew the touch of tormenting heat, it hissed into nothingness. Shocking cold encompassed me. Water—whence it spouted I knew not, only that falling sheets of it pushed outward at the Master of the Plain of Desolation and forced him to retreat before it. So we went—the falling water accompanying me.

I paid no heed to our direction or surroundings, for I was sure that I must concentrate on one thing—holding as close as I could to my inner enabling. Whether he wished it or not he played guide and I was content to have it so for now.

We descended stairs, a ramp, sloshed through rooms, the water running stream-wide now. I knew that he was marshalling his resources to keep out of its touch without losing me. My own power built steadily; I could only hope his was dwindling.

There lay a wide-open portal behind him, great enough to dwarf us. Above the swishing of the water I heard an unmistakable sound. Though there were no war drums to arouse a fighter into frenzy, we were moving straight into a furious battle.

Allitta:

To the west a portion of roofing sloughed away and was gone. I shivered, not only from the chill of the wind-borne water but from fear. My perch could be breaking up about me. I crawled away from the gap in the roof, just as the hole was enlarged.

Even through the ever-rising sound of rushing water I could now hear roars and screams, battle cries that I could understand. Some who served in the forces of the Outer Regions were surely now engaged. Another piece of roof was gone; the hole was enlarging in my direction. Now it formed a recognizable square. And from that—I staggered to my feet even as Kassca, her fur sleeked with water, sprung to me.

Behind her came Ravinga and Wiu—save that this was a Ravinga I hesitated to hail. Could I be deceived by some Power to see one I thought I had known well, now more regal than Yuikala?

Chapter 30

Hynkkel-ji:

Spray blew over us; now I could see behind Quinzell men and rats locked in deadly struggle. The Dark One threw out his arms. Around him the mist of water thickened like a wall. My strange weapon failed as the mist barricaded him. I was no longer a menace.

"Hynkkel!"

In spite of the need to watch Quinzell I glanced to my left.

Ravinga—and Allitta. Their clothing clung soddenly to their bodies. They might just have emerged from the river. Between them a weapon sliced viciously—a trio of knives formed its head and a wisp of cloth fell from Allita' s shoulder.

The doll maker—or was it she?—pointed sharply. I knew it was a warning and instantly redirected my attention to Quinzell.

Though he had not joined the melee below, I saw his attention was divided between his forces, engaged with those I recognized as my own following, and me.

Though I now distrusted it, I swung my weapon up once more, butt against my chest, and fired. My aim was true; my target close, but there came no result. Light shone only for a moment then disappeared. There followed a backlash, smashing at me. I stumbled, unable to control a body so suddenly weak that I found myself on my knees, slammed against one of the pillars framing the Palace entrance. Again my sight was darkened—Once more time turned backward—So it had been before.

Through the air a body hurtled, not dead or wounded, but landing with a warrior's skill nearly upon me. My brother stared down.

"Your are hurt?"

My shoulder scraped the wall. I had not loosed the power rod, but kept a firm grip on it. I tried to use my left hand to help regain my feet, but the weakness hindered. A firm grasp brought me to stand shoulder to shoulder with Kalikku.

"YALA, YALA, YALA!" Even the growing thunder of the water could not drown out the familiar war cry.

Somehow I was able to stand firm beside my brother, looking down into the battlefield.

Allitta:

When I saw Hynkkel go down I think I whimpered. In that moment I could have flung myself at that mist-obscured figure he confronted and clawed him. Then I saw a human warrior join Hynkkel. All the while, the Dark master of this city raised his hands to point fingers right and left, aimed always at man-rats. Each he so indicated was sorely wounded. One lacked an arm and another had a great hole in his chest. Neither fell, but continued to fight, sweeping knife crowned spears such as our men had never before faced.

There were men of the Outer Regions down. I saw rats tearing them to pieces and looked away. Hynkkel had drawn his brother close, so he could speak directly in his ear. Kalikku shook his head. Hynkkel raised the rod he held even as his brother tried to thrust him back.

Hynkkel struck out and wrenched himself free. He tottered once as Kalikku let go. I saw his brother attempt to catch him. Then another took a hand. I had not realized that Ravinga had gone, though we had been so close together. There she stood blocking any move of Kalikku's.

My hand went to my breast. The gift jewel was again warming. Another warrior—the young officer Jaclan—had now gained a lower step. Blood streamed from an arm, but when a man-rat speared at him, his blade swung and he was a step higher.

Before me lay a scene of scarlet horror. This was such a blot that even the Essence Itself might rise to dash away. Still the streams of rats were gathering as fast as the ever-rising water.

Ravinga stood on the step above Hynkkel, yet I did not see her offer him any aid, if she could. I clasped my amulet between both palms; its heat grew. Then—step-by-step—avoiding Ravinga, I became shield mate with Hynkkel. I raised my closed hand over my head, biting my lips until I could taste blood, for I felt as if I nursed a blazing fragment of the desert sun. Desert Sun—I could see it hanging above us!

A shaft of blistering-hot light streamed from between my fingers. It did not strike directly at the misty head of the Dark One but at an angle.

Wisps of steam—Hynkkel's weapon raised a fraction. Behind our enemy rats and men, no longer engaged, were falling back.

Quinzell swayed a fraction, then steadied. His face sharpened to resemble a rat's. One of the three-pointed spears sailed at Hynkkel. I swung my jewel on its chain. I did not really see any contact between the two as I snatched it back. Still the spear upended its length with no hand on it and fell. At the same moment I was roughly and hastily shoved aside by Kalikku. Before his hands left my shoulder Hynkkel shouted, his voice ringing out.

"The time is NOW!"

With both hands he held the butt of the weapon to him; he might have so caught at a sword that had plunged into his breast.

Hynkkel-ji:

All I could focus my sight upon was that shaft of water mist and its core, with the blazing light beating upon it. I do not remember aiming. A faint touch of memory—So it had been before—and my defeat had followed!

The mist collapsed and the light beam was also gone. Before me the Lord of Desolation tensed. I was well aware he prepared to leap for my throat. My hands fell to my side, weak and useless after my last small effort.

A hand holding a sword arose, between the enemy and me. I knew that he could not be slain by steel. My own weapon had rolled to the bloody space below.

Now a ball of light flew into sight before me. Somehow, when I flung up my hand I captured it.

What followed assuredly could not have happened in any world I knew.

Quinzell paused to laugh at me—and met a spray of water. His mouth opened to emit such a scream as of a victim on the rack. The water was visible, as it struck his body, a greenish blotch running down from the base of his throat. The flesh it touched began to soften and slough away. Though he did not fall, larger and larger portions of skin and sodden flesh dropped from his frame. His face remained solid. I could only believe that Quinzell was not human, but perhaps a construct, a doll such as Ravinga made so skillfully. If so—his head—

Bones gleamed whitely. I could see the lift of ribs where skin pulled and curled away. Still his eyes glared and though he uttered no further cry, I was aware he continued to live.

Lived and fought. It was my turn to cry out in agony and nearly yield. For that other invaded my mind, striving to take me over. Somewhere there came warmth, a promise of help. I did not know why I lifted my hand to my head, where a fire within my skull ate at me. But I too held fire and it vanquished those other flames.

Facing me now was a skeleton, near clear of flesh. Only the head remained intact. Intact, alive and containing a rage so great as to be palpable. Was this demon of the Desolation truly immortal?

"Hurl!" The command did not ring in my head but in my ears.

Hurl what? I could scarcely accept that which suddenly weighted my hand once more—another ball of fire and light as before. In hope and fear—I threw!

Shrieks and screams—not voiced by me nor by the thing I fronted. Before me the skeleton threw up bone hands to claw at features, which disintegrated under their touch. Still this thing of the Dark kept its feet, red eyes of a demon regarding me from the fleshless skull.

"Zdzislaw!"

The skull twisted to look past me, its jaws opening to display pointed teeth, mouthing words. I clutched my own head, for ringing within it were the deadliest of curses. I could stand no more. Pointing straight at the bony horror, I cried:

"By the power of the Light and the Essence—be gone!"

My answer came in a shower of bones that gave eloquent testimony: the Dark Will remained no longer!

On the Steps of the Palace:

She, who was Ravinga in the here and now, stood before the great doorway at the very edge of the steps leading down to the battleground. Water drained away now, carrying the bodies of rats. Countless numbers still lay heaped like dunes of noisome offal. Those of the Outer Regions who had died defending the freedom of their land lay in the Palace behind her, decently prepared for ever rest. It was the gray of first twilight and she was stooped, as well she might be, as though a burden greater than any guessed had fallen from her. A questioning trill, a pull at the hem of her robe—she reached down and Wiu settled against her.

"Done, little one, and well done—here! But all is not yet finished." She had spoken aloud and another who had come to join her hesitated. "What remains—? Is there still evil in the Desolation?"

"There is another evil, more to be faced, House Head of Vurope."

"That being?" Hynkkel had joined Allitta.

"There is rebellion in the home lands. We shall be met with hostility when we try to return to Valapa."

"Yuikala," said Allitta.

"Shank-ji." Hynkkel did not echo her but spoke another name.

Then he added, "If so, we lose when victory appears ours. Yet," his shoulders raised in a shrug, "I am pledged to my duty before the Essence. I hold no others to fight my battles— Already I must answer for those who died here."

Hynkkel-ji:

There is a point past which a man may bow his head, drag his feet, yet, because he is a man and has given his word, he must go on. I accepted this on the fifth day after our battle with the Dark One. Only a portion of my task was behind me. That I would go on, perhaps to my death, I did not question.

Two others of my followers were sore wounded, though I was certain that Ravinga's tending had drawn them back from death. My brother went with a bandaged shoulder; Ortaga's right hand lacked three fingers. They refused to yield to their wounds, but ever followed me as I explored the Palace.

There were supplies in plenty. We could remain here for months if we chose, but I did not. When Allitta described to me the going of Murri, I had a hope that I must not nurse, that he had gone to rouse the Pride for our help. But I must not count on such good fortune.

My father, I was certain, had the force of our Queendom and others loyal to the Emperor alerted. He might be already engaged with the rebels. How many warriors he might gather I could not even guess.

I must not linger here much longer, though I longed to watch as this land came to new life. The water, which had broken from the earth, had largely drained from the city to gather in a pond larger than any I had ever seen. Around its shores sprouted greenery, growing so swiftly I truly believed the Essence was at work changing our world.

Kalikku and Jaclan rode to scout that poisoned and dreary land, which was all we had ever seen of the Plain of Desolation, for we knew we must somehow cross it on our return. They reported that the land had been deeply churned and a large stream was breaking from the base of a rocky spur to flow south. No longer was there any noxious odor in the air.

We saw no more live rats. A number of the larger ones we had found among the dead. And man-rats were discovered limp and dead during our explorations of the city, as if they had perished with their creator. Ravinga studied these closely and retired to solitude for a day. She had only emerged within the hour and I was able to ask my questions.

Yes, we have those who choose to retire from the usual life of our world to serve only the Essence. But this maker of dolls was not one such. She held apart in a way that instilled awe in me.

"You knew this place before; you knew that dealer in evil. Who are you? Who was he and what is the truth about this?"

"This is the lost sixth Queendom," she returned calmly, then turned to Allitta. "Give, my Heart Daughter, that which lies upon your breast."

From the breast of her travel robe Allitta obediently produced the ball of light that had served me. I had thought it a fashioning of crystal, but now it was opaque, and surely much larger than I had remembered.

Ravinga took and held it out for us to see well. I realized that it was unlike any gem I knew, even those which are deemed to hold spirits. Though it was white, beneath its surface swam knots of color: red, green, blue, and warm gold. Each might have been a spark from the crown of a Queendom. Ravinga turned it around—those sparks came and went.

"What—" Allitta did not complete her question.

Ravinga smiled. "It is what has not been seen since the Dark set its brutal shadow on this land. Men once called it an opal."

She handed the gem back to Allitta saying: "Keep it until there is need."

Allitta:

I received for the second time that talisman and understood that I had become thereby a guardian of a treasure.

We waited still to count off some ten days until the wounded, under Ravinga's tending, were healing. The triple horned oryxen were, by Hynkkel's order, turned loose. We found others, which were thriving, having been sent to graze by the pool where greenery continued to spread.

At last Hynkkel summoned a council that included all of us, even Kassca and Wiu, who settled with us. Not counting the seriously wounded there were only ten of Hynkkel's followers remaining. We also had four of Shank-ji's force. (He had left, we learned, earlier). The remaining ones we found chained in one of the underground pits. Their treatment had changed their allegiance—for they went on their knees before Hynkkel after being found, praying forgiveness, offering their lives to serve him.

Hynkkel had stared straightly at each in turn, copying a trick I had seen Murri use. I caught a hint of thought search and shied away, as this was Hynkkel's task alone. He made his choice and took them under his command.

We had gathered in one of the state rooms of the ancient Palace and now Hynkkel laid before us his decision.

"I must go forth from here, back to Valapa if I can. There is still conflict in our land that must be met and the city must be made harmless. We do not know what has been happening elsewhere. There may be many changes to come for the Queendoms and the Empire.

"I am sworn to what I must do, but I lay none of my duties you. There are supplies in plenty here, water wealth beyond belief. As you have seen, the weapons of the Evil One have, during the past few days, rusted and are unusable. No rats have been sighted, nor any of the monsters developed from them. If you choose to remain, do so. I can offer you no safety beyond the Plain, only danger and of a kind I can only guess."

He stood silently staring down at his hands where they lay on the table. Then he lifted his head and, without looking at any of us, said: "Choose!"

Thus it was that our company rode out of the Plain of Desolation that once was, none remaining behind. The wounded rested in padded slings between pairs of oryxen.

Clearly even the desert lands were altered. For a space we traveled along the stream sighted by our scouts, beside running water that no man had ever dreamed could exist. Along its banks abounded fresh green growth, which our mounts greeted with honks of delight.

It was Hynkkel's plan to return first to Kahulawe for the sake of the wounded. However, on our second night beyond the Plain we heard out of the shadows of the dunes an ear-splitting yowl. Many cat voices must have joined together. Hynkkel slid from his saddle and plunged through the sand to where Murri came to meet him, followed in turn by his awesome sire and dam. Having embraced his furred brother, he was brought to his knees by Murri's weight. Standing again he went to the huge Myrourr and his equally massive mate Maraya to pay them royal homage.

In our second council the great cats joined and Hynkkel questioned the coming of the full Pride—in a camp of their own just beyond ours. He pointed out if they were to go into battle for him, the old hatred between man and Sand Cat would resurface, perhaps worse than before. They agreed reluctantly that Murri would go with our party as would be expected, but their force would keep out of sight. However Myrourr stated firmly by thought touch that they would not let one of their kin, their sworn brother, go into danger alone.

They also brought news. Shank-ji had gone to Valapa. There had been a rebel rising there and the Queen had given command of the city force to him, saying Hynkkel was surely dead and Shank-ji was by blood right and warrior training the proper choice.

There had been fighting in the streets. Hynkkel's father, with only a small company, most of them the guards he commanded, had been sent to scour the desert for Hynkkel and search for rats. So General Meguliel had been driven out of the city and was now encamped a day's journey from Valapa. Kalikku volunteered to ride ahead to their camp. With our wounded to care for, we could make only a slow pace.

The Sand Cats became our eyes, sweeping out in three directions to make sure we were not trailed, or flanked by any enemy. It was not known whether any of the other Queendoms had joined in the revolt and sent their guards to swell the rebel army. I served Hynkkel by collecting the reports of the Sand Cat scouts.

It was a weary time of waiting for enemies or reinforcements. The latter came first. At daybreak on the fifth day we overtook a caravan bound for Valapa. The caravaners greeted Hynkkel with more than just recognition. I saw he was rather overwhelmed by their rejoicing over his survival, since he had braced himself to believe most of the Outer Region dwellers saw little that was promising in him.

The caravaners took our wounded to transport in greater comfort. Seven of their company swore guard oaths to Hynkkel and we were loaned a number of extra mounts, so now we were able to make better time.

Still, save for our own company, we seemed now to travel through a deserted land. Then Kalikku returned with an officer of his father's command to say that though Shank-ji's force of rebels remained on the great rock island of Valapa, there were signs that they were close to action.

Hynkkel now rode with this small division of the Imperial Army. Ravinga and I rather withdrew to ourselves.

For the first time since I had left the ancient city I felt less duty-ridden. Soon I could think of a future. But what future? What had I to return to if Shank-Ji and the Diamond Queen were finally defeated? Hynkkel had named me before the court his chosen Companion—assuring me that it was only temporary action, which would cease to exist when trouble was behind us.

I was House Head in my own right but, I discovered now, I had little desire to return to that standing. Well, I could only wait and see.

Hynkkel-ji:

For the first time in my life I met my father as an equal, man to man. He listened without question or interruption to my story. I realized that much he must have already heard from my brother. Also it was told in segments, for we had major plans to make concerning Valapa. He slowed his gait when I mentioned that the Pride of Sand Cats followed us. I hastened to assure him that their part of our army would not attack unless ordered. It was my hope that seeing such an array of one-time deadly enemies might have a daunting effect upon the rebels.

To my surprise he seemed to find that amusing. He smiled as he shook a finger at me. "You have a desire to see some squirming in the enemy lines; is that it? Well, you may; you may."

I now regretted stops for food and rest—to get there—to face this encounter—to come through it or fail—that was my only wish. If once in a while a vague dream of the future intruded, I walled it away at once.

Chapter 31

In the Desert Land Near Valapa:
The Diamond Queen and her guards had put their mounts on a hard climb to the top of one of the smaller rock outcrops. Below them stretched a relatively level space that even lacked any drift of dunes. There were the forces she had helped to assemble. With them was one whose banner man carried both the Imperial Banner and that of her own Queendom on a single standard. Shank-ji had not waited for his messengers to the other Queendoms to bring in more recruits. Let this barbarian General from Kahulawe make his move—all he would win was his death—a dishonorable one, since the army below marched in the name of the Emperor. She had no doubt that by night Shank-ji would take the throne unchallenged.

Between two north dunes there was movement as a mounted party appeared. Four riders moved, but only one came to the edge of the proposed battlefield. By either side of his oryxen paced Sand Cats. She had seen many skins, but these two desert dwellers were near as large as the oryxen. Now she could sight a third beast, one nearly as large, pacing as a rear guard.

Though she could not discern the rider's features—he wore no uniform but the worn clothes of a common desert roamer—she knew him. Her mouth twisted. So—he *had* survived.

No flag of truce fluttered beside him. However, as rider and cats came to a halt facing the assembled army, one of the officers urged his mount forward and drew up a short distance from the man of the desert. She burned to hear what was being said!

Hynkkel-ji:

The last time I had fronted Shank-ji had been when the two of us dared the leap for the crown of empire—the last and most dangerous of the trials. He had lost a hand to the swinging plates of the great mobile. I had won—not that I wanted to. Now his standard bearer edged out of the first rank and came a short way into the open behind his leader so that the double display of flags was clearly visible.

I waited. Let Shank-ji declare himself. Yet it seemed he was in no haste to do so. Perhaps this also was a test. He wished to goad me into speech. If so, I had won again, for at last he raised his voice to the pitch of a field commander.

"Lurker in the dunes, you and yours come no farther."

I deliberately sent my oryxen forward several paces, the cats moving sedately with me. His mount snorted at their approach.

"You speak for whom, Shank-ji?" I hoped my mildness of tone might rouse his temper. An angry man is less than one under control.

"For the Empire of the Outer Regions, for the Diamond, the Ruby, the Emerald, the Sapphire, the Topaz—"

"And these all follow you now, Outlaw?"

There had been no movement in his force when he had listed those allies. He held the Diamond, yes, but I saw no others.

"Usurper!"

I answered ever more mildly. "You show me an army. It is my turn to reply."

I then whistled as an outland herd keeper to alert his charges. I could not see what was behind me, but I well knew that those I faced could count. Our pitifully small troop was following me into the open, but in such a way as to suggest it was but the advance of a larger force. While on the tops of the dunes, walking with consummate skill, came the pride of the Desert Cats parading with inherent dignity.

There was a stir in the other ranks. Oryxen, unused to cats, bucked in fear as their riders strove to keep them from bolting. The line at attention broke and there was a confusion of shouted orders, cries and the bellowing of beasts.

"Murderer," Shank-ji shouted at me, "you would set the cats upon us? We have all hunted them. Their skins line our dwellings; we tread them under our boots!"

My three companions growled deep in their throats. I did not look but I was sure fangs appeared, claws extended into the sand at our feet.

"They will defend themselves, even as you would, Outlaw. There will be no fangs at your throat unless you invite them. You made a common cause with rats and the Dark One who commanded them. So, you have no right to curse as enemies those of the Pride."

My companions threw back their heads and their combined roar brought to a halt for a moment the tumult behind Shank-ji. I might have used the weapon of the Dark One to silence his warriors. I raised my voice so that those in the rebels' front ranks might at least hear me.

"Is this one your choice of a leader, Men of the Diamond? One who made a pact with Evil, served the Dark One, and later ran, leaving men who followed him faithfully to torture and horrible death? Let those he abandoned now testify."

I did not move but from either side rode those we had discovered in chains, waiting to be transformed into man-rats at Quinzell's pleasure.

They advanced at a slow walk until they were lined in front of Shank-ji, facing the army.

"Do you know these?" My voice rasped now.

"Yes," one of the three shouted. "Do you know me, Almik? I have shared storm shelter with you."

"And me?" shouted one on his left. "We ate together before the Devil One's monsters dragged me away, Jibben! We joined the guard on the same day."

The third of their company pressed a fraction past the others. His arm went up. With a forefinger he jabbed the air in Shank-ji's direction.

"I gave allegiance to you, Lord. But did you raise your voice to save me when the man-rats took me to be added to their company? You, Kelash, who are of my own House." Now he pointed to the line. "And there stands Kwaku also—"

"Now I am known to others." He waved his hand toward where I sat my mount. "I am known to the August One who found me in chains; the one who slew the Dark One with the Great Power he commanded. I know the August One; I know those who follow him."

The man who had spoken first took advantage of all eyes being on the speaker. He brought his mount around and with the skill of a well-trained fighter made it leap toward Shank-ji. In his own hand he held a knife. But he did not reach the rebel leader. Shank-ji was on the move—at me—a sword in his left hand.

"No!" I shouted at the cats, already crouched to spring. I had no sword, but I would fight my own battle to the end. I slipped down to my wrist the armband my sister had fashioned for me. It was heavy and it was truly mine. Into its making had gone, I knew, all the good fortune Melora could wish me.

The cats obeyed but, though my mount was used to their presence, Shank-ji's was not. It reared before it reached us and its rider had to fight for control, dropping sword to grab at the reins tight looped about his handless wrist. The oryxen, plainly terrified of the cats, reared again, and this time its hind hooves skidded in a patch of sand. It came up against my mount who snapped with ready teeth and bellowed.

I was out of the saddle to spring at Shank-ji, who was yelling as he jerked viciously at the reins. My mount snapped, huge teeth missing Shank-ji's thigh by scarcely more than the thickness of his breeches. He still fought to keep his seat and I knew it was in his mind to ride me down if he could. Only the rage of the two oryxen, bred to be savage enemies in battle, defeated his purpose. I slammed against his leg, the edge of the metal band now across my knuckles tearing cloth, bringing blood. He screamed, dropped the reins to grab at a knife in his belt.

His mount reared again and he rolled from the saddle. I caught and pulled him away from the hooves of the two oryxen now fighting in earnest. My battle—not to be resigned to cat or enraged mount.

We hit the ground together and rolled apart. Freed from ceremonial robes or bulky uniform, I was glad of my ragged clothing, for I was on my knees as he thrashed to rise from the slippery sand. He now faced me, his face a mask of savage rage. We were both swordless and knifeless. Knowing his superior strength and warrior's training outmatched me, I attacked. My upswept hand with its metal-clad knuckles struck his face just above the eyes and I dragged it down with all the strength I could summon. I met with bone. He screamed for the second time and threw himself at me so that blood and fragments of torn flesh spattered as I sidestepped. Avoiding his blundering rush, I swung at the back of his head. Once more I felt I had delivered a crushing blow.

He staggered on a step or two and went down face first. His legs kicked twice but he made no attempt to rise. His furred headgear was gone, having been knocked off at my first blow. I looked down now at a deeply gashed head, splintered bone. Lifting my hand I saw more blood—my own. The edge of the metal band had also marked me. I need not turn him over—Shank-ji was dead.

At the Edge of the Battlefield:
Yuikala's hand flew to her mouth. She must get away! She knew as well as if they had shouted at her that the warriors below, deprived of their commander, would not attack unless the enemy threatened. Perhaps many of them had been dubious of the cause from the start. That—that—outlander down there would be assured of safety now. She looked over her shoulder to her guards, not daring to allow herself to wonder if they would still obey her orders. The barbarian's personal conquest would plainly bring him renown among the warriors—his victory in hand-to-hand combat—the

method that had historically settled many major disputes between Houses and was accepted as final.

"Ride!" she ordered curtly. "Back to Valapa."

However, she was not to retreat very far, for there were two riders waiting for her, and with them one of the great cats, a female who stood a little apart watching. They blocked the way.

"YOU!" she spat at the one nearest the cat.

Allitta:

When Hynkkel made his decision to front Shank-ji in person, Ravinga drew me aside, saying: "He is right, this mate of yours. But there is another who must answer to us. Come—"

She rode on so quickly that I did not have time to say that the Emperor was *not* my mate, nor was I, in truth, anything to him. I had been trying for some time to avoid thinking of our own tangled future, but it must be decided soon.

We rode some distance westward before turning south, coming so to the back of the rebel army. None marked our going; they were too intent on Hynkkel. Again we turned, this time east, and only a short way ahead I sighted the well-marked trail to Valapa. Here Ravinga reined in. What or whom she awaited, she did not tell me. She was silent and that assuming of an invisible mask told me she was drawing on inner strength to face some danger.

Though I sought to be alert to my surroundings, my thoughts were also entangled. When I had first met Hynkkel in the days when he was close to being outlawed by his House for his aversion to becoming a warrior, I had believed him of little worth. I knew that Ravinga appeared to have an interest in him, but I could see no reason for it. Yes, he was very able in dealing with animals and suited probably for caravaner.

The changes in his life had come without warning. Amazement at his ability to survive the rigors of the trial for Emperor was my main emotion when he won his way to the throne. Then events moved very swiftly and mostly by chance, or so I believed. I had come to study him more closely when the secret of the river became ours. Now I could see how stupid had been my earlier judgment. Most of our heroes in the Outer Regions had gained acclaim in battle. Hynkkel's had come in another way. One who held brotherhood with the Sand Cats had powers far beyond the sword and spear. I was sure that his like had not been known before, though Ravinga had hinted in some far past he had faced the Dark One before, though then he had been defeated.

I made a silent petition now to the Essence that the protection of Grace would now be given to him who was the Champion of the Light.

My thoughts held me so that I had stared back to that battlefield without truly seeing movement. The Sand Cat who had joined us padded closer and Ravinga shifted in the saddle.

A mounted company rode toward us—at its head was the Diamond Queen. Her swift pace suggested retreat and my heart began to pound.

Ravinga made no move to give her and her followers any room to pass and gain the road to Valapa. Yuikala was forced to rein in and face us. As Ravinga, she might be wearing a mask—her face was pale and expressionless but her eyes raked us with undisguised hate. It was toward me she looked now and her voice was meant to be a lash.

"You!"

I made no answer but there came a growl from the cat, echoed in lesser volume by Kassca who pushed around the edge of my cloak to face the enemy.

Ravinga moved her mount a pace or so forward. Yuikala's oryxen showed his fear of the Sand Cat, snorting, shaking his head and striving to back away.

"Well met, Highness," Ravinga used the formal court speech. "There is that to be said here and now."

She waited a moment and then uttered a single word— one I had never heard. Her reins were dropped and her mount stood quietly as she lifted her hands and gestured.

The Queen lost all mask-like control. Her mouth opened as though to shriek. Instead she snapped her jaws together before she spoke another unknown word:

"Zacaki," The whip edge had left her voice.

Ravinga nodded. "So you are one who knows, as I have suspected. The twists of the Dark hold you."

"Sand devil!" the Queen's voice scaled upward to near a scream. "Essence—take this one who would rend the world apart!"

Wind touched me, lifted the ragged edge of Ravinga's cloak, but did not linger with us. Leaping across the baked earth, it seized upon Yuikala. Her mount reared and the reins snapped in her hands. She pitched from the saddle and before she could regain her feet, the oryxen plunged, bellowing, away from her. Sand arose to encircle her. Covering her face she screamed. She did not run, I believed; rather the wind and sand dragged her. Now we saw only a pillar of sand that tottered from side to side toward the waiting desert.

Two of the guard would have followed her, but Ravinga waved them back. "She appealed to the Essence. Now she will answer to what she summoned and that will decide." We watched as the erratic pillar disappeared.

In the Palace of Valapa:
Hynkkel-ji:

Much lay behind, but more waited ahead. I had been able to rid myself of those who had come to welcome me and was alone in my old chamber. The ringing music of mobiles chimed loudly. I wanted nothing more than a place I could sit in silence. However, if one can stuff one's fingers in one's ears, one cannot so stifle thoughts.

My world had changed, in great part from my own efforts. There was a new Queendom in the Outer Regions—for it there must be a Queen, a trusted one—for that I had the answer. The future of those who had rebelled must also be settled. There must also be exploration of the under waters. Already all the algae pools of the Queendoms were swelling, giving birth to streams.

The Sand Cats were safe from men, their own lands granted them, not to be invaded. As this thought, Murri rubbed his head against my arm. There would come others to bond with his kind and good will would come of it.

A flood was rising about me—a flood of decisions, orders to be given, explorations to be made of the onetime Plain of Desolation. Already I sensed the coming of the overwhelming fatigue.

There was one door curtain I had not raised since I had been shown to these quarters at a time, which now seemed long ago. I shrugged off the heavy robe that had been my wear before the welcoming court. Feeling more at ease, I pushed aside that curtain.

Allitta arose from the cushions. She did not seem surprised at my coming. Yes, there was my promise I would release her. Release *her*—no! But I feared that she would release me.

Allitta:

This was the meeting I knew we had been moving toward for many days. There was a strange warmth in me—a warmth not unlike that which had come from the amulet. What—? I was—not in heat—there had been no warning. I curbed the desire to reach for him, the longing that he would take me into his arms.

Suddenly he smiled and threw up his hands in a gesture one would make when a difficult task has been safely accomplished. Then he did reach, but I eluded him in spite of my longing.

"I will not be a Companion," I summoned my pride.

"A Mate—" his voice was caressing, as were the eyes meeting mine.

"But the Emperor—"

"This land has seen many changes during my short reign." He was laughing and the strain had disappeared from his face. "There will now be an Empress; never question that."

Later I raised my head from his shoulder where we lay at ease among the cushions.

"Ravinga?" I asked. She had brought this happiness to me; she must never be forgotten. He picked up my thought—perhaps it would always be this way with us.

"She will not be. There is to be a Sixth Queen in the Plain of Renewing as it is now known. The Essence will grant her and it all grace. We shall name it the Opal land."

Thus began the Empire as it is now and was once long ago: Six Queendoms under an Emperor who brought them peace.

Biographical Sketch
Andre Norton

Andre Norton has written and collaborated on over one hundred novels on her more than sixty years as a writer, working with such authors as Robert Bloch, Marion Zimmer Bradley, Mercedes Lackey, and Julian May. She has received the Nebula Grand Master Award, the Fritz Leiber Award, and the Daedalus Award. She currently lives in Murfreesbore, Tennessee, where she serves as Director of High Hallack Library, a research-and-resource center for writes and students of popular literature.

In 1990, Miss Norton made the acquaintance of Karen Kuykendall after being given a copy of one of her books of fantasy illustration, which were set in a universe of the artist's own creation. Upon learning that Karen had never organized into novel form the complex and extensive background to her "Outer Regions," Andre undertook to do so herself. The result war *Mark of the Cat,* Which was published in 1992. Following Karen's death in 1998, her chronicler returned in her honor once more to the world of the Four Kingdoms with a sequel, *Year of the Rat.*

Biographical Sketch
Karen Kuykendall

Karen Kuykendall studied illustration and motion picture design at Art Center and Chouinard Art Instituted, Los Angeles. She held as M.A. in Education/Art History from the University of Arizona and was for nine years a teacher of English, history, and art.

Ms. Kuykendall's unique creations, which she evoked in multiple media including costumes, sculpture, paintings, jewelry, and dolls, were frequently inspired by her fantasy world of the "Outer Regions." In 1992, that universe received an additional incarnation as a novel when fantasy Grand Master Andre Norton translated the artist's vision from a visual to a verbal form as the novel *Mark of the Cat*. Many of Karen's pieces are now held in private collections in the United States and Australia. Examples of her work are also on permanent display at the Mesa Museum near her long-time home in Case Grande, Arizona. She died in 1998, after a long and valiant battle against cancer.

Come check out our web site for details on these Meisha Merlin authors!

Kevin J. Anderson

Robert Asprin

Robin Wayne Bailey

Edo van Belkom

Janet Berliner

Storm Constantine

Diane Duane

Sylvia Engdahl

Jim Grimsley

George Guthridge

Keith Hartman

Beth Hilgartner

P. C. Hodgell

Tanya Huff

Janet Kagan

Caitlin R. Kiernan